My Lord Beast

Other Five Star Titles
by Mary Lennox:

The Moon Runners

My Lord Beast

Mary Lennox

Five Star • Waterville, Maine

First Edition
First Printing: April 2005

Published in 2005 in conjunction with Tekno Books and Ed Gorman.

Set in 11 pt. Plantin by Liana M. Walker.

Printed in the United States on permanent paper.

Library of Congress Cataloging-in-Publication Data

Lennox, Mary 1944–
   My Lord Beast / by Mary Lennox
      p. cm.
   ISBN 1-59414-328-5 (hc : alk. paper)
      1. Inheritance and succession—Fiction. 2. British—India—
Fiction. 3. Trials (Murder)—Fiction. 4. Poor women—
Fiction. 5. Widowers—Fiction. 6. Nobility—Fiction.
7. Revenge—Fiction. 8. England—Fiction. 9. India—Fiction.
10. Romantic suspense fiction. 11. Historical fiction. I. Title.
PS3612.E55M9 2005
   813'.6 22   2005043217

Dedication

For my mother, Geraldine Zipperstein, who opened the portal into the world of books and led me through.

Acknowledgments

Special thanks to Jackie Floyd, Amy Tolnitch, and Sarah Hankins, dear friends and critique partners who have never let me get away with anything less than my best. I'm also grateful to Laura Resnick, who, in the midst of a nightmare move, read the story and discussed ideas with me.

Special gratitude goes to my agent, Jeffrey Rohr, and to Denise Dietz, my extraordinary editor, who found something she liked in this book, went out of her way at a difficult time for me, and then helped me make the story better.

And finally, with love and pride, many thanks to Drs. James Glazer and Catherine Glazer, and Phoebe Glazer for so many things. And to James and Cassie, thank you particularly for letting Aubrey be yellow and still live to fight the good fight.

Prologue

Aubrey Drelincorte returned from a vast, empty darkness to a low-pitched growl rumbling in his ear. He lay still as stone against the jungle floor, one cheek pressed to the earth, and willed his sluggish brain to kick into action. Something made that sound again—a deep, anticipatory purr. The ground beneath Aubrey's cheek vibrated and the hairs at the back of his neck stood on end.

He dared to open one eye. Pinpricks of pain burst through his brain at the slight motion. His pistol, one of two he always carried into the jungle, lay warm in his limp hand. Why? he wondered fuzzily. When had he fired the gun?

His vision swerved to a shape about three feet away. His wife, Susannah lay there. Her eyes were open and clouded. And her face was a frozen mask of hatred and fear. Blood trickled from a small wound in her chest. A bullet wound.

God in heaven. His stomach lurched. Blood beat in his ears in a surging, hissing tide, blocking out all other sound. *He couldn't have done that.* His heart leaped in fear and doubt and a horrified self-loathing.

Then, out of the corner of his eye, he caught a movement near Susannah's body. In the dusk of twilight, a great leopard

9

crept forward and crouched over her with proprietary intent.

Bile rose in his throat, stinging and hot. *Dear God, dear God.* Soundlessly, his lips formed the words.

The predatory cat's jaws opened as he settled lower to feed. Sharp teeth caught the last light in the instant before they would plunge into her shoulder.

Aubrey reached down into his belt and grasped his second pistol. The leopard's head shot up. In an instant, the beast rose into a crouch. Snarling and screaming, it sprang and landed atop Aubrey. Aubrey's finger jerked hard. The bullet plunged into the leopard's forehead, cutting off its unearthly scream. In a dying lurch, its forepaw swung down, slashing across Aubrey's face and down his chest.

The shot and Aubrey's cry sent the birds shrieking from the trees. Ram Dass and the servants filled the clearing at a run, white turbans gleaming beneath the light of their torches. Frowning, Ram knelt beside Aubrey, his fingers at the pulse in his throat.

"Still here," Aubrey managed.

"Yes. God is good." Gentle fingers found the hole in Aubrey's shoulder and pressed a pad to it.

Aubrey heard the slap of long, sharp knives against vegetation. Ram lifted him up and others slid a makeshift litter beneath his body. He had carried a man away from a hunting accident like that just weeks ago. That man had lived, just as he would, by God. Breme and justice depended upon it.

He felt the tug, the rise of the litter. The men carried him past Susannah's body, out of the clearing, and into the desperate struggle of the next months—the only months, he realized now, that probably remained of his life.

Chapter One

England, February, 1843

Lilias Merrit stared blindly out the window of her small chamber, her shoulders slumped, her faded day dress still half-buttoned. She knew she had no right to feel this miserable. Her beloved older sister, Pamela, wasn't dead, after all. But with her desertion, life had taken on tragic hues to match the cold, gray day outside the window. This morning, Pamela, her dearest friend and ally, had gotten married.

Strubbs, her old nurse, walked into the small chamber. She picked up the bridesmaid's gown lying on the narrow bed, fluffed the rose satin confection, and placed it in the wardrobe. "Your papa wishes to speak to you, Miss Lily."

Lilias's hands froze on the last of the buttons of her worn woolen gown, then resumed their work. Whenever her father chose to remember her, it inevitably meant trouble.

She sighed and took the shawl from Strubbs, hugging it tightly about her gown. With Pamela's absence, the house seemed cold, as though the dead of winter had seeped into every corner.

As she entered the parlor, Geoffrey Merrit stood before the fire. He was still clad in the wedding finery he had insisted they buy.

Even in the three years since the Disaster, her father had managed to look every bit the successful London merchant he had once been. "Appearances are all," he had said innumerable times, and Geoffrey Merrit lived by that creed.

His blond hair was barely streaked with gray, and his blue eyes still held their sparkle. His face was ruddy and handsome. Pamela had inherited her beauty from him.

"I'm here, Papa," Lilias said. Her father turned, glanced quickly at her, and then away, as was his custom.

"An excellent wedding." He rubbed his hands in satisfaction. "It is a pleasure, indeed, to have one daughter so well married."

Your pleasure, Father, is in the bargain you made with Squire Trevell for his generous marriage settlement. You sold your daughter to a man fifteen years her senior. Glumly, Lilias waited for her father's no doubt troublesome decree.

It came with a swiftness that made her gasp.

"One wed, the other about to be," her father said. "Done well, my girl, to catch yourself a wealthy farmer."

"I have done nothing of the sort, sir, as well you know." Lilias gritted her teeth and pressed her lips together, containing the outbreak that would set her father off into a lecture.

Her father grinned. "Never did know how the lads looked at you, Lily. Landham's been looking for some time. Saw it at every hunt and every county assembly. Been expecting him to press his suit this last fortnight."

Landham! Richard Landham was a handsome, rather crude man. Lilias suspected him of a complacent self-love, no doubt because the girls of Tilden village admired his fine looks. But she always felt anxious in his company, and disliked the way his gaze slid up and down her body in too intimate a manner.

12

"You can't accept him, Father," she said. "If I marry, it will be to a man I respect."

"My dear girl, everyone in the community respects Landham. Next to Trevell, he's the wealthiest man in the county. Besotted with you. Keep you in fine style—promised me that."

Her father beamed as he had in years past, when he'd concluded a favorable business transaction. "Look around for better, if you wish. I go to London for the next month. When I return, I figure I'll accept Landham for you."

For once, he looked her full in the face. Then he winced, as though the very sight of her hurt. What had she done to make him dislike her so?

"You've always been proud, Lily. Unattractive trait, that. No doubt inherited it from your grandfather. Serves you ill in this small village. And this village is all we have, 'til I stake my claim on London again. Landham's a fine looker—he ain't a gamester, nor a drunkard," her father said softly. "Not got the polish of the lads you used to know, but a good fellow."

"I'm not a snob," Lilias said. She wasn't, was she? She was just curious about the world, and eager to learn, and sometimes . . . bored and restless, especially since Pamela's hasty betrothal and subsequent marriage.

And she didn't mind Landham because he was a farmer. It was the way he rode his horses with a hard hand and sharp spurs. It made her wonder how he would treat a troublesome wife. "I don't know that I can be happy with Landham."

"Don't wish you unhappy, Lily," her father said with a sigh. "But see here, my girl. He's offered a fortune for you—a thousand pounds. That's proof of his tender feelings, should you need it.

"Besides," her father added with more than a touch of impatience, "Landham's sworn that he'll respect and care for you. I trust him to do it. Man of his word—all Tilden knows it."

In spite of the hurt, Lilias drew herself up. "You wouldn't force me to this, would you, Papa? I've worked since I was old enough to nurse Dr. Thomas's patients. I bring home all my salary from Tilden's school. I've tried to be helpful, indeed I have. Have you no care for me?"

Her father's mouth dropped. "Never would I force you, Lily. Asking you to consider the man, that's all, and I do it for both of us. You'll be settled with a fellow of substance and importance. And with the money from Trevell and Landham, I'll begin again." Her father brushed an imaginary trace of lint from his sleeve, and refused to meet her gaze.

"This is highly unfair."

"Life's unfair. But see how the wheel can turn again? Three years ago, I was a ruined man with two daughters to feed and clothe. Had nothing but this country cottage. I know, your mama loved it, but I never favored rusticating." He stared into the fire, blinked, and cleared his throat.

"Now, I'll return to London with a nest egg to seek my fortune again—your fortune, if I succeed."

Her father flushed, but squared his shoulders. "But maybe I'll fail. Then you'll be condemned to Tilden for the rest of your life. County's got bloody poor pickings in the marriage mart. Better to have you settled properly now, with the best of the lot." With an awkward hand, he patted Lilias on the shoulder.

"Don't fret, child. With what Landham's invested in you, he'll be careful of your happiness."

"As careful as he is of his animals?"

"You're too tender of heart, Lily. Comes from only having one horse. Landham's like any farmer—a little rough with his stock. But he gave his word on the matter." His face bright-ened. "Tell you what. See Landham while I'm gone. If you find you can't bear him, I'll not accept him. Now, that's fair, ain't it?"

He cast her another quick glance. "Not a beauty like our Pamela, but there's much about you a man would wish. If you find Richard Landham pleasing enough, apply yourself to the task of charming him. That's the ticket, my girl."

As though she would! As though, she thought glumly, she could. Charm was not her strong suit. She was too blunt, too proud. Papa had reason to be disappointed in her.

"There now," he said, smiling as though he had settled all to both their satisfaction. "I'll journey to London tomorrow. With any luck, I'll find lodgings and a few servants who won't rob me blind. Settle everything one way or another when I return."

With an impatient wave of the hand, her father turned characteristically brusque again. "Go, now, Lily. Think of the future. Think of your trousseau—make it a modest one, mind you, but with lists of bonnets and furbelows and gowns, won't you have a fine time 'til I return?"

Deep in thought, Lilias walked to the small stable behind the house and led Starfire from his stall. The gelding, a magnificent chestnut with flaxen mane and tail, had been hers from her twelfth year.

One month, and her life might change, utterly. It always amazed her how so much could remain unspoken in a conversation with her father. To borrow shamelessly from Jane Austen, on the surface lay his sense versus her sensibility. But beneath it all was his accusation of both her pride and her prejudice.

Lilias leaned her head against Starfire's shoulder, breathing in the comforting scent of well-tended horse. It would be lovely if, just once, she could do what Papa wished.

If, just once, she could please him, as Pamela always did.

And this year, she had already displeased him mightily.

To her father's horror, she had begged Pamela not to marry John Trevell, but to run away with her, instead. It had all happened in such a rushed fashion. One evening, Pamela had gone off to a party of whist and conversation at Squire Trevell's house, only to fall ill and remain there, chaperoned by the squire's maiden aunt, for a week. And strangest of all, she had not wished to see Lilias or her father the whole while.

When Pamela returned, pale and quiet, she announced her betrothal to the squire, and their wishes to wed by special license within a week. Papa had gone into paroxysms of delight and almost danced a jig around the parlor. Lilias, shocked, and—she had to admit—hurt that Pamela had never confided her interest in the squire, had protested mightily. But Pamela, with a sweet smile that enhanced her fragile beauty, declared herself grateful to John Trevell and determined to wed him.

Papa would be pleased if Lilias wed Landham. Not as pleased as he was with Pamela, but then, she wasn't Pamela. Could she learn to like Landham in a month?

Lilias bridled Starfire and threw herself upon his back. She wasted no time on a saddle. The last of the light would be gone in an hour and she needed to seek Gran Megan's excellent advice at the gypsy camp.

As she passed the village of Tilden, Lilias pulled the horse back into a trot and began to look out for the children who would be sledding now, with no thought to the road. Rounding the bend, she saw them scattered on the snowy hillside, their noses and cheeks as red as their woolen hats.

"Miss Mer-rit! Watch this."

Lilias smiled and waved at Nicholas Simms, who threw

himself on his sleigh and swooped down the hill to stop just in front of her. Starfire stood still as a statue until the boy jumped up. Then he nuzzled Nick's ear. The boy laughed and petted the horse.

"He's a good 'un, he is," Nick said, as he began the long climb back up the hill.

"Look out for Jenny Baker, Nick," she called after him, pointing uphill. Jenny waved as she lowered herself onto the sleigh and got a push from a friend.

Once past the Tilden Hill, Lilias squeezed the horse back into a canter and thanked whatever angels looked after difficult girls that her father had not sold Starfire after the Disaster.

The gypsy camp rose on the plain ahead of her, a neat settlement of wagons and campfires. At the sound of Starfire's hooves, dogs burst into a chorus of barking. Women and men looked up from their work about the fires. Suspicious glances changed to smiles, and hands that had reached for knives and whips waved in greeting.

"Lily! Good fortune to you! Come, you'll stay and sup with us, no?" Val, Gran Megan's strapping son, came forward and held her horse's reins as she slid off.

"No. I've not time for anything, it seems. Oh, Val, I'm in a scrape. Please, where's Gran?"

Val led her to the brightly painted wagon and knocked upon the door. It creaked open and Gran Megan's head appeared, her long, silver hair shining over one shoulder in the pale winter light. Slender, supple, and strong for all her fifty years, Gran moved through the wagon with the grace of a far younger woman.

A warm smile creased cheeks still mystically free from heavy wrinkles. "I knew you would come, Lily. I have tea waiting, and you will tell me all."

Lilias breathed a deep sigh of relief as she climbed into the wagon. The warmth and soft lamplight surrounded her with the promise of sanctuary.

Gran sank gracefully onto a tufted pillow behind a small table and motioned Lilias onto one opposite her. As Gran poured the dark, strong tea into a mug, Lilias quickly told her about her father's expectations.

Gran handed the mug to her. "Drink," she said. Lilias obeyed instantly. One tended to do so around Gran.

When she'd drunk the bitter brew, she scowled into the depths of her cup and handed it to Gran. "A month, Gran. And then my life will either change forever or I'll have failed again. What am I to do?"

"Why, what your father told you. If you don't want Landham, you'll refuse him, which is my advice to you, anyway. You've a fine mind and a good heart, my girl. You need time to grow into them. There's much better waiting for such as you." She swilled the leaves about in the bottom of the mug.

"Stuff! I'm plain as a post compared to Pamela, and she's stuck with Squire Trevell."

"Who loves her heart-deep and has the look and the liveliness of a much younger man."

"Well, she did say she was happy with the squire, but I still think that an age difference of fifteen years is more than a bit. Perhaps I shouldn't have said so to her, but I did."

"And how did she answer you?" Gran Megan's bright eyes assessed her.

Lilias shrugged "She spoke of his 'delicacy of feeling.' That she appreciated his 'courtly, gentle attention,' and then she paled, and then she blushed." Lilias wrinkled her nose. "At which point, I pressed her to describe those aspects of the squire's attentions that made him eligible for sainthood."

Gran's mouth quirked. "And what did she say to that?"

Lilias frowned. "She just went pale again and changed the subject to what her marriage would mean for Papa and me." Remembering the conversation now, she felt a pang of guilt, for John Trevell really was a good man.

"And now she's gone on her wedding trip, and I have no sister to advise me. So it's either disappoint Papa or marry Landham."

She bit her lip. "I'd rather not marry anyone, you know. I want . . . something else, something . . ." *More,* she thought. The world beckoned, if only she could find a way to experience it.

"Hmm." Gran narrowed her eyes as she studied the tea leaves. "Just as I thought. No need for that sacrifice," Gran said, smiling up at her and placing the cup back on the table. "Something else will appear on the horizon, if you just have the courage for it. But while you think on the future, you should know something, Lilias. We'll be leaving this place soon."

Lilias's heart turned to lead in her chest and slowly sank into the vicinity of her stomach. With the gypsies gone, there would be no haven where she was accepted exactly as she was.

"When?" she cried.

"Oh, in a few days, I'd expect," Gran said, in a cheerful voice. "When his lordship's safe home and calls for us to come."

"His lordship?"

"The earl, him that lives at Breme. About twenty miles to the west, Lily Lamb. Don't you remember?"

"The one with the music?"

"Aye, I was sure you'd remember the music. This lord en't the father—he's dead these ten years. But the son, Lord

19

Aubrey. He's coming home, and ask for us he will."

Lilias knew Gran was right. With the Rom, information traveled from place to place faster than it would by post.

"Lord Breme's a good man—a sure sight better to me and mine than those around here, I'll say." Gran's dark eyes glittered and her voice rang with contempt. Then, her expression changed and she swirled the dregs about in the cup she held, rechecking.

She looked up at Lilias, a mysterious smile playing at the corners of her mouth. "For now, my lamb, you go home. Keep a lookout on the road past Tilden Hill. It's going dark, and those on the road may not be as careful as they should."

Aubrey's gaze swept the land outside the coach window. The landmarks were fast dimming, and the white snow took on a blue tint in the deepening twilight. Right on schedule, the shivering began. He slumped back against the squabs of the coach, as Tom Coachman whipped the team of four into a brisk canter.

Ram Dass sat opposite, serene as always. The bag beside him contained the quinine and the unguents he insisted upon rubbing into the scars on Aubrey's face and chest, where the leopard had ripped the flesh open. To his left, Will Lessing, his secretary, sat with a traveling desk on his lap.

Twenty more miles and he'd be home again. Home. . . . After the inquest, there had been long months aboard ship, and then days spent at coaching inns from Portsmouth. But tonight, he would sleep at Breme, far from the gossip and speculation now racing through society.

"Three hours 'til home, my lord," Will Lessing said. "Shall we take the time now, before the light goes, to peruse the list I have prepared?"

Aubrey barely heard him. He glanced idly at the shops and

homes in the village of Tilden as the coach raced through. Neat houses built of golden Cotswold stone lined either side of the road. Lamps lit up the windows against the coming darkness. He felt a stranger here, in a place where he'd played on occasion as a boy. He'd been carefree and reckless then, with a certainty that life would always be good.

"The list? Certainly, Will." Aubrey noticed a faint, very faint twitch of contempt on Ram's lips. He ignored it. Ram could look askance all he wished upon the course Aubrey was determined to take, but he would not prevail.

Aubrey nodded to the secretary. "Proceed."

Will took a sheaf of papers from his traveling desk. "Lady Caroline Berring. Her fortune exceeds thirty thousand pounds, to offset her questionable birth. She's a lovely girl of eighteen, with a pleasant and unquestioning character."

"I believe you mean to say 'dull,' Will."

Will pressed his lips together. "Now that you mention it, my lord." He cleared his throat. "Next, Miss Margaret Hall. Tall, and handsome in the classical English style. The daughter of a wealthy wool merchant, Miss Hall is in fine health. She has been trained to manage a large household and does so with ease."

"Perhaps she would wish to manage her husband as well," Aubrey said lightly, despite the body-wracking chills. Vaguely, he felt the cup of medicine Ram placed in his hands and drank the draught.

"I did get a sense of that in her character, my lord."

"Will, tell me what you think—clearly. Time is of the essence. Please be concise." He was sick of it—the illness, his barely controlled temper, his inability to think.

"Yes, my lord." As Will's voice droned on, Aubrey glanced idly out of the carriage window. It mattered little to him whom he married, as long as it was accomplished soon and his bride could provide him with an heir. Even if his plans to waylay Hindley worked, he had six months at most before his cousin and heir returned to England.

So much of the terrifying ordeal in the jungle was a blank to Aubrey, but one thing he remembered clearly. As his men had carried him out of the jungle, Aubrey had made two vows. The first was that he would survive. And the second was that Rupert Hindley would never get his hands on Aubrey's fortune or his home.

A movement flashed in the half-light ahead and brought him to with a start. A shadowy figure on horseback raced toward them on the road ahead. Highwaymen, he thought. Or perhaps assassins. He and Ram exchanged glances and slipped their pistols from their coats.

"Will," he said quietly with a look at his secretary's white face. "Can you shoot?"

The lad swallowed hard and nodded.

Ram had opened a small case. He took out two more guns, and handed one to Aubrey and one to the secretary. Aubrey held out his hand for a knife, as well, and shoved it into his belt.

Hindley's work already, Aubrey thought as he scanned the road for more than the one rider. He assumed there would be at least six, like the ones Hindley had hired to kill him on the road to Delhi. What irony, if he should have survived everything, only to die so close to home. He pulled the coach window down and braced his arm on the ledge to steady the pistol against the next bout of fever chills.

Then, in amazement, he blinked. Only the one rider raced toward them, a woman, it seemed, from her height and figure. She waved her arms wildly, cape flowing behind her in the wind. Aubrey banged the roof of the coach and relaxed his hold on the trigger.

"Tom," he yelled against the sound of hoofbeats and wind and the loud groan of locked wheels. The carriage swerved across the road as the coachman shouted at the startled team. Still clutching the pistol, Will grabbed the inkwell while papers scattered to the floor.

"The gun, Will," Aubrey said, pointing to the secretary's shaking hand. Will slipped the gun onto the seat and leaned back, shutting his eyes.

"Aye, my lord. I see her!" Tom was hauling hard on the ribbons. But the horses, given their head for so long, were slow to respond. The woman kept on coming. Aubrey's heart began to pound against his chest.

"Halt!" she cried in a ringing voice as she wheeled her horse sideways, blocking the road. The chestnut rose on his haunches, pawing the air, his mane flashing silver in the moonlight. The team hesitated at the sound of her clear call. Tom shouted a curse and tugged with all his strength. The coach slid to a stop, wheels screeching.

"Holy hell!" Tom roared. "Are ye mad, woman?"

"Oh, do stop that cursing!" The hood of her cloak hid much of her face, but the young voice was cool and crisp. And educated, an odd thing in a woman alone upon a wintry road at nightfall. "What person ordered this carriage to race down this road?"

She's furious, Aubrey thought. The little idiot almost caused a disaster and *she's* furious.

He was about to call out when, to his surprise, Ram opened the opposite door and stepped down onto the road. "My master is ill," he said in his soft, lilting accent. "The coachman wished to get home quickly for that reason."

"Oh." She leaned forward just a little, then checked the movement, betraying both curiosity and an inclination toward politeness. Someone must have taught her not to stare.

23

"I beg your pardon," she said in a much softer voice. "The children are sledding down the hills to your left and right just beyond the turn."

She pointed to the curve in the road only thirty feet away. Aubrey caught his breath as he realized what calamity she had just averted.

Ram bowed to her. "My thanks and those of my master, Miss . . . Would the lady be gracious enough to give me her name?"

"Miss Lilias Merrit," the woman said. Aubrey could hear the smile in her voice. "And yours, sir?"

"I am called Ram Dass."

"Um. . . ." Her horse showed just a hint of restlessness, with a half-hearted paw at the hard road. A light clasp of her hands on the reins stopped that behavior. "I apologize. There are so few books in the village, and none on India. But you are a Sikh, or perhaps a Lascar, are you not? Do I say Mr. Dass, or do I use your full name?"

"I have been a soldier, yes, but now I serve my master. And if Miss Merrit will be so kind, she will use the full name."

"Oh, yes, of course. Well, I am pleased to have met you, Ram Dass. My apologies to your master, and my wishes for his recovery."

Her head tilted back. She must be looking up at poor Tom from the shadowy folds of her hood, Aubrey thought.

"Do remember the children, Coachman." She turned the horse and trotted him toward the coach. Aubrey slumped back into the squabs as she passed and rode down the road behind them.

Then he turned, leaned his head through the open window, and stared at her straight back as she rode away. She rode astride. With, if he was not mistaken in the dusk, no saddle. And still, she had signaled the horse to rear.

The door shut as Ram climbed in, settled into the seat opposite, and closed the window firmly. The coach rocked forward at a slow pace.

Aubrey was filled with the most inexplicable desire to laugh, long and hard. "Rather cheeky assassin."

His thoughts lingered on Lilias Merrit, who went out on a winter eve with no groom, when a gentlewoman would have taken her carriage and an abigail. But she spoke like a lady, and had just taken to task the owner of a coach and four with a gold crest emblazoned upon it.

"Miss Lilias Merrit," he mused. "A courageous chit."

"My lord?" Will Lessing asked, his hands busy opening the inkpot and dipping his quill. "You wish to consider this lady?" His voice held surprise.

"Oh, by all means. With that healthy set of lungs, she's a fit bride for the beast."

Will shot Aubrey a troubled look but, overall, remained quiet beneath the onslaught of his sarcasm. He dipped the quill again and scratched out something he'd just written in his infernal notebook.

Aubrey felt like a cad. He wouldn't have mocked a kind and courageous lady in the past. It came from the constant strain of waiting for Hindley's next move in the game.

He shut his eyes and slid back against the squabs of the carriage. In truth, he wouldn't consider a woman like the lady on the road under any circumstances. What little part of him remained civilized admired her. And he refused to wed a woman who aroused any emotion in him, particularly admiration.

Chapter Two

Lilias trudged through the village in deep snow, her head down and her feet freezing in her boots. Aversion to meeting Landham made her take the fields to the village instead of the road past his prosperous farm, adding another half-hour to her journey. In the last two days, she'd honestly tried to do as her father wished. She'd been kind to Landham at Mrs. Thomas's dinner party. She'd even taken him as partner last night at whist. But while there was nothing about Landham she could dislike, she couldn't quite like him, either. When push came to shove, she just didn't trust him.

"Lilias!" Anne Thomas, the doctor's pretty blond daughter, ran toward her, waving her hand wildly. "Have you heard? Lord Beast has returned to England!"

Lilias reluctantly surfaced from the bog of problems she must solve in two days. "Lord who?"

"Lord Breme, of course. Where have you been this last se'ennight? We're agog at the news. Can you imagine that man having the nerve to set foot in England after what he did?"

"Exactly what did he do?"

"Lord Breme murdered his first wife, did you not hear?

Shot her dead and then . . ." Anne leaned close and her voice dropped to a dramatic whisper. "He mutilated her body."

"Nonsense." Lilias fought the frisson of fear that rose inside her. She knew the villagers had probably exaggerated the grisly stories beyond any semblance to truth.

At Lilias's skeptical look, Anne nodded vehemently. "Oh, you may be certain about this. He's a demon. A worshipper of death. A monster. A beast. And there is more . . ." Anne paused and her pretty blue eyes widened. "He seeks a bride so he may do it again."

In spite of her problems, Lilias couldn't help but laugh. "You mustn't believe such rumors, Anne. If Lord Breme murdered his wife, the queen would have him arrested and hanged."

"Perhaps she will at any moment." Anne frowned, her mood seemingly ruined by Lilias's refusal to be affected by her news. "Laugh all you wish, but you'll see. The man is a beast, and he will end up with a noose around his neck.

"Now," Anne said as she put her arm through Lilias's and walked beside her toward the schoolhouse. "Come home to sup with us. Papa will invite Mr. Landham if you wish it, and perhaps he'll bring a friend."

Lilias smiled. Anne might be a featherbrain bent upon flirtation and gossip, but she never could hold a grudge for more than a minute. "Not tonight, I'm afraid. I must return home with my purchases." Her basket of foodstuffs weighed heavily as she contemplated the long journey back to the cottage.

"Miss Merrit," Dr. Thomas's voice called out to her as he approached. "My very best wishes, my dear," he said, shaking her hand. "From what I have heard, you will soon trade your father's hearth for that of your future husband."

Lilias cringed inwardly. "Any rumors you might have heard to that effect are untrue, sir."

Dr. Thomas smiled at her and winked. "As I heard this rumor from Mr. Landham, I believe it to be true. He and your father raised a glass at the Bull and Bear and agreed on the betrothal contract the night before your father left Tilden for London, my dear."

Papa agreed to the betrothal? Dr. Thomas's voice seemed tinny and distant. "You seem to be the only person not to have heard the news. Although we all hope Mr. Landham will permit you to continue your work with the children." He broke into a kindly chuckle.

"Permit?" Her heart drummed loudly in her ears.

"Of course, my dear child. You will have more pressing obligations after you are married." Dr. Thomas smiled. "Anne and I wish you joy, Lilias. Your future will be a happy one."

"I haven't agreed to anything, yet," she said, staring at her boots, trying to control the sudden wave of fury that swept her.

A shadow loomed over the snow at her feet. She glanced up sharply to find the large, well-favored man she'd been avoiding in front of her, legs wide and hands tucked into the belt at his waist.

"I'll walk ye home, Miss Merrit. Lilias, if I may," Richard Landham added, with a wink to Anne and Dr. Thomas.

At their indulgent chuckles, her anger surged higher. "You may not, Mr. Landham." She mustered as cool a voice as she could, considering the bile that choked her throat. Holding her skirts close so even those might not touch Landham, she slipped past him.

He followed at her heels.

"What do you mean by spreading it all over Tilden that Papa has agreed to your suit?" she hissed at him, turning to glare as she walked farther from Anne and Dr. Thomas.

Landham merely laughed and strode on beside her, his boots crunching loudly in the snow. "Y'er a spunky one, Lilias. That's why I want you. And have you I shall. Yer father's bent on it, same as I."

"He is merely considering your offer." *Oh, God, let that be true,* she thought furiously. "Do you know, Mr. Landham, that I despise the word, 'spunky.' It is usually used by a man in an attempt to compliment a creature he believes inferior to him. You have spunky horses, spunky hounds, and I suppose that now you wish a spunky woman."

Lilias stopped dead in her tracks and turned toward him. Her promise to her father flew away like so much blowing snow. "Well, you'll not have me, sir. You ought to look around for a more acquiescent mate. It will save you time and embarrassment."

Landham's face flushed deep red and his eyes narrowed. He lunged forward, grabbing her arms in a grip she felt through the layers of woolen cloak and wide sleeves. She winced at the pain. He crushed her against his chest and took her mouth in a hard, punishing kiss. She struggled, but his grip only tightened. Fear surged, and she pushed frantically at his chest.

"Landham," Dr. Thomas's voice cried out from behind them. "We shall see Miss Merrit home." At his disapproving tone, Landham let her go.

Lilias put a shaking hand up to her bruised lips.

"Remember that, my girl," Landham said in a low, threatening voice. "Remember that when you think of refusing me what I want."

Without a word, Lilias turned and ran toward Dr. Thomas as though the hounds of hell were on her heels.

Gran Megan stood in front of the brightly painted wagon.

The firelight glowed upon it and limned her bright silver hair with a halo of light. Lilias slipped from Starfire's back and straight into her open arms.

"Please, Gran. Take me with you."

Gran set her back, staring at her face. Her fingertips softly touched Lilias's lower lip. "You've a nasty bruise, there. What happened, love?" Gran's voice was as gentle as a summer breeze.

"Landham." Lilias spat the name. "Earlier tonight he showed me what I may expect from him."

"Aye. That one's been sure of his place at the table since he was a child. I suspect he didn't like the word 'no.' "

"He didn't." Lilias's mouth curled with the bitterness settling deep inside her.

Gran pulled her into her arms. "I told your mother, and I told you, Lily love," she said as she stroked her back. "You always have a home with us."

"Only give me a ride to Breme-on-the-Wold, Gran." Lilias, convinced that Landham would come against the Rom if they gave her sanctuary, had worked it all out beforehand. "I'll take the stage to Bath. I could become a dressmaker's assistant, perhaps, or a lady's maid. Just until Papa comes home and I can sort this mess out."

"There is another possibility, child, and I'll ask you to consider it very carefully. You know the lord's safe home?"

Lilias nodded. "Everyone speaks of it in the village. Although from what I've heard, Lord Breme is the closest thing to a dragon or a monster we have in these parts."

Gran looked long and hard at her. "And what else have you heard, Lilias?"

She shrugged. "Oh, the usual misconceptions and rumors, I suspect. You know how Tilden's villagers love to condemn."

"You don't believe the stories?"

Lilias gave a huff of derision, in part, to hide the little shudder she could not manage to keep from herself. "The tales lack logic. How could a man who'd murdered his wife return to England, expecting no notice of his crime? Even the lords must stand trial for murder."

Gran smiled. "Logic, is it? Ah, 'tis better than ignorance, no? Well, then, into the wagon with you. Val will see to your baggage and the horse. We'll be off with the sun to Breme and you must sleep a bit first. When we're on the road, I'll tell you what you might do."

"As long as I don't have to lie, cheat, or steal—with apologies to Val and the Rom—I'll do it."

She shuddered, and ran the sleeve of her coat across her mouth in a futile effort to be rid of Landham's touch. Her lip started throbbing again. "I'll beg in the streets before I put myself beneath the thumb of that swaggering brute."

Dear heaven. Papa would be so disappointed in her. Again.

Chapter Three

The jungle was still warm at twilight. He heard the bats take wing and Susannah's little shriek as one of those diminutive aerialists swooped close. Susannah motioned him farther into the jungle with a smile. He resisted, but somehow she compelled him forward into the gloom. Just ahead, he sensed a fissure in the earth—a deep pit. Down, down lay darkness. "Darkness visible," he whispered, and wondered at the irony.

For as he stood swaying at the edge, he understood that he was looking into the mouth of hell. His hand shook. He felt the heavy metal grip of the pistol in it.

"The pit is what you deserve," she said. She was waiting, expectant, her glittering smile full of hatred and anticipation.

"No," he told her.

"Do it," she said. "You think there must be some mistake. Poor, delusional bastard, still looking for a way out of the guilt. You've already done it once. Do it now and know yourself."

Nooo . . . Choking in repugnance, his gaze riveted upon the pistol in his shaking hand. He shut his eyes in negation, but as the sharp crack of the shot reverberated through the jungle, his eyes opened again. Susannah stared down at her chest. Dark blood blossomed there, then flowered into a wide, grisly pattern on her

32

white gown. She choked, and her expression froze into that mask of shock and hatred emblazoned upon his tormented thoughts. She slowly, slowly sank to the ground.

Aubrey awoke gasping, as the sound of the shot reverberated through his brain. Sweat ran down his back and his chest, soaking his nightshirt. He covered his ears to drown out the cacophony everywhere around him.

Ram walked in, took one look at him, and went to the washstand. Shaking his head, he wrung out a cloth and placed it on Aubrey's burning forehead.

"Make them stop," Aubrey whispered.

"It's an absurd order. Let them play," Ram said. "The music will do you good. Try to listen."

From the ballroom below, the harpsichord's notes pounded like a hammer in his head. He could barely concentrate through the pain. "No. Tell them to leave the ballroom now, and to lock the door behind them." The music had to stop or he would go mad.

"You're thinking of Dr. Bingham's ridiculous prognosis again, aren't you?" Ram said, bringing him back to the present and the pain lacing through his head. "I told you at the time, Aubrey. That man's a quack, no matter how many honors he's got from the Royal Society. The sooner you let the music in, the sooner you'll let yourself remember."

But what did Ram know of it, other than blind loyalty? Aubrey had read once that dreams never lie. So there was only one explanation, he thought with a shudder of self-loathing. He was a cold-blooded murderer.

"Tell them to stop," he cried out, stretched taut by the sound and the pain.

Ram ran for the door to Aubrey's bedchamber and opened it on William Lessing, his hand lifted to knock.

"Give me a minute." Aubrey's voice came out grating and harsh in the large room, a symptom of the bloody illness, and an insult to his ears. Although the fever was heavy enough to drag him under, he stared with throbbing eyes at the ceiling, afraid of the dreams, afraid of himself.

Will entered and crossed the room with hesitant steps, coming to rest beside the bed. He held his lap desk before him like an acolyte holding a sacred relic. But his face was pale and his hands trembled.

Below, the cursed sound stopped and a door shut with a decisive clap. Although his head still throbbed, Aubrey found he could breathe again. He frowned, concentrating on Will's uncharacteristic behavior. Damn. It was bad news and would take a month to get it if the boy didn't relax.

"Sit down, Will." Aubrey motioned to a comfortable wing chair near the bed. Will drew it up and settled himself.

"I hope you are much improved this evening, my lord," Will said, as he fumbled with his notes from the desk.

Aubrey shrugged. "It runs its course. Now. Have we a report from Captain Treadwell?"

Will's face, if possible, grew paler. "Despite the embargo most captains honored, Mr. Hindley found a Dutch ship in Calcutta. It will take him three months to arrive in London."

"I see." The bleak, empty hollow expanded inside. He had thought he'd have more time. Six months at least, to protect everything he cared about.

He had to stop the damned recurring nightmares and think. Ram told him fear and self-doubt put the dreams into his mind. Ram insisted that someone else had been in that jungle with him and Susannah. After all, Aubrey had been shot too. Yet the nightmares were so clear, so damning.

How could he possibly know for sure whether he was even worth defending, if he could not remember?

But to go to the gallows and give everything to Hindley? Never.

Will pulled out a handkerchief and blotted his forehead. Visibly, he steeled himself to continue. "We know Mr. Hindley still seems bent upon your demise. I believe he'll instigate a trial, but we can't be certain. If he chooses murder, he need not even be in London. After all, he had time to plot while waiting for the inquest in Delhi."

Yes, Aubrey thought. He knew Rupert Hindley's character with a certainty that justified his own moves in the game. "I must decide quickly upon the next countess. What more have you learned?"

Lessing straightened his shoulders. "As much as I could concerning Miss Merrit, my lord."

"Miss Merrit? Why in heaven's name would you concern yourself with her?"

Lessing looked confused. Then his face got very red. "My—my lord, I thought you wished her placed at the top of the list."

Breme's high towers and crenellations rose huge and grim against the cloud-torn sky. Lilias trembled as she approached the dark castle. The wind wuthered through the bare branches of massive oaks on the lawn. The moon sailed forth from the clouds, revealing lead-paned windows staring out at her like so many blank and inimical eyes.

"This is not a good idea," she muttered as she tethered Starfire beneath a large portico at the side of the castle and sought the servants' entrance. There didn't seem to be one, at least none that she could see. She eyed the massive main doors with aversion.

But Gran Megan's voice still echoed in her ears, insistent and compelling. "If Landham seeks you in Bath, he'll find you and none will stop him from taking you. Only a man of power can protect you. Only a man like Breme."

She needed asylum. 'Til the end of the month, or perhaps after, if her father disowned her for ruining his hopes. She straightened her shoulders and strode to the doors. It took both hands to lift the heavy iron knocker. Its sound seemed an echoing knell through the thick oak doors, announcing her doom rather then her arrival.

She placed her ear to the door and heard footsteps clicking on what sounded like cold marble. One of the big doors creaked open and she peered into a cavernous hall, lit only by a single candle held out to inspect her.

"I believe I have made a mistake," she managed. She turned away from the shadow holding the flickering light, her foot poised to scamper back to Starfire and the safety of the Rom.

She heard a voice, soft and lyrical in accented but fluent English. "Miss Merrit," said Ram Dass. "We are honored. Come in, if you please. I shall tell my master you have come."

Aubrey stared at Will Lessing in amazement. "The top of the list—Miss Merrit? Will, I was only bamming you, and very obviously. I thought you understood."

"I'm sorry, my lord. I was certain that you jested, but Ram Dass insisted." Will cleared his throat. "I shall go on to the next young lady."

Aubrey opened his mouth to push Will on through the blasted list. And shut it again. He was curious about the woman. "Since you've gone to the trouble, Will, at least tell me what you've learned."

Will opened his notebook and retrieved a folder. "Miss Lilias Merrit. Younger daughter of Geoffrey Merrit, by all accounts a handsome and successful merchant who lost everything in the winter storms on the Atlantic several years ago."

Aubrey nodded. "An impoverished merchant's daughter." Still, those modulated, aristocratic tones he'd heard on the Tilden road didn't quite fit the picture of a tradesman's daughter, no matter how wealthy. "I suppose he could afford the best governess for her some time ago."

"Indeed, my lord." Will returned to his notes. "Miss Merrit's mother died when she was quite young. Her sister was recently married and is gone from Tilden upon her wedding trip. Miss Merrit, however, has of late been betrothed to one Richard Landham, a successful landowner with a fine manor house quite close to Tilden."

In the silence that followed, Aubrey could hear the faint ticking of the ormolu mantle clock. He almost laughed at the niggling little pang of disappointment that struck his belly. He didn't even know the chit and he regretted her story's turn into a dead-end.

Oh, he knew too well that women married for money and position. However, the conventional choice didn't seem quite fitting for a woman who rode like a Valkyrie through the night and challenged a coach and four. What she'd really challenged was his imagination. During these last few minutes of speculation, he'd felt almost sane.

He pursed his lips. "I suppose it must be the redoubtable Miss Hall, or Lady Caroline Berring," he said lightly. "If you will make inquiries tomorrow, I shall send you to visit both families as quickly as possible."

"Of course, my lord." Will scraped his papers together, rose, and bowed, turning to go.

A rap sounded at the door and Ram strolled in, his white turban glowing from the soft light behind it in the hall.

It was difficult to tell how long Ram had been gone. Aubrey had enough trouble holding on to his clarity of mind in order to dictate letters to his solicitors, and a particularly important one to Sir Samuel Paxton Green, barrister, known as the Fox for his clever defense of his clients.

The room was beginning to spin when Ram motioned Will out. Vaguely, Aubrey heard the door shut after him.

"There is a lady to see you," Ram said.

Through the shards of light flickering in time to the throbbing of his head, Aubrey could swear he saw a twinkle in Ram's dark eyes.

"At half-nine on a winter's night?"

"Indeed. She is named Miss Merrit. Miss Lilias Merrit."

Aubrey shut his eyes, pressing finger and thumb against the bridge of his nose in a vain attempt to push back the pain. "Not a clever joke, my friend."

"I am not joking. Miss Merrit will be with us some time, Aubrey."

"The devil, you say!" Aubrey pushed himself up from the pillows, a sense of outrage momentarily blotting out the pounding in his head. "Can't have a woman like that around here." Visions of enraged fiancés demanding satisfaction and the ensuing lurid stories in the dailies throbbed through his mind in rhythm with the vise clamping against his forehead.

"Too late for that. I've hired her for the next month, and I have a feeling she'll be of much use to you."

"Hired a gently bred woman? For what?"

Ram shrugged. "A companion, a nurse, what have you, she'll do it."

"I'll be damned if I'll—"

"Well, I can't play nurse anymore, old fellow. I'm going to be busy enough looking after your sorry hide, and you know it."

Aubrey clenched his teeth. "Any time you wish to return home . . ."

Ram raised a brow. "I'll return to whichever home I choose when my job is done, and not a moment before. Now, drink the potion and go to sleep. We'll deal with Miss Merrit in the morning."

Aubrey pulled the bell by the bed.

"Oh, no you don't," Ram said, shaking his head. "You're burning up with fever. Tomorrow."

"That woman is in my house, alone and unchaperoned. I will see her tonight." The valet came in, took one look at him, and went white, himself.

"Get my clothing, Jackson. And quit fluttering. For God's sake, is everyone in this castle acting in a Cheltenham tragedy? There's a fine inn just three miles from Breme. She can stay there, after I've explained the impossibility of her request."

Lilias ordered herself to stop fidgeting with her gloves as she waited in the cozy study where Ram Dass had placed her a half-hour before. Outside the closed study door, scurries, scuttles, and whispers from the winding corridor set her teeth on edge. As soon as she'd entered Breme Castle, she'd gone past the far edge of anxiety and slipped right into irrational terror.

The door opened silently and the Indian servant bowed. "Miss Merrit honors his lordship with her infinite patience. If miss will follow, I will take her to Sahib Lord Breme."

Lilias had been weak with relief at the prospect of work for the next month, even though Ram Dass could only guarantee the position for a week. But after the rumors and the deep gloom of the castle, she'd hoped to face her employer in the light of day.

Begin as you mean to go on, she chided herself, and straightened her back into a posture she hoped showed dignity and at least an outward display of calm.

"His lordship is kind to see me at so late an hour."

Ram Dass bowed again and led her into the hallway. The candle sconces had all been lit as she waited, revealing the rich intricacy of the wall paintings.

She and Ram Dass seemed to walk forever. She spent the lengthening moments wondering anxiously. Why would a man like Breme bother himself with the likes of an unknown servant, whom he could easily meet tomorrow? Unless the more ghastly rumors of idol worship, torture, and ritual sacrifices were true!

Mentally, she shook herself. Good heavens, the man's only proven crime to English sensibilities had been to write with respect about India and its neighbor, the small, independent country of Zaranbad. She had wished to read his books, but the library in Tilden had refused to carry any.

Ram Dass turned left and escorted her up a curving stairway to the second story. There, he turned right again, confusing her already helpless sense of direction further. How was she going to find her way out of this confusing maze? Perhaps, like Theseus confronting the Minotaur in his lair, she ought to have brought a ball of string with her.

Ram Dass stopped and knocked at an arched doorway to her left. A deep voice sounded from within—a sort of rumble wherein she could not make out the words. Ram Dass opened the door and bowed, indicating that she should precede him into the darkened room.

A brace of candles glowed upon a table halfway across the room, producing a small circle of light that only emphasized the gloom surrounding it. The flickering firelight was the only other illumination in the room. After the bright hall, the effect was one of being thrust into stygian darkness. Her nerves jumped beneath her skin at this loss of light, as though something worse than a mere interview loomed.

When she heard the soft click of the door latch behind her and turned to look, Lilias realized Ram Dass had left her.

She was alone with Lord Beast.

Slowly, in the dim, silent room, her eyes adjusted. She made out a tall shape sitting within the winged shadows of a large chair to the right of the fireplace. A table stood beside the chair with what looked to be a glass upon it.

"Miss Merrit, I presume?"

The voice was rough and rasping. It had an uncanny, almost inhuman sound. Steeling herself, she remembered that Ram Dass had said his master was ill. Perhaps that accounted for it. She shivered, and tried to cover the movement by smoothing her skirt with damp palms.

"Yes, my lord." Lilias pulled together the manners her governess had instilled not so long ago and gave the man in the shadows what she hoped was a graceful curtsey.

"The same Miss Merrit of the adventure outside Tilden three nights ago?"

Her eyes widened in surprise that a man of wealth and importance—a lord—would mention the incident upon Tilden road. Did he do so out of resentment that she had upbraided his coachman? Inwardly, she winced, but pushed on in an attempt to change the subject.

"Indeed, my lord. I had been visiting friends that night, the same ones who brought me here today—the Rom."

"You are a friend of Gran Megan and her family?"

She tried to detect the emotion behind the reverberating growl. Interest? Curiosity? No, merely impatience, she concluded.

"Yes, my lord, as was my mother before me." Lilias cleared her throat with a little cough. Although her hands itched to wring the folds of her skirt into shreds, she forced them to lie still at her side.

It was like a bad dream, this polite conversation in a darkened room with an unseen man. His voice sounded like the rasping purr of a lion. She pictured something terrible sitting in the chair, a monster with that deep, rumbling tone emanating from some gigantic chest. She veered between the desire to flee and the need to complete her task.

Need won out. "I apologize for the late hour. Gran Megan suggested I apply for a position immediately, and as my wish is to spare her any more responsibility for me, I agreed."

"Ram Dass spoke out of turn. I don't need a well-bred nurse-companion."

"I would be grateful for employment at Breme, even though I recognize its time limit. If you need someone to fill other positions, I shall be happy to do so for the next month." She was rushing on and on, she knew, but could not seem to stop. "I am well trained in all aspects of housekeeping. Indeed, I have shared responsibility for my father's home in London from a very young age. I am versed in preparations for a dinner party of forty. I can easily work with your staff—"

"I already have a housekeeper." The voice impatiently broke into her monologue, as though the dark essence in the chair grew weary of toying with her.

"I see." Her heart thudded and then began a slow descent to the region of her waist as she stiffly curtsied and turned toward the door. As she took her first step, the brutal determination on Richard Landham's face haunted her memory.

She wheeled again to face the shadow in the chair. "Perhaps the housekeeper needs an assistant. Or I could work as an upstairs maid. I am not proud, my lord."

She saw the quick slash of a large hand, a ring flashing in the firelight. She heard the odd rasp of his breath, then another, and peered through the darkness toward the sound of it. The firelight played upon a dark-clad knee. The large hand that had moved with such swiftness lay upon it—long, graceful fingers at rest, the ring a dull glow of gold. The hand had a yellow-orange tint, presumably from the firelight.

"A lady can't become an upstairs maid. I shall call my carriage for you. The coachman will take you to Tilden, or, if you wish, to the Lion, a respectable inn in the neighborhood."

Oh, lord. This was worse and worse. Desperation shoved her in the very direction she didn't wish to go—toward the mysterious figure in the darkness beyond.

"Ram Dass warned me you would not wish me here, given my . . . ahem . . . background. He also said there is no one else in the neighborhood to care for you, and that he cannot do so now, himself. It will take you at least a week to find a good nurse, my lord. I worked for two years with our local doctor before becoming schoolmistress for the children of Tilden. If you need my references, here they are."

She shut her mouth abruptly, humiliated that the catch in her voice made her sound like a beggar. She moved closer, the letters of reference trembling in her hand, and placed them on the table beside his chair.

"Not much on compliance, are you?" His hand rose to his face. His thumb and finger pressed against a forehead almost hidden beneath an unruly lock of hair. "Bring me light, so I can read them."

At the deep rumble, she walked back to the candelabrum.

She lifted the branch of candles and edged forward, pulled along by determination, held back by the darkness and the tales. The light illuminated shelves of books to her right as she approached the chair. It shimmered and shook a bit as she moved. She was ashamed that this man should know that her hand trembled.

When she arrived before the chair, the graceful hand rose again and reached for the candelabrum. It brushed against her own, a touch of gentle certainty, warm.

Too warm. Fevered, she thought. Willow bark tea, tonight. Then he grasped the metal and she relinquished her unsteady hold.

He set the brace of candles on the table beside the papers. "You wish to stay without a chaperone in this castle, in close proximity to me? Then you ought to know what you're taking on."

The rough, mocking tone jarred her resolve. She took an involuntary step back.

"Come, now. I know you're curious. Look your fill." He raised the brace of candles. The light threw his face into stark relief.

She stared, smothered the first gasp. Black, angry slashes marked the left side of his face, giving it a sinister, bestial look in the glimmering light. Beads of sweat slipped down over that ravaged cheek. And all of his skin, to what should be the very whites of his startling blue eyes, was the color of an egg yolk.

Chapter Four

Damnation, Aubrey thought. She was comely—even with her mouth hanging open in shock. No more pretty women, he thought. He'd sworn he wouldn't have one in the house. Not for a week, and certainly not for a month. At least his overwhelming urge to protect her had fled at the look on her face. What the hell was Ram thinking?

And then her mouth clamped shut, and she just . . . looked, as though he weren't a beast sporting a leopard's love tap—his own little mark of Cain—on his face. As though he were a man, albeit from her expression, a not very pleasant one. Well, what did she expect when the room swam and the only real thing in it was this woman—darkness and light made beautiful?

She wasn't at all in the insipid pink and gold English style. There was something exotic about her, with those fathomless eyes and skin the color of moonlight. He could not . . . must not allow anything like her near him, not when he couldn't afford one more scintilla of—all right, call it by its rightful name, mad fear. Fear of the future, fear of what he could do, had probably done. Fear of the monster he must be inside.

His head was spinning. It wouldn't be long before he'd

succumb to the fever. Tomorrow he'd give her the sack. To-night, he had to get rid of her before he fell over in a pool of sweat and shaking.

"Call Ram Dass," he said. "Now."

She was quick, he'd give her that. Within a moment, Ram was kneeling beside him, and the girl was looking over Ram's shoulder, handing him some vile concoction and in-structing him to drink it, like a nanny with an obstreperous child.

He'd be damned if he'd let her treat him that way. After a word to Ram, she slipped from the room. When Ram half-carried him into the hall, she was nowhere to be seen.

Good. That woman must not see him in this condition. She was leaving tomorrow.

Lilias did not run from Lord Breme's lair. That was be-cause, she noted wryly, her legs were too weak to manage anything above a walk.

She followed the butler through hallways, dark labyrinths she would never be able to find her way out of.

What had she gotten herself into? She pushed down the panic that roiled through her stomach and caused her heart to stutter against her chest. Funny, that his looks had been a shock, but not a terrible one. The sense of claustrophobia that gripped her now had descended at the end of the inter-view, when she'd heard his voice change into a tormented, bestial groan. He sounded like a soul writhing in purgatory. As though the villagers were right, and the powerful lord of this castle was indeed a mad beast.

Lost. Oh, dear heaven, she was lost.

Of course you're lost, you ninny, she mentally scolded. You've never been in this place and it's huge. By daylight, you'll learn it. You are perfectly able to fill the position without this stupid tendency toward a swoon. It's only for a month, at most.

The butler wound farther and farther through the maze of corridors and stairways, burying her in confusion and an anxious sense of hopelessness.

Where else could she go? She couldn't remain with the Rom, for there was always the chance that Landham would find her with them and punish them, as well as her. She had no other option than to convince Lord Breme to keep her for a whole month. And beneath that realization came the understanding that she might have successfully exchanged Landham's brutality for the questionable protection of a man far more frightening.

When she finally reached her chamber, she sat in the elegant room like one turned to stone, while her brain ran round and round, going nowhere. A silent servant—didn't anybody speak in this place?—put her dinner tray on the highly polished mahogany table by the blue velvet armchair in which she sat, but she did not eat much and what she swallowed tasted like sawdust.

"There's nothing to fear," she whispered. "Nothing to fear. Nothing to fear." With trembling fingers, she picked up the heavy key and locked the door. After a long day of hard travel, exhausted, she lay down upon a four-poster bed with its brocade canopy, silken sheets, and soft pillows. And stared out the window, while the stars progressed across the cold, indifferent sky deep into the night.

Ram prepared the quinine and brought it to Aubrey, as his valet helped him out of his soaking shirt.

"It is the hope of this humble servant that Sahib will not exert himself to such a degree again."

Aubrey gave him a laugh tinged in mockery as Ram

washed his chest and arms with tepid water. With his wave of dismissal, the valet left the room and shut the door behind him.

"My exertions were in vain, as you knew they would be. She's bent upon taking over your duties."

Ram smiled as he toweled off the water. Aubrey almost missed the look of satisfaction as his head bent forward in exhaustion. He hung on to the washstand in front of him with both hands in order to keep upright.

"Good. You finally realize Miss Merrit will remain here as your companion." Ram's voice grew serious. "She's going through something very bad, Aubrey. You must have sensed her desperation for the position."

He had felt it. He just didn't trust it. Even when conscience niggled with the dim possibility that she might be no more to blame for her need than he was for his monstrousness. "For the week, but that's it," he warned Ram. "Companion, nurse, guest—what have you," Aubrey managed to say from within the folds of a nightshirt Ram had thrown over his head. "I suppose you've won, for now."

With strict instructions to his legs to stay upright, he walked to the bed on his own two feet and slipped beneath the light sheet. "But don't crow about it. These night sweats won't last all that long. I can feel the difference already. She'll be gone sooner than you think."

"I have a feeling Miss Merrit will not marry this Landham."

"That's not our concern, is it?"

"And why not? Lessing says her betrothed is a landowner of good reputation and wealth. It was known that her father approved the match—that the bridegroom was eager for the wedding. And now she comes here, in the middle of the night, and begs for work. I should think that's a matter of concern for any civilized and curious man."

Aubrey gave Ram a sharp look. "Why would she do that—leave the safety of home and kin to take a menial position?" Aubrey stared at the fire, the first piece of a puzzle dangling seductively, just begging to couple with another, and then another, if he could only find them.

"There could be a simple answer," Ram said. "Maybe she sees more than others and consequently wants more than security. Terribly un-British of her, but there you have it." Ram tapped his finger against his forehead. "Take me, for an example. The English in India saw only what they wished to see—an Indian, a menial, about to come home with you to lead a better life in the most civilized country on earth."

Ram's English, clipped and cultured as it always was when they spoke alone, was tinged with a fine contempt, and Aubrey felt shame that his words should be so true.

"But not Miss Merrit," Ram continued in a milder vein. "She saw me through the darkness of that night and knew me for a specific sort of Indian. And tonight she remembered me and spoke to me with respect, something the rest of them can't do, for every Indian is a wog to them."

Aubrey knew what he meant. Miss Merrit was different. She seemed not to pre-judge anything, not even a monster who looked more than a bit like the beast that had marked him. Had it not been for that and for her look of desperation, he would have given her a lecture upon the folly of running away from home after what must have been a lover's quarrel.

Hadn't it?

Temptation leaned over his shoulder to whisper into his ear: *You've always been a selfish cad, with an ocean's worth of curiosity.* The company of that woman was like a tonic. No, more peaceful, like a respite from the pain. Only at the very end of the interview had he remembered why he was in England, ill and fighting for his life. And why that life might not be worth fighting for. And as she inexplicably refused to run screaming at the sight of him, why not take advantage of the situation? Perhaps, with her around, he might even begin to think clearly about his next moves.

It would give her time, too, to miss her farmer—Landham, was it? The man would only treasure her more if he had to do without her for a week or so.

He shrugged. She'd take one look at him in the daylight and give notice, anyway. "I don't want her to see me like this," he said, and cringed at how pathetic he sounded.

"Very well. Although that woman strikes me as rather accepting. For once, since this travesty began, you might find sympathy from a fellow creature."

"I don't want her sympathy. A week at most, and she goes. Do you hear me? I don't want a vulnerable woman about the place. You know what I might be capable of."

Ram's eyes narrowed. "You don't remember. But that doesn't mean you're guilty, Aubrey."

Why did Ram have to be so bloody insightful?

If he told Ram about the details of the dreams, would he lose his only friend? He didn't know. It was safer to take the coward's way out. "It doesn't mean I'm innocent, either," he said, purposefully vague. "Oh, for God's sake, man, go to bed."

"Aubrey . . ."

"This conversation is over, Ram." Aubrey turned his face to the wall and closed his eyes. He heard the quiet click of the door latch and rolled onto his back, stacking his hands behind his head and staring out the window at the murky darkness. It promised to be a long night.

Lilias awoke to a bright sun and a tap on the door. A maid

silently let herself into the room, curtsied, and placed a tray of toast and tea on a table beside the bed. Another maid arrived with a coal hod and made up the fire.

With a silent curtsey, both headed for the door.

"Thank you, ahh . . . I don't know your names."

"Mine's Jane, miss. I'll see to your clothing and your baths and anything else you need," said one, a red-cheeked girl with a snubbed nose and a wide smile.

"I'm Sarah, miss." The short, dark-haired scullery maid sniffed once and lowered her gaze to the hod she carried.

"Just got here, did you?" Lilias said sympathetically.

"Yes. I miss my mum something terrible."

"Sarah," hissed Jane.

"No, that's all right." Lilias climbed down from the feather bed and pulled on her wrapper.

"And it's late, so it's even colder when I finally have the time to pr . . ." Sarah yelped as Jane's elbow jammed her ribs. Jane gave Sarah a quelling look, and she gulped.

Lilias narrowed her eyes at Jane. She wondered if poor Sarah had to sleep through the cold winter night in a room without a fire in the grate. Did Lord Breme truly treat his servants so shabbily? Who knew what he was capable of, if even a few of the rumors were true? She suppressed a shudder. She'd better try to discover more before she agreed to stay for a month.

If he even allowed her to do that. That stultifying sense of hopelessness threatened again, but she shoved it down by concentrating on Sarah's problems. "My mama died when I was seven, and I miss her every day," Lilias said, changing the subject back to the scullery maid's initial complaint. "Do you live close enough to see yours on your half-days?"

Sarah broke into a watery smile. "Oh, yes, miss. She's the midwife in Breme-on-the-Wold. I can walk over every other

51

Tuesday. I'll see her again next week. In a year, Mr. Jeffries says, if I work hard, I'll become an upstairs maid. Then I'll get a half-day every week."

So. The silent butler of last night was Mr. Jeffries. "I'm glad. There, you see? The future always makes the present look better."

"Yes, miss." Sarah bobbed a curtsey, and Jane swept her through the door, poured tea for Lilias, and turned to the wardrobe to take out Lilias's gown.

A short time later, however, as Lilias attempted to find Lord Breme's room through the maze of corridors and stairways, her courage deserted her. Breme's endless halls were just as confusing as they were last night and the worry of seeing him again, with every scar and that tormented expression made clear, had her going hot and then cold. Finally, after three false turns and two unnecessary flights of stairs, she found the door to Lord Breme's room. She swallowed once and cleared her dry throat, then knocked briskly and waited for his summons. It didn't come. She knocked again. But there was no sound from the room.

She chewed on her bottom lip, anxious and uncertain. He'd looked bad last night. Aside from the monstrous scars and coloring, he had looked very ill. What if he were lying alone, helpless to answer and at death's door?

But maybe he needed privacy for something—taking care of his bodily needs, for instance.

After a few moments of uncertainty, she cleared her throat, called out, "Good morning, Lord Breme," and sailed into the bedchamber.

A man lay shadowed in a huge, ancient bed, its tall headboard carved with a hunting scene of stags and hounds, its green velvet curtains held back by maroon and green silken cords against the four posts. She could barely make out his face, but the hand that plucked at the coverlet was the same long-fingered, graceful hand she'd seen in candlelight last night.

"You didn't knock." The voice rumbled deep, impatient.

"I . . . I did, my lord. You didn't hear me."

"I see no one has taught you not to correct your betters," he said, then shrugged. "Better that you've come, I suppose, as I've had second thoughts. This is a very bad idea. You should leave. Immediately."

Her hands clenched together to stop the trembling. She had nowhere else to go.

"Do you understand, Miss Merrit?" he asked her, his voice soft. "You're the wrong woman for the job. Go home, where you belong."

Her heart pounded loudly against her throat. "You have to keep me," she heard herself saying in a quavering voice. "You can't find anyone else at such short notice."

"You're telling me what I have to do?" His voice rumbled louder in what she interpreted as growing outrage. She took two steps back, then stood her ground. He was ill. He couldn't even get out of bed. He couldn't hurt her now.

What about later? Her pulse stuttered.

"You realize I don't have time for this . . . this impertinence."

"Yes, my lord," she whispered, then cleared her throat past the lump of fear that clogged it. "But the fact remains that you need a nurse and I need this position."

In the silence that stretched out between them, she heard the wind wuther against the windowpane and shivered in a room already too warm.

"It's on your head, then," Lord Breme said, finally. "But I warn you. I'll use you and abuse you before I send you back to that farmer. You'll be grateful to see him after I'm through with you." The beautiful hand waved a dismissal. "Leave me now."

Lilias raced for the door and out into the hall. Another one like Landham. Wait—how did he know about that? How could she stay in the same house as a—a cruel, murderous ravisher with a superhuman ability to spy out his servants' secrets? Would he shove himself against her and hurt her as Landham had done? Would he simply shoot her, or would he prefer to strangle her? What could she do? Where would she go?

Then she remembered how he'd looked last night, the heat of his hand as she gave him the candelabrum, his voice, raw and tortured by the sickness. Until he was a good deal better, he'd not have the strength for his . . . unnatural inclinations.

She found the stairway down. Her foot hovered over the first tread.

She needed a week to determine where she would go next. She desperately needed money to get there.

Slowly, she took the first step, and then the second. As she descended to the floor below, the trembling subsided. It was simple, really. She must convince the cruel, mad, lascivious, but incapable Lord Breme that she was the right woman for the job. She had to be nice.

But not too nice.

And she had to leave before he became . . . capable.

"You told her you'd use her and abuse her?" Ram asked later that day with a quirk of his brow.

"In my present mood," Aubrey said with asperity, "about all she can expect is a fit of temper at least twice a day. I simply don't have the time or the energy to be polite."

There was a quiet rap at the door. Somehow, he knew it

was Miss Merrit, come to take up her saintly duty. He just sensed it from the exasperating I-don't-wish-to-bother-you-with-a-loud-sound kind of knock that one could barely hear. Why didn't Ram realize how it humiliated him for that woman to see him as weak as a child and as hideous as a beast?

He sat upright in the armchair when all he wanted to do was crawl back into bed and pull the covers over his head. He continued to keep his back ramrod straight in that chair as time ticked away. It seemed he stared at the door for at least an hour, his head swimming with the beginning of the fever.

It did not open. He was certain he'd already told her to enter.

"Well, what are you waiting for?" he rumbled. "Come in, Miss Merrit."

She entered with a serene smile on her face and her hands clasped so tightly in front of her that her knuckles were white. "Good afternoon, my lord."

Scared and too proud to admit it, was she? He almost felt sorry for her. She must have had second thoughts. He might be rid of her sooner than he'd supposed. The thought should have relieved him, but it left him with a flat sort of feeling.

She looked at him with the same concentration Ram used when he tended the scars. "Have you eaten?"

"I don't wish to eat."

"I'm not surprised," she said softly, putting her hand against his forehead.

Her hand felt cool against the heat, and would have soothed him if he hadn't been still sitting up, damn it, in a starched shirt, cravat, waistcoat, and trousers because a lady had entered his room.

"Then why'd you ask?" he croaked, sounding sullen and

55

beast-like at the same time. He hated his voice even more now that she heard it.

"I needed to know just how ill you were. You're too sick to get out of bed, that's certain."

"Can't go to bed. There's a lady present." His voice came out in a rumbling mumble, he realized vaguely. The room was much too bright.

She had the temerity to smile—just a little smile that he might have missed had he not been perusing her face so carefully. "I'm not a lady. I'm a servant—a nurse."

He narrowed his eyes against the glare and stared at her. The sun shone through the tall window, limning her hair, until the red and gold strands gleamed amidst the darker chestnut. He liked looking at her.

With a great effort, he managed to cross his arms. "Don't look like one. Won't get into bed with a lady." That didn't sound right, did it? The sunlight revealed the lush curves beneath the modest blue wool gown she wore. It sounded just right, he thought, and smiled through the haze at her.

Her lips pressed together and her brow wrinkled in what seemed a worried frown. "I'm only your nurse, my lord," she said. "I'm a nobody."

"Right," he said.

"So, I would be the right person to help you into a night-shirt and then into bed."

"Not bloody likely."

"If I can't help you, what use am I?" she asked in a voice that seemed to tremble. She seemed afraid, but not, at the moment, of him.

The room began to swim. He had to get back into bed before he humiliated himself and fainted at her feet. "I don't need your help!" he shouted. "Get out!"

"Then Ram Dass will have to help you, and he's too busy to do it."

"He'll do it today." Across the room, Ram stood with his back to the scene playing out in front of him, and pretended to study a letter.

Aubrey could see the telltale tremor in his shoulders. Damn. If he were Ram, he'd be laughing, too.

"For the love of God, woman, I'm not a child," Aubrey growled.

She crossed to the door, then turned to face him, hands on her hips, chin in the air. "You could have fooled me," she muttered, in a voice so low nobody but he, with his acute and discerning ear, would have heard her. In a swirl of petticoats, she was gone.

The next morning, Lilias wound her way through the maze of Breme Castle to Lord Breme's door, determined to smooth over her rocky beginning.

"Miss Merrit?" Lord Breme's rasp was cheerful, at least.

"Yes, my lord," she said, encouraged.

"Go away."

This interchange continued, unvaried, for the next three days. Apparently, Lord Breme had agreed to keep her here without actually using her services. Furthermore, Ram Dass had left Breme three days ago, and had just returned this morning. That meant that someone unskilled tended him, or perhaps that he wasn't being looked after at all.

Each night she'd worried that he might succumb to the terrible fever that wracked him. Banned from his chambers, she paced the floor of her room, ready to aid him. Guilt swept through her at that thought.

It didn't matter who he was or what he'd done. He was simply a patient with a dangerous illness, and in pain. She was trained to help him. In spite of what she thought of him, she had to change their nurse–patient relationship immediately.

Consequently, she lay in wait outside Lord Breme's room for Ram Dass. When he walked out into the hall, she hurried up to him.

"Is he still very ill?" she asked.

Ram Dass nodded, his lips set in a grim line.

"How can I get him to accept me as his nurse?" She huffed out a sigh. "I don't wish Lord Breme to come to harm, Ram Dass, and I am truly skilled. I must find a way to make him accept my help."

Ram Dass nodded again. His turban reflected the soft light of the hall in a nimbus. She laughed to herself at the picture of Ram Dass, Hindu saint.

"His lordship's nights are very long and difficult. If you read to him a bit, perhaps that would make the time pass more easily for him, and then he might trust you near him. I'll come for you when he needs you, miss."

She grabbed onto that idea like a lifeline. "Oh, yes, I should like that very much."

As darkness approached, she waited for Ram Dass to come to her room. Her nerves skittered. The clock ticked toward midnight, strangely loud in her ears. Then she heard the quiet knock on the door.

When she opened it, Ram Dass, holding a candle, stood in the hall. "His lordship needs distraction now. Will you come?"

Ram turned and walked down the hall, clearly expecting her to follow. She grabbed up a couple of books she'd found in Lord Breme's magnificent library earlier this evening and ran after him.

The dark hall was full of strange noises. Creaks and wutherings and shufflings whispered down the corridors, and the cold seeped up stairways. As the hair rose on the back of her neck, she moved closer behind Ram Dass. She tried her best to ignore the darkness and the eerie sounds, but a moan of the wind against the windows made her start. By the time they stood before Lord Breme's door and Ram Dass motioned for her to enter, she didn't hesitate. Anyplace was better than that hallway.

"Stand by the fire and warm up, woman." Lord Breme's irritable growl came from the shadows of a wing chair to the left of the fireplace. As she walked toward the fire, she peeked into the recesses of the chair.

Dark circles smudged beneath his eyes. His hair lay lank and damp on his forehead. She felt a surge of sympathy for him, in spite of his impossible ways.

He stared up at her, the blue depths of his iris almost black. "You look like you've seen a ghost. Before me," he added with a curl of irony on his lips.

"The castle makes sounds." Embarrassed, she looked down at her hands clasped about the books. Somehow, now that she was here with Lord Breme, the idea of ghosts seemed silly.

"Most people would say they're just the sounds an old castle makes. I like to think they're house spirits, like the Russians have."

"House spirits?"

He nodded. "The servants think a benevolent spirit guards the house. It shifts and turns in its sleep at night. They set out bread and drink for it, to keep it happy where it is. Sit down there."

"You were in Russia?" She found herself sitting before the fire in the seat beside his. A small table between them held a candelabrum and some liquid in a glass.

He nodded shortly.

59

"Have you ridden in a troika over the snow?"

"I've driven one. Less difficult than a coach and four, as far as I was concerned."

With a shock, she thought of him as he must have been, before the horrifying incident in India. She pictured him standing in the racing sleigh, skimming across the frozen snow beneath the light of a full moon. She imagined him effortlessly guiding the horses, a strong and graceful adventurer in a Russian fur hat and cloak, with no scars. "Were there wolves?"

He quirked a brow. "Yes. You ask a blasted lot of questions for a nurse."

She pursed her lips and blew out an impatient whir of sound. "I read. I live in a little village. I have nobody else to ask about things. How fast did you go?"

"Fast. That's all for tonight."

She wished to hear more, but he just sat and stared at the fire, his lids drooping.

"You brought books?" he asked.

"Two," she said, startled that she'd forgotten her need to impress Lord Breme and gain acceptance as his nurse.

"Ram says it'll pass the time. Maybe it will. What have you got?"

"Poetry. I thought you'd be too weary for philosophy, or even a novel."

He waved a negligent hand and reached for the glass. "Have at it," he said. "For all the good it'll do."

She opened the Tennyson, pulling the brace of candles closer to her for the increased light.

"This one's "The Lady of Shallot," she said, and began to read, sneaking a peek at his face when she came to the end of a stanza. He sat staring at the fire, his elbow resting on the arm of his chair, his hand supporting his chin.

Somewhere at mid-poem, she noticed his mouth had tightened. She paused.

He said, "Why Lancelot yet again? That strutting peacock! What about King Arthur, for God's sake? Can't Tennyson find anything to say about him, other than he's cuckolded and he dies?"

"But don't you wish to know what happened to the poor Lady?" Lilias wished very much to know, and there were only a few stanzas left.

"I know what happens. And any woman who dies because of that puffed-up popinjay deserves what she gets. Read something else. I'm sick of this one."

Lilias pressed her lips together to keep them from trembling. He was ill. He was weak. There was nothing to fear.

Instead, she leafed through the pages of the second book, by one Robert Browning, and chose a poem that was not too long. " 'My Last Duchess,' " she began. " 'That's my last duchess, painted on the wall. / Looking as though she were alive.' "

She'd only read two lines and realized she'd made a terrible mistake. Like a spectator at the scene of an impending accident, she froze, reading on because she was too rattled to stop.

" 'Sir, t'was not / Her husband's presence only that called that spot / Of joy into the Duchess's cheek,' " she continued. Heavens, what should she do? Was brazening it out better than admitting she knew about his past?

She stole a look at him. In the dancing firelight, she could see the tightness of his shoulders and the bunching of his biceps. If she could just get through this without making him realize that even an isolated village like Tilden knew of the dreadful rumors. But was that better than this clockwork recitation of jealousy, cold fury, and revenge?

With a growing sense of doom, her voice sped over the lines, until she raced through the poem, mad to end the tormented, coiling tension for both of them.

Lilias darted another glance at Lord Breme. Like the single tolling of a bell, fear thrilled through her.

Even in the dim light and despite the jaundiced tinge, his face had drained of all color. His eyes were glittering, blue shards. He seemed so alone, so shattered. Yet she, the author of his anguish, was within arm's reach. It would be so easy for him to stop her, with those clenched fists, with those powerful, muscled arms.

She smothered a gasp and half-rose, whether to flee or to go to him, she didn't know.

"Go on," he said, in a voice so brittle, she thought it might break like a crystal goblet crashed against a wall.

Slowly, she sank back into her chair, while her muscles cramped in fear.

" 'I gave commands. Then all smiles . . .' "

"God, no. Stop," he said.

" 'Stopped together.' " She corrected automatically, her wits slow with the frozen, mechanical dullness of an antelope cornered by a lion. She kept her eyes on the page, her hand spread across it as though she could blot out the words.

A tight silence filled the room. Lilias stared at the open book, afraid to look up. Like a striking cobra, a hand shot out and ripped it from her lap. As she scrambled from the chair, Breme flung the book into the fire.

Wildly, she backed toward the door, every muscle poised for flight. Breme rose and staggered to the window. His back was to her, but she could see the tremor in his shoulders as he bowed his head.

"You know about it, don't you?" he said. "I take it the tale is all over the county by now."

"Yes," she whispered, edging even closer to the door.

He turned his head a little and his image was caught in a gilt-edged mirror hanging on the wall close to his left. His movement arrested, he stared into it, seemingly frozen by the black slashes of his scars in a pale, strained face and the anguished glitter in his eyes. He looked fell and wild, some creature out of a tale told on All Hallow's Eve.

"Am I a madman, then? A beast without heart or conscience or soul? How could I do that? God help me, I couldn't do that!" His arm rose, the signet ring on his finger flashing in the candlelight. With a crash, his fist drove into the looking glass, shattering the reflection into a hundred jagged shards of glass.

His hands rose and he bent his head, burying his face in them. He uttered a low, harsh cry, and in that moment, Lilias flinched, from fear and from the naked revelation of his agony. Blood ran in narrow rivulets from the back of his hand to his cuff, staining it black in the dim light.

Help. They needed help. She ran to the bell pull and yanked on it. "My lord," she said in a shaking voice. "Come, you've hurt yourself. Sit down. Let me bathe your hand. Oh, your poor hand."

He let her lead him to a chair, and sat when she pushed him down into it. Then she ran to the pitcher and bowl on the washstand, and carried them to the table beside the chair in which he sat, his face averted from her.

And all the while, her heart thrashed against her throat like a bird beating against iron bars. She wanted to run from the room. And, irrationally, she wanted to take him into her arms and hold him, telling him it would be all right.

Instead, she bent over him, pulling sharp slivers of glass from the back of his hand, murmuring soothing words all the time. "You're weary. You're ill. You don't know what you're saying. You'll rest, and it will all be better."

The door flung open. Ram Dass walked into the room, reaching them with his long strides in a matter of seconds.

"Let me help Sahib," he told her, and took the cloth from her nerveless fingers.

"Not too bad, my lord. But a few scratches, that's all." His voice was soothing, reassuring, as he took over the job of cleaning Breme's hand.

Lilias stood, staring. Her legs seemed to be rooted to the floor, like a creature's in a bad dream.

As Ram bandaged the hand, she and Breme stayed like that—still as figures in a frieze or a painting, for what seemed a long, terror-filled moment. Then, slowly, Breme turned his face toward her. His eyes were bleak, empty voids.

"Leave me," he said in a broken whisper.

Her legs became her own again. She fled, flinging the door shut behind her.

Chapter Five

She awoke at dawn with the headache. For the first time, she missed Tilden, where she had never suffered a megrim. Torn remnants of fear lingered beneath it, like ragged clouds flying in a dark sky.

Last night she had made a terrible mistake and driven them both into a maelstrom. He had looked so frighteningly strong standing at that window. And afterwards, almost maddened by despair. He could have broken her in half if he'd wanted, but he hadn't. She'd hurt him, it seemed, unbearably, and all he'd done, really, was to turn against himself.

God, had he killed his wife? The picture of Lord Breme standing by the shattered mirror with his head in his hands haunted her. But what if he weren't a monster, simply a man in excruciating pain? With a thudding heart, she watched the hands of the ormolu clock move slowly toward her appointed hour with Lord Breme.

She longed to help him. Ever since Mama had died, she'd had daydreams of running into a burning building and saving people, or jumping into a pond and pulling a drowning child out to safety.

She was terrified of him.

Perhaps she shouldn't see him today. Yes, that would be good. No, that would be giving up.

"Aagh." She shuddered, groaned, and rolled over, pulling the quilts up to her neck and throwing a pillow over her head, a fool trying to shut out reality. But it refused to stay out. Jane came in with her breakfast, and Lilias rose and dressed.

When the hour chimed, she heard a soft knock at her door. She opened it to see Ram Dass looking at her with a hint of something new. It seemed like respect, the kind perhaps that men give each other in battle. "Lord Breme wishes to see you."

She gulped. "I wonder if that's a good idea. Perhaps Mrs. Nettles would be more . . . soothing."

"I think you must go to him. And I think you should try again to attend his needs. He would not hurt you, Miss Merrit." Ram Dass's gaze burned with a deep conviction. "I would stake my soul on that."

Slowly, she let out the breath she'd been holding. "That was not my main concern. I believe . . ." Oh, it stung to admit it! "I think I might hurt him more than help him."

"I disagree, and I know him better than you do. Furthermore, you must begin in earnest to attend Lord Breme today, for with my other duties, I can no longer do it. He understands and he is asking for you. Shall we?" Ram Dass spoke in a commanding, perfectly clipped public school accent that she'd never heard him use before.

There was no decision to make, it seemed. She squared her shoulders and followed.

As they walked down the corridor together, Ram Dass said, "If you would honor this servant by listening closely, I will tell you what to do."

Lilias listened to the Eastern lilt of his words and wondered if she'd just imagined that upper-class precision a moment ago.

She took a deep breath. "Yes, please, and also tell me about the ointment you concocted. Of what is it made?"

"The ointment has a base, very smooth and soothing, made of a moss from Zarastan that heals infection. Also, there is bacilicum powder, and a special root taken from an area near the palace. . . . Of the King," he added, after a short pause.

"You seem to know a great deal about healing."

"I always wished to become a doctor," Ram Dass said.

Lilias smiled, almost forgetting what, or rather who, lay at the end of this walk. "Your father must have been very proud of you."

Ram Dass shrugged. "No, miss. He had other plans for me. But enough about this humble servant." Ram Dass went on with the particulars of Lord Breme's treatment.

Wounds, thought Lilias, stuck on grammar in lieu of thinking beyond the next step down the corridor. Ram Dass mentioned *wounds,* whereas she would have said *wound.* Was this simply a matter of translation or did he count each slash by the leopard's claws a separate wound?

Ram knocked at the large heavily-carved door and then pushed it open gently.

I shall not bolt, she thought, and squared her shoulders. Lord Breme's hoarse voice greeted Ram. She wondered if the fever had left him. Oh, dear heaven. Here she was hoping it had not. If he felt stronger than he had last night . . . if she angered him . . .

The door swung to. She followed Ram Dass into the room and stopped halfway across the floor, her feet silent in the deep pile of the Persian carpet.

Lord Breme stood at a small desk with his back to them,

sipping from a bone china cup and reading a newspaper. Nothing gave credence to the events of last night but the neat bandage wrapped round his right hand.

The next thing Lilias noticed was the brilliant gold of his hair. In the meetings they'd had, she had missed that, and a good deal more, she thought, as she took the liberty to peruse his form.

Tight black breeches hugged slim hips and long, muscular legs. A full-sleeved shirt of thin linen stretched across his muscled back and tucked in at the trim waist. He wore neither waistcoat nor cravat.

As he turned to greet Ram Dass, she saw that his shirt was open at the neck, revealing a sprinkle of golden hair. Hair, on his chest.

She had never seen a man without his cravat before, and the sight made her feel strange, warm and taut. Her body must be reacting to her fear.

She dropped her gaze from the graceful lines of his strong throat.

"Thank you for coming, Miss Merrit. I must say, I'm surprised."

She drew out the curtsey to hide her embarrassment and looked up into his eyes. His expression was calm, and she smoothed her face of any trepidation she might feel.

As she continued to hold his gaze, she noticed how very blue the irises were. The yellow color was still there, perhaps a little lighter than before, but she was expecting it, and somehow, today, it did not seem the most important thing about his face.

The high, broad forehead, the square jaw, and the straight nose were much more noticeable. The scars that slashed from high cheekbone to jaw stood out, as well, in stark, black lines. All in all, this man must have had quite a *good* face before his terrible accident.

Lord Breme suffered her perusal. "Look your fill, Miss Merrit. Then ask your questions and be done with it."

The abrupt voice in that jungle rumble jangled the last of her nerves. "If I might . . . how long will you be . . . yellow?" Her hand shot to her lips. "I'm so sorry. I have a tendency to blurt." When had she become so very, very stupid?

"I have never seen a case like yours," she amended, in a futile attempt to salvage the situation.

His lips curved in a tight smile. "The malaria hangs on for a while and brings on the fever at night. Which reminds me. You are not to come to me again at night." The yellow color deepened to orange. His lips pressed together, but not before she'd seen the full lower lip tremble.

"Yes," she said softly and blinked against the sting at the back of her eyes. Which caused her mind to flounder about for something that would distract them both from difficult subjects. She ended up staring at his cheek.

"Does it hurt?" She had moved closer, she realized. And now leaned toward him and raised her hand, feeling sorry for the poor, seared flesh. She stopped just short of touching him and blinked again in confusion.

The world seemed to be turned upside-down.

"As much as any greeting from a leopard," he said with an impatient wave of his hand. "Ram Dass takes care of it."

He straightened, an obvious sign of his desire to end the interview. "Let's get on with it, Miss Merrit. You see me as I am. Do you think you can still bear to deal with my needs for the rest of the week?" His yellow eyes searched her face, making her feel as though he could peel back the layers of her skin and look straight into her brain. "About the Browning," he said gruffly, "I've already ordered another, if you wish to read the whole thing."

Good lord, he'd twice mentioned last night. Frozen for a moment by nerves and sympathy, she ducked her head and then sneaked a glance at his face. He was studying a spot on the wall behind her left shoulder as though it was the most interesting thing in the world. His face was taut, and his eyes were bleak and empty.

"I find him actually more interesting than his wife, but many feel he's not as talented," she managed to answer in a perfectly ordinary voice.

His shoulders relaxed and he nodded. "We shall have to try another of his poems, then. Until now, I've not been able to make inquiries as to your comfort here. I take it all your belongings were brought from the Rom upon your arrival?"

She shot another quick glance at him. Was that a roundabout apology for last night? "Yes. A footman delivered them." Beside her made-over gowns, she had brought the three things of value she owned—Starfire, her mother's pearls, and the violin.

"Very good. Do you like your rooms?"

He was indeed coming quite close to civility. "They are beautiful, my lord." In truth, they were fit for a lady, not a servant.

"And, Miss Merrit—that chestnut gelding of yours?"

Her eyes widened. "Yes, my lord."

"I had the grooms bring him from the gypsy camp to the stables this morning. In case you might wish to ride on occasion."

His courtesy touched her as no formal words of apology could. To give herself time, she cleared her throat. "Ram Dass told me how to tend your wounds," she said. Looking nowhere but at her cuffs, she unfastened them and rolled them up. "Is the pitcher filled with clean water?" she asked Ram Dass, looking anywhere but at Lord Breme.

Indeed, she wished almost that he looked like the beast from last night. He stood there—tall, proud, surprisingly kind beneath the frightening façade. He suddenly seemed so far above her in station and courtesy as to make her stomach clench in self-consciousness.

Ram Dass indicated the bowl and pitcher on the washstand. The servants had cleaned both of the blood from the night before. Grateful for the chance to turn her back upon Lord Breme, she hurried to it and began to wash.

"I shall be able to attend to your illness, my lord." Thank heavens her voice sounded professional and cool. "If you will be seated, I'll begin."

"Yes. Of course," he said in the same clipped, perfect tone that Ram Dass had used in the hall. She shook her head, wondering what secrets the two of them shared.

Lord Breme shoved his fingers through his hair and stared, not at the chair but his bed.

Another quiet knock at the door produced a footman with a note for Ram Dass. He opened the missive and then looked up at Breme. "I must attend to this, Sahib. I leave you in Miss Merrit's capable hands."

The water Lilias poured into the bowl sloshed over the edge. She steadied her hand and just managed not to crash the pitcher down on the washstand.

A quick glance at Lord Breme's face showed the same helpless consternation that washed through her. "It can't wait?"

Ram Dass, shrugged apologetically and showed him the missive.

Breme nodded sharply. "Go ahead," he told Ram Dass, and she heard the click of the door behind the servant. As she wiped her hands on the clean cloth, she heard Lord Breme's resigned sigh and then his muffled footsteps across the deep Oriental carpet.

She turned to find the ointment and then back to the chair. Nobody there. Her gaze swept the room and came to a screeching halt at the huge, four-poster bed. Breme lounged upon the pillows with a resigned expression on his face.

"If you must tend my wounds, Miss Merrit," he said, his torso rising with the grace of a large cat in the huge bed, "let us proceed quickly."

As Lilias watched with horror and fascination, he lifted his arms and stripped the shirt from his body.

Chapter Six

Lilias Merrit's hands slipped from her hips.

Her exotic eyes widened and her soft mouth formed a soundless little *oh* as he threw the shirt halfway across the room. "The sooner begun, the sooner done," he said. The heat he felt rising from his chest up his throat and over his face must surely show. He felt like a pox-scarred stable boy given his wish to be alone with a buxom dairy maid, knowing all the while she'd find him disgusting.

The way she stared at him made him realize just how terrifying a sight he must be. Damn it, if Ram hadn't left, she would have still had wits enough to hide her reaction.

He'd spent half the night realizing what he'd looked like to her—a madman, brutal, cruel, dangerous. Well, then, let her think that. He couldn't convince her otherwise.

"No more shilly-shallying, Miss Merrit. Just get on with it," he said and stretched out, closing his eyes and turning his head away from the repugnance he expected to see in her gaze. He felt the bandage on his chest lift.

"The first weeks must have been very difficult." Her voice was close, and soft with a sort of sympathetic normality. He could actually smell the sweetness of her breath—honey and tea and apples all mingled together. A subtle perfume emanated from her body as she bent over him. Humiliation and a hot spark of desire swirled him into a confusion of feeling.

"I don't know," he said gruffly. "I was under most of the time with fever from the bullet wound."

"Yes," she said as she gently washed his cheek. "It healed very well, though."

"Ram Dass knows a great deal more than most physicians."

"I'm beginning to realize that," she said. There seemed to be a smile in her voice.

He darted a glance at her. She climbed up into the bed and knelt, arranging her skirts around her. Leaning over, she dipped a clean cloth into the bowl she'd put on the bedside table and then wrung it out. She re-applied it to his chest and kept it there, soaking away the ointment and his self-consciousness in the steamy warmth of the cloth. She had good hands—soft and strong at the same time. She seemed to know just how to touch him.

"Feel better?" she asked, giving him a real smile this time. It lit her face with a piquancy he'd not noticed before. She was close enough that he could identify her scent—fresh soap and delicate lily of the valley.

He grunted a yes as she began to apply the ointment, her brow furrowed just a bit, her lower lip caught between her teeth. She looked like a little girl making letters on her slate. From where he lay, he could see the soft curve of her cheek and the delicate fringe of her dark lashes as she looked down at his chest. Her fingers were soothing, each touch a light caress, leaving his chest with seeming reluctance, to dip into the ointment and return, stroking, lingering. Her touch heated his bare skin as, after months of lying dormant, imagination awoke and wreaked havoc with his senses.

He heard the light hitch in her breathing, saw that her breasts rose and fell quickly, as quickly as did his chest. Was it possible that the current of desire she'd awakened in him swept her along as fiercely as it carried him? He almost laughed at his stupidity—a poor beast hoping for a womanly response when all she could feel for him would be pity at best.

She bent her head closer to her work, her hands stroking and warming the springy hair on his chest. He suppressed a shiver of delight. His groin tightened in response. So much so that all she had to do was look and she'd know.

She was a nurse. She was betrothed to a man by all accounts a virile and handsome fellow. She'd laugh, or run in horror.

"There," she said in satisfaction. "I believe that's just what Ram Dass told me to do. Shall I call for him to see, or shall I bind you now?"

Visions arose that belonged only in an eastern bordello. That part of him with a mind of its own stirred and grew.

He had to get her out of here. Now. "That's enough, Miss Merrit," he said in a loud, rasping shout, and almost cringed at the sound he'd made. "Ring for Ram Dass."

Color rose to her cheeks and she lowered her gaze. "But my lord, I haven't finished. I'm sure I can do it better, if you'll only give me more time."

Bloody hell! Any minute she'd look down at his trousers and see how well she'd done. "Go away, Miss Merrit!" he shouted. "You only make it worse!"

She sprang from the bed and pulled the bell. Still backing, staring at him with those huge, fearful eyes, she made her way toward the door. It opened and Ram walked in. Utter relief and then shame played across her expressive face. With an act of will, she wiped it clear. Again, she was the cool, dispassionate nurse who had come in this morning, expecting to please her patient.

He prayed she had no idea how she'd pleased him.

She curtsied, studiously avoiding his gaze, and then quickly slipped out the door. He was left to face Ram's surprise. He rose and walked to the table. Under the pretense of getting the damned bandage, he adjusted his trousers.

Ram stood by the window, impassive and mute. The silence grew a bit unnerving.

"I told you she wouldn't work out," Aubrey said, just to goad Ram into beginning the inevitable battle.

"Well, you certainly must have made it clear to her. At the moment she's racing toward the stables like the devil's after her."

"She's too young, too cheeky, too—"

"Comely. I've seen you look at her, Aubrey. And given your oh-so-English sense of propriety, you are afraid of what you want to do with her. At least be honest about it."

"What are you, now? My procurer?" At the thought, Aubrey seriously considered striking the best friend he had in the world. "I would no sooner make this woman my mistress than I would slit the throat of an innocent child."

Ram still stared out the window. "I'm more the sanctity of marriage type, old fellow," he said. "Actually, you could do worse than a marriage of convenience with this girl."

"She has no connections, no money. Society would cut us both. You do realize how desperately I need society's approval in these next months." He shut his eyes in exasperation. "And more to the point, it would be like taking a downy young chick and placing her in the fox's den." Images assailed him—Lilias Merrit prey to the gossip, the intrigue of society. "Ram, you'll have to get rid of her. Pay her for a month's work. Just be sure she's gone by nightfall."

"She's come out of the barn," Ram said, ignoring him. "Whoa, she mounted without stirrups—just swung on, light as a feather. She's galloping off in the direction of the gypsy camp. What a seat that girl has on a horse."

Ram still gazed out the window, as Aubrey wished to do. "The hell with society," Ram said. "Given the circumstances, you'll not find someone to suit better than Miss Merrit. She'd give you the courage to stand up to all of 'em. And she's proved she won't turn tail when things get difficult.

"This illness has made you a damned fool, Aubrey," Ram continued in a conversational tone, his hand moving to his pocket. "You need a wife. Fate put a woman right before you who's kind, brave, and honorable. Even half-gone with fever, you want her. But you are so irrational from sleepless nights and self-flagellation that you'll kick her right out of your life without considering the possibilities. You need rest and reason in order to plan your next move, and I shall give it to you.

"Just remember, my friend," Ram continued. "I'm doing this for your sake." He turned, lightning swift, and raised his hand.

In the light streaming through the window, Aubrey saw the flash of metal, and then felt a sharp, burning pain as the bullet ripped through his shoulder.

Chapter Seven

Starfire galloped on, leaping the stone wall that separated the lawn from the wilder wood beyond. Lilias drank in cold wind, needing the rush of sound past her ears to drown out Lord Breme's angry roar, the jangle of her fear. As well, she needed to erase the picture of him stripped to the waist and lying on a rumpled bed, his head turned away from her, his body flowing with sensual grace.

"I'll use you and abuse you," he'd warned her, and she'd stayed, despite the shock and tension of last night, because standing alone in his bedroom and looking at him had been nothing like being with Landham.

Where had it come from, that shivery, warm tingling inside, a curious desire to run her fingers across his chest and discover if his skin was soft, like hers? And how she'd touched him! Not as a healer, but as a woman touched a man she wondered about. It made her groan in humiliation now to remember it.

Storm clouds raced across the sky, tumbling in the wind with a wild confusion that matched her own.

Oh, God, she thought in humiliation. She'd stroked him like a courtesan, and he'd responded by shouting and raging.

No wonder her wits had deserted her.

Perhaps Breme Castle, itself, was making her depraved. She had to give notice immediately. By letter. For she knew one thing for certain. She would walk all the way to London before she had to face Lord Breme again.

She slowed the horse with leg and rein, and looked around her. She had galloped through the thick wood and over fallow fields to the gypsy camp, set up at the edge of a clear, cold stream.

"Lily!" Gran Megan waved from her wagon, and Lilias rode over to her, slipping from Starfire without a word and throwing herself into Gran's open arms.

"I should never have come to Breme," she said against Gran's shoulder.

"Come you inside, Lily lamb. Tell me all about it."

She couldn't—how she'd felt in that moment with Lord Breme—heavens, how she'd *touched* him. Like a drowning swimmer, she grasped the first spar that came her way.

"He is unbearable—rude, cutting—he shouts! I have to leave here," she said as she sat inside the wagon a few moments later, staring at the steaming tea Gran had just poured her.

"Drink your tea first, and give me the cup."

Gran's face wore the determined look Lilias had seen before. She drained the cup and handed it back, wanting this over. If she slipped back into Breme Castle and packed, she could be gone before nightfall.

"A short time of happiness, then a struggle, a journey, a slim chance at the end." Gran looked up, puzzled. "That's all they tell me, but for one other thing."

Lilias laughed. "I'm afraid you've told me somebody else's fortune, Gran. This morning was certainly not a time of happiness, short or otherwise."

"No, lamb. This is definitely your fortune. But see how the leaves swirl together there?"

She held the cup out. Lilias peered into it.

"What does the pattern look like to you?" Gran asked.

Lilias narrowed her eyes. "Well, I don't see flowers, or swans, or even leopards. I just see two letters intertwined."

"Exactly. And what might those be?"

"There's an A and then there's an L, almost like a twiggy monogram on silver." She looked up at Gran, whose face had a very odd look on it.

"This isn't just your fortune, Lilias. It's Lord Breme's, as well. His Christian name is Aubrey."

"Nooo." Lilias shook her head repeatedly. "That could be an H, not an A. And the L could be a sideways V."

Gran gave her a long look. "You're looking for an exit where there's none."

Lilias opened the door to the wagon and dumped the cup out on the ground below. "I don't need one. It's neither my fortune nor his. It's nothing."

"You have to go back, lamb. It's fate."

"I don't believe in fate."

A sound broke outside the wagon, a man's voice shouting, and the answering calls from the gypsies. Val stuck his head into the wagon. "Lily! There's a footman from the castle outside, and he's fair set to lose his mind if you don't come right now."

Lilias climbed down quickly. One of the footmen who normally stood by the great doors of the castle rushed over to her, incongruous among the Rom in his green and gold livery. "Thank heaven you're here, miss. You must come at once."

"What is it?" Lilias grabbed Starfire's halter and swung herself up on his back.

"Oh, miss." The footman's face crumpled in a look of

horror. "His lordship's been shot."

Lilias raced through the front doors of the castle and ran up the broad Tudor stairway, the footman at her heels. Heart pounding, she turned left on the landing.

"No, miss!" the footman shouted. "This way."

She turned around and raced after him, down the endless corridor, up another stairway, and finally, she burst through the door to Lord Breme's chambers.

Ram Dass stood beside the large bed. Breme lay very still, his eyes closed. She swallowed past the knot of fear in her throat.

"How bad is it?" she asked Ram Dass.

"It's not bad, just a flesh wound. He's very lucky. I've given him laudanum."

The breath she'd been holding escaped in a rush of relief. His still face had looked so defenseless. With the long lashes shadowing the plane of his cheek and the tender lower lip softened in relaxation, no one would ever take him for an unfeeling brute.

Ram Dass gave her a solemn look. "I must be gone from Breme to find more protection for Sahib. Will you be able to nurse him? For you must treat the malaria while he is weak from the shock of the wound."

"Of course, but you must tell me what to do."

Ram Dass gave her a list of the drugs she would need.

"Along with the quinine," he said, "you must give him an infusion of Quinghaosu."

"That sounds very exotic."

Ram smiled. "Actually, it is made from a simple plant and has been used in China for over two thousand years. But I have found it a very powerful weapon against the disease . . ." He paused, then added, "A bed has been made up for you in the dressing room. I hope this does not offend your sense of modesty, but it is necessary."

"I understand. I've stayed overnight when nursing some of the children in the village."

"Good." Ram Dass took her hands in both of his. "Miss, he is unhappy because of the malaria and . . . difficulties he faces now. I hope you will realize that beneath all of that beats a heart as kind as that of any fine, honorable man."

A heart as kind? Oh, no. She wasn't quite ready to accept that bit of praise as truth. She pursed her lips and stuck out her chin. "I shall nurse him just as carefully, no matter what his disposition."

Ram Dass gave her a smile. "I see you refuse to believe that now. But I think that you will eventually find Sahib a good man and a good master. If only he rests long enough to awake himself again," he added, his face going grim.

To awake himself again . . . What was he really like, she wondered, as she sat at his bedside and looked down at his sleeping form. *A good man and a good master.* The servants loved him. And he had been kind to her. Before she disgraced herself.

She smiled down at him and brushed back the strand of hair that fell over his forehead. "Perhaps you are like a prince suffering beneath an evil spell. I know you won't thank me when you awaken," she whispered. "But perhaps I can ease the burden a little. You'll never know, of course." She thought of her father, and all the little things she'd tried to do for him, only to realize nothing she did would make him really look at her.

"Although, occasionally, it would be nice to be thanked." She laughed a little and shook her head. What a silly hen, to be talking to him as though he might actually understand.

She took a deep breath and smoothed the coverlet over his

chest, watching the rise and fall of it, reassured by its even rhythm.

He stood on the stairway down into the ballroom, trembling from the sickness and a sense of grim foreboding. He tried to turn, to go back, but something compelled him to move forward. Slowly, he drifted down the stairs. A butler dressed in black took Aubrey's cloak in his clawed hand and announced him with a diabolical grin.

The music jangled against his nerves. Loud and raucous laughter, high shrieks of merriment with an edge of hysteria, screeched from all sides. The stench of sweat and decay wafted in the air and, despite the candles blazing from the onyx chandeliers, the place seemed a vast, dark, echoing cavern—a void from which he could never return.

Wraiths danced around him in a wild bacchanal, garbed in aristocratic dress from different centuries. A woman waltzed by in a bloodstained gown, her perfect, beautiful face framed by blond locks writhing like snakes. She threw her head back and laughed up at her partner, a tall, thin man sporting beauty marks on his dead-white cheek and chin. They only half covered the scars from the pox. He was dressed in a satin frock coat and an elaborate powdered wig. They both turned to Aubrey. Their eyes, rimmed in red, glittered like coals.

"Where am I?" he whispered in horror.

"Don't you know, my lord dolt?" Susannah scolded. "You're where you belong, my dear. Where you put me, you bastard."

She smiled, a cold, sneering twist of the mouth. "You're in hell."

"No!" he screamed, flailing, pushing away arms that held him fast. But he was weak. He couldn't get free. He choked back a sob, trying to block out the laughter, the cacophony of off-key instruments, the shrieks.

Through the discord and the panic, a lone voice reached him. A contralto, he realized—pure, every note true. A simple song, one that didn't make him cringe with agony.

"Flow gently, sweet Afton, among thy green braes . . ."

A good song—from the nursery, when his mother would come to sing him goodnight. He held on to it, and the ugly, grating sounds slowly faded. The voice was a rope, pulling him upward, toward light, and the cool, clean world above this endless waste. And he was back in a ballroom, but not that evil place. Breme's ballroom, full of sunlight, its line of French doors looking out at the park, abounding in the fresh, bright green of spring. He was home.

The sky darkened, the whining wind whipped about the house, and Lilias watched her patient's face with trepidation. He'd twisted and moaned just a short time ago, possibly suffering a hallucination. The song seemed to quiet him.

Ram Dass had assured her Lord Breme would not be violent. It was only the laudanum. It would soothe him, and he must continue to take it every six hours for the next few nights.

He had awakened twice and been quiet each time as she gave him the laudanum and bathed his face and chest. The clock on the mantle chimed midnight. In spite of Ram Dass's assurances, she waited for the first sign of a returning fit, her back tense in the wing chair beside the bed, her feet poised to spring upward, her hands at the ready to restrain him should it be necessary. She scoffed silently. The man in the bed was well over six feet and promised, after recovery from his present illness, to weigh close to fourteen stone. There was little she could do to restrain him if he were to struggle more than he had a short time ago.

His lids fluttered open, a sweep of extravagant lashes rising. She held her breath. He looked at her for a long time, the deep blue of his irises wondering and clouded with the drug. Then he smiled, a slow, deep curve of sculpted lips exuding dreamy charm, the kind that mesmerized, that compelled.

"You," he said, a whispering rumble, a soft caress of sound.

She smiled back. What else could she do?

"I thought it was you," he went on, that musing tone a delight to the senses. "It was wonderful, that last part. There were girls and men. Dancing in the ballroom. And then there was just you."

"Just me." She repeated it out of pique. Other women danced and flirted in beautiful gowns. She nursed the sick and taught children. She wore dull gowns and led a life to match them.

"Mmm hmm. You wore bright colors—silk, flowing trousers, a bodice. You had bells on your ankles and kohl outlining your dark eyes. Your feet were bare, the arches high and graceful."

His rough voice caught her in a dream. She felt the tingle of shock and excitement ripple down her spine. *It's just the laudanum talking,* she reminded herself sternly.

"The music started slowly: a drum, a sitar, and tambour. The bells about your ankles chimed each time you beat the floor with your feet to the rhythm of the drum. You whirled, faster and faster." He smiled and shut his eyes. "Miss Merrit. Oh, Miss Merrit. You dance divinely."

Her breathing grew shallow and quick. Her heart beat faster. Genie, sorcerer, magician—how could a picture so shocking make her long for more? She leaned forward, hand outstretched, drawn to the magic of his voice and the pictures he painted from fever dreams.

His hand reached out from underneath the counterpane

and grasped hers—not tightly, but firmly enough that he pulled her from her chair. "Come closer," he said in a voice somehow vulnerable. "Sit beside me. It's all right. I can't hurt you tonight."

For no reason, she thought of a child in a nursery where goblins might hide, asking for one more story.

She climbed onto the stool and then the high Tudor bed, sitting back against fluffed pillows and the heavily carved headboard, her legs stretched out before her. She relaxed against the downy comfort, the muscles in her back slowly easing in the warmth and softness of the big bed.

Lord Breme smiled and murmured deep in his throat. As the clock ticked on, he seemed to fall back to sleep, shifting on the feather bed. His shoulders rolled toward her and then his head settled in her lap. Her hand rose to gently dislodge him. Without opening his eyes, he found it. Arm across her thighs, he covered her hand with his, snuggled his cheek more deeply against her lap, and let out a sigh that sounded like repletion.

She stared ahead in the darkness. She could extricate herself from her perch beside him. But he was sleeping, he was happy. Why disturb him? The clock ticked on. Was its rhythm anything like the beat of the music as she danced in his dream? Against her tentative fingers, the shining gilt of his hair felt like heavy silk. She listened to the beat of the clock, while from nowhere reasonable, a slow smile tugged at her lips.

Four days later, Ram swung into the room, not a bit of shame in his graceful slouch.

"How are you, old fellow?" When he reached the bed, he took Aubrey's wrist in thumb and forefinger and checked his pocket watch.

"I've been looking forward to thanking you, Ram," Aubrey said. "With great relish."

Memories flooded his brain. The sound of Lilias Merrit's voice declaiming Pope with sly humor, the night when she sat beside him while he told her things about school or summers at Breme before his parents died in the carriage accident. The gentle hands that held him until the bout of chills and shaking stopped. He'd liked it at the time. Now, it filled him with frustration.

Those days were a detour, a little path toward sanity. And he resented the sense of loss that came over him now they were ended.

"Of all the stinking, dirty tricks—"

"Quiet. I'm counting." Ram whipped a doctor's frown his way.

Aubrey ignored it. "I ought to bring you up on charges with the foreign office."

"I'm an excellent shot, Aubrey. The ball only creased the skin, and due to your enforced rest, you're doing beautifully. By the way, I've hired some detectives—Desmond Mann's men."

Aubrey nodded. He knew of the old Bow Street runner and his agency.

"The staff was most concerned, particularly Miss Merrit. Did she tell you how pleased I am with your condition?"

"Did I tell you how displeased I am with your cure? Of all the high-handed, dirty, double-dealing, idiotic schemes. What the hell were you thinking?"

"I was thinking that you were half out of your mind with fever, most of it due to your worthless indulgence in guilt. I merely gave you the time you needed to come to your senses."

Aubrey's blood began to beat heavy and dark through

his veins. "You went too far."

"*I* went too far? Look at yourself! Pushing forward in your schemes without really examining the past. Abusing poor Miss Merrit, who needs your protection, by the way, from that fellow, Landham."

Aubrey rose from the bed, shaking from reaction beneath the stupid nightshirt. *Avoid strong emotion,* Doctor Bingham had told him. "Why? What's happened?"

"Nothing. Only I've made inquiries. He's one of those crude, self-centered toughs who take over a gathering as soon as they walk into it. The word is, he doesn't like it when he's crossed. The barkeep at the village tavern says that he's hurt a few men rather badly."

"And you think he'll do the same to Lilias?" The thought sickened him.

Ram nodded. "I do. Whether or not she thinks so is another matter. Women are often fools over men until it's too late. I'm sure she's worrying over which would be worse for her, a man who will be sure to abuse her or a position as a slavey to some cold aristocrat who'll work her into an early grave. As I said before I shot you, there's a third alternative. Perhaps, if you cannot bring yourself to wed her, you might send Miss Merrit away with enough money to guarantee her an independent life."

"I need her here for now," he said, confounding himself.

"You'll be recovered soon. After that, she will have to take her leave, Aubrey."

"No."

Ram quirked a brow. "You would not compromise her by keeping her here?"

"Of course not," he snapped. Something else . . . he wanted something more from her. The peace, the release from the strain of all that plotting, the easy conversation, the pleasure of watching her expressions change from thought to thought. He wanted more of it.

Ram stared at him. "If she stays, you must take her to wife," he said flatly.

He hadn't thought that far, Aubrey realized. "On the one hand," he said, beginning to pace, "she's intelligent, kind, and as stubborn and strong as any man. She'd know how to protect what was hers. After all, my main reason for taking a bride was to get her with child. Lilias Merrit likes children.

"But on the other hand," he continued, "if I take a penniless merchant's daughter to wife, the ton won't see her pretty face and piquant intellect. They'll see a man so evil that no woman of wealth or station would accept him. Then they might well brand me a murderer."

"Soon you must choose one hand or the other, Aubrey. Now that you're thinking clearly, turn your thoughts to it."

Ram gave him a significant look and, without another word, left him to do just that.

Trouble was, he didn't wish to think about it. He was just recovering. If he wanted a little more time to sort out his life, why the hell shouldn't he take it?

Chapter Eight

Lilias arrived in a rush at Lord Breme's door the next afternoon. Totally understandable that she'd lost her way and ended in the wrong wing, she thought. Breme Castle was as full of twists and turns as the maze at Hampton Court. She followed the line of footmen who brought four huge trunks through the door and set them down in the middle of the floor.

"Good to see you, Miss Merrit." Lord Breme glanced up at her from behind the desk, and then raised his brow at the footman by the door. "Cancel the search party, Frederick."

"Good afternoon, my lord. You seem better today," she said, as Frederick bowed and closed the door behind him.

With a look at his wrinkled brow and the intense expression in his blue eyes, she decided to forego apologies for her tardiness. Why was he looking at her as though she were a difficult problem he had to solve?

"Your trunks have arrived," she said, stating the obvious in an attempt to turn his attention elsewhere—in short, anywhere but at her.

"Why don't you open the first?" he asked her. "You'll need these." He crossed the room, his long, graceful strides the movements of a man used to exercise.

He offered his hand, palm up, with the keys in it. She hesitated. When he was very ill, she'd touched him without thinking: soothing him, bathing him, and changing his bandages. Each touch made her feel more of a kinship with him, one she knew would naturally disappear as soon as he began to gain strength.

He was better, now. This touching was not wise. Heat rose to her cheeks in a guilty blush. Staring at his upturned palm, she reached out for the keys. His hand was cool, firm beneath hers. His fingers drifted against her wrist, the heel of her hand, and stroked the palm as she slid the keys from him. Her hand, nay, her whole body tingled.

She saw the flare of heat in the depths of his blue eyes. Cheeks burning, she busied herself with the first trunk, turning the key in the lock and opening the heavy lid.

A treasure trove of exotic scents wafted from the trunk—jasmine, ambergris, sandalwood, and perfumes she didn't have names for, whose scents made her feel excited and languid at the same time. She inhaled deeply, and then slanted a swift glance at Lord Breme.

His knowing smile sent another traitorous blush to her cheeks. No one looking at him, sitting upright in a wing chair, would take him for anything less than a perfect English gentleman with his frock coat, waistcoat, cravat, and well-pressed trousers. A perfect English gentleman but for his dangerous eyes and the dark, piratical slashes on his chiseled cheek.

But she knew better. No gentleman had ever watched her with such intensity. No man had ever made her feel so tongue-tied. No man had ever made her feel anything the way he did.

"You lived near the jungle?" she asked, breathless as she

drew back the muslin wrappings from the top of the trunk.

"I lived in many places in India, but yes, the lawn of my bungalow in Bengal gave onto a jungle." His voice sounded strained.

She wrinkled her nose, keeping to the conversation playing on the surface of some other communication playing out between them. "I suppose you had snakes. I don't like snakes." She pulled out the first item, a long stretch of bright, shimmering orange fabric, bordered in cloth-of-gold four inches thick on each end. The sari was barbaric, opulent, shouting riches and shameless, bright color. She stroked the cloth.

"Cobras," he said, watching her hands on the gold threads. He crossed one leg over the other, then shifted in his seat.

"Are you uncomfortable, my lord?" she asked him, concerned.

"Yes," he ground out.

"Is there anything I can do to ease your discomfort?"

"Not at present." There was a sense of tension in his pose, as though any moment, he would spring. "Snakes. We were discussing snakes. There were others that were poisonous. But there were elephants, too. And monkeys in all the trees about the lawn. And birds, brilliant in color, calling to each other all morning and all evening."

"Did you ride an elephant?"

Aubrey shut his eyes to erase the erotic picture of Miss Merrit's fingers on the cloth, the supple curve of her back and shoulders as she turned and laid the sari on the table beside the trunk. Hard and aching from the sight of her, he almost laughed aloud at his folly in believing that what he wanted was only the peace he felt with her. What he wanted had nothing peaceful to it.

Without looking at her, he could hear her smoky voice, caught by the picture of the East he had made for her. He realized with a start that Lilias Merrit was fun. Fun to talk to and fun to tease.

"In Rajasthan, the nobility drape their elephants in ropes of pearls and use saddle cloths of gold-trimmed silk. I have ridden one like that at sunset down a wide street where all the fine houses were made of pink stone. The whole earth seemed to glow pink and gold."

"Oh, my."

He opened his eyes. Her hand lay on a bright red silk sari, trimmed with gold embroidered in patterns of flowers, their petals opened wide. She raised the garment to her cheek, brushed against it, buried her nose in the scent of sandalwood that rose from it.

"You have done this nursing business before," he said, abruptly changing the subject to rouse her from her sensual delight in the material, and thus rescue himself from the torment of need he felt when watching her.

"Mm hmm," she said, breaking into his thoughts. "My very first nursing experience was with my sister. She took a bad spill four years ago. Much to my relief, she was fit as ever again in a few months. But she was a terror after she began to mend."

"It must have made you just as cross, to spend all that time nursing a termagant."

The look she gave him was full of surprise. "When my mother died, I was only seven and Pamela was a mere twelve. She put aside her childhood to take care of me. She told me bedtime stories. She dried my tears when I cried and helped me with my studies. And all that time she was alone, but for me."

Rising, Lilias placed the sari beside the other lengths of

cloth. "She's the dearest person in the world."

"And your father?" His curiosity about her continued to surprise him. Perhaps it was the merciful normality of the conversation.

"Well," she said briskly, "I believe this trunk is empty. Would you like to go through the next, or would you rather remove to the library for tea?"

"I wish to remain here," he said. "I believe we were about to speak of your father."

His voice, he noted, had that hint of command in it that he'd used at times in India, when he and Ram took their men on a mission. It had always brought unquestioning obedience, both from the English and the Indians under his command.

Lilias Merrit pursed her lips. "Papa is pragmatic. Ambitious. Decisive. Intelligent but not intellectual."

An expression flashed across her face before she could mask it. Anger, maybe. And sorrow.

"The next trunk, I think," he said, swerving from what seemed painful to her.

Beneath her modest collar and high-buttoned bodice, her breasts rose in a sudden inrush of breath. Then she nodded and raised the lid of the second trunk.

So, Aubrey thought, still intrigued, but oddly touched. She would not speak of her father. Nor had she said a word to anyone about the fiancé. He knew that because he'd asked Jeffries. Perhaps she wasn't like the rest of the girls in her village—all of them mooning and sighing over Richard Landham.

For her part, Lilias busied herself with the next trunk, stalling for time to recover. Two more weeks and the month would be over. Had her father lied to her about withholding his consent to Landham's suit? If so, would he ever speak to her again when she refused to marry Landham?

She drew back the folds of the muslin wrapping. Within lay more strange and wonderful treasures—intricately inlaid boxes that smelled of cloves and incense, warm, soft shawls embroidered all over with flowers and leaves, and small ivory figures, some of them sporting two too many arms.

"Oh, my. What is this?" she blurted before she thought. Then she blushed and put the statue hastily on the desk. The little lush goddess in a wicked state of undress looked at her with a secret smile that both fascinated and shocked.

Lord Breme gave the carved ivory figurine a long glance and then slanted a look at her from beneath the fringe of his lashes. A smile just as secret played at the corners of his mouth. "She is called Lakshmi, the goddess of wealth." He looked at Lilias again. "And fertility."

She cleared her throat. "Heavens. What an odd combination." Intrigued, churning with embarrassment, she glanced at the statue again.

"Not in India," he said. "She—ahem—rather, her expression, reminds me of you, in your less cautious moments." He watched her closely, his eyes dark and intent.

Her cheeks burned. To be compared to an idol—and a barely-clad one at that!

"I am not a bit like this statue," she said in a cool, clipped tone. Then her curiosity spoiled the effect completely. "But why not in India?" she asked him.

"Because his wife's fertility means wealth to a farmer—all those extra hands to help him, you see. And so many children die young in India." He rose from the chair and walked toward her. "I suppose you like children."

She froze, then circled away until the large trunk stood between them. But after all, what he wanted was not propinquity, but a finely-wrought statue of a panther from the trunk. He retrieved it and set it on a bureau in the room. It was so lifelike that Lilias expected it to spring from the bureau at any moment.

"What woman would not like children?" She held the little goddess carefully, staring down at the rounded limbs, the sensual pose.

"Several, I would suspect. They can be a nuisance at times. And a burden. Young creatures need protection."

The way he attended her reminded her of the panther, guarded and still, but ready at any moment to spring. "Of course," she said. "That is the duty that goes along with the joy."

His smile caught and spread, the scars on one side of his face dark, vivid slashes, the other cheek and jaw sculpted and perfect. "Yes. I was right about you that night on the Tilden road."

What did you think about me? she longed to ask. Instead, she stared out the window at the coming dusk.

A knock sounded at the door and Ram entered. Lord Breme set down his last armload of exotic spices and teas. "You need to see me?"

Ram nodded silently.

Lilias blinked, feeling as though she was awakening to another reality. "I'll leave you, then, my lord," she said as she walked toward the door.

"I'll meet you in the library at, say, half-five, Miss Merrit," Lord Breme said. "We'll take tea."

He held the door for her as she swept through, and walked beside her a little way. Why would he show such attention to a servant?

She turned right, in the direction she was certain led to the library. Partway down the hall, Lord Breme's hands closed on her shoulders and held her at a standstill, her back to his chest. "Miss Merrit, I could not help but notice that you seem to be a trifle . . . geographically impaired." His breath was soft and warm against her neck, stirring the curling tendrils and making her pulse race in her throat.

"I don't know how anyone would not appear so in this enormous maze of a house," she shot back, held in thrall by the light touch of his hands. He bent his head so close to her cheek, she almost felt the curve of his lips.

He turned her slowly to the left, his chuckle a whisper away from her ear. "May I offer some advice?"

She suppressed a shiver of excitement and gave a slight nod. Her hair brushed slowly and lightly against the stubble on his cheek. It wasn't until she took a breath that she realized she'd been holding hers.

"Whenever you come out of a room, turn the opposite direction from the one you are certain is correct. That ought to solve the problem."

"Right." She nodded once, firmly.

He released her, his hands slipping from her shoulders with seeming reluctance. She left him without a backward glance, heart pounding against her throat. Whether it beat in fear or elation, she knew not.

"Jeffries gave me some letters for you. They're from London."

"Thanks, old fellow. Just put them on the desk," Aubrey said, carefully placing the little Indian statue on a niche where he could see it from his desk. He wondered if he was right about Lilias Merrit's resemblance to the statue. If one were to slip the gown from her shoulders, would her breasts be as round and lush?

He walked to his desk, dipped a quill in the inkpot, and made a notation on the letter he'd just read to discuss with

Will later. Then he picked up the sheaf of mail and looked through it. As he opened the wafer, he realized Ram had yet to say a word.

Aubrey's eyes narrowed as he read, and his guts twisted. He dropped the letter to the desk and picked up the next one, slitting the wax seal.

The first had been from White's, his club in London. This was from The Explorer's Club. Both had the same message: "This unfortunate event and the rumors . . . must take action to protect the members from unpleasantness . . . just temporary, until the matter is resolved . . . ."

Ram picked up the discarded letter and read it. "The bastards."

There were three more letters from the boards of various clubs and organizations, all the same: polite requests for Aubrey's resignation. He walked to the fireplace with the stack and dropped the letters, one by one, into the blaze, watching the edges curl, then smoke, then finally burn to ashes. He shook his head slowly.

Until that night in the jungle, it hadn't occurred to him how it would be if the world he had always considered his own shunned him like a pariah. And these were the men he had to win over to his side in order to survive.

He'd had everything, and Hindley was taking it all from him, bit by bit.

"They never asked Lord Bellamy to leave," Ram said in a growl, "and he was rumored to dance with witches on the dark of the moon and torture virgins in his tower."

Aubrey glanced at Ram. His face was stark and a muscle twitched in his jaw. It struck Aubrey that Ram would understand this prejudice better than most. Oh, at Eton, with all the brawls in which he'd stood beside Ram, he'd known how difficult it was for his friend growing up. But now, deep in his gut, he understood exactly what it was like.

"Even absent, Hindley's been busy," Ram said. "He's no doubt bribed several impecunious friends to spread rumors even worse about you."

"Yes," was all Aubrey could manage. Inside, feelings he refused to identify churned. Ruthlessly, he shoved them deep, deep down. He'd spent the last four days in a fool's paradise and he had no time to waste. He had to think, to plan. To survive, or at least protect Breme.

"Send for Will, Ram. It's time to set the wheels in motion. I'll want as many of the nobility in the area as will accept an invitation to dine next week. There will be several more parties as soon as I'm able to travel to London."

Ram gave him a look filled with pity. "We can fight this. You'll remember. You don't need to rush into marriage with anyone on that list."

Aubrey shook his head and gritted his teeth. "And if I don't remember? I'll easily look the part of Bluebeard unless I gain a wife of whom the ton will approve. And that just might sway enough of my peers to find me innocent. The women on my list are the only possible candidates to give me that. Along with an heir to checkmate Hindley. As for Miss Merrit," he went on, ignoring the pity on Ram's face, "all it takes is money to give her a future without her farmer, if she wants one."

The clock ticked on. *Too late, too late, too late.*

Before he'd expected it, inexorable as fate in a Greek tragedy, the deadly game had begun.

At half-five, once down the stairs and past an elaborate salon, Lilias looked about her. The library was just down the winding hallway, she thought, although she'd not approached it from this direction before. She was about to move past the next closed door, when she noticed the remarkable carving above its cornice. There, upon an elaborate marble frieze, putti frolicked, playing horns and violins and flutes.

She stopped before the closed door. Perhaps it wasn't locked. She lifted her fingers to the latch. It gave smoothly, and she peeked inside. French doors draped with heavy green velvet curtains lined a very large room. Chairs were set against a mirrored wall. It might have been used as a ballroom, but the floor was filled with music stands. Violins, violas, cellos, and bass were placed beside each stand and sheets of music lay on them. In the center stood both a magnificent harpsichord and a pianoforte. And opposite were chairs in lines and rows. A hundred people could sit and listen to an orchestra in this room.

"Magnificent," she said softly. This was where the music had come from those many years ago, on the summer when she'd been seven, and grieved for her mother, dead since winter. She had stopped speaking—had not spoken for six months, Pamela later told her.

Val, Gran Megan's son, had brought her to the castle's neatly scythed lawn. Night had fallen, dark and napped as velvet. Stars bloomed overhead. She could make out Orion with his belt, Castor and Pollux. And just when she thought there was beauty in the world, after all, the music began, so achingly lovely that she'd cried deep, choking sobs. And spoke again, afterward.

Lilias ran to the violin section. Her hand reached out of its own accord and lifted a violin and bow from the stand in front of her. Her mother's was a fine one, but this was better. Italian, she thought, and old. She examined it carefully and found the Guarneri marks within the sound box. Unbidden, her gasp of awe echoed through the room.

Her fingers itched to pluck the strings. She did so softly.

The notes resonated against the domed ceiling and the walls. The room's perfect acoustics caressed the sound like a lover.

"What the hell are you doing in this room?"

At the soft menace of the voice, she jumped, clutching the violin in a nightmare fear that she might drop it. "I saw the instruments above the door," she said. "It wasn't locked. I thought it would be all right if I—"

"No. You're not to be here," growled the master of the castle.

The heat of his anger scorched her from all the way across the ballroom. She turned to the music stand. With trembling hands, she put the violin back slowly, with great care.

She touched the music on the stand. Not a hint of dust came off upon her fingers, as though this room were cared for daily.

"I won't touch your instruments if I practice here. I have my own violin."

Breme's mouth pressed hard together in a grim line. Outside the long wall of windows, clouds masked the setting sun, throwing the room into gloom that dimmed even the bright gold of his hair. His deep voice echoed, as though from a cavern. Staring at his scarred, brooding face, Lilias felt she'd fallen into the kingdom the ancients called Hades, and that the king of that place stood before her, pronouncing her doom. She bit her lip to stop the trembling.

"How often must I say it? This room is forbidden you. Do you understand?"

A reasonable woman would curtsey and nod and run. Not this woman.

"Why? After all the concerts that must have filled this room with beauty, I mean." Her voice caught the corners and came back to her ears richer. Oh, she would die happy if only she could play in this room. One look at his face convinced her she might very well meet her end if she challenged him again.

"From here, the sound travels everywhere in this house," he said curtly. "You will not play here, because I do not wish to hear it."

Lilias colored at what must be an implication of her lack of polish. Well, the man had grown up with two parents rumored to be virtuosos. She pressed her lips together to keep the words back, but to no avail. "I'm not all that terrible a violinist. If you'd only hear me play once, I'm sure we could arrange a time when I wouldn't disturb you."

He regarded her with a raised brow, the glowering lord of the underworld transformed suddenly into the cool and arrogant aristocrat. "Your schoolgirl screeching would disturb me at any time, Miss Merrit," he said, clipped and cold. "Do not think to disobey me in this. This discussion is over."

Pamela had often warned her against the sin of pride. But Mama had been brilliant, and Mama had told her she would be even better when she grew up. She felt her skin prickle, and quite consciously kept her hand from clenching. She had never wished to strike someone more in her life.

"Schoolgirl screeching? You have no idea how I play. Of all the rude, insulting—"

"Come, now. Surely you can't expect me to believe you play with much finesse." He scowled at her and her blood beat hot.

Yet, as he quickly moved to the door, he no longer looked condescending. He looked like a caged beast, fearful, desperate to run but forced to remain and attack anything that came close.

"Who was your teacher? Your mother, I believe, and a rustic tutor thereafter. What did you learn? Country airs, no doubt. All very well for the schoolroom, but your violin's uninspired caterwauling is not welcome here."

He held the door open. "Come," he said, his tall frame unyielding. His tone was so mocking and so imperious, she almost refused to obey. But it was Lord Breme's music room. Stiff with resentment, she walked through the door.

As he pulled it shut behind them, she found herself shaking.

"A warning, Miss Merrit. Don't wheedle. Spare me any wounded looks or tears. Others far more adept than you have tried and failed to lure me into accommodation. You'll not be able to wrap me round your little finger on this or any other matter. I shall not be swayed. Do you hear me? I shall not be swayed from my path!"

In the space of half an hour, he'd changed again. She hated him for his arbitrary insults, his tirades, his frightening reaction that shook her sense of security. Most of all, she hated what he had reduced her to. She was a servant again, no more. He could insult her at will, and she was helpless in the face of his power over her.

For the first time, she felt the walls of Breme Castle closing in on her like a prison.

Desperately, she shoved them back with the only weapon she had—fury. Whirling, she faced him, chin up. "In Tilden, they jest, and say, 'My lord Beast.' Recently, I've thought that they were stupid, that you were nothing like that. But it's true. You are a beast."

Lord Breme slowly looked her over from head to toe and quirked a sardonic brow. "You think to retaliate by insulting my vanity as I have yours? You won't score points that way, Miss Merrit. You may have a misapprehension of how you play, but I am completely aware of how I look."

"How you look? How you look?" She shimmered with heat and rage. "I am not referring to your face, you dolt. I am speaking of your behavior. And in that, you are beastly, indeed."

She whipped about and strode away on legs that wanted to shake, toward the first stairway she came to. She was on the second stair when she heard his voice.

"Farther down the hall, Miss Merrit, and to your—"

"Don't you dare," she whispered too low for him to hear, but at that point, her courage deserted her. She picked up her skirts and ran up the stairs. In spite of her fear, she'd traverse the entire castle before she gave him the satisfaction of taking directions from him.

Aubrey strode toward the barn, his greatcoat swirling about his boots in the wind, his thoughts churning as fast and hard as the clouds above him in the dark, stormy sky. The stable lad, already alerted, had Domino, his black stallion, saddled and ready for him. The gypsy whip Gran Megan had given him years ago was clipped to the saddle. As Aubrey swung up on his back, Domino tossed his head, eager to go.

The black had plenty of energy. It would take a firm hand and concentration to hold him back the first few miles. Good.

He had a wedding to plan. And a trial to face. This last embarrassing outburst in the ballroom proved one thing.

Miss Merrit had to go. Just by being here, she weakened him. He forgot his duty, his heritage, his revenge.

He moved the horse into a trot for a mile or two across the fields, then slipped the reins a notch and leaned forward. Domino broke into the rocking, long strides of his canter toward the gypsy camp. The wind whipped past Aubrey's face as he upbraided himself. He'd wasted precious time when all that lay before him—the neat farmsteads of the tenants who depended upon him, his servants, the bright castle and land that was his home—faced a danger more potent than any since Cromwell's troops had laid siege to it. Those men hadn't succeeded because his great-great-great grandfather had better things to do than make himself indolent with dreams and wild with lust.

The gypsy camp lay just beyond this field. Gran Megan would know what to do about Lilias and where to send her. If Landham truly were a brute, he'd make sure she was safe from him. But she had to go. Today.

At a noise from the woods to his left, Aubrey pulled Domino's reins and the horse halted. Voices came from the woods, a man's voice shouting angrily and a woman's shriek of pain. Aubrey wheeled the black, unclipping the whip. Galloping through the forest, Aubrey bent low on the black's back, the limbs of trees whipping close overhead. Aubrey passed an overturned basket, the winter herbs in it spilled to the ground.

In a clearing ahead, he saw quite possibly the most handsome man in England standing, legs spread. He was crowding Gran Megan against the hard trunk of a tree and his hands were wrapped around her throat. She struggled weakly in his grasp.

"Yer lying, you old besom!" he shouted. "I know you took her. Tell me where she is!"

Aubrey flicked his wrist. The whip unfurled with a snap and wound around the thug's throat. Aubrey tugged. The bastard flew backwards, landing on his back, choking.

Aubrey looked down at the man flailing on the ground below him, his hands clutching at the whip round his neck. Aubrey tamped down the urge to pull a little harder on the whip and rid the world of this piece of offal.

"Have a taste of your own medicine," he told the man on the ground.

"My lord," Gran said on a sob. "Praise heaven you came."

"Who is he?" Aubrey asked Gran Megan.

"Richard Landham," Gran said, and with those words, complicated everything.

Aubrey leaned over and gave Landham a long, narrow-eyed look. "I am Breme. The Rom are my sacred charge, Mr. Landham. I protect them as I would my family, and I do the same for anyone living on my land. From now on, men will be watching for you. If you come within my borders again, you will pay with your life. Do you understand me?"

Aubrey let the lash slip just a bit, allowing Landham to breathe without struggling. Slowly, the whip slid from his neck. Landham rose to his full height, an inch above his own, Aubrey guessed. Landham's face, now taking back its normal color, really was quite handsome, but the look in his eyes spoiled the picture.

"She took what's mine," he said. "I've a right to come for her."

Aubrey smiled. Landham turned white again. Looking down at the pistol Aubrey pulled from his greatcoat, he swallowed audibly.

"You have no rights here." Aubrey jerked his head to the left. "I see your horse in the trees yonder. Get on him and get out of here, before I put an end to your miserable existence."

Landham ran for the horse. He was up and gone in a matter of seconds.

Aubrey stared after him. Then he lifted Gran Megan before him on the black and took her back to the gypsy camp. Within moments, the women were tending her inside her caravan.

Val's face looked like doom when Aubrey refused to let him join the men who mounted up and rode out to follow Landham.

"If you find him, you'll kill him. Do you think your mother wants you to hang?"

Val shook his head, a desperate look in his eyes. "Someone's got to kill that man. He's poison."

"Someone will, Val. And probably soon. But let it be someone else—most likely a brute just like him will finish him off. Meanwhile, I'll send men to guard the land and I'm asking you to join them. Between us all, we'll keep your mother and Miss Merrit safe."

And there was the conundrum. He'd have to keep her now, damn it.

What to do? he thought as he trotted homeward. If he saw any more of her, he'd be either lust-filled or edgy at a time when he needed his wits about him. He had to find Lilias Merrit a safe haven as far away from Breme as he could get her.

Chapter Nine

As it happened, after Lilias left Lord Breme, she ended up, not in her room, but in the kitchen. By that time, most of the hot emotion had subsided, and the old stubborn streak reared its head. And in her present mood, she greeted it with flags waving and a brass band.

As she entered, Cook turned, surprised, in the middle of icing a cake. Mrs. Nettles, sitting at the kitchen desk, looked up from her writing. Sarah, helping Jane put together a tea tray for one of the footmen, smiled at her, if a little hesitantly.

"Oh, miss. Is there anything amiss? Frederick here was just bringing your tea in the library." Mrs. Nettles smiled at Lilias. "I put some macaroons on the plate for you."

Anything amiss! "Lord Breme is no doubt ensconced in the library by now. But if I may, I'll take tea here, with all of you."

Sarah looked at Cook and Mrs. Nettles, who cleared her throat. "If you'd like that, my dear, I'm sure that's quite all right. Please, sit here, with me." As Frederick left the kitchen with a tea tray for one, Mrs. Nettles spoke of the castle and the wonderful repairs Lord Breme had authorized for the next year. Jeffries, entering a short time later, glanced from

Lilias to Mrs. Nettles. Some private communication must have taken place, for he took his seat at the head of the kitchen table and drank his tea without a word.

The tea was soothing, the cakes and biscuits comforting and sweet. Lilias relaxed, listening to the talk around the table. Slowly, she became aware of a startling difference in this household from the one she had helped to direct before the Disaster.

The staff interacted in a surprisingly democratic fashion. Oh, there was no doubt that Mrs. Nettles and Jeffries ruled below stairs, but the conversation was so pleasant, and each person, even Sarah, the newest member of the staff, was accepted almost as an equal.

No one had as yet forced conversation upon her, but Lilias felt as much a part of the cozy group settled around the table as Sarah seemed to be. So she ventured a question on her own.

"Mrs. Nettles, you know everything about Breme. Is there any place in the castle where one might make noise and not be heard in the family quarters?"

If Mrs. Nettles was surprised by the question, she didn't show it. "Oh, now, I would think that the attic would be soundproof, if that's what you're looking for. In the old days, some of our people used to go up there when they needed a bit of quiet to rehearse. Now, we all use it at different times, due to the—ahem—difficulties with the ballroom."

"You all rehearse?"

"Oh, yes. In the days before Lord Aubrey went abroad, we used to play quite regularly. And some of us preferred not to be heard until we got our parts just right. Why, I remember old Mr. Quick, the head gardener. He played the clarinet—one of the best musicians I ever heard. He was that precise, he was. Such a perfectionist. Do you remember that Mozart

Clarinet Concerto, Mr. Jeffries?"

Jeffries chuckled. "Oh, my, yes. Mr. Quick spent hours in the attic with that one. We didn't hear his part until the dress rehearsal. He was playing for the king, you see, Miss Merrit. Old George, himself. The roses suffered that summer, I must say. But his performance—ah, pure magic."

Lilias looked from Jeffries to Mrs. Nettles to Cook. Their faces were wreathed in smiles of reminiscence. The younger ones leaned forward, fascinated.

Now she understood. The heavenly orchestra she had heard those many years ago had been made up of Breme's staff. No wonder there was such a sense of equality among them. A fine musician would recognize and respect another in this group, whether she was a scullery maid or a lady's maid.

How did this happen? Did the earl distribute instruments to the tenants' children? Did he hire a master to teach them? The possibilities charmed her, making it difficult to hang on to her outrage. Still . . .

In the end, it only took her two days to learn the shortest way to the attic. Two uncomfortable days, in which, except for her unavoidable duties, she kept away from the broodingly unpredictable Lord Breme. It was really quite easy to disappear in a castle of two hundred rooms, particularly when it was obvious that Lord Breme didn't wish to see her, either.

Now she understood Sarah's complaint about the cold. Lilias, wrapped in her cloak, took the narrow stairway up into the cold, drafty attic and carried her mother's violin with her. After all, that beastly man had not forbidden her to play. He'd only said she must not use the music room.

"Where the devil is Miss Merrit?" Aubrey stopped in midstride about his study. Neither Ram nor Will answered him.

He'd seen little enough of her over the last few days. A good thing, that. He hadn't wanted to see her, had avoided calling for her, in fact. She probably feared him now, he thought with a pang. No wonder.

He felt like a cad.

She came when called, but she was . . . aloof. That delightfully musical laugh was silent, the wonder on her face when they talked of books and exotic places had disappeared, the spark that glowed to life when he looked deep into her eyes was extinguished. He wondered if the whole gender of women knew how to bring a man low without trying, or whether it was just one of Lilias Merrit's special talents.

"Sir Samuel Paxton Green will come down to see you next week," Ram said, ignoring his question. "He's quite insistent that you concentrate upon remembering every detail of that day in India, Aubrey."

"I am trying," he told Ram. "I shall continue to do so."

He shouldn't mind that she hated him. It was for the best, after all.

But when he had to summon her, she came to him with a red nose and cheeks. What was wrong with her? A little, anxious ping went off in his mind. Was she ill? Should he call a doctor or ask Ram to look at her?

Dashing off another set of notes at a small desk, Will shot him a glance and pursed his lips. "The invitations have arrived from the printer. Would you like to see them?" Will, too, chose to ignore his question.

"I'm sure they're appropriate."

Ram leaned against the wall and continued staring out the window. Just then, Jeffries rapped at the door and walked in with a tea tray, his face cool and expressionless.

Aubrey refused to question their silence. He was in a foul

mood. He kept remembering how she'd looked in the music room, with pain in her eyes before it turned to fear.

He picked up a silver letter opener and tapped out a tattoo against the desktop. "Not fair," he muttered.

"What, my lord?" Will looked up from a letter he was proofreading.

Yes, he had lashed out at her in the ballroom. He'd been scared, damn it.

Beastly, she'd called him. He couldn't get that out of his head.

He scowled down at the carpet. "She's in a snit, and I won't have it."

Reaching the fireplace, he plunged the poker into a log with more than usual force.

"Who's in a snit?" Ram asked in his most condescending voice.

"I'll thank you to mind your own business," Aubrey said, dropping the poker into its frame. "Impossible," he said again. The plan, and nothing else, he reminded himself for the hundredth time that day.

Will looked up from the desk, puzzlement in his eyes. "The dinner party, my lord? I need your orders for the guest list. I . . . I take it you wish to continue with the plan?"

"Why would you think otherwise? Those invitations must go out today. And Ram must get the special license as soon as I've made my decision." He paced another turn round the library.

"You look warm, Aubrey. Are you feeling well enough?"

Ram's voice cut into his thoughts. "Where the bloody hell is Miss Merrit?" he snapped.

Ram's dark eyes were cool as he gave Aubrey one of his inscrutable perusals. "She is in the attic."

"That arctic wasteland? What could she possibly want in

the attic this time of year?"

As an inquisitive boy, he'd only explored up there a few times in winter, when his breath froze in the air and frost formed on the floorboards so that they crackled with each step he took.

Ram examined his nails, as though they were far more fascinating than Aubrey. "She plays her violin where the master cannot hear and be displeased."

Jeffries, Ram, and even Will frowned at him. Aubrey felt himself dangerously close to a guilt wallow.

"That woman's so stubborn, she'd catch pneumonia to prove her point. Jeffries, send a footman to get her."

Jeffries, too familiar to meekly accede, stood his ground with a sniff of disdain. Jeffries could sniff 'til the cows came home, Aubrey thought. He'd be damned if he'd have music in this house or Lilias Merrit shivering in the attic.

"Music, reckless sporting contests, anything that triggers deep emotion within you must be banned," Dr. Bingham had told him. *"Above all, avoid congress with a woman who arouses your deepest emotions."*

Stay sane. Win the game. Avoid music. Avoid pretty, penurious women.

"My lord," Will said, with a longing glance at the door. "If that will be all . . ."

Aubrey waved his hand in dismissal. Will rose and scurried out, glad to be rid of him and his foul temper. Jeffries bowed ironically and went out, as well.

"Some of the staff listen at the foot of the attic stairs," Ram said.

"Don't they have better things to do?" Aubrey turned away and walked toward the window.

Ram huffed out a sigh strong enough to fell a tree. "You know, Aubrey, you're a very private person. I don't normally interfere with you because of that."

"Was that an ironical statement?" He rubbed his still-sore shoulder.

"This abhorrence you have of music—it ought to be gone by now, old fellow."

Aubrey snapped his fingers. "Just like that, you think? How lucky for you if you ever experience the same thing."

"So I'm only guessing here, but it seems to me there's something more to it."

Aubrey pressed his forehead against the windowpane. The cold air made the heat and the closeness in the room almost bearable. "It hurts," he said.

He felt Ram pause behind him. "Physically hurts?"

He nodded and shut his eyes.

"Then I can only guess at two possibilities. The first is that you don't want to feel anything. For a man with your prospects, that's somewhat understandable. But I don't believe that's the reason."

The silence drew out until Aubrey couldn't stand it anymore. "And the other theory?" He turned to face Ram.

"The one I think is correct?" Ram's eyes, deep and serene, held his gaze. "That you're afraid. Afraid you don't deserve the pleasure it brings you. That you don't deserve happiness in any form. I believe you could apply the same theory to your determination to immolate yourself upon the altar of a miserable marriage."

Aubrey's heart stopped, then beat like the slow, tolling knell from the church belfry. He turned his back on Ram. "Go to hell," he said. "And shut the door behind you."

The next two days passed in a mad rush of activity. Aubrey met with solicitors and barristers. He issued orders, separated his personal shipping fortune from that of the estate, revised his will, set up a trust for Lilias Merrit, and carefully reviewed his strategy. The plan, set in motion, flowed smoothly.

The unacknowledged battle continued with Miss Merrit. He tried to ignore her sessions in the attic, but the thought of her exiled in that cold, dark place made him wince. He approached Mrs. Nettles—the only servant who still smiled at him—and asked her to put some of those woolen gloves with open fingertips and warm wraps in the attic room where Lilias rehearsed. At night he stared at the shadows thrown by the firelight, and felt as though all the warmth had been sucked out of his life.

The next afternoon, he asked Ram to stay after Will had left to post the invitations. "How's the concert in the attic going these days?" he said.

"You ought to hear her."

"The thing of it is, Ram . . ." He stared down at his hands. "You were right. I'm afraid."

"I'll go with you, Aubrey. I'll help you get away, if the pain gets too bad. I'll make sure nothing happens to her."

"I don't know . . ." Music. The lure was almost irresistible. Even the sound of a country dance would be like coming home after a long exile.

"It would just be an experiment of sorts," Ram said quietly. "Think how you'll feel if nothing happens."

He turned to Ram, his heart in his throat. "You could keep her safe?"

"How long have you known me, Aubrey? Have I ever done anything to betray your trust?"

"Other than shoot me?" Aubrey took a deep breath. His hands shook slightly as he drew them through his hair. "Ask the servants to leave the area." He would die before he let them see him howling like a crazed wolf the way Hindley had described him, the way Dr. Bingham thought he might.

Ram squeezed his shoulder. "All right." He shut the door behind him and Aubrey sank into a chair, staring dully at the Persian carpet.

What had he just done? Would it be worse to know? God help him. *What if Lilias heard him and saw him for what he might be?*

He gave Ram time to disperse the servants and then climbed to the attic. Time slowed, as though he walked through the nightmare he couldn't keep at bay. But Ram met him at the top of the stairs, and then walked with him toward a room halfway down the hall. Ram, forever loyal, and for now, stronger than he.

There was only silence, and for a moment, he was afraid that she had left, that he would have to buck up the courage to face this ordeal again tomorrow. He sank against the wall. It was cold at his back, and his breath came out in a cloud.

When the first, sweet notes of the violin came, he was no longer cold. Sweat poured from him. His body tightened, the fear rising as pain split his head.

The darkness of the jungle. The sounds of the night creatures, the bats winging past, and the insects. Susannah, triumphant and cruel in the dying light, words he couldn't make out. Someone behind her—danger. The feel of the pistol in his hand.

His body clenched, resisting.

"Listen to it. Stop shutting it out." Ram's soft, insistent voice broke through the haze of agony.

He swallowed hard and forced himself back, into Breme and the cold, and sound wafting from the room beyond.

Ram sat patiently across from him, one knee bent, his arm resting upon it, his gaze steady on Aubrey.

116

He forced himself to breathe slow, steady gusts of air. The music twined around him like a budding vine, sweet, protective, holding him up against the fear.

The pain lessened. Relaxing against the wall, tentative at first, he opened himself. And the music poured in, confounding him. The beauty of the piece was overwhelming. For a moment, he didn't think of what she played.

Then, with a shock, he recognized the slow second movement of the Mendelssohn *Violin Concerto*. She had made it her own, drawing from the notes all the lyricism, all the magic. He closed his eyes, enraptured, as the violin spoke to him with its almost-human voice. Time ceased. He was conscious only of the music flowing over him, lifting him from the terror and the anguish of the past months.

Halfway through the virtuoso display of the third movement, he jerked at a tap on his shoulder. He felt as though some protective layer of his skin had shed, and every sensation was so sharp it hurt.

"She's been up here for a while, and will probably stop soon," Ram said. "We'd better go."

"Yes," he whispered.

They returned to the library in silence. After he shut the door, Ram's smile was replete with satisfaction. "I told you so. That damned charlatan Bingham and his society lunatics!"

Aubrey still couldn't trust the fragile relief. But he knew who was responsible for it, and what she had given back to him today.

She deserves better than Landham. She deserves better than me.

"Ram, is there an excellent mantuamaker in Breme-on-the-Wold?"

"A dressmaker?" Ram laughed. "How should I know?"

117

"Would you find out for me? And if so, would you send the carriage to her and ask her to come out to the castle?"

"If you wish." Ram gave him an odd look.

He walked to the fireplace and spread his fingers to the warm blaze, his mind working at a solution to the problem at hand. "And my godmother. I'll write her immediately. She must come to the dinner party. And eligible men." He ignored the involuntary twinge in his stomach, and threw himself into the plans. "Better send for Will. And when he's left, would you ask Miss Merrit if she would take tea with me?"

Yes, in the short interval left to his life, he could take a little time to ensure her happiness.

Chapter Ten

She came a short time later, with her customary red cheeks and a red nose. He rose, fighting the temptation to rub some warmth into her.

"You'll get the ague in that attic, and then *I* shall have to nurse *you*," he said, as he poured out a hot cup of tea and handed it to her.

Her brow wrinkled in confusion and then her eyes narrowed. He looked down at her hands, clenched tightly in her lap. She apparently had geared herself for another scathing set-down. "I don't wish to get out of practice, and you don't wish to hear me play," she shot back. "The attic is just fine. I like it up there."

Just fine. Women were always saying that when they really meant: *You are a pig of the lowest sort.*

Aubrey stared into his cup. He recognized stubbornness when he saw it, and Lilias Merrit had a rather huge supply on hand.

"I'll have a maid sent up there to light a fire each day for you. Just tell me when."

"That's not necessary," she said, her lips pressed into a pinched line—a spinster's martyred expression.

"I am not the emperor Nero and you are not about to be thrown to the lions. Kindly remember that, when you play each day in your warm, comfortable attic room."

She twirled the melting sugar cube around in her cup with her demitasse spoon, biting her lower lip and watching the swirling liquid as though all the answers in the world were hidden in its depths. Then she huffed a dramatic sigh, and looked up at him with thoughtful curiosity.

"The staff talked with me, my lord. They fondly remember the days before you married and traveled, when each evening after tea they would gather in the music room and create wonderful music. They all wish you will begin the custom again."

Last night he'd remembered those evenings, full of sound and beauty—his mother with the flute, his father at the harpsichord, himself with the violin. He sat a little straighter, remembering. Music, so recently the cacophonous signal that set the demons loose, might just become a weapon of protection in his pathetically empty arsenal. It had been months since he'd played. Perhaps. . . . His fingers itched to pick up an instrument.

His lips twitched and he couldn't keep back a smile. She didn't hold a grudge for long, it seemed, as long as there was a prospect of him giving in to what she really wanted. He'd have to remember that.

She was leaving soon. He wouldn't have to remember anything about her.

"My lord?"

He glanced over at her.

"Are you quite all right?"

"Of course," he said, clearing his throat.

"It was just—the way you were grinding your teeth, I wondered if you were in pain."

"Not at all," he said, through clenched jaws.

"Oh," she said with a smile. "Good. The servants, my lord. The music," she reminded him.

"Ah, the music. I've been thinking about that. And about your position here, Miss Merrit. I wish to discuss both with you today."

She sat up ramrod straight. "If I have displeased you, my lord . . ."

"No, this is about something else entirely. I am planning a house party for next weekend. I thought a musicale would be fitting. As I seem to have recovered from my aversion to music, I rescind my order regarding the ballroom."

"Well. That's quite—"

"Kind of me?" Again, his lips quirked and there were crinkles of merriment at the corners of his eyes.

Reluctantly charmed, she glanced down at her hands.

"You'll be invaluable in aiding me, both by preparing the staff and house. Mrs. Nettles has explained to me that she is getting too old to take on this task alone. I suggested you help her. She was quite pleased with the idea."

To Lilias, glancing up with a surge of relief followed by a sense of . . . well, a sense of disappointment . . . the request was the answer to a knotty problem. She had been too vain to realize it until now, but the clash of wills between them had been highly inappropriate. If she were honest with herself, Lord Breme, certainly rude and occasionally frightening, was her employer.

Furthermore, the role of assistant housekeeper was more fitting to a person of her station. Unlike the position of nurse–companion, it was an anonymous post, shielding her from both the stares and whispers of the guests, and from her unruly emotions.

It was just that the voice asking this of her was velvet deep and lyrical, and she found herself shocked by her reaction to it. She, a woman who prided herself upon her independence, would not become that ridiculous cliché—a servant who lived through her master.

Mentally, she shook herself. The man merely told a good story, and he had more intelligence than the foolish men of Tilden. That was all.

"Will you do so?" he asked her.

She looked Lord Breme in the eye, into his startling, co-balt blue eyes, fringed with impossibly long lashes, a dark sable at the tips, lighter as they touched the lids. She smiled in a stiff panic, right at the forbidding scars she had tended. It did not help. She liked looking at him, was moved by it, the way she'd like looking at a beautiful painting, despite the slash across the canvas.

It was a good thing Papa would return from London in a fortnight. She only prayed that he would forgive her for re-fusing Landham.

Papa would let her come home, she tried to reassure her-self. He must.

"Of course, my lord. It is fitting that I learn all I can from Mrs. Nettles. It will help me in the future to have you include mention of my work as assistant housekeeper in my refer-ence."

"You'll be more helpful to me if you can also attend the festivities. I'll expect you, of course, to sit at table and keep things moving along properly."

Lilias laughed, rather than give in to hysteria. "But that's impossible! You can't wish a servant to sit at table with your guests."

"Nonsense." He waved his hand, dismissing her quite-reasonable worry. "I've ordered a few gowns for you. To all my guests, you'll merely be my interesting neighbor, Miss Merrit of Tilden."

She shook her head, waves of panic engulfing her. "It's a mad scheme. Someone will see through it."

His laugh was tinged with a bitter ring. "Compared to some of my schemes, this one is the height of reason. No one knows you. You look and act more like an aristocrat than most of the ton. You have enough wit and backbone to carry it off. And you have insisted that your musical ability exceeds the average."

"Musical ability?" Lilias's head was beginning to swim. What did this have to do with anything?

"I need another soloist for the Bach *Double Concerto*. You know it?"

Lilias nodded, staring at him in shock.

"I offer the position to you if you're really as good as you insisted several days ago. But only if you'll agree to my perfectly reasonable request." He smiled, tempting and shining as Lucifer. "What do you say, Miss Merrit? Want a chance at that concerto in the ballroom? I believe you noticed the quality of the acoustics."

The ballroom . . .

His smile deepened. "You'll play the Guarneri, of course."

Unresisting, she slid into temptation, nodding her head wordlessly.

"Excellent," he said, looking down at the papers on his desk. "Perhaps you'll begin immediately. Mrs. Nettles is waiting for you in her office."

Despite the whirling of her thoughts, Lilias curtsied and walked to the door with what she considered admirable dignity. She turned to the right and made her way down the hall, skirts and petticoats sailing along with her. A pair of strong, beautiful hands cupped her shoulders. Slowly, Lord Breme turned her about until she was facing back in the direction she'd come.

"This way, Miss Merrit," said the velvet voice in her ear, soft, amused, more intimate than it had any right to be. Then the hands jerked away from her shoulders. "Terribly sorry." The voice behind her had tightened like a drum.

"Right." She lurched away from him and walked on without looking back.

"Tom, if you'll pay for the oysters and then carry these parcels to the carriage, I shall move on to the butcher's and meet you again there," Lilias said.

Tom Coachman tipped his hat and picked up the first parcels. Lilias walked out of the fishmonger's and looked about her at Breme-on-the-Wold's pretty shop buildings of Cotswold stone. Many of the owners had gone out of their way to provide exactly what Lord Breme wanted for the dinner party, she thought with satisfaction.

She'd done well enough in her new position. Mrs. Nettles and she had been all over Breme with a battalion of maids and footmen. The castle shone from top to bottom. The guests would arrive this evening, and by then, Lilias would have the last of the delicacies ready for Cook to work into magical dishes from the places Lord Breme had visited in his travels. Ram Dass had been a particular help in this endeavor.

As she walked toward the butcher shop, Lilias thought the party, now that she felt a bit more like herself, was a fine idea, almost as fine as her total immersion into her role as assistant housekeeper. She rarely saw Lord Breme, although once, walking past the ballroom, she'd heard him and been amazed. The sound of his violin had been like a powerful, mesmerizing voice, the notes full and rich, tripping with the certainty and passion of a true master.

Somber, she'd run up several flights of stairs to the attic, preferring to practice for hours in secret rather than reveal a note to the ear of such a virtuoso.

Lilias looked up to see a shopper barreling straight at her. The large man, a muffler tucked about his chin and a cap pulled low on his head, did not stop when he saw her in his path. He kept coming, as though he would run her down. Quickly, she moved out of his way, but he veered and caught her by the shoulders, jerking her once hard and pulling her with him into an alcove created by the bow window of a draper's shop.

"So this is where ye've been keepin' yourself. I guessed ye'd fled east, but not where." She froze, and stared up into the eyes of Richard Landham. "A good thing I needed some new harness today. I'd a missed ye for sure."

He squeezed her arms so hard she was afraid he'd snap a bone. "Unhand me, Landham," she said between her teeth. "Or I shall scream."

His grip lightened, but did not lift from her. "Ye do so and I'll just explain it's a lover's quarrel. Who do ye think they'll believe, Lilias? You or me?"

She whimpered, knowing whom they'd believed in Tilden.

He pulled her forward, his breath hot on her face. "Ye've had yer time. Now ye're coming home, girl, and ye're going to do as I say."

She opened her mouth and screamed for all she was worth. People stopped and stared. One man stepped forward, ogled Landham's height and breadth. When Landham narrowed his eyes, the men stepped back and walked quickly away.

"Told ye so, sweetheart. Come along with me, quiet-like. Scream again, and I'll make you sorry."

Chapter Eleven

She screamed again. Landham muffled the sound with his mouth. His hand wrapped about the back of her neck. The other crushed her against him, almost choking the breath out of her. She tried to struggle, but he was so big. People shifted quickly around her and no one stopped him. She thought she might faint.

At the edge of her consciousness came the sound of heavy boots at a run.

She fell limply against the alcove door, and gasped. Air, sweet, cold, and Tom's voice: "Here, now, what are you doin' with Miss Merrit?"

And Ned, the stable lad, piping in: "His lordship's gonna be right bleedin' furious, you mess with Miss Merrit again, you effin' bugger."

"Ned!" Lilias rasped in amazement. She'd never heard the boy say a bad word, and those were really bad, were they not?

"Lord Breme, is it?" Landham backed away a few yards, his eyes narrowing. "So, that's the way of it, Miss High and Mighty Lilias Merrit. Ye'r too good for the likes of me, but ye'll sell yerself to be a beast's light skirt."

Scowling, he jabbed his finger at her. "Ye've done it now,

girl. I'll not take another man's leavings. There are plenty of flowers not been plucked yet for this man."

Landham grabbed her elbow in a bruising grip and whispered into her ear. "When Breme boots you out and ye'r all alone, I'll find you. And do what I should have done a long time ago. Who'll protect you then, girl?"

Turning on his heel, he strode away. Lilias held herself erect, one hand against the solid wood of the door for support. The trembling shook her from head to toe. Landham shoved his way down the street, elbowing passers-by who got too close. They scurried aside, saving their curious stares for her. She stiffened, pushed away from the door, and found her legs did support her.

"Thank you, Tom. And Ned." Somehow, she couldn't get up the strength to be humiliated by what they'd just witnessed. She swallowed the metallic taste of blood and probed gently at the inside of her cheek with her tongue. She'd bitten it, beneath the cruel pressure of Landham's mouth.

Her father had thought to marry her to a man whose kiss was an assault.

"I am very grateful for your aid. Let's finish our business. Cook needs these supplies as soon as possible."

"An' that's what happened, my lord," Tom Coachman finished, standing before Aubrey with his cap twisted in his hands and a worried expression on his round face. Ram leaned his shoulder against the wall, his hands crossed over his chest, listening intently to Tom's story.

"Landham kissed her?" Aubrey's fists grabbed the edge of his desk so hard the knuckles turned white. "Did she welcome it?"

"Well, I don't know she wanted it. When we came out of the fishmonger's, I heard her make a noise. That's why Ned and me ran over to her." He thought for a moment. "But it was like a little scream. Maybe like, you know, when you take a girl by surprise and she's so glad ye did."

Aubrey pushed away from the desk and tried hard to measure his steps to the door and back, carefully holding his hands behind his back. "I see. Anything more you noticed?"

Tom shrugged in a helpless manner. "I was down the street, so I didn't see. All I know's we got there and I pulled at him and he let go. She sort of leaned against the shop door. Maybe like he hurt her." Tom rubbed his chin, considering. "But maybe, you know, like when you kiss a girl who fancies you and her legs get wobbly and she sort of sags against ye 'cause she likes it."

Something rose up inside him—red and passionate and furious. "Was she relieved to see you, Tom?"

"My lord, I couldn't tell. She's not one to show how she's feeling. But he did, when he heard she was workin' here. He called her names. He said he'd not . . ." Tom turned beet red from his chin to the top of his bald head.

"Out with it," Aubrey said, barely stifling the urge to shake it out of the little coachman.

"Not have another man's leavin's. He broke with her, my lord."

"He said this in the middle of town?"

Tom looked up at the ceiling, considering. "That he did. Shocked her, I reckon. Upset her."

Well, she was free. He just wished he could reassure himself that she was glad. "Thank you for telling me, Tom."

Tom bobbed a little bow. "I jest thought you ought to know, my lord."

"You were right. If there's anything else, let me know at once."

The coachman nodded again and made for the study door.

"At once, Tom." Aubrey rose as the door shut. He crossed to the window and restrained himself from doing something to relieve the pressure.

"I got a more detailed report on Landham yesterday," he told Ram. "A man of substance in the community, the detective told me. A sportsman, generally well liked. A handsome devil, the detective said." Aubrey knew all about that part of it.

"You did a good thing to write Lady Amelia, Aubrey. Miss Merrit is out of it now."

"I'm not at all sure that she'll stay out of it. What if she's too besotted to realize what he is? What if he finds her, if she apologizes and explains? What if he believes her and takes her back to Tilden?" Each sentence burst out of him as he trod the carpet back and forth, bashing against possibilities he couldn't control like an animal against the bars of a cage.

He stopped dead in the middle of the floor, staring at the bleak winter sky outside his window. "By God, Ram. Last time I saw Landham, he had his hands wrapped round Gran Megan's throat, choking the life out of her!"

Ram's voice was firm. "There's only so much you can do, old fellow."

"She should stay here, where I can keep an eye on her."

Ram laughed, a short, sharp sound of mockery. "I'm sure your new bride will be delighted with that arrangement."

"Jesus." Aubrey strode to the desk and poured out a glass of brandy.

"Call it off," Ram said. "You're trying too hard, and rushing into marriage won't help your cause. I have a very bad feeling about this weekend."

"You know what's waiting for me a few months hence."

"Take your chances with your peers. Rest and let your

memory awaken. But don't marry, not yet. We'll find another way."

If his memory awakened, it might well mean certain doom. For he could never live with the guilt. "Leave me as I am, Ram." He stared out at the coming dusk. The window-pane reflected his face with the ugly scars, the eyes glittering in agitation. He raised his glass in mocking salute. *Gentlemen, I give you the mad, the murderous, Lord Beast, in all his Satanic glory.* "Marriage to an acceptable woman and hope of an heir is my only recourse," he said.

Outside the study, footsteps ran up and down the stairs. The maids were making ready the last of the rooms.

He pulled the bell to summon Will. In two days, it would all be settled.

And the woman who stood up to him, laughed with him, and tempted him would be gone. Wealthy enough to choose whomever she wished as a husband. Except him, not that she'd ever want him.

"Cook needs to see you, miss," a footman called as Lilias slipped up a back stairway toward her chambers.

"I'll be with her shortly," she said in what she hoped was a calm voice. A moment later, she opened the door to the privacy of her bedchamber.

She did not wish to speak to anyone until she had composed herself enough to put the incident at Breme-on-the-Wold behind her.

What if Landham went to her father with his lies? She tried to tell herself that her father's opinion had been so negative for so long, it now meant little to her.

But it wasn't true, as the knot in her stomach testified. Geoffrey Merrit was a shrewd man, a hearty, larger-than-life figure whom she'd idolized as a child. His disapproval stiffened her back, but it hurt all the same.

With her hand still on the latch, she stared in surprise at three gowns placed carefully across her bed. One was a delicate light-blue woolen afternoon dress with pristine white lace cuffs and collar. Another was a maroon silk gown. The skirt was trimmed in black lace, but the puffed sleeves, which came only to her elbow, had no trim at all. This gown must be for tonight's musicale, for their fullness allowed maximum movement of her shoulders and arms, and they lacked the dripping lace that would hamper her playing.

The last, made of dark gold velvet with a low, square neckline and long, tight sleeves, fairly shouted beauty and expense. New petticoats, stockings and unmentionables lay beside the gowns, lacy and delicate, the likes of which she had not seen in three years.

She stroked her hand across the nap once, then pulled on the bell, and Jane came almost immediately. "There has been a mistake," she said. "The mantuamaker must have misunderstood Lord Breme's instructions. These are much too fine."

"Oh, no, miss," the maid said with a dreamy sigh. "I took Lord Breme's order to the ladies in the village. He was very clear in his instructions. Are they not the most beautiful things you've ever seen?"

The extravagance of the gowns was barbaric, opulent beyond belief. Fit for a countess, not a neighboring gentlewoman. "I need to speak to him. Immediately."

Jane dropped a curtsey. "He's in the study, miss. I'll tell him you're coming directly. He'll like that you wish to thank him, indeed he will. He's had little enough of that in the past."

Lilias took a few moments to steady herself before rapping on the study door. The maid's words unsettled her resolve to lecture him upon the propriety of making munificent gifts to one's assistant housekeeper. They made her wonder what his life had been like with his young countess.

Lilias had a lot to thank him for. The attic room in which she played was not only warm. Colorful silk and woolen hangings now covered its cracked walls. Soft, thick Oriental carpets lay over the worn floorboards, and comfortable chairs and a sofa offered respite. The lamps were lit when she arrived each day, as though some genie watched over her and knew her erratic schedule.

But these expensive gowns might arouse certain . . . suspicions. She rapped upon the door and stiffened her spine when she heard the deep voice bid her enter. He stood with his legs wide, hands clasped behind his back, staring at the fire.

She blinked, momentarily stunned. Not having donned his tailcoat yet, he was dressed in formal dark trousers, a white linen shirt, cravat, and a white-upon-white waistcoat. His shining hair was brushed into place, and every line of his body was graceful, strong, aristocratic. She was caught in the moment, with a sudden, empty ache swamping her.

Tonight marked his return to the world in which he belonged. He stood there, a tall, fine specimen of a man in his strength. He didn't need her help anymore.

The latch clicked softly as she shut the door. He turned his head and searched her face, his eyes watchful and grave.

"I trust you had a pleasant trip to Breme-on-the-Wold, Miss Merrit?"

The question unnerved her, bringing back the terrible encounter with Landham. "It was successful, my lord," she said in as cool a voice as she could muster. "All the supplies for the dinners, breakfasts, and luncheons are now in the pantry. Cook is particularly pleased with the turtle for the soup."

His brow furrowed for an instant. He looked as though he

were about to say something else, then nodded abruptly. "Good. I have absolute faith in Cook's abilities. But you wished to speak to me?"

"Yes." She took a deep breath and steeled herself. "I have been given to understand that the gowns in my bedroom are what you expect me to wear for the weekend, my lord."

"They are." He watched her, dark lashes fringing his eyes, hiding his expression. But he held very still, as though waiting for something.

"The gowns are . . . are very beautiful. Indeed, they are more beautiful than anything I have ever seen."

He ducked his head, looking at the carpet between them with a crooked grin. "I'm glad you like them. I expect that you'll wear the maroon tonight."

"I understand." Good lord, she actually squeaked. She took a slow, deep breath. "But that's just it, my lord. I cannot wear it, and I cannot go in to dinner with the guests. I daresay that your life of traveling has made you forget the customs of your countrymen. But I must respectfully remind you that in masquerading as a mere gentlewoman neighbor, I cannot wear a gown of such value. However kind . . . however very, very kind it was of you to gift me with all of this, it would be unseemly of me to accept any part of it."

He frowned. "I'm counting on you, Miss Merrit. Everything depends on the smoothness of this weekend. Who will direct the servants? Who will ensure that the guests are comfortable, if you will not?"

She shook her head wildly. "You don't really need me. Mrs. Nettles knows just what to do, as do all the servants. The festivities will go off without a hitch."

Slowly, he looked her up, then down. "And the musicale? Have you anyone to substitute for the second violin?"

Her heart sank. The Guarneri lured her like a siren, and

the thought of someone else playing that particular piece was too miserable to bear. She looked down at her toes and bit her lip.

He seized upon her distress. "Well, that is the exact reason why I need you to appear tonight in that maroon gown, at my dinner table, and opposite me in the ballroom."

What exactly was he about, slipping into that charming smile as smoothly as a seal into water?

His expression shifted again as his gaze grew serious. "This party is very important to me. I am not sure that I can do this without your help."

When he asked like that, how could she deny him? But her stomach jangled in dread and remembrance. That morning four years ago, Papa had returned from his warehouse with the news that all was lost. She had only been fifteen and not yet out in society, but that day had changed their lives, utterly.

When their neighbors and friends had come to ransack through their home on the day of the auction, she had overheard their sneers and their pitying whispers. There had been no other shield for her but a rather stiff-backed pride.

"Don't you understand?" she said softly. "If I masquerade as something other than myself, it's tantamount to admitting that I am less than I should be."

Lord Breme's voice was just as soft, but very sure. "You are more than all of the fools who will gather in my home this weekend. It is more than fitting that you be my honored guest. In all of what I must accomplish in the name of duty, I shall have done one thing tonight to be proud of. I demand—"

"The fact that you are my employer," she interrupted, blazing with her own heat, "does not give you the right to demand that I pretend to be what I am not. If you wish it, you have my resignation."

His face was taut beneath a deluge of emotions so swift and so contradictory that she could not follow them all—frustration, determination, despair. With that last, a terrible urge to give him whatever he asked overwhelmed her.

"Then I ask it," he said, as though he'd read her mind. "Just for this weekend. You are my neighbor, come to dine and to stay the night. My wealthy neighbor, I shall make clear. The guests live far from Breme. No one will ever guess you aren't exactly what I say you are. It is what you should be, after all."

In the silence that followed all the strange simmering of emotion, Lilias had a foolish fancy that the very stones of the house paused to listen. In the waiting silence, temptation whispered seductively. If Papa had kept his fortune, she'd be in London tonight, wearing a beautiful dress and dining with people whose conversation would prove interesting. And as he said, no one would know her.

"All right," she said.

"No one will know me," she repeated softly to herself as she made her way up the stairs, around another confusing turn to her room. But this had been a terrible day and the fear that it might turn worse niggled at her.

She thought of the beautiful dresses waiting for her in her bedchamber. She had never worn anything like them. Well, of course, she thought. She'd been too young for such a gown before the Disaster. Excitement and pleasure rose in her. To be free to dress and act as though she weren't in desperate straits for two nights was too delicious a chance to pass up.

After all, it wasn't as though anyone would know. Nothing could possibly go wrong.

Chapter Twelve

Aubrey greeted his guests in the rose drawing room, doing his best to appear urbane and clever. Lady Caroline Berring, with her auburn hair and heart-shaped face, was appealing, if one fancied a shy child. She stood behind her mama, the handsome and quiet Lady Berring, who had produced this daughter seven months after she was widowed. But the ton had always whispered that Caroline's hair was exactly the color of the Duke of Hartford, an extremely close friend of the widowed Lady Berring.

Caroline had taken one horror-stricken look at Aubrey's face, stuttered some greeting or other, curtsied, and disappeared into a corner, trembling like a rabbit caught in a snare. He almost felt sorry for her.

"How do you find winter after all that heat?" Lady Amelia Tate, the gray-haired, indomitable widow of England's ambassador to Portugal, asked him.

"I do find England rather cold after India's tropical heat," Aubrey said to his godmother. "I miss it. Living in a foreign country can be rather enlightening."

Lady Amelia smiled and leaned heavily on her cane. "New customs, new friends, new ideas, my boy, and a certain freedom. I know what you mean."

Mr. Franklin Hall, slick barrister and overly fond papa, stood near the entry beside his daughter. Miss Margaret Hall was a tall woman with a typically blonde English prettiness and a bold carriage. At the moment, she closely examined the candlesticks and silver sculpture on the mantle, no doubt with an eye to their weight and their worth.

Ram, in his guise of dutiful and discreet Indian servant, stood in the corner, keeping an eye on Miss Hall, whom he no doubt suspected to be plotting petty larceny.

"Perhaps you'll take a stroll about the room with me," Aubrey said, planning to stop and introduce Miss Hall to Lady Amelia, whose power in society was legendary. No doubt Margaret would be thrilled. Then his gaze swept past Margaret toward the entrance to the drawing room just as Lilias Merrit arrived. Her dark eyes held those exotic, mysterious depths as she moved forward in a glide of petticoats and maroon silk.

In her everyday woolens, Lilias Merrit moved a man to desire. But dressed in this shimmering gown, she shone with a radiance that seemed to light the entire room. The deeper voices around him hushed as the other men caught a glimpse of her.

"Dear heaven," Lady Amelia whispered beside him. "Gwendolyn."

Aubrey turned to her in alarm and found her staring at Miss Merrit, her hand covering her lips.

"Godmother," he said softly. "Is all well?"

Lady Amelia smiled up at him, her blue eyes bright with a mist. "All is very well, dear boy. The young lady who just entered the room, Aubrey. Is she the one you wrote to me about? She's crossing to the far window."

"She's the one," he said.

"Could you introduce her to me, dear?"

"I shall bring her to you." So much for Margaret Hall for the moment, he thought with relish. Lilias Merrit stood quietly before the window, appraising the guests. She nodded to one of the footmen, who immediately approached one of the ladies and offered another glass of ratafia.

He made his way toward her. Bowing over her hand, he raised it to his lips. He breathed in the scent of her—fresh wildflowers and something beneath it, wilder and sweeter.

"I welcome Beauty to my castle," he said, pleased with the masquerade and the chance it offered to give her effusive compliments.

She laughed. "A pretty speech, my lord, were I a beauty."

"It's no lie, Lilias."

She made a moue of regret with her pretty, lush mouth. "You may no longer be yellow, my lord, but I shall always be brown."

He laughed and shook his head. "You are many colors—sable to gold to russet," he said, his eyes gliding over her upswept hair, then down her forehead, her cheeks, her lips. "Pink and cream and rose. A man could count them all and never weary of it."

Startled, her gaze flew to his.

"Come," he said, ignoring her blush and his recklessness. He took her hand and placed it in the crook of his arm. "Lady Amelia wishes to make your acquaintance."

Once he'd taken her to his godmother, he relaxed his guard for a few moments, enjoying the interchange between them while Lilias and Lady Amelia talked about the differences in customs in some of the exotic lands where her husband had been posted.

Lady Amelia rapped her cane lightly on his arm, breaking his concentration. "You mustn't forget your other guests,

Aubrey. Miss Merrit and I shall get along famously together."

Hearing Margaret Hall's shrill laughter across the room, he stiffened his shoulders.

"Go along, dear. We'll settle in for a lovely chat," his godmother said firmly.

Aubrey nodded and turned to march into the breach toward the blonde chit and her father, who looked at him with identical acquisitive expressions.

"Lady Amelia," a gravel-voiced man said behind him. "Breme, so good to see you looking well again after the terrible tragedy."

"Sir Edward." Aubrey turned with a short bow to one of his neighbors, bluff old Sir Edward, a man he'd known since he was a boy. "Miss Merrit, may I present Sir Edward Havenhurst?"

"Charmed." Sir Edward bowed over Lilias's hand with a flourish, looking as though he'd meant what he said. "Lovely addition to the evening, my dear. Makes me remember how this castle rang with gaiety not so many years ago."

"I take it you have happy memories of times here," Lilias said.

"Oh, indeed. For years, and then of course, after Aubrey's marriage. Such lovely country house parties. They went on for days and days. Young Lady Breme was a brilliant hostess. Such fine ton—a leader of fashion, a diamond of the first water. An invitation to her charity ball was more precious than gold. Ah, that lady! She had a sweetness about her that touched every heart."

"I suppose she was musical," Lilias said in a small voice.

"Oh, she did not play, nor did she sing. But in the ballroom, she was light as a feather, as I recall. The men flocked to her like bees to honey. A real enchantress. What a tragedy."

Lilias looked down at her borrowed finery. She was a fraud in the house of a lady who had been a diamond of the first water.

"Never would believe for one minute that the boy had aught to do with it," Sir Edward was saying in a firm voice. "Too sweet-natured from his cradle, he was."

"I agree with you, Edward. Now, could you tell me who that young gentleman is in the far corner," Lady Amelia said, taking his arm and stemming Sir Edward's flow of talk. "Perhaps you could bring him to us and introduce him."

"That's Beverley. Heard he took a first at Oxford—literature, I believe. Your Miss Merrit must definitely meet him, my dear lady," Sir Edward said with a bow, and left them to return with the eldest son of a viscount, who, it turned out, was quite interested in the poetry of Tennyson.

Later that evening, after a dinner worthy, Lilias thought, of a king's table, the guests entered the ballroom and arranged themselves on the gilt chairs set up in rows before the west end of the room. What a difference there was between the large, empty ballroom she had seen two weeks before and this glowing chamber. The brilliant light of hundreds of candles in the large Venetian chandeliers illuminated the room. Castle Breme's servants filled the west end, smiling and chatting with each other, tuning instruments, applying resin to bows, leafing through sheet music on individual stands. The ballroom hummed with life.

She stood in front of this marvelous orchestra and slowly recognized its players. There was Mrs. Nettles at the harpsichord, a lovely lace collar and cuffs affixed to her dark gown. Jeffries, with a bow, took his place as first violin. Even Ned, the stable lad, held a child-sized violin.

Lord Breme strode to his place directly beside hers at the

front of the orchestra and removed his dark formal evening coat. He bowed to her, smiling, excitement shining in his eyes.

"I haven't heard you practice once," he whispered, and the smile widened into a grin.

She rolled her eyes. "I won't disappoint you, my lord."

The smile became gentle, surprisingly so. "I know that," he said. "Ready?"

She gave an abrupt nod and swallowed the lump in her throat. The Bach *Concerto for Two Violins in D Minor*. Her mother had loved it; they had played only the *largo* together, her mother far superior on the lower notes, and she trying her best on the higher. She had played it a thousand times since, and in these last weeks, she'd worked to become more adept, thinking of her mother, missing the second violin terribly, especially in that movement.

She forgot her fear of discovery and the magnificent former Lady Breme. She was to play a piece she loved. In this room, with its glorious acoustics and a full orchestra of people who had been kind to her from the beginning of her stay at Breme.

With a deep breath, she picked up the Guarneri violin she had so lovingly plucked the first time she had visited this ballroom. Jeffries gave the note and they tuned their instruments together, the strings sweetly echoing in the vast silence that engulfed the room.

Lord Breme sent her a glance, a question. She nodded. He turned to Jeffries, who tapped out the beat.

Sound burst upon her—magnificent notes of the *vivace*, the second violins introducing the vigorous theme, a fugal exposition. She and Lord Breme came in to answer their question, moving along the clear melody in bursts of color and light, flinging the musical phrases back and forth between them. It was unlike anything she had ever experienced, that merging of glorious music. She heard every instrument and all of them together at the same time. The bold, bright joy of it only made her fingers more nimble. The sound of the Guarneri filled her to bursting, its bright upper registers and full lower notes a delight to the senses.

The final chords of the first movement ended before she could do more than exist in a celestial sphere of harmony and rhythm. Lord Breme rolled up the full sleeves of his white shirt in order to keep them from interfering with his playing. Then he picked up the violin again, his muscled forearm graceful as he lifted the bow.

He shut his eyes for a moment, as though he were letting the music fill him. He was a mystery of contradictions, with his strong, broad shoulders and beautiful, sensitive hands. His stillness commanded the silence for a long pause, and then the bow swept across the strings and sounded the first, sweet notes of the *largo*.

With those first notes, some mystical curtain raised, and Lilias saw him as she never had before. With every note, it seemed as though he asked her a question from his heart. She felt her own heart open to him completely, listening. The tones and the lyricism of his playing moved her to answer in kind above him, soaring slowly, held aloft by his music. His notes supported hers, and lifted them in a graceful *volte*.

This was the sound of longing.

Their music twined together like lovers, gaining in depth and richness, a courtship without words. He led, she followed in the dance, yielding, yearning, until the end, and silence.

They stood a few feet apart, staring at each other, breathing in unison, as though they had just run across Salisbury plain and entered the sacred circle, hand in hand. As though there was nothing in the world but the two of them, and everything between them was clear and beautiful and right. Someone cleared his throat, and Jeffries took up the theme of the last movement.

As for Aubrey, a sweet, heady sense filled him as he gazed at Lilias across the small space that separated them. Something had changed. He had no idea how or why. But he felt sure her heart beat to the same tempo as his did.

In some corner of his consciousness, he heard music and then it died.

"My lord? Miss Merrit?" Jeffries's whisper brought him up short. He'd missed his entry into the *allegro*. Lilias turned beet red and she raised her bow.

Jeffries tapped the rhythm, and with a nod from Aubrey, the orchestra began again.

Aubrey snapped to and came in beneath Lilias. Oh, she led him a chase, leaping over the initial motif with wild abandon, changing from coy to clinging, her notes sometimes sweet, sometimes stormy.

Great, brilliant shards of joyous light filled the darkness, chasing away the monsters with blasts of glorious sound. He had wanted to secure a future for her that would communicate his gratitude, but she'd turned the tables on him once again. The last notes surged through the room, alive, triumphant.

Her eyes shone. All the light of the room seemed to emanate, not from chandeliers, but from her.

With a bow to her, he took her hand and turned to the audience. Reality exploded with the thunderous applause of his guests. Margaret Hall sat in the front row, her eyes narrowed in a venomous stare at Miss Merrit, upon whom it was wasted.

She was smiling at Jeffries, and, dropping Aubrey's hand,

curtseyed to him and the orchestra in a silent tribute to their playing.

Aubrey frowned. With an arrogant lift of one brow, he commanded Margaret Hall's attention. Her face colored to a blotchy red and she looked down at her lap. Satisfied that he could at least cow the harpy, he reached again for Lilias's hand, motioning to Breme's orchestra behind him, and they all bowed to the continued applause. He heard shouts and cheers as he and Lilias bowed again . . . Lilias, his many-faceted nurse–companion/assistant housekeeper/violin virtuoso.

He breathed deeply, catching the sweet, wildflower scent of her, feeling a delight that had nothing to do with anything he'd felt before. It reminded him a bit of those hot summer mornings at Breme, in the meadow near the forest. He had a sudden memory of himself as a child, arms out at his side, falling back on the tall grass, unafraid, knowing it would break his fall in a soft cushioning mound. Knowing that, at the same instant, sprinkles of dew from the surrounding flowers would shower his face and body with cool, fragrant drops of water.

What a perfect combination of security and anticipation.

Yes, something had changed. He'd put himself into her hands, so to speak, and she had placed herself in his. It had to do with trust. For the first time in his life he felt an open trust between a woman—this woman—and himself. It was better than sex.

Well, he thought ruefully, not quite. Which left him thinking how the act would feel with that same openness of emotion—no barriers, no fears—to shed the protective covering and crash through to the core.

The orchestra struck up a waltz.

"Miss Merrit. Ripping good fiddling." A young man who'd spoken to her earlier tonight bowed over her hand.

"May I have the honor?" he asked.

Lilias blushed and glanced Aubrey's way—just a shy, quick assessment, a start of hesitation. As he watched, she straightened, smiled up into the callow blackguard's eyes, and just like that, Aubrey was left alone to accept the compliments of people who crowded around him.

He turned to a footman standing nearby and took a glass of champagne from him. Retiring to a corner in the ballroom, he watched Lilias Merrit waltz about the room with one man and then another. He smiled, chatted with his guests, and all the while wished nothing more than to end this charade he'd set in motion, and send them all to perdition.

Lilias tossed in her bed, listening to the music and laughter floating up to her from the ballroom. After a few dances with some of the men at the party, she'd retired for the night.

She brushed her hair hard, trying to brush away the confusion. She had a sense of having turned an irrevocable corner. Sometime during that concerto, she'd stopped seeing him as a lord and herself as a servant. She'd begun to wish for impossible things, like music, and moments of intense debate over how slow an *andante* should be, and lazy conversation in sunlit meadows.

She gave a laugh—her audacity went so far beyond what was permissible. All she had to do was recall Sir Edward's awed expression in the drawing room tonight as he praised Susannah Drelincorte.

Who did she think she was, trying to pass as one of these people? Compared to Lady Susannah, that paragon of grace and beauty, she was a fraud, a drab, a pushy fool attempting to gull society for a weekend. This was all wrong.

"Someday," she whispered, "I want the love of a kind

man, an honest, hard-working, gentle man, not an arrogant, unpredictable aristocrat who believes he has the right to shout or smile with no thought to whom it might . . . discompose. I'm fine the way I am, thank you very much, without beautiful gowns and dinner parties."

But the mattress felt lumpy, the pillows too soft. She finally fell asleep just before dawn, to rise late and dress in the frilly gown of a wealthy lady. A gown with wool as soft and as blue as a summer morning.

With a glower, Aubrey gazed down the long dinner table at Lilias Merrit, seated between two of the eligible men he'd invited specifically for her.

Unfortunately, he realized in the drawing room before dinner that he had been right about the velvet gown he'd chosen. The color brought out the gold in her hair and the nap of the cloth contrasted with the glowing darkness of her eyes. The gown was a stern, plain, magnificent contrast to the ruffles and furbelows worn by the other women in the room.

The tight sleeves covered her arms to her wrists, the tight bodice wrapped her slim waist, and the long skirts hid even the toes of her slippers. But ah, the square neckline. One's gaze went to it. One felt a shock of delight at the sight of creamy skin. A vulnerable, graceful throat enhanced by a necklace of rose-hued pearls, a peek of soft curves above the bodice, only enough of a glimpse to tantalize, to make a man dream of taking the gown down from her shoulders slowly . . .

He shot a look of pure venom at hapless, shy Lord Beverley to her right and Giles Jepson, a wealthy landowner from Kent, to her left. Both men were supremely interested in the same square neckline. At least Beverley had the decency to blush when he caught Aubrey's look. Jepson merely grinned.

A surge of pure possessive fury caught Aubrey by surprise. But why shouldn't he resent their attentions? No matter that he'd invited them for just this purpose. It was one thing to plan Lilias Merrit's rise from obscurity to desirability, and quite another to witness it.

He turned to Lady Amelia to wipe away the picture of Lilias, the prized bone between the two dogs he'd placed beside her.

"I had a lovely hour with your Miss Merrit, dear boy," Lady Amelia told him.

"Not mine," he said a bit too insistently. "Where was she this morning? I didn't see her at breakfast."

"She didn't come down until you gentlemen were well off. How was the shooting?"

"We had decent sport," he said with a shrug. He wasn't very fond of hunting, but it seemed to please his guests, and after all, one purpose of the weekend was the resurrection of Aubrey Drelincorte as a fine, sporting fellow.

Lilias seemed to be avoiding him, leaving him with two or three of the candidates on his list—most obvious among them Margaret Hall, who now smiled at him from where he'd seated her, far down the table, close to Lilias. He hoped Miss Hall was less of a problem for his nurse–companion/assistant housekeeper than for him.

When, after ices and cakes, Lord Breme suggested the ladies retire to the drawing room, Lilias gave a silent sigh of relief. The dinner was a success. As soon as she had seen Lady Amelia to a comfortable seat on the sofa, she would leave the drawing room, slip into the kitchen, and celebrate the triumph with the staff.

Lady Amelia thanked her as she settled a cushion behind her back and set a throw close-by in case she felt a chill.

"Your mama raised you well, Miss Merrit. It's unusual in this day and age to see a young chit observant enough to know what an old woman needs."

Lilias blinked against the sting of tears. Mama would have enjoyed this evening. If not for her family's cruel pride, she would have had many evenings like this. "Thank you," Lilias said. "Mama could have taught etiquette to an orangutan, and he would have graced a drawing room with nobility."

"Nonsense." Lady Amelia patted her hand. "One needs good material with which to work."

"I was not very good, I'm afraid. It is said that every young lady must sketch well. I positively cannot sketch, I cannot play piquet—indeed, I cannot remember which cards have already been tossed up—and I learned Greek but not French. I assure you, my mother had a hopeless task."

"And how did she succeed?"

Lilias hoped if she ever lived to be of an age, she would look a bit like Lady Amelia, whose blue eyes crinkled at the corners in the most appealing manner.

"She gave me an hour in the stables for every successful dancing lesson. And whenever my embroidery looked not quite a tangled mess, she taught me to play the violin."

"Oh, Miss Merrit." Margaret Hall's strident voice carried across the large drawing room. All other voices hushed. Ram Dass, in the midst of pouring tea for Lady Caroline and her mother, glanced up sharply.

Miss Hall slowly strolled across the space between them, a thin smile on her perfect pink mouth, her fan languidly waving in the air. When she reached Lilias, she gazed down from her superior height, a malicious gleam in her eye. Lilias felt the first warning of something difficult coming. Miss Hall's eyes had been cruel and speculative after the concert last night, too.

"You live in the neighborhood, Miss Merrit?"

Lilias nodded and caught Jeffries's gaze. The butler came forward with coffee. "I do. And you, Miss Hall?" It was jarring that someone as classically pretty as Miss Hall, with her fashionable roses and cream complexion, her round blue eyes, her golden curls, should be such a calculating bit of goods.

"We have a home in London, of course, and Papa is interested in an estate in Kent—Branderleigh, I believe. The family fell upon hard times. They ought to accept much less than it is worth."

Lilias inwardly cringed as she imagined the plight of the people who must give up the home they'd held for countless generations.

"Tomorrow afternoon, we shall travel to view it."

"How charming for you."

"But I am pleased to say that I have finally placed you, Miss Merrit."

"I beg your pardon?" Lilias drew herself up and gave Margaret Hall a cool stare, but her heart began to beat against her chest like a drum.

"You have an older sister, I believe. Miss Pamela Merrit." Margaret Hall's voice was soft and insinuating.

Lilias nodded. "She is my sister, yes. Lately married to Squire Trevell of Tilden."

"Ahh," Miss Hall said with a knowing smile. "She did very well for herself, considering the straits your family fell into some years ago. You see," she continued with a sly glance, "Pamela and I frequented the same parties in London. She spoke of a younger sister, then. Next I heard, your family lost *everything,* and I never saw poor Pamela again."

As Margaret Hall continued, her low-pitched voice rose in a triumphant shrill. Lilias's heart sank to her belly. Rooted to the spot like some cornered animal, she cast a glance about the drawing room. Open-mouthed ladies hung on every word.

"And because you are dressed so *very well*, I assumed you must be someone other than Miss Pamela Merrit's impoverished younger sister."

Margaret Hall stared first at Lilias's pearls and then at her gown. She laughed, a harsh, loud sound. Although Lilias wished to sink into the floor and fade away forever, something inside her insisted upon standing tall.

"However," Margaret Hall continued with a sneer, "it occurred to me that gown might be a gift. Yes, a gift from a close friend, no doubt."

Lilias felt the blood drain from her face. She felt exposed, branded, and dirty. She wished to run away and hide forever.

Miss Hall turned her head to see the room full of women hanging on her every word. Reconsidering, she turned back to Lilias with a malicious simper. "But silly me to question! I've heard these arrangements are *de rigueur* among the ton."

There was a gasp from a corner across the room. Lilias glanced wildly in that direction, at the bloodless face of Caroline Berring. Lady Berring's hand slid up to cover her mouth, her eyes wide and tragic. Ram Dass straightened. For a moment he looked like an avenging king, who, with one word, could have Miss Hall's head struck from her body.

Lilias had heard, of course, from the servants, of Lady Caroline's whispered parentage. But no one in society would have dared do more than whisper, until now.

Lilias felt her blood rise, hot and furious. Words a lady should not speak welled up, but she didn't care who heard them. Behind her, Lady Amelia stood up slowly.

"My sister and I have known poverty, Miss Hall, but never the need to destroy lives in order to appear the more acceptable," Lilias said. "You have humiliated yourself beyond redemption with your offensive words, your exceptionable manner, your unseemly insinuations. I suggest you retire for the night while the rest of us endeavor to forget your tasteless display."

"My words were doubtless of great interest to the company here," Margaret Hall said, turning with a rapacious smile to the others. Several women had gathered closer to the Ladies Berring and sniffed, turning away. Too late, Margaret Hall recognized her mistake. With head held high, she walked quickly from the room.

Conversation began at once, a discreet background somewhere in the distance as Lilias tried to calm her racing heart. Ram Dass sent her a look of warm approval, but as her anger drained, the sick humiliation returned. She had a terrible fear she'd burst into tears.

She stood silent, counting the minutes until she could leave.

Lady Amelia squeezed her hand. "Oh, Lilias, how proud of you dear Gwendolyn would be."

Lilias turned in surprise. "You knew my mother?"

"She was my best friend," Lady Amelia said. "After her marriage and her family's rejection, my papa would not permit me to see her. Once, when I slipped out and found her direction, your father told me she was not receiving. Between my father, your father, and hers, I never managed to see her again."

"Thank you for telling me that, my lady. I wish Mama had known." Lilias checked the mantle clock. Enough time had passed. "I shall say good-night, as well."

Lady Amelia laid her hand on Lilias's arm. "I must speak to you in the morning, after you have had time to compose yourself. I shall not leave Breme until I have done so."

Lilias managed a curtsey and crossed the room quickly. Only one more duty, she silently promised herself, and then she could retire to the privacy of her bedchamber and hide beneath the bed all night, if she so desired.

She must get away. Her mind raced with jangled thoughts as she fought for sense. If Lord Breme gave her a good reference, she might set up as a temporary companion or housekeeper in some remote corner of the country. She could only pray that, by next week, there would still be a family in England who had not heard of Miss Hall and her accusations. Then her heart sank even further. Would Papa refuse to acknowledge her at all after this terrible day?

As she stood at the kitchen door, she could hear the low, hushed voices of the staff within.

"You know why he's doin' this," Tom Coachman said. He sounded angry. "The only thing that'll save the castle is an heir, an' quick."

She was sure they spoke of Lord Breme. What trouble was he in?

"But those women," Mrs. Nettles said with a sniff. "They're all wrong. When he's got a perfectly good . . ."

Lilias felt like slapping her own face to make herself stop sympathizing. After what he'd exposed her to tonight, Breme and his problems could go straight to Hades.

She cleared her throat loudly and pushed through into the huge kitchen, unable to raise her eyes from its intricate, brightly-colored tile floor. Then she plastered a smile on her face and looked up. At the sound of the door shutting, all eyes turned to her.

"Mrs. Nettles, Mr. Jeffries, all of you, the evening has been a complete success," she said, keeping her voice even with an effort. "The soup and turtle were extraordinary, Cook, as was the lobster *en croute*. You all outdid yourselves

152

and made Lord Breme extremely proud."

Mrs. Nettles pursed her lips and looked about the large, brightly-lit room at the solemn nods of all fifty faces. Propelling herself forward, she drew Lilias toward the table. Jeffries had already pulled out a chair. Lilias didn't know whether she sat of her own accord or whether Mrs. Nettles simply pushed her down into the chair. The rest of them—upstairs maids, footmen, even the kitchen boy—gathered around, giving her speaking looks of sympathy.

They know, Lilias realized with a jolt. Of course. Staff knew everything that went on in the house.

Mrs. Nettles shoved a cup of tea toward her. "Drink up, miss. It will do you good."

A bubble of hysterical laughter rose in her throat. Hastily, she swallowed it down with the tea. "Mrs. Nettles, I'm not one to discuss much of a personal nature. I appreciate your attempts to comfort me, but it isn't necessary."

Mrs. Nettles patted her hand. "Just listen to what we have to say, that's all. This bold piece of work—Margaret Hall—she did what she did out of jealousy. Because she's one of them on the master's list of candidates."

"Candidates?" Lilias said blankly. If the evening had not already taken on a dreamlike quality, it did now.

"Aye." Tom Coachman turned his head to spit his disgust and reached for his handkerchief. "Them he might marry."

The sounds in the room began to pulse. The necessary heir . . . saving the castle. It all began to form a clear picture in her mind. "Lord Breme plans to marry?"

"Aye, very soon. And he's wrong about that list. They're all wrong for him."

"We wanted you to know, miss. So you can change his mind."

"About what?" Her chest hurt right over her heart, and she couldn't rub it in front of the staff.

"Marryin' the wrong lady, of course," Tom went on.

Everyone else nodded in unison, as though now she would understand and do something about this . . . this. . . . She feared if she asked another question, she would stammer.

"I see," she managed. She needed to leave. Now. "I'll . . . I'll just . . ." She gestured vaguely as she rose and walked out the door. *Breathe,* she told herself fiercely.

And fled up the stairs and down the hall until she arrived, breathless, at the door to her room. Once inside, she slammed the door shut and, sobbing, threw herself on her bed.

Chapter Thirteen

"Where is she?" Aubrey quietly asked Lady Amelia as he scanned the pink drawing room in vain for Miss Merrit. Something bad had happened. He could tell from the muted conversation and the troubled looks that had greeted the men upon their entry.

"Who, Miss Hall?" Lady Amelia's gaze probed as she asked that question.

"Of course not," Aubrey said through gritted teeth. But Margaret Hall was missing, too. What mischief had she wrought? "What happened? Is Miss Merrit ill?"

"I suggest you ask her." Lady Amelia stuck her chin in the air and refused to say another word.

"Ram," he said a moment later after crossing the drawing room. "Where's Miss Merrit? What's wrong?"

"Ask her." Ram turned to Lady Caroline, his expression gentle and concerned. "When you wish to retire, my lady, I'll have the cook make a soothing tea for you."

Thus, Aubrey had to go through the coffee and tea business, and a conversation with uncomfortable pauses with the Ladies Berring in an attempt to soothe them. From their agitation, and the uneasy glances of the other women in the room, his worry hardened into certainty.

Disaster had struck while he was gone.

When the clock finally struck the hour, he bade his guests good night. Doffing his dinner coat and his waistcoat, he waited in a frenzy of impatience and anxiety for another full hour until the house ceased its creaking and sighs, a sign that no one was awake and would notice him creeping into Lilias's bedchamber. After several glasses of brandy and a parade of possible lurid scenes in which Lilias played victim to Margaret Hall's cruelty, he opened his door.

With sure, silent steps, Aubrey made his way in darkness through the familiar halls of Breme. The door to the blue room was locked, but he had foreseen that possibility, given whatever the hell had happened in the drawing room. He pulled out the keys he'd asked of Mrs. Nettles and, with a click of the latch, was inside.

A February full moon flooded the sitting room with light. Lilias stood staring out the window, so deep in thought, it seemed, that she hadn't even noticed his entry.

"What happened?" he asked her.

At the sound of his voice, she stiffened and whirled around. "What are you doing here in the middle of the night? Are you out of your mind? What more will people think?"

He ignored this, in favor of more pressing matters. "Are you ill?" he asked her, moving closer to examine her face.

In the light of the moon, he could see everything—how her eyes were huge with misery, how her hands were fisted at her hips, how the fabric of her high-necked white nightgown was so thin it showed every lush curve of her body. While his body burned in reaction, his heart tore at the realization that the gown was so old and worn.

She pretended to consider his question. "No, I am not ill. Outraged, mortified, disgusted—all these I am. I take it I am to congratulate you, my lord."

He considered whether this discussion had better wait until daylight. But then the anger emanating from her persuaded him that he'd be wise not to turn tail.

"You know about the list," he said cautiously.

"I do. If I were you, I would eschew Miss Hall. She's already examining the silver plate. Why in God's name would you think to make such a person your wife?"

It was the tremor beneath her cool sarcasm that made him reply. "I need an heir. Rather soon, I'm afraid." He heard himself, knew he sounded cold and uncaring, when all he'd wanted was her understanding.

"I'd trust a python before I'd trust that woman with a helpless child."

He had heard a good deal of sarcasm from her, but never venom. "What did she do to you?"

"She made me furious, but I don't count. In her desire to hurt me, she overset the Ladies Berring—both of whom wouldn't hurt a fly. My advice is to take Lady Caroline." Lilias's voice trembled.

He found himself trembling as well. "I don't want Lady Caroline. What did Miss Hall say to you?"

She flapped her hand in dismissal of his question. "Your list is ridiculous."

He strode forward until his boots were toe-to-toe with her slippers. He wanted to shake her until she told him. Then he wanted to take her in his arms and promise that no one would ever hurt her again. "What did she say?"

Her eyes flashed fire. "I was a fool to think no one would recognize me."

"Lilias, so help me, I can't be patient about this."

She drew herself up. "Miss Hall told the entire drawing room that I was your . . . your . . . she implied I was your mistress. She assumed correctly that you bought the dress for me. She must have thought that even my mother's pearls were . . . were payment from you."

Lilias stepped away from him. "I must leave here tomorrow. I hope that you will give me a good reference. You might mention that I have successfully served you in two positions. It will make me a better *candidate* on the *list* of future employers."

"No." The word burst from him. She couldn't leave him this way. Where would she go? What could she do? Who would protect her?

"No?" Her laughter was tinged with shock. "By insisting I mingle with your guests and wear those gowns, you exposed me to humiliation no woman should suffer—from a person inferior to me in every way!"

He put out his hand to her. She slapped it away.

"Do you think because I'm poor and at the mercy of my employer's whims I have no right to dignity?" she continued. "I am as fine, as worthy, as your titled guests! Better than most of you! Did you ever think I might have a family that this will touch? My sister, my father—oh, God, my father—what will he think of me now?"

His hands ached to hold her and tell her it would be all right. He stood like a fool, torn between the light that was Lilias and the doom that Hindley brought closer every day.

Or worse, the fear that he was in fact a madman who shot his wife in cold-blood and now attempted to get away with it.

She was better off as far from him as she could get.

"After tonight's debacle, there will be whispers in the London trade circles for months." She turned away from him and pressed her fingers to her forehead. "I need to disappear. I need a good reference to gain work with some isolated invalid. And now you don't even think enough of me to give me that?"

He wheeled her around and lowered his head until they were nose to nose. "I know perfectly well what you are, Lilias."

She stood her ground, her face blazing. "Empty words. I have to go. If you give me a reference, I shall be acceptable for hire by someone far from London. You know it as well as I."

"You are not going off to work your fingers to the bone over some complaining old woman or some rustic nobleman's brats."

She was hot with anger. He could scent it, the sweetness of wildflowers, the heat of her skin emanating from the folds of her thin muslin gown. It added to his own anger, his passionate need to make her *see*. The most elemental part of him strove to come closer, to merge, to lose the darkness in the joining.

"My future is none of your business," she hissed.

"Everything you do is my business," he ground out. His hands slid up her arms, clasping them above the elbow. He could feel their softness through the gown, the tensile suppleness from her riding. She was femininity and strength, heightening the hot flow of his blood. "You are my business— mine."

"How dare you, you, you autocrat, you dictator, you . . ."

"Because." He pulled her toward him, slowly, knowing it was madness, giving in to the powerful surge of his blood, wanting, needing just to touch, to hold, if only for a moment. She stood close, her eyes fixed on him with a look he couldn't decipher, her lips parted. They both breathed in unison, in, out, almost tasting each other's breath in that small space between them. His hand cupped the back of her neck to hold her still.

"Because of this," he whispered, and finally, after eons of wanting, kissed her.

Chapter Fourteen

She should move. She should shove him, with both hands. Those were the last thoughts Lilias had before his lips touched hers. Then there was nothing but sensation—the softness of his mouth brushing over hers, soothing and exciting at the same time.

He held her firmly against him with one hand, his arm a support as her body yielded and melted into his. His lips brushed her cheek, the shell of her ear. She felt his warm breath against it, and bit back a cry of shock and pleasure. Her legs felt weak. She lifted her arms to grasp his shoulders, clinging to his strength to hold her against the tide of sensation that swept her beyond herself.

She was so close to him she felt his heat. Against her ear, his soft sigh spoke of mysteries she could only long to understand. His tongue tasted and licked delicately, his teeth nibbled. It made her feel things deep inside, weak, and wanting. He surrounded her, warm, strong, overwhelming her with pleasure. A sigh of delight escaped her parted lips, and she arched her neck to him in surrender.

He bent to what she offered and made a sound deep in his throat, of satisfaction and need. Her mind could barely register more than a rising response to every stroke of his fingers on her cheeks, on the tendrils of her hair, at the nape of her neck, every kiss against the hollow of her throat.

"God, Lilias," he said, "I had to sit there and watch Lord Beverley moon over you all night, and that man, Jepson, sneak looks down your bodice."

"Who?" she murmured, lost in the sensation of his lips heating her skin.

"Good." His laugh was half a groan. "Don't remember them."

His arm enclosed her more firmly as he drew her into the curve of his body. Through her thin nightgown and the fine linen of his shirt, she felt his sculpted chest against her breasts and the rippled muscles of his torso. He was like a living statue, fine and strong and gentle. His other hand stroked her neck, the curve of her ears, her brows, with yearning, gentle fingers, learning all about her, creating sensation wherever he touched.

And then his hands shifted down her back to clasp her buttocks, pushing her so close she could feel him hard and hot against her belly. She cradled him, murmuring, loving the feel of him, the warmth and moisture of his mouth, his light kisses on her collarbone.

"This is right," he whispered. "This is how it should be."

No one had touched her with gentleness and this amazing communication, like a warm river flowing through his flesh to hers and back again, taking part of her with it, and returning to her again, full of his essence. This was nothing like the fearsome experience with Landham. As he stroked the roundness he held, and the backs of her thighs through her nightgown, she was well beyond fear, and propelled by a glorious anticipation, a tight tension winding deep through her belly, and lower.

A step creaked in the hallway. They froze. His arms tightened protectively, his head shot up to look over her shoulder toward the door. They barely breathed as the footsteps moved toward the door, then past it and down the corridor.

Terror gripped Lilias. She backed out of his arms and stared down at her body. Her nipples—good God, she could see her nipples hard and peaked through the thin muslin of her gown. She crossed her hands over her chest and stared up at Aubrey Drelincorte, a lord, a proud, powerful man. He stared back, his face unreadable in the dim light. But she could imagine what he was thinking.

She had just accused him of ruining her reputation, as though this were only his fault. But now she remembered all the times when touching him had been a guilty pleasure. When verbal sparring with him added a spice to her life she had never tasted before. When just being with him gave her a sense of adventure beyond any other.

Dear heaven. If she stayed here, she would become what Margaret Hall had accused her of being.

The footsteps did not return. "You must leave now," she told him. "We must never do this again. I shall be gone before morning."

His gaze traveled past her, to the window and the darkness beyond. "Don't go to Landham. Promise me that much at least."

"Landham? How did you know?"

He turned to her, his indigo eyes glittering in the candlelight, the grim set of his mouth and the slashing scars making her cold. "I understand why you smiled and simpered at the men seated beside you at table tonight. I understand why you'd run from Breme through cold and darkness to flee from my kisses—the monster's touch." Abruptly, he turned away, stalking toward the door.

She heard his voice, soft and dangerous. "But what I want to know is why you shamelessly kissed your farmer, a man so much lower than what you deserve, in the middle of Breme-on-the-Wold. Do you want him so much that even in daylight . . . by all that's holy, Lilias, do not go to Landham!"

"So after you take what you want, you dare accuse me of being a flirt, a wanton!"

"I didn't say it right. But whatever you think of me, Lilias, promise me that you won't go to Landham."

His face, ah, his face with that empty, bitter bleakness to it, that drew her and frightened her at the same time.

She looked down at her hands, helpless in the face of this darkness. She swallowed the hurt from his words, although her heart felt as though it was cracking in two. "I'll not go to Landham," she said around the quiver in her voice. "Now go, for the sake of whatever reputation I have left."

"I'll go," he said in an unsteady voice. "And I'll make it up to you, Lilias. For this . . ." His hand gestured, vaguely, as though he was unable to find words that quite described their situation.

"Make it up?" A rake said that when he wanted to get rid of his mistress. She stiffened and backed away from him. "All I want from you is my reference."

He stepped back and nodded at her, a jerk of his head. "I'll write the bloody reference." Heading for the door, he opened it and peered into the hall. He moved with graceful decisiveness.

In spite of the fact that every muscle in her body trembled with rage and mortification, she wondered in a wild fit of jealousy how often he'd done this before, with other women who came as guests to Breme. The door clicked shut behind him. She couldn't hear his footsteps as he walked away. The sense of wonder and delight she'd felt in his arms sank into miserable oblivion.

So. He thought her fit for his other list of women—the ones a man toyed with and bedded and deserted, while he courted the women good enough to marry.

Lilias lit a brace of candles and set it upon her dresser, counting the coins in her reticule. She'd escaped from Landham and she'd get away from Breme. She packed her trunk, wearying herself with her own list—of coach stops, of present wages earned, of trades other than that of nurse–companion–assistant housekeeper, in which she could quietly recover from hating him, and hating herself more for her stupid dreams and moral laxity.

Ram lounged in a chair in Aubrey's room a short time later, his aspect saturnine and amused, as it always was when they were alone. "You look like you've just envisioned your next incarnation, my friend. In which you're returning as a cockroach."

"In this life, I am already a cockroach," Aubrey muttered. "I thought to give Lilias a future, and I came damned near close to ruining her. Thank the gods that Lady Amelia will take her under her wing. Her influence should negate what happened here tonight."

He turned away from the look of deep understanding that Ram gave him. He could deal with the constant anxiety, the single-minded sense of purpose that propelled him forward. But Ram's compassion unmanned him.

"You deserve a good life, Aubrey. You deserve to wait until the trial has proved you innocent before you tie yourself to someone you'll despise."

He thought of his seething jealousy at dinner. He thought of Susannah, bleeding to death on the jungle floor.

"My Lord Beast . . ."

Ah, Lilias. Some vengeful god put you on that road all those weeks ago, to show me what a chance I have lost forever.

She'd never know how she'd soothed his fears and awakened his most passionate desires. In his present mood, that fact seemed to top his list of regrets.

Heavy-lidded from a sleepless night, Lilias heard one of the carriages depart from Breme. She looked out the window to the drive below. If she were inclined to wager, she would bet a great deal of money upon the fact that the smart, close carriage belonged to Miss Hall and her father. She almost hoped Lord Breme had succumbed to her very obvious campaign for a title. It would serve him right.

Unaccountably, tears welled, spilling down her cheeks like rain. She raised her hand to her mouth and stared out at the grounds. To her left, she could see the castle wing that held the kitchen, where Mrs. Nettles and the kitchen maids no doubt prepared dinner.

They would be laughing at some joke or other. It would be warm there, with wonderful aromas rising from the pots. If she were there, they wouldn't look at her with disapproval or think her odd.

She realized that was the worst thing about leaving. At Breme, for the first time since her mother died, she felt free. They understood her and they still liked her. They . . .

He. She bit back a sob, acknowledging the worst. Lord Breme, that short-tempered, self-centered, arrogant, insulting dolt, had seen her and sparred with her and laughed with her and made her feel valuable, just as she was.

Until last night, when he'd made her feel as cheap as a sailor's doxy on the London wharves. She mopped at her eyes and cheeks. Resolutely, she raised her hand to pull upon the bell to call for a footman to take her trunk, only to hear a soft knock on her door. She blew her nose and tucked back a stray lock of hair and opened the door.

Lady Amelia stood at the threshold, an astute understanding in her bright blue eyes and a determined tilt to her chin. "I see you're packed, my dear. Excellent. My carriage is almost ready. If you'll come down to the hall, we shall be off in just a moment."

Lilias's mouth opened and shut and opened again. She snapped to and shut it only long enough to muster thought. "You are kind, my lady. Too kind. Tom Coachman has promised to take me to London, where I might find my father and then a position."

"Nonsense." Lady Amelia waved her hand in airy dismissal. "You're coming straightaway with me. Do you think I'd allow that too-too handsome jack-a-napes to handle your introduction into society?"

Lilias stared at Lady Amelia, then reached out to touch her forehead. "I think you'd better sit down, my lady. You're not feverish, but I fear the weekend has been a bit overwhelming for you." She led her ladyship to a soft chair and placed cushions at her back. "I'll ring for tea. Perhaps you oughtn't make the long drive today, but rest here."

"I should love tea before we leave." Lady Amelia laughed up at her. "But let me reassure you. I'm entirely in my right mind."

Lilias shook her head slowly, a sick, shamed heat rising to her cheeks. "Then you couldn't possibly know the truth of my situation." She stared past Lady Amelia to the window and the snow-covered lawn beyond it. "Margaret Hall was correct. I'm the assistant housekeeper, my lady. And a good one, at that. But the dresses, the weekend . . . it was all a masquerade."

"I've been aware of that from the beginning, my dear," Lady Amelia said softly. "It makes no difference at all. You're coming to London with me."

Chapter Fifteen

Aubrey stood at the window and watched Lilias climb into Lady Amelia's coach, her skirts sweeping into the dark interior. Frederick shut the door and the coachman loosed the reins. The matched black horses trotted off smartly, no doubt eager to go on this bleak winter morning.

He'd known she would leave today. He just hadn't considered how black the hour of her departure would be. Once she'd met Lilias, however, his godmother had been delighted to take her away from him.

In silence, he watched the carriage all the way down the long drive until it disappeared at the first turn past a tall boxwood hedge. At a huff from the armchair in the corner of the room, he looked away from the window.

Ram stood up and gave him a look of disappointment. "Will returned last night from London with the contracts signed. All they need is your name on them. He got the special license, too. Just fill in that delightful barracuda's name and you can kiss the rest of your life good-bye."

Aubrey stared out again at the empty drive. "I'll manage her." And he'd make damned sure his lovely Margaret said not one word against Lilias Merrit.

"And what a pleasure that will be," Ram said in a voice laced with sarcasm. "She's like an ill-tempered mare. Correct her, and she'll remember forever. She'll wait 'til you're not looking and step on your foot hard enough to break it."

"Thank you, Ram. I'll be sure to keep my guard up."

"You'd better, with this sweet flower of womanhood. From what Will told me, the Halls were one step from prancing about a tastelessly ornate sitting room, in which no doubt you will be called upon to impress your father-in-law's guests from time to time. The Cits do love their bagged aristocrats."

"And since when have you become such a snob?"

"Since the day in Delhi when you saved my hide from that damned mob. Made me think of my father's class distinctions with respect. And since when have you lost your nerve?"

"If you don't think it takes courage to wed that Gorgon, you have less intelligence than I thought."

Ram shrugged. "It takes no damned courage at all, Aubrey. It only takes a stubborn penchant for pessimism. I could see it in your face last night. You've never wondered what will happen if you're still alive in three months' time."

He nodded. "The thought never crossed my mind." In truth, he had never allowed its presence. It would drown him in guilt to think he might actually get off.

"Well, it would be the gods' typical irony if you find yourself saddled with a shrew of a wife for the next thirty or forty years."

Even to himself, Aubrey's laugh sounded forced. "Your father's mistake was educating you at Oxford rather than Cambridge. You've become an incurable romantic. You know the plan, Ram. You know the ton. I can't deviate." He let out a harsh breath, the frustrated acceptance of a man caught in the snare of his own making.

"Wait, for the sake of your serenity, which you also need to help you through this mess. Wait and try to remember."

"Quit harping and leave me," Aubrey said. "Even our friendship has boundaries."

"I'm going." Ram strode to the door and pulled it open. He turned and gave Aubrey a look of exasperation. "I've seen both worlds, Aubrey, and yours is better. You are wealthy, you are free of encumbrances. You can choose whom to wed. But fear has made you a fool."

"And you are an encroaching wind sucker. Call for Will, if you please. I want this over and done with."

It had been cold and dreary in the house for the week since Miss Merrit's departure. Aubrey had gone over the terms of the betrothal settlement with one of his army of solicitors earlier, which was depressing enough.

And now this bad news from Lady Amelia. Aubrey stood by the study window, puzzled and alarmed, perusing her letter by the light of a weak winter sun.

In spite of my attempts to introduce Lilias into society, things are not going well. Friends who know of my plans refuse to visit. I cannot believe that the rumors spread by that Malicious Person you so foolishly invited into your home have risen through trade circles and begun to circulate through the ton. It is a somber day when the daughter of a man who started life as a butcher's assistant would heft more weight with society than the granddaughter of a duke.

Aubrey's eyebrows shot up. The *what* of a duke?

At a ruckus in the hallway outside his study, he lifted his head and headed for the door. It burst open to reveal a large, red-faced, elegant looking man of middle age, a sword and scabbard affixed to his person. He pulled both Jeffries and a footman along in his wake.

"You are Breme?" the man demanded.

"I am." Reinforcements in the form of five more footmen came to a screeching halt outside the study.

"On guard, Lord Beast. You have ravished my daughter!"

Impatient to be done with the madman, re-read his letter, and perhaps race to Lilias's side, Aubrey made the mistake of saying, "And which daughter would that be?"

With a cry of rage, the fellow lunged at him. Strong hands wrapped around his neck and squeezed in a chokehold that could fell a giant.

Chapter Sixteen

With an upward jerk of his forearms and a slide to the side, he broke the hold. One well-placed swing cold-cocked the lunatic.

"My lord?" Jeffries's voice quavered an octave higher than usual.

"A bucket of water, if you please, Jeffries," Aubrey told him.

The bucket arrived. Aubrey applied it in one judicious heave to his visitor's face.

The man sputtered and heaved himself up on one arm, with a gingerly rub to the jaw. "Damn, that was a good 'un, sir."

"And you are . . . ?" Aubrey waited while the fog cleared from the man's eyes and the rage returned.

"Geoffrey Merrit, you scurvy piece of filth." He staggered to his feet and pulled off his glove. In a vain attempt to aim for Aubrey's face, Merrit fanned the air to the left of his head. The glove sailed across the room.

Lilias's father, Aubrey thought, avenging her honor. The day just got better and better.

Merrit blinked in the direction his glove had taken.

"I hate the waste of a perfectly good life over a quarrel I don't even understand, sir," Aubrey said. "If you will kindly explain your reasons for this challenge, we shall know how to go on from here."

"Ruined my daughter, you reprobate," Merrit spat. "Kept her here as your mistress and dispensed with her when you decided to marry. By God, Landham spread it all over Tilden village, and I personally heard it bandied about London. Realize what you've done, you selfish bastard? No man will have her now! I demand satisfaction, sir, and I intend to get it."

"Landham defamed her in Tilden?"

Merrit's eyes were two coals. "Aye. She can never return."

"And everyone in London knows this, as well?"

Nothing could be worse than this, Aubrey thought. All his good intentions, and some not so good, had put Lilias in the position of a pariah. She couldn't even find employment if the rumors had reached such a level. She was ruined.

She was the ruined granddaughter of some damned duke.

Combined with the crushing guilt, a sense of reckless elation filled him. He had tried, God knows he had. He had struggled with desire and emotions he had not felt since his parents had died. But fate had caught up with him. It seemed the best he could do was give in to the inevitable.

With Lilias. A grin tugged at his lips.

"What do you plan to do about it, sir?" Merrit asked.

"First, convince you that you need not settle this in a duel."

Merrit put his head in his hands and shook his head slowly, back and forth. "Won't make a difference to me. Got nothing to lose."

"Come, man." Aubrey steered him into a seat. "Everyone has something to lose."

Merrit moaned and shook his head. "Already lost it all.

Pamela's settlement money, gone in a flash. All my hopes for a new life for Lilias, gone. I'm better off dead than having to see her face when I tell her."

Aubrey sat down at his desk. "You'd better tell me about it, Mr. Merrit. I'm sure we can come to some agreement that will recoup your losses."

"You blackguard!" Merrit half rose, shaking his fist. "Do you expect me to sell my daughter?"

"Of course not." He motioned to Ram, who negligently leaned against the doorsill, his arms crossed, a grin on his face. "I think we need a solicitor," he told Ram.

"I'll get Morton. He's still here reading the fine print on the—I take it—former contract." Ram turned into the hall. "Good thing you didn't fill out Miss Hall's name on that license," he called over his shoulder.

The doubts and fears howled at Aubrey. But the elation slapped them down. He nodded to Lilias's father. "There is only one thing to do, and it must be done quickly."

"Then you'll fight?" Geoffrey Merrit rose to his full height, putting himself on a level with Aubrey, and glared at him.

"Face my future father-in-law over weapons at dawn? Not bloody likely."

Merrit, still off balance, blinked like an owl. "What?"

Aubrey laughed, more than a little unsteady himself. "You and I will sign a contract, Mr. Merrit. Then I leave directly for London to make an honest woman of your daughter."

Only one little problem remained. How in hell was he to convince one fiercely independent, damnably stubborn woman to accept his proposal?

From the cushioned window seat in her bedchamber, Lilias drew the ivory damask curtains and looked out upon

Grosvenor Square. At this dark hour of four in the morning, the London fog swirled about the hocks of the vegetable sellers' horses, the skirts of the maids setting out for the flower market, the carriage wheels of the late-night revelers just returning from a ball or a midnight assignation.

During the last week, in spite of her soft feather bed, she had awakened during the night to sit in the beautifully appointed chamber and stare out this window. She told herself it was because she was used to the quiet of the country and had a predilection for fresh air at night. Thus, through the open window, the constant rattle in the street below and the bells of London disturbed her sleep. She told herself a lot of silly things, in order not to admit she was a familiar tune—the female in a melancholy decline.

She shopped, chatted in a pleasant fashion with Lady Amelia, tried to aid her without understanding what problem weighed on her hostess more heavily as the week progressed. She concentrated upon the memory of Lord Breme's behavior the night before she'd left, and tried very hard not to remember his music the evening before.

She needed to forget him, to put an end to the empty hopelessness that was like an arrow to the heart. She tried to be cheerful, thinking that would dispel the heavy lump in the pit of her stomach. Only alone in the darkness before dawn did she admit to herself how very much she missed Breme.

A commotion in the street outside gained her attention. A coach and four, its wheels grimed with road dust, pulled up to Lady Amelia's townhouse. The fog dissipated slightly and the gaslight revealed a crest on its side. But the dirt covering it made it difficult to determine who owned the vehicle.

However, the short, square form and the bald crown of the coachman as he removed his hat and wiped his steaming round face with a kerchief were unmistakable. Tom

Coachman jumped down from his perch and opened the door. A man, tall, broad shouldered, hair shining like mellow gold in the lamplight, stepped lightly out. His black cloak swirled as he turned. His gaze swept the house.

A shock of recognition struck Lilias like a lightning bolt. She ducked behind the curtains. From their sanctuary, she peeked out, her heart thumping.

Too late. Instinct, or something like it, had brought that sharp regard to her window, and there it remained.

He stared for a moment, then blew out a breath, as though he had been holding it. His sculpted lips curved in a slow smile of satisfaction. He strode up the stairs. The crash of the knocker echoed through the house.

Lilias threw on a wrap and headed for the top of the stairway. In the marble hall below, the butler arrived, hastily slinging on his black coat over his nightshirt. A moment later, the door flung open and Lord Breme strode inside.

Lithe and vibrant, he seemed to fill the whole entry hall. She backed away from the stairway and hid, pressing against the corridor wall, her eyes shut in a completely ineffectual child's gesture of self-defense.

"I never knew you for a coward, Lilias Merrit," he said in a voice filled with reckless impatience. "Show yourself."

Oh, God. After everything poor Lady Amelia had done for her, Lilias was stuck in a farce in the middle of her entry hall, at—she looked at the ormolu clock on the table beside her— half-four in the morning.

She rushed to the top of the stairs and leaned over the balcony. "Hush, my lord," she hissed down at the figure standing with legs spread and cloak flung back, fists on his hips. "People are staring."

It was true. Servants had crept into the hall, nightcaps and dressing gowns askew in their haste.

He shrugged, impossible man. "Let them."

She crept down the flight of stairs until she stood two steps above him, her face level with his. "My lord," she whispered, "what could you possibly want at this hour?"

He grinned. "You." In the middle of the hall, with the servants gaping, he swept her a low bow and took her hand, lifting it to his lips. "Miss Merrit. Would you do me the honor . . . the very great honor . . . of becoming my wife?"

Two of the maids sighed.

She narrowed her eyes and leaned forward until they were nose to nose. She sniffed, a terrible suspicion taking hold. "You're sotted."

He shook his head, grinning even wider, white teeth flashing. "I haven't had a drop. Will you marry me?"

Lady Amelia's cheerful call from above interrupted her sigh of exasperation. "Hallo, dear boy. Finally come to your senses, have you?"

Lilias craned her neck to see Lady Amelia beaming down at them over the stair rail in her blue wool dressing gown, her plait of white hair hanging over her shoulder.

"If you two are going to finish this properly, you ought to have a bit of privacy." Lady Amelia motioned negligently to the right. "Take the study, my dears. You know where it is."

Aubrey took Lilias's hand and tugged her up the stairs. At the landing, she heard the click of a door. Lady Amelia had disappeared into her bedchamber.

Lilias slanted a glance at Aubrey as he turned his head and tugged again at her.

"Come on, Lilias. So many plans, so little time."

From the brilliance of his laughing eyes to the width of his grin, he looked inordinately alive. No doubt about it; he was definitely enjoying himself. She shook her head, suddenly angry that he should make her heart race, as though this was no joke.

"What need for privacy, my lord?" she said, pulling her hand from his. "The whole house knows our business now." She folded her arms across her chest and tapped her foot.

Aubrey's brow shot up. Pointedly he looked her up and down and then leaned toward her. "You're so much smaller than I, Lilias. Light as a feather, I'd say. Easy as pie to sling over my shoulder. We can go into the study quietly," he said in a soft voice, "or we can go with a bit of fuss. Either way, we're going."

She gritted her teeth and looked at the servants in the hall below, craning their necks to watch the spectacle. Tightening the belt of her wrapper, she wheeled, climbed the flight of stairs, and turned left.

And felt arms that pulled her back against a muscled chest, enclosing her with gentle strength. She felt the warm huff of laughter against her ear and then a kiss on her bent nape. "My darling girl. Your other left."

My darling girl? Horrible, irreverent man, to make her shiver like that. She wheeled about and quickly found her way to Lady Amelia's small study. He was right behind her, opening the door for her and throwing his cloak on the single chair in the room. He motioned to the loveseat with a rather imperious wave of his hand.

Who did he think he was, expecting her to drop into a seat meant for close contact with the enemy? She shook her head hard and remained standing, chin up, arms crossed, in an admirable, she thought, attitude of cool reserve.

He measured the distance between them with a speculative look. She backed up a step and he followed with two. She backed up another and held her hand out in a warning gesture. He stepped forward just once, but it was one of his big strides. He definitely had narrowed the gap.

"Stop right there or I'll bolt."

He shot a glance at the door. She let out an exasperated breath and he stood still, giving her an ingratiating look from limpid blue eyes—the man was born to tread the boards.

He stopped where he stood, cautious now that he'd apparently noticed her fists at the ready.

"Why?" she asked. "Why now?"

She waited for something typical—a dictum, or at least a cool, logical reply—but it didn't come. Now his smile was warm and sweet as honey in the sun.

"Because I didn't wish to wait until morning to reach you."

She narrowed her eyes. Humor would get him nowhere. "Why do you wish to marry me when a week ago Miss Hall held your *sincere* affection?" If her voice dripped with sarcasm, so what?

He acknowledged the hit with another quick grin. "And it's going to cost me a pretty penny to get out of that one, let me tell you." He took a small step closer.

She sniffed the air again, wondering if he'd lied to her about his recent alcohol consumption.

"Then why go to the trouble?"

"I need warmth and companionship?"

"You could get a dog."

"Damn," he said. "You're going to be difficult, aren't you?"

After the last week, she had a right to be. "Give me honesty, if nothing more."

Aubrey took a deep breath. In his urgency to get here, to take her in his arms again and see if she felt as heavenly as she had a week ago, he'd come up with nothing that would convince her to accept him.

Well, she wanted honesty, didn't she? It made it easier—no messy delving into why he had raced here like a madman through the night. He didn't know the answer to that one himself.

He took one last step and captured both her hands.

"I want you, Lilias," he said without preamble. "I've wanted you badly for a long time." Bald words, they were, not full of poetry but, somehow, the truth.

The words hung in the air between them, fragile as Murano glass.

"I am aware of that," she said quietly.

Watching the pain cloud her eyes, he knew that she was thinking of the night before she left him. "I was a cad," he said.

She nodded. "Truer words were never spoken."

He let out a frustrated breath and planted both fists on his hips. Since he'd realized both her lineage and her plight, he'd been running full tilt toward her, only to be pulled up short of the goal by a veritable mountain of stubbornness. "Damn it, Lilias. If you'd told me you were a duke's granddaughter, we'd have been married two weeks ago."

She shook a finger at him like a scolding schoolmistress. "When it comes to so serious an undertaking, that shouldn't matter, you insufferable snob."

He glared back at her. "It does matter. You knew I needed society's approbation in this marriage. Only your pride kept you from revealing your lineage. Had I known, I would have been delighted to 'eschew Miss Hall,' as you put it."

"Get out. Get out and never come back again."

He realized he'd made a muck of it before the last words were out of his mouth, but he couldn't stop. Where had all the noble phrases he'd rehearsed gone? He was only left with this frustration to make her see the situation for what it was and to stop fighting him. So that he could take her into his arms and finally breathe again.

He took two steps toward her. She backed away and he followed her all the way to the wall. He watched her face for the moment of recognition that she had nowhere to go, and then he leaned into her, imprisoning her with his weight, his size. She evaded, averting her face. His hand reached out, cupping her chin and gently turning it so she faced him again.

"I want you and you want me. I could feel it when we played the double concerto. I could feel it when we kissed. It's an excellent feeling. I want it back. And I can tell by the way your pulse is beating right here . . ." His finger stroked down the sweet, smooth skin of her cheek, her chin, and ended at the carotid, pulsing to a beat as fast as his own tripping heart. "I'm not alone in that realization. You'd better face it, Lilias."

"What a delightful declaration," she said with a sarcastic lift of the brow. "How can I express my gratitude?"

"By accepting the truth. What we have together is good. It's better than good. And we can have it at Breme. You like it there. I know you do."

Her face softened. Encouraged, he went on. "Think of your future. You'll be wealthy, free from worries, capable of helping your sister. And your father, rather than rotting in Newgate as a debtor, will have money and the means to work again in the profession he loves."

Her face drained of all color. "What do you mean?" she whispered.

"Your father's business ambitions are destroyed," he said as gently as he could. "He pinned all his hopes on one ship, and it sank off the coast of Africa."

"Destroyed? Oh, Papa," she said in a broken voice.

Her expression grew bleak. He grabbed her hands, trying to calm her.

"No, no. It's all right. We came to quite an amicable agreement. The marriage settlement, Lilias. It'll give him enough to live on for the rest of his life, and enough to get his hand back into the game."

Her mouth fell open, then shut with a snap. "You bought me?" she asked in a voice of rising fury.

"No, never!" Aubrey knew he had to tread carefully now. She was staring at him, wide-eyed, and he realized this honesty she wished would hurt her more. "I wanted to come for you anyway. You see," he said, propelling her toward the loveseat and pushing her down onto it, "Lady Amelia wrote. She was beginning to suspect the reason why her friends have suddenly refused her invitations. At the same time, your father paid me a visit."

Her mouth dropped open. "My father! Why, in the midst of his own troubles, would he bother with me at all?"

"He did more than bother, my girl. He challenged me to pistols at dawn."

"You're bamming me!" She laughed.

Aubrey's heart wrenched for her. What must she think of her place in her father's heart to be so disbelieving?

"I am not. Landham gave everyone in Tilden to believe that I ruined you. Similar rumors spread by that viper, Miss Hall, have taken London by storm. All the more so because I am somewhat . . . notorious among the ton."

Her disbelieving smile cracked. She looked bewildered, sitting in her gown staring out at nothing. Shock, Aubrey thought. Too much too fast.

"Then I am truly ruined," she said in a low voice. "Oh, poor Lady Amelia. I've stayed here, only hurting her more."

She turned anxious eyes to Aubrey. "If I leave now, will she regain her friends?"

He sat down beside her, pulling her against him hard, his hand rubbing up and down her back, soothing, his other hand curled against the nape of her neck, surrounding her with his strength, his support. And all the while, his mind seized upon the way to use her soft heart in the most disgraceful, manipulative manner to get his way.

"We can make it all right for Lady Amelia if we act quickly. Our marriage will solve everything. You will be a countess. Nobody will look disparagingly at Lady Amelia for having a countess visiting for a mere week before she was engaged."

He pulled her closer and buried his face in the sweet curve where her neck met her shoulder, exulting in the slow softening of her body against his. "Oh, Lilias. Your father was furious at first, and only saw the right of it after several judicious glasses of whiskey and my assurance that I would never do anything to hurt you. And I won't." He raised his face from her hair and looked down at her, conscious of the solemnity of the vow he was making. "I'd cut my own throat before I hurt you, Lilias. That much, at least, you must believe."

With finger and thumb, he lifted her chin. "You must marry me, Lilias. There's no other way."

Her brow furrowed. "I don't understand. Why come here? Why save my father from prison? What do you get out of it?"

"I already told you what I get. Most importantly, I need an heir for Breme. Rather quickly. The child's gender doesn't matter. The castle isn't entailed to the first-born son. A girl may inherit, as well. That is what I need."

She flinched at his brutal honesty and pulled away from him, her eyes narrowed. "Once this is done, it can never be undone. Don't you understand? There has to be more than just carnal pleasure. There has to be respect, and I'm not sure I trust you to give me that. Go ahead," she said, lifting her chin to that stubborn tilt. "Look into my eyes and tell me you respect me."

No, this was all going wrong! His hands cupped her shoulders, giving her a little shake. Without his volition, the words poured out. "Listen to me! That night before you left, when I came to you, I said those things because I was jealous, Lilias. Of Landham. I was furious. I never meant to imply that you were in any way a . . . a light skirt."

Her eyes widened in shock.

"Jealous?" she whispered.

He nodded dumbly, horrified that he'd let it slip. But as he watched her, the anger faded from her eyes.

"Truly?"

He nodded again.

"Yes," she blurted.

He narrowed his eyes. "Yes, what?"

"Yes. I'll marry you."

Desperate to make her capitulation a reality she would remember, he pulled her into his arms and kissed her with all the pent-up desire of the last, lonely week. As soon as his lips touched hers, she slipped her arms about his neck and clung, warm and willing and passionate.

He felt the breath he'd been holding go out of him as though he were a punctured balloon. He held her against him, the soft curves of her breast against his chest, her heart beating in rhythm with his. He stroked her back, her sides, loving the feel of her.

"Do you have any idea what you do to me?" he whispered, brushing his lips against the curve of her neck. "Just let me have this and I'll be ecstatic."

She gave a deep sigh and nodded, then pulled away. Carefully, she pleated the skirt of her nightdress. The clock ticked off seconds, minutes, as she worried the muslin of her gown and bit her lip, thinking it through.

Finally, she lifted her head and looked at him with a steady gaze. "When?"

"At Breme, I thought. Two days hence, by special license. Ram's making the plans now."

"Two days. That's very fast." She sounded breathless. "I have another demand to make. The marriage depends on it." She squared her shoulders. "I shall need time to adjust. To the changes, you see." Her clear-eyed regard disappeared, hidden beneath lowered lids and a lush fringe of lashes.

"Time for what, exactly?" He had a cold feeling in the vicinity of his belly.

"I should like to wait to consummate the marriage."

He'd been here before, with Susannah. Pleading shyness, she had demanded a long engagement, with all the parties and fuss that went with it. Because she seemed so ethereal, almost too delicate for a man's passion, he had consented to give her time to get used to the idea of the marriage bed.

She'd taken the time to indulge in lascivious carnality. With her lover, Hindley.

Aubrey looked down at Lilias's face, wondering for a moment, then dismissed the thought. Lilias was not Susannah.

But it hurt, all the same. "Lilias," he said slowly. "You understand I need an heir as quickly as possible."

She glanced up quickly, then away again. "Yes."

The silence deepened, broken only by the ticking of the clock. Dread filled him at what truth he might have to face. Hadn't she liked his kisses? He'd thought so. Was he mistaken—again?

He took a painful breath. "Do you find the thought of coming to my bed distasteful?"

A blush, very rosy, very bright, crept up on her neck and face. Her mouth made a little *oh* of dismay. "No. But whether or not you see it as I do, to my mind you bought me."

He barked out a laugh. "My God."

She scowled at him in response. "I have my pride, you know."

He frowned back at her. "A good deal more than you need, in my opinion."

Her dark eyes flashed. Yes, he thought, much more pride than was necessary.

She pursed her lips. "The marriage act is very intimate, isn't it? A woman who feels she's being herded into marriage, no matter how good the intention, needs time to get used to the situation."

He swallowed. "How long?"

"A month."

A month! He felt his lips press together in a tight line. His own wife-to-be, bargaining over how long she could stay out of his bed. The insult to his pride was almost physically bruising. "Too long." His voice sounded stubborn and curt, even to his own ears.

"Two weeks, then."

"A week, Lilias. I can't give you more than that."

For any number of reasons. The child, first and foremost, of course. But no other bridegroom tolerated such self-abnegation. Must he, because of her misplaced pride? Or was it because he looked like a monster?

She bit her lips and glanced up at him. "I just . . . you have been the master and I the servant, my lord."

He laughed, a sarcastic sound. When the swift look of hurt crossed her face, he relented. His wasn't the only bruised pride, here. He held out his hand and took the one that fidgeted with the folds of her wrapper.

Raising her hand to his lips, he gave her a somber look, to reassure her that he took her seriously. "I know I'm not easy to get on with. I know I've fought with you far more than I've flattered you. But with you, I have never been master, and since the first night I saw you, Lilias, I have never thought of you as a servant."

Her lids swept down, the long lashes hiding her dark, expressive eyes from him. "But I have." Her shoulders rose and fell. She lifted her head and regarded him solemnly. "All right, then. A week."

A week—she wanted a damned week. Equal parts gentleman and fool he was to agree, but how in hell would he to get her to marry him otherwise? In the end, with no reassurance to give her and with his own, insistent need, he took her in his arms and kissed her, shutting his eyes, drowning them both in his passion. He dove so deep, there was no thought but one.

This woman felt as though she'd been made for him.

The instant spark springing to life between them was right. He knew with every brush of his fingertips along her sides, her hips, that this one body would be magnificent beneath his, that her legs would be just the right length and strength to wrap round his hips, that they would fit. Everywhere. Like two halves of a whole.

A week hence, it would be done, never to be undone.

He brought her closer, lifting her onto his lap and turning her into his body so she lay nestled in his arms, her legs curled upon the seat. He buried his face in the shining mass of her unbound hair, breathing in the warm, soft scent of her. He ran his hand down the length of it, to the curve of her hip, and up her side beneath it, silken strands against the back of his hand, the soft slide of muslin against the swell of her breast at his palm.

She pulled away, breathless, gazing at him in solemn question. In the lamplight, he could see the dark circles beneath her eyes. She'd been unhappy this last week. Maybe she had missed him. His chest swelled at the thought.

He'd given her a promise.

Aubrey shut his eyes. He made a sound deep in his throat, frustration and need both. She murmured something and rubbed her cheek against his chest. His hand slipped back to her waist. He held her against him, every part of him taut and eager and denied.

Damnation. It was going to be a long week.

Chapter Seventeen

"Ooh, miss! Isn't it the finest loveliest gown you've ever clapped eyes on?" Jane laid Lord Breme's offering out on the bed and stood back, clasping her hands in awe.

Lilias nodded, swallowing the lump of cold, hard fear in her throat. Shivering in her chemise, corset, and petticoats, she moved nearer the fire. What was she doing, marrying a man who could produce a confection of lace and ribbons and creamy white satin overnight? A man who had paid a king's ransom for her, to hear her father tell it.

"I can scarce believe it was done in a day," Jane chattered on as she brushed Lilias's hair. "Just look at that perfect seam, stitches so tiny you can barely see them. Just think how long those seamstresses worked to get that lace to hang just right on the sleeves."

Lilias knew why Breme was marrying her. Two things motivated his proposal—honor and lust. She should be grateful. Without him, her father would be in Newgate and, twice disgraced, she'd be out on the streets.

This marriage was convenient for a lot of people. She swallowed the rather unwieldy lump in her throat. He hadn't even said he respected her.

When Mama and Papa were together, her father had watched her mother with the most adoring look on his face. Lilias's heart sank to her belly.

She didn't expect that from Breme, of course. But she didn't know this man whose quicksilver changes in mood left her spinning in confusion, whose bleak, dream-tormented nights made her long to take away the demons that haunted him, whose sweet kisses made her body and her heart melt.

"Some of us will play today at the reception," Jane said as she helped Lilias into her white satin dancing slippers.

"I'm very glad, Jane," she managed.

Two days gone of the bargain. In five more, she would go to his bed. She'd always thought that when she gave her body to a man, she should be ready to give him her soul. How could she protect her heart while sharing his bed?

Oh, it was all so mercenary. And she'd agreed to it. Not because he'd saved her father and offered her a way to undo the damage she'd done to Lady Amelia, but because, she realized with a sinking heart, she shared his lust.

She may even have instigated it. *Good lord, Lilias,* she thought. *What a Delilah you turned out to be.*

At her sigh, Jane whipped her head from rapt contemplation of the gown. "Are you well, miss?"

"Of course," she said with what she knew must be a weak attempt at a smile. She fanned her hot cheeks. It would be all right. She could love this heir they planned to produce together. No, no. Better not think of that just now.

She knew how to be helpful. She'd had practice for years.

It had worked with Breme before. When he had been ill, she'd been able to quiet him when nightmares held him prisoner. After all, he had not gotten rid of her, had he? Was that what she was worried about? That he'd tire of her and run off to India or Russia or Timbuktu?

Jane helped her into a silk wrapper that did little to warm her or allay her nervous fears. A knock sounded at the door. Jane opened it and Lilias let out a gasp of joyful surprise as her golden, beautiful sister scowled darkly at someone in the hall and sailed into the room.

Lilias ran into Pamela's embrace and amazed herself by sobbing so loudly she was certain the entire house could hear her.

"Out," Pamela said over her shoulder to Jane, who scurried to the door and slipped from the room. Then Pamela just held on tight until the worst was over.

"You don't have to do this, my love. You may come away with John and me right now." Pamela reached into her reticule and pulled out a lacy handkerchief.

Lilias wiped her face and shook her head. "I'm just so very happy to see you. I thought this would be such a hole-in-the-wall affair, with no one to witness but Jeffries and Mrs. Nettles. The vicar won't even let Ram Dass be witness, because he says Ram Dass is a heathen, but I know him ever so much better than anyone else and I like him."

"But Lilias, dear heart. To marry Lord Breme! Think of the rumors—his reputation. You cannot mean to trust this man with your life! When we returned from our wedding trip and Papa told us about it, we determined to help you escape this terrible fate. But Papa seems to like Breme, impossible parent that he is. All dressed in his finest, and puffed up like a peacock, and saying he will give you away. Let us flee this travesty immediately."

Lilias began to shake her head and couldn't seem to stop. "I would never leave Lord Breme on the day of our wedding. How would he feel?"

"Why would you care about such a man's sensibilities? They say that at best, he is mad, and at worst. . . ." Pamela folded her arms and stared at her in sorrow.

Each muscle and tendon in Lilias's body quivered. "He is neither mad nor capable of what you suggest. Never speak of this again to me."

"Ooh, noo. I see it now," Pamela said slowly. "The man took advantage of your tender nature, Lily. Plain and simple, he made you sorry for him, didn't he?"

In the space of a few moments, Lilias went from tears to outrage to a sense of the absurd, all part of wedding day hysteria, she supposed. "Of course not. Why would a man like that have to make anyone sorry for him? He's brilliant and funny and rather fine-looking and—"

"With that dreadful disfigurement, you think he's fine-looking?" Pamela gave her a look that said she had just proved her incompetence and was ready for the asylum.

Lilias frowned. "They're just scars. He is really a rather comely man, especially now that his color has returned to normal."

Pamela pursed her lips. "His color? What was it before, pray?"

"Yellow. He had malaria. But he's quite well, now."

Pamela turned thoughtful. "You think he's attractive? And it isn't because he's given you that beautiful wedding gown and has fifty thousand a year and is a peer of the realm?"

Lilias's stomach curdled from guilt. "Of course I find him attractive," she hedged, then gulped, a mournful little sound in the still room. "And what's worse, he knows I do."

Pamela's face went dead white. "Lilias! He didn't do anything to hurt you, did he? To make it impossible for you to escape his clutches?"

Impatiently, Lilias shook her head. "I am still untouched—well, practically so—oh, Pamela, do be sensible.

You are, after all, a married lady now."

Pamela shut her mouth with a snap.

"He has not ruined me, I promise you." Lilias rose and paced the room. "It's just that I have no fortune, no real education, no title, nothing to recommend me, and he has everything. You heard what he did for father?"

Pamela nodded.

Lilias sniffed into the handkerchief again. "I am sorely overset at the prospect of this uneven match. It is a disaster."

She twisted the linen square and stared at Pamela, tears still sliding down her cheeks. "What if he ends by hating me?" she whispered.

"Then I shall challenge him, myself," Pamela said in a reassuring voice. "I told him so, just before he showed me to your rooms. I walked into this place and told him that if he makes you even a little unhappy, I shall see him hounded to the ends of the earth." Her hand cupped Lilias's cheek gently. "You really do have a place with John and me, my love. Think again if this is what you wish."

Lilias nodded slowly. "I have agreed to marry him and I shall. I am just not very courageous, when push comes to shove."

Pamela enfolded her in a tight hug. "I shall not be content to see this deed done today, Lily, no matter what you say. But if you promise me that you will come to me if you are unhappy, I'll at least sleep a little easier."

"There will be no need for me to come, but I promise anyway." Lilias wondered how she could be both touched and impatient with her own sister. "Now." Eager to change the subject, she led Pamela to the sofa and pulled her down beside her. "How do you like being a married lady?"

Pamela blushed in a soft, becoming way, just as she did everything else in life, Lilias thought with fondness.

"I like it excessively. John is so gentle and kind to me."
Her expression became strained and unhappy. "But Lily,
there is something that I must tell you. I am . . . I am increasing."

Lilias stared at her, open-mouthed. "Increasing? You are
with child?" As the words sank in, she felt a wonderful swell
of happiness wash through her. "Oh, Pamela! What a lovely
wedding gift for me! I'm to be an aunt, am I? Oh, I shall have
to learn to sew immediately! And knit, as well, I suppose."

Pamela smiled weakly. "Yes. I suppose you will." She
glanced down at her hands, twisting on her lap. "But Lily, I
think there is something wrong."

Lilias frowned, her thoughts already turning to the
practicalities. "Have you been to the doctor? Have you been
ill? Have you taken a fall?"

"There's nothing I can put my finger on," Pamela said,
but she didn't meet Lilias's eyes. "Something just doesn't feel
right," she said in a rush. "Dr. Thomas has insisted that all is
well, but . . . I'm a little frightened, that's all." She turned
away, fussing with a bit of lace at her wrist. "It's probably just
foolishness, but I can't shake the feeling that . . ."

Pamela was not usually at a loss for words, Lilias thought,
concerned. Something was really bothering her. "Perhaps,
because soon I'll be a countess, and therefore permitted my
eccentricities, I can help you, for a change," she said with a
smile she hoped was reassuring. "I'll see what I can learn."

"Oh, Lily, thank you. You have always been able to ferret
out pertinent information."

But the worry lingered in her sister's expression and added
to the sense of unease concerning her wedding day.
"Pamela," Lilias said, taking her sister's hand, "is there more
you wish to say?"

Pamela's smile trembled as she looked down at their

joined hands. "You know me well. I can't sleep at night for thinking something bad will happen to this baby. And to me. I hate to worry John about this. He's been so patient and accepting. Would it be selfish to ask that you come to me when my time comes, or if anything should happen before that? I don't know how I should get through it without your help."

Lilias squeezed her sister's hand. "I promise, Pamela. I'll come, no matter where I am or what I'm doing. I'll come to you if you need me."

Pamela threw her arms around Lilias. "You are so good to me, Lily." She pulled out a handkerchief, dabbed at her eyes, and sniffled into it.

"Now," she continued in a businesslike manner. "Since you're bent upon this wedding, I have some things for you. You have mother's pearls, but I thought you'd like to borrow my earrings to go with them. And I have a little blue handkerchief and a new pair of gloves I bought for you in Brighton. But I was so overset about the wedding, I left them in the coach. I'll find John. He's with Papa in one of the drawing rooms. He'll get a footman to bring them in."

Pamela walked out the door in a swirl of skirts. Lilias, pacing before the fire and muttering to herself, didn't hear the click of the latch in the sitting room next to her bedchamber.

"You look beautiful. And in need of persuasion, all over again." Aubrey's voice was a deep velvet purr.

He leaned against the doorjamb, his arms crossed. Dressed in his shirtsleeves and dark trousers, he was elegance and power, what she wanted and what she feared. Her traitorous heart lurched with joy as he walked toward her.

Her palms itched to touch him. She wiped them on her wrapper. The feel of the thin silk brought her back to a realization of how she was dressed.

"What are you doing here?" she asked, backing up a step. He took two, ending up right in front of her. It constantly amazed her how quickly this man could move.

"Minimizing the damage." He grinned, jerking his head toward the door where Pamela had disappeared.

She shook her head, puffing out a deep sigh of frustration. "I already told Pamela this wedding is going forward. And it's bad luck for the groom to see the bride on their wedding day."

"Only when she's dressed in her wedding gown. And you're definitely not dressed."

Aubrey pulled her closer still. His midnight gaze slid down from her face to the place where the lapels of her dressing gown now gapped open. His finger followed, delicately tracing the line from the curve of her neck and down.

She tingled, arching her neck, eyelids fluttering shut as he lightly stroked the swell of her breasts above the corset. She felt his breath warm and soft against the hollow of her neck. She should fight this, she thought vaguely, then didn't think at all. "You said a week," she sighed, leaning toward his touch, suspended in sensation and delight.

"The agreement didn't specify a cessation of all contact."

Kisses grazed along the line of her throat, teeth nibbled lightly, and then his tongue flicked in the hollow. She made a soft, involuntary sound. Through the chemise, she felt his hands drift over her breasts in exquisite caresses. His touch branded her with heat. She fumbled at the buttons on his shirt, wanting to touch him back. Her nipples ached, the barrier of the corset and the chemise a torment.

As her hands caressed his skin, he groaned deep in his throat. His mouth covered hers, his hands slid from her breasts to her buttocks and pulled her forward into the shelter of his hips. She felt the hard heat of his intent and gave a breathless sob, shocked by the sound of so much need coming from her throat and by the straining movement of her hips as she pushed closer still.

He lowered his head and brushed his lips against the soft mounds of her breasts. Heat streaked through her like lightning. Her limbs went weak with the pleasure of it. Her fingers laced themselves into the silk of his hair.

"What are you doing to my sister?" Pamela's sharp voice cut through the haze of ecstasy and need.

Aubrey's head shot up. He pulled Lilias against him protectively. Her face felt as though it was on fire. She fumbled with the ties to her wrapper, securing it around her tightly, and ventured a quick glance in the direction of the door, where her sister stood like an indignant nanny. She fought the urge to giggle in a fit of embarrassment and nerves.

Pamela scowled darkly at Aubrey. "How could you?" she said in a voice quivering with angry disapproval. "Get away from her this instant!"

Aubrey's mouth quirked. "It's your sister's fault. If she were less desirable, I might be able to control myself." He planted a quick kiss on Lilias's head and freed her gently. With an ironically polite bow to Pamela, he left the room.

"Pamela," Lilias began, "he's teasing, you know."

Her sister bit her lip, looking as though she were about to cry. She was very red in the face. "I never told you about this part of married life, Lily. Now there is barely time. But there are three things you must understand."

Pamela drew her down into the sofa and sat beside her, tightly holding onto her hand.

"Number one, men have . . . animal urges. The best men can control them. Number two, the responsibility to remind husbands of this belongs to us ladies. In our actions and our words, we must be soft and gentle at all times. That way, our husbands will treat us with utmost gentleness and respect in public and in private."

But when he kisses me, I don't want gentleness. I want his hands all over me, Lilias thought in despair. *Oh, God. He'll never respect me.*

"Number three," Pamela continued, "this behavior may be impossible for some men. I greatly fear Lord Breme may be among those too crude to understand. He may be among those men who take what they want without thought or kindness."

Lilias wanted to sink into the floor. She was living a lie. Her sweet sister, who had given her all the love and attention their mother would have lavished on her, thought she was a lady.

But Lilias's reaction to Aubrey's slightest touch proved one thing conclusively. She was a strumpet.

Pamela gave her a dark look. "If your husband proves among the baser breed of men, you must hope for the best, my love."

"And that is?"

"A mistress."

Not on your life, Lilias thought. And stared down at her hands in dismay, knowing she was doomed to be counted among the baser breed, herself.

Chapter Eighteen

Lilias stood in the antechamber of the church, peeking through the closed double doors in horror as her father grinned and pushed a huge bouquet of lilies and pink roses into her limp hand.

"Quite a turnout," he said. "Breme certainly knows how to put on a show."

It was an understatement. The back two-thirds of the church was packed with visiting nobility, the men peering with pinched disdain through quizzing glasses at the first rows, filled primarily with the staff of Breme, the gypsies, Lady Amelia, Ram Dass, Pamela and John Trevell. Those inhabitants of Breme-on-the-Wold who had not found seating stood at the sides.

Her father suddenly let out a bark of laughter. "Holy Hephaestus! There's your grandfather, sitting as stiff as a corpse in the front row. Why he don't look a day older than when he kicked me out of his house, and me with even more money and better prospects than any of your mama's suitors. And your Aunt Edith is right beside him. Always was a timid little thing, but sweet-tempered. Well. Breme certainly has a sense of humor."

Her mother's family, after all these years! A whimper escaped her tight throat.

Geoffrey patted her hand. "Don't fret, gel. He'll do well by you. You believe that, no matter what lies that bastard Landham's spreading now. When I think how that brute took me in with his money and his everlasting love talk, and me an old trader from infancy, practically! Well, what's done is done, and luckily, no real harm to you, Lily."

He stared down at his polished boots and then gave her a direct gaze. "Hope you'll forgive me, my girl. Do wish you happy."

"Papa," Lilias said in surprise, "this is the first time you've looked at me!"

Oh, heavens! Had she actually blurted that out aloud? "Forgive me, Papa. I'm a little nervous, you see, and . . ."

Her father's mouth had dropped open. "I don't look at you, Lily? Well." He cleared his throat. "No wonder if it's true. Look just like your mama, you know. I couldn't give her what she deserved—her old friends, her family—she gave it all up when she wed me."

He looked down at his boots and then at Lilias again. "And then, after I lost everything, you couldn't have your music lessons anymore, when even these ears could hear you had your mother's gift. Instead of parties and lessons with girls your age, you had to work all the time. Don't suppose any man would be proud of what he'd done to his little girl. Don't suppose he could look her in the face."

A moment must have passed as Lilias tried to absorb what her father had just said. She swallowed hard against the lump in her throat, reached up on tiptoe, and kissed her father's cheek. "I'm so glad you have come to give me away, Papa."

Her father turned a bright red. And smiled, straight at her. Her father cared about her. Maybe, someday, the man waiting for her at the altar could, too.

As she turned again to peek through the double doors to the church, the congregation rustled in anticipation as Lord Breme took his place at the front of the church. He had dressed in a dark, formal suit and stood tall and proud. Through a tall, leaded pane, the sun shone upon him, gilding the thick fall of his hair, emphasizing the dark, slashing lines of the scars across his left cheek.

With his intense blue gaze, he looked at the double doors as though he could see her, his stance expectant, a line of tension about his mouth. The organ burst into a piece by Bach.

Geoffrey took a deep breath and huffed it out again. "By God, let's give 'em something to remember, Lily!" With a steady hand, he took her own and laid it upon his arm, and they walked through the double doors.

During that long walk down the aisle, she never took her eyes from Lord Breme. She noted first the softening of his sculpted lips as the door opened and she came through on her father's arm. As she drew close, Lord Breme's hand reached out to her, and finally, she felt the light squeeze of reassurance as she took her place beside him.

Afterward, Lilias remembered little about the ceremony that joined her life forever with this man who was still a mystery. The vicar spoke. She answered when required, in a calm voice she hoped. Lord Breme's voice had been firm as he spoke his vows.

One thing she did remember—the powerful, heady kiss they'd shared at the end of the ceremony—the taste of him, sweet and tart like the best wine, the warmth of his body, the strength of his arms. They seemed to hold each other upright in that moment, against the staring crowd of strangers and the uncertainty of the future.

Later, at the elaborate wedding breakfast in the Great

Hall, the castle put on its most magical appearance. Garlands of flowers hung from the ornately carved balcony of the minstrel's gallery and from the backs of the winged griffins that topped the landings upon the stairs and protected the House of Breme. The music flowed as constantly as the champagne. The gypsies neither lifted the aristocracy's purses, nor pilfered the silver, as her father feared. As smiling members of society greeted her politely, she thought perhaps that she might find a way to make this uneven marriage work.

Her grandfather, Alfred Crosby, Duke of Ayres, immaculately dressed in a dark-blue formal suit, his thick white hair perfectly brushed, was as stiff and distant as he had seemed sitting in church.

"My felicitations," he had said in a dry, cool voice, without any trace of warmth or recognition. He peered sharply into her eyes and she met his glance, she hoped, without a trace of the unease she felt. "You'll do, my girl. You look like your mother, and your grandmother as well. When the Season begins, call upon us at Ayres House. Bring your husband along."

The invitation was many years too late, in Lilias's opinion. "I don't know that I shall get to London any time soon, sir," she said in a voice that matched and met his cool tone.

Her grandfather's lips curved up in a slow, rusty movement, as though he rarely indulged in a smile. "I've portraits, my girl. Of your mother when she was just your age. Of her when Gwennie was a little thing—couldn't have been more than three then, and already prettier than a summer's day. It might be worth a trip to see 'em." He rapped his cane on the floor and walked stiffly off, his shoulders straight and tall.

Lilias glanced sideways at Lord Breme. He was contemplating the floor, a grin tugging at his lips. "Intriguing bit of bribery, don't you think?"

"No," Lilias said in a soft but fierce aside. "I think I prefer my father's materialism to my grandfather's pride."

Her Aunt Edith was a pale, small woman with a tendency to wring her hands. "You look so much like your mother," she said with a soft smile. "I am so glad to see you at last." With a ducking motion, she moved closer, grasped her hand, and placed a kiss on Lilias's cheek.

When she traveled down the reception line, Lilias took the little note her aunt had left in her hand and tucked it into the wrist of her glove. Later, when the line had finally trickled to nothing, Lord Breme took her hand and led her to an alcove set off from the Great Hall by maroon velvet curtains. She sank into the carved Elizabethan chair. Shy suddenly at being alone with him, she pretended to study the table beside her, an inlaid French piece from the last century.

"I'll get you something to eat and drink," Lord Breme said with a smile in his eyes. "There are several more hours of this to endure."

She nodded gratefully and, when he left her, leaned her head against the chair's wood back, placing her hands on its arms. The little piece of paper moved against her palm, where it had slipped down. She unbuttoned the glove and took it off, then opened the paper and read the few words written on it. Quickly, she looked about for someplace to dispose of the note.

"Your aunt gave you that?"

She gazed up into the cool eyes of Lord Breme, holding a plate and a glass of champagne. She nodded, caught by his careful, expressionless gaze. He said nothing more, but she saw the way his hand clenched the stem of the glass. For that reason, she hid her embarrassment and shame, and met his gaze as she held it out to him.

He placed the glass and the plate upon the table and took

the note. For a moment, he was silent, staring down at the small message. Then he looked at her, his lips curved in harsh irony and his eyes were bleak. "It is always reassuring to have your family close ranks behind you."

"They know nothing." She bit her lip, took back the paper from his outstretched hand, and lowered her gaze to her lap.

Come to us if you are in need, her aunt had written.

His hand came out, gently raised her chin, and caressed her cheek. But his eyes glittered dangerously, leaving her mute with despair. "You have only yourself to blame, my dear," he said. "This is the reaction you must expect when you place yourself in the hands of a beast."

Pamela smiled up at her husband as he placed the merino shawl about her shoulders. They sat in their own cozy drawing room after the carriage ride home from the wedding. She relaxed against the brocade back of the library chair, safe again within her well-ordered home. John had pulled his chair closer to hers. He knew she found it reassuring—his size, his strength, his gentleness.

"Dearest, you look weary," he said.

"It has been a long day," she replied, pouring tea for him, adding the cream and passing it to him.

"You barely ate a thing at the wedding luncheon," he said, as she poured another cup for herself and added a lump of sugar. "Cook made the biscuits especially for you. Eat them slowly and you'll feel better."

"Yes," she said vaguely, picking up a sugar biscuit and biting into it as her mind mulled over the revelations of the day. "John," she began, and then felt the blood rush to her cheeks.

John's voice was as soft and comforting as a down quilt.

"What's troubling you, Pamela? You know you can tell me anything. Anything at all."

"Do you think Lilias will be safe with him?"

"Breme? I think he cares for her a great deal more than he'll admit. I think he'd defend her against any threat."

She smiled at him, grateful and awed still. "As you have done for me."

Then she gazed into the distance, clutching her teacup. It rattled against the saucer, and she put it down, folding her hands in her lap. "But the way he looked at her throughout the ceremony, and after, too. Edgy and hot and impatient. The way he came to her before the wedding—she was in her dressing gown, John, and he . . . he . . ."

"He embraced her?"

"Yes. He touched her." Pamela made a helpless gesture with her hand and then clasped it hard again with the other. "And kissed her. I think he would have done more had I not interrupted him."

"And how did Lilias react?"

"She seemed to like it. Is it possible, John? Do good women enjoy this? Welcome it?"

He rose to kneel before her and lifted her clenched hands in his.

"Pamela," he said with that gentle patience that made her wish to lean into his strength forever. "When I think of . . . well, I want to rage and tear the world apart. And I can do nothing, because doing anything would hurt you more."

Slowly, as though he were releasing a bird from a snare, he unlaced her fingers and kissed each one. When he looked up at her, there was a world of understanding in his deep brown eyes. "Yes, my love. Good women enjoy this. I am a patient man, and an optimist. I swear to you, Pamela. Someday, you will find this act between us a thing of joy."

Two days after the wedding, Aubrey sat alone in his study and cursed himself for a fool. He knew it was unfair to Lilias, but he didn't care.

He burned for his wife and he couldn't have her. It was easier to stay out of her way than to be in the same room with her: wanting, hurting, and resentful because of it. So he prowled his study, defensive and prickly, counting off the days of satisfaction he'd forgone, when there were so few left. He'd come racing to London to find her because of two things—an heir and the peace she brought him. At this rate, there would be no heir. And if this was peace, then hell must be full of it.

His nails drummed a tattoo against his desktop. Jesus! Lilias and her chaste goodnight kisses and her use of her original suite all the damned way down the hall from him, and three days more to go.

Because she wanted him to prove to her that she wasn't a servant. Damned if it wasn't the other way around, with him aching and waiting, hat in hand, when he had every right to consummate this union with his wife.

He was tired of the servants' quizzical looks and Ram's ill-timed advice.

"Aubrey, she looks at you at supper," his friend said in exasperation last night.

"Stuff it."

"As though she's wondering what it would be like to have her bluff called, to be mastered, so to speak."

"Shut *up*," he'd said and spent the rest of the night with a brandy bottle.

But she did look. He caught the glances, the downward sweep of lashes hiding her eyes when he looked full at her.

Did she wonder? Did she fear him? Did she miss Landham?

A perverse vanity prompted him to keep his bad side to her at table. He was what he was, after all. She'd better get used to it.

A rap at the door broke through his thoughts, which had been circling his head like a tiger in a cage for two days. He wasn't sorry for the interruption.

"It's about Lady Breme, my lord." Ben, the detective he'd hired as a footman for his muscle, his wits, and his ability with a pistol, stood in the doorway.

"What about my lady?"

Ben's square, bluff features held a look of concern. "She's set for going off to Breme-on-the-Wold, and she wants to ride alone. Would you like that I ride with her?"

He thought for a moment. Lilias had spent the last afternoon holed up in the library, he knew from Ben. Perhaps she simply wanted a dash across country on that chestnut of hers.

"Let her go, Ben. But follow her at a discreet distance."

Ben nodded. "Aye, my lord. I'll not disturb her."

"Good. Report to me when she's safe home."

Ben gave a little bow and shut the door behind him. Aubrey shook his head, as though to clear it. He needed air, himself. He'd visit the tenants, see to the condition of their farms and their houses, take note of their new children. Fresh air wasn't the answer to what ailed him, but it was a way to expend the frustrated energy he'd built up.

Lilias rode Starfire into the small clearing past the village where Sarah's mother, the midwife Betty Mathers, lived. The little stone house, set in front of a wood and beside a stream, had a white plume of smoke rising from its chimney. Lilias breathed a sigh of relief. Luckily, someone was at home.

Yesterday and this morning, she had searched the texts in

Breme's library for information on childbirth and the months that went before. When her research came to nothing, she remembered Betty and eagerly seized on the idea of visiting her. It was a chance to get away from the castle and fulfill her promise to Pamela.

Lord Breme had become strange and silent with her since the morning after the wedding, when she had suggested they ride out after breakfast.

She so wanted a special time with him, to assuage her fears that the marriage was only one of convenience and duty to an inferior. Instead, she had barely seen him at all. Was he already regretting his choice of a bride?

She sighed and gave the horse a glum pat. Four days married, at sea, and rudderless. She used to know who she was—Lilias Merrit, nurse, teacher, musician. Now, she was the bought-and-paid-for granddaughter of a duke. Who, until four days ago, had refused to acknowledge her existence.

The cottage door opened and a wizened little woman stood in the doorway, wiping her hands on a clean apron. "Good morning to you, my lady. 'Tis a little soon for you to be calling upon me, isn't it?"

She smiled and slipped from Starfire's back. "Indeed. But I have questions for you anyway. Sarah told me you might spare me a bit of time."

"Aye, and gladly. Do you come in."

"Thank you. I'll just tether my horse."

Betty Mathers waited until she'd affixed the tether and then stood to the side of the open door. "Come into the parlor, my lady. And ask away."

Lilias ducked her head beneath the low entryway. She followed Betty into a bright little parlor and took the rocker the midwife indicated.

Sinking back into it, she told Betty Mathers about Pamela,

her fears, and her symptoms. Betty listened quietly, then spoke.

"Sounds like she's a little more than a month into her time, you see. One of two things will happen with that babe, my lady, and I can't say which yet." Betty's pleasant face was serious, intent. "But I'll tell you either one will be for the good, and neither will hurt your sister."

"And those two things?" Lilias leaned forward in her chair.

Betty Mathers shrugged. "Either the babe's formed right and it'll settle two or three months hence. Or there's something wrong with it, and she'll lose it."

Lilias froze at those words. Pamela's expression when she spoke of the child she carried had been so fearful and sad. This would be a tragedy for her.

Betty leaned forward and patted Lilias on her hand. "Sometimes it just happens that way, my lady. Nature provides when the babe's not healthy. The womb knows it won't survive in this world, and it slips the babe before it has a chance to suffer for long."

"And the mother?"

"Ahh. The mother—she can have another child. And this child most times will be strong and fit, and she'll not have empty arms all her life."

Betty Mathers gave her a searching look. "But I'm thinking you didn't just come for that, although your sister is dear to you. What else do you wish to ask of me?"

Betty's expression was so relaxed and so understanding that suddenly there were a dozen questions Lilias wished to ask. So, sitting in the quiet, bright parlor of the midwife, she began.

Aubrey stacked the papers neatly on the desk in his study

and smiled at Will Lessing. "I think that's enough for today, don't you?"

"Thank you, my lord." Will stood and stretched.

Aubrey looked behind him to the window overlooking the park and realized that the late afternoon sun slanted through. They'd been perusing figures for several hours, determining profits and a few losses due to a storm at sea that had almost sunk three of his ships. Overall, the picture looked good. He'd done better than last year, which had been a banner year for his shipping and trading interests.

He noted with a grimace of irony how very much work a man could hide in if he were miserable. "My lord?" Ben, the masquerading footman, stood outside the study, a quaver in his voice.

Aubrey looked up at the troubled, square face of the footman and motioned him in. "Shut the door behind you as you leave, Will," he told the secretary.

When they were alone, Aubrey sank into his desk chair and folded his hands together on the desk. "Is there a problem, Ben?"

"My lady is home safe."

"Oh? And why do you look as though Valhalla will fall tomorrow?" When the detective didn't answer, he prompted him with a growing sense of doom. "What happened in the village, Ben?"

"It was where she went, my lord. I thought I must tell you." The man's face had gone bright red.

"Where?" Why was it that people couldn't just spit out the bad news and have done with the interminable, nerve-pulling wait?

"To the midwife's cottage, my lord. Not that I think there's aught wrong with it. But you told me to follow, and to report, so I have, now." Ben's expelled rush of breath signaled the end of his revelations.

Aubrey's fingers tightened on each other like clamps on a vise. "No doubt, there's a good reason. Thank you." He motioned to the door in dismissal. He heard it click shut and Ben's footsteps receding down the hall.

Aubrey rose, whirled in one fluid motion, grabbed up a heavy crystal paperweight, and threw it hard against the mantle. It crashed into a thousand pieces. But the motion offered no relief from the beating of his blood, and the fury pumping through him.

Betrayal, the kind he'd known once before, smirked at him from where the splinters of glass shone in the heat of the fire. He saw it all again—Susannah's maidenly shyness before their marriage. The lightning swift change on their wedding night. The disdain in her voice, the disgust on her face, long before the leopard had branded him with these scars.

"Peasant," she'd sneered, tightening her wrapper over the body he'd just discovered knew a good deal more than his seemingly innocent bride had admitted. "A peasant's hands, a peasant's huge, clumsy body. You so lack Rupert's finesse. Do you imagine for a moment that I would have gone through with this charade had my parents not forced me to do it?"

He'd stared down at his big hands. Before, he'd been proud of how they could manage a horse or yoke oxen to the plough. Proud that they could coax the most delicate notes from violin or harpsichord. The fingers and palms seemed to grow larger as he stared. Ham-fisted, he thought.

She'd thrown her head back and laughed, her eyes glittering with hatred. "Just be grateful. The midwife assured me that I'm not carrying his child. Would you have guessed if I'd passed it off as yours? I would not have hesitated to do so.

And you, with your nose in your books and your music and your tiresome estate, would never have known the difference."

A sound came from him, a guttural, beast-like rasp from deep in his throat. Fool that he was, he'd allowed it to happen again—the illusion of innocence, and now, the visit to a midwife. As he wrestled with the possibility that another man's bastard grew in his wife's belly, his life slid out of control. Again.

Landham was a handsome devil.

Was she with child?

Everything inside him screamed no. She'd been reluctant. Reluctant? Hell, facing ruin, she'd refused to marry him. And then she'd changed her mind. When he'd said—when he'd admitted his need for her.

He counted the months since she'd fought with Landham and arrived at Breme. Long enough to suspect she was pregnant with another man's child and go to the midwife for confirmation.

By God, married, celibate, and cuckolded before the week's end. If she were carrying Landham's child and would not tell him, he really would go mad.

Lilias stood by the fire in the library, glancing at her husband each time she thought she could get away with it. He sat in a library chair, his eyes intent on a book. She liked to look at him—the way he sat, one leg crossed over the other at the knee, his long body elegant, harmonious.

There was no sound in the room but the ticking of the clock and the soft shhsh of the page as he turned it, thumb and forefinger slipping along the paper, power and grace unleashed in that small movement. The lamp's glow caressed the gilt of his hair.

"Seduce him," Betty had told her. "It sounds as though it won't take much."

She had thought while bathing to wear the beautiful gold velvet gown he had bought her. She had asked Jane to dress her hair with special care, and had strung her mother's pearls through the curves and loops of her coiffure.

He hadn't noticed anything. Indeed, he seemed weary, like a man who'd struggled with some dark cloud, and come away drained, but victorious. Only once, at dinner, had he attended her sharply, when he'd asked about her afternoon.

If she'd felt comfortable with him, she would have mentioned Betty Mathers. However, with her uncertainty, with his strange changes of mood, she hesitated to tell him anything of an intimate nature concerning Pamela. Especially when Pamela had been so dreadfully rude to him at the wedding.

But when she finished talking, his mouth set, and his eyes gazed beyond her, infinitely sad and empty. What had she done? What had she said? How could she bear to live with a man who would not tell her what he wished of her? The hall clock struck the hour of eleven. Lord Breme did not look up.

"I bid you good night, my lord." Strung to the breaking point, she took a deep breath and turned to leave.

Halfway toward the door, she paused, swung around, and looked at him. He sat so still and ignored her so exquisitely. She turned and walked back until she stood before his chair. With a slap of her hand, she sent the book flying. And took two steps back when he sprang up, his nostrils flared like some jungle cat scenting game at last.

"I'm sorry if that was an old and loved tome. But I assume from your silence that I've done something to displease you. I wish you will tell me what it is, so that I might make amends." There. She'd gotten it out, quavers and all.

His face was suffused with color, his eyes narrowed as he stared at her. He turned his back, the muscles taut and stiff through his whole body.

"You wish to know?" he said in a voice tight as a hunter's trap. "Come with me."

He picked up the candelabrum on the table beside his chair, a silver branch of three candles. She followed, through the hall, up the wide, ornately carved stairway above the tiles in the entry hall, through the long corridor, dimly lit with sconces. He stopped at his door and pushed it open, waving her into the darkened room.

Only the glow of the fire made the dim shapes in the room visible. For a moment, the darkness took her back to the beginning, her first night at Breme, fighting the fear of the monster awaiting her in his lair. She could walk away and leave him to his strange, silent melancholy. But the longing for the sometimes maddening, mysterious man she'd known before the wedding was too strong. She took a hesitant step.

"Don't be afraid," he said. "Regardless of gossip, I do not beat my wives. And I can't seem to drum up enough of the requisite fury to murder you tonight."

At that, her chin shot up and her legs carried her through the door.

"What's the matter, my sweet?" His voice was light, mocking. "It's the same room as always. You've been in it many times before."

"I'm not afraid of you," she said. It seemed she was only afraid for him.

"Perhaps you should be afraid," he said grimly, striding ahead and bringing the light with him. The room took on its familiar trappings—the tables beside the pair of wing chairs facing the fireplace, the wardrobe tall on one wall, the massive, ornately carved Tudor bed.

The bed, she thought with a wild leap of her heart. Her hands ran down the front of her gown, straightening the folds. Was her hair still pretty, or had it come down while she fretted? The door shut with a decided click. He placed the candelabrum on the mantle and moved toward her, as finely made as any man had a right to be. Faintly menacing and graceful, his shadow rose on the wall behind him.

"Lilias, why did you go to Breme-on-the-Wold today?" he asked in a soft voice more menacing than a shout. "Whatever you tell me had better be the truth, and I shall try to deal with it." But this close, she saw the set of his jaw, and she wondered wildly just how he intended to deal with it.

Rattled, she said the first thing that came into her mind. "Because the books in your library didn't have sufficient information."

"You went to use the lending library?"

"No, of course not. I—"

"Let me save you the trouble of confession. Why did you visit the midwife, Lilias? Are you carrying Landham's child?"

"Am I . . ." Suddenly, it all made sense—his silence and tension tonight, his refusal to even look at her. She put her hand up to her chest, near her heart, as though she could rub the hurt away. That he should know her so little—should respect her so little—to believe *that*.

"You had me followed!" She raised her hands to strike, and he captured them.

"Did you marry me to give your child a name? If you tell me now, it will go better for you. Are you breeding?"

She hated his belief that she could marry him while foully lying about something so important. She stared straight at him, while tears beat hot and stinging against her eyes.

"No," she said. "I. Am. Not." She hated that last, bald word for something that people only mentioned in polite, almost spiritual terms. Enceint, increasing, with child. "Breeding!" *Like a stupid sheep,* she thought furiously.

He let go her wrists and stepped back. "Well. That's something, anyway."

"I should hope so! You had me followed!" she said again, still stinging from the insult.

He gazed at the wall behind her. "For your safety, I thought. Until today. I am inclined to believe you, at least about the pregnancy." She opened her mouth to speak. He put two fingers on her lips, his brows raised in mockery. "We'll deal with any other tearful explanations later."

He shrugged, smiled a little, a throw-away, ironic curve of his beautiful mouth. "You may have been an innocent, seduced and abandoned. Why should I not choose to believe that, if I wish? It's preferable to this hell I've been living in for the last four days."

"Hell?" As she breathed the word, his assumptions, his behavior, all of it paled beside the surge of surprise that washed over her. Betty was right, it appeared.

His bald declaration and the intensity in his dark blue eyes acted as a mirror, revealing her to herself in an image she had never known she had.

He was angry. He was hurt. He'd ignored her because he wanted her.

"I don't bloody like the sensation, Lilias. I don't plan to experience it again. Expect that you will always be guarded, except when you are beside me, or beneath me, so to speak. That's the other thing about to change, Lilias."

His beautiful voice had deepened, its timbre so seductive it would have tempted Eve into racing right out of the garden and into his arms.

"Come here."

Chapter Nineteen

The reckless, sensual light in his blue eyes held her gaze. She could almost wish to give in to the velvet music of his deep voice, the promise of his body, his grace and strength and mystery. But . . .

"Just a minute," she said in a clipped tone.

He took a step toward her. Now, he was so close she could feel his heat. Anger? Lust?

She held up a hand, palm out. "Not so fast. I have it on excellent authority, my lord. What we are about to do can be special, if there is trust between the people involved. You've just made some very insulting insinuations. I am, to put it mildly, furious. And I intend to hear your proof, so I can judge you as you have judged me. Perhaps I shall be a bit more rational, however."

He looked poleaxed, she noted in satisfaction.

She narrowed her eyes and placed her hands on her hips. "Let's hear it, my lord. Even a suspected felon is allowed to defend himself."

He drew himself up, gave her a glare. The shimmering heat seemed a bit dissipated, but not yet cooled. "You were betrothed to Landham. Landham kissed you at Breme-on-the-Wold, and then repudiated you. When you visited the midwife—"

"You naturally assumed the very worst, didn't you?"

He took a breath. For a moment, it looked as though he was about to tell her something more. Then his lips pressed together in a thin, angry line.

"And with Landham, was it?" She heard the contempt thick in her voice. "That pig didn't kiss me. He crushed my mouth so hard my cheek bled, and, I might add, he almost smothered me. I had bruises along my ribs, and then I had to hide them and go to your blasted dinner party, where that awful Hall woman . . ." With a start, Lilias snapped her lips together.

"Look what you've done now," she muttered. "I'm whining."

His lips quirked, once, twice.

"You had the gall to accuse me of wantonness and deceit, and now you're going to laugh at me?" she said, outraged.

"I apologize," he said. Then, unaccountably, his face grew solemn. "You should have told me, Lilias. I could have protected you from him."

She sighed, too strung apart to continue the battle. "Apology accepted, I suppose. Men are strange creatures, especially where pride is concerned. And as for protecting me, you have done that now."

He gave her a long look, his face taut, nostrils flared. "I won't dwell upon whether you loved Landham or hated him. But you're mine now, Lilias. And I simply cannot wait any longer." He shrugged, a helpless gesture. "I can't."

They stood close, breathing in unison, almost quivering with expectation. The very air seemed charged. She had no doubt about what he meant. She thought about how his kisses dispelled the memory of Landham's assault. Her confusing, vibrant, difficult husband could make her forget her own name with the power of his touch.

It seemed the wrong time to draw a line in the sand. "All right." Her breathless voice didn't sound like her own.

"Good." With deliberation, never taking his gaze from hers, he picked up the candelabrum and blew out the candles. The room was plunged into darkness broken only by the dim light of the fire.

She stood still, almost blinded by the sudden loss of light. She felt rather than heard his movement, circling her. Felt it in the solid warmth at her back, the hands that rested at her throat, stroking upward, across her cheeks, over her eyes, brushing her very lashes in the lightest of caresses. Felt him pull her back into the curve of his hips. Even through the layers of skirt and petticoats, his intention was hard and evident. His every touch held the power and the precision to draw shivers of delight from her.

"Don't hold back from me, Lilias. Please." His warm, sweet breath huffed against the shell of her ear and she trembled.

This was what she had asked Betty Mathers to tell her about, and Betty had given her the knowledge that relieved the fear—that she would be awkward, that she would somehow never be as desirable as Lady Susannah had been.

But Lilias hadn't told Betty that this man could make her body go limp from the touch of his tongue on the nape of her neck. She hadn't said that his hands, learning the shape of her, could make her turn in his arms and crowd into him with a yearning to get closer until there was nothing between them—no distance of clothing, or station, or wealth.

His hands on the small buttons of her gown were swift and sure. If she could think at all, her newly-found feminine pride would sink like a frigate in a winter storm.

Strong fingers slipped between the velvet opening, parting it all the way down her back as he slid the gown from her shoulders. Cool air caressed her, and then his soft, warm lips kissed the sensitive spot where her shoulder met her neck, sending her with a little sound of delight past thought and into pure feeling. His hands were busy at the strings of her corset. It landed on the floor with a ping of satin and whalebone.

He pushed her away from him. The firelight revealed her, she realized with a blush. It played on her skin above her chemise and petticoats, with her gown at her waist. He, on the other hand, stood shrouded in darkness.

"Beautiful," he said with a hitch to his voice.

He was a seductive phantom, raising her arms out to her sides, stroking down the curves of her breasts, circling her waist with his hands. The gown fell into a heap of soft velvet at her feet. The petticoats followed.

"What are you doing?" she asked him, a foolish question, but her mind whirled with sensation. Heat filled her, embarrassment and a secret, tingling thrill deep in her belly. She was on blatant display before a shadow lover. Before her husband, who seemed to know more about this act than any man had a right to.

He knelt before her, every movement sure and swift. He lifted her feet and removed her slippers, then her stockings, with a slow, seductive brush of his hand from calf to knee and higher, the gilt of his hair glinting in the firelight, just a whisper away from her breasts. At the thought, they ached with anticipation. She held her breath, loving the feel of him, the brush of his fingers.

His hands rose beneath the chemise, lifting it, grazing her thighs in little circles that made her arch her hips toward him and cry out, grabbing hold of his shoulders. At his touch on the ribbon at her waist, the tie loosened. Her unmentionables slipped to the floor in a shhsh of sound.

He pulled her forward. Warmth behind her from the fire. Warmth of his body before her, so close she wished nothing more than to melt into him. He rubbed his cheek against her breasts, kissing the valley between, molding them with his hands. His incipient beard was rough against the softness of her skin, his moist lips a balm.

Heat swirled through her, taking her breath.

"It isn't fair," he said in a voice that shook slightly. "Ah, Lilias. That you should be so beautiful." His deep voice was muffled against her.

"Don't stop," she said. Although with every touch of his hand, her limbs went weak. An emptiness inside cried out to be filled. She felt a slick dampness between her legs that she was helpless to control. Her breath came in gasps of desire.

He rose with uncanny grace and helped her step from the pool of satin and velvet at her feet, then stepped back, her dark lover—every line of his body tense with anticipation. "Take off the chemise," he said, his voice dark and deep.

His bald admiration filled her with pride. Never had she felt so feminine, nor so exposed.

"But I'm almost bare and you are still clothed," she said in a breathless voice.

His coat, waistcoat, and shirt were off in less time than it took to draw a deep breath.

He planted his long leg on a footstool and bent to remove his boots and stockings. The muscles of his back were so defined that they rippled in the dim light of the coals.

He stood again, hands at his waistband, and removed his trousers. Her gaze swept his long legs, tight with muscle, but the darkness hid that part of him between, and she wished with avid curiosity and the last remnants of anxiety to see and understand that mystery. His arms spread wide at his side, as though to say, this is what I am.

"Now you, Madame."

"Light the candles," she whispered, longing to see him.

His laugh was a soft chuckle of resistance in the darkness, and his hand rose to his cheek in an oddly self-protective gesture. "Don't push your luck, darling. I remain in darkness, with only you illuminated, to my deepest delight. The chemise, if you please."

The thought that he could see her—all of her—while remaining a mystery to her made her shiver and, God help her, pant in short, breathless gulps of air. She fumbled at the straps, and the whole gauzy bit of muslin slipped from her and landed at her feet.

With a swift lunge, he bent to her, one arm beneath her knees, the other at her back. She felt the earth give way beneath her feet and the room tilt. She threw her arms about his neck, threading her fingers through the soft, thick locks of his hair.

The sheets lay cool beneath her back and bare legs. He covered every inch of her from shoulder to breast to toes. Her hands caressed him and found the soft, absorbent linen of the bandage, smaller now. Her fingers skimmed over the muscled chest, and he made a deep sound, almost a purr of pleasure. His sudden arch brought hips and thighs against hers.

The hard ridge of his desire moved against her hip, and testing, she rubbed against it just a little. He groaned as though she had destroyed him.

"Oh, no," she cried, an involuntary sound of concern. She tried to ease away, without hurting him more, but his arms clasped her and held her there, beneath him.

"Do it again." His voice came tight and soft, not with pain, she realized, but control. She relaxed. It felt wonderful and wicked, this communion of skin to skin. Her arms closed about him and stroked downward, from the long, clean lines of his back to his hips and lower, learning the tight curve of his buttocks. He was so strong, yet he made her feel safe in his arms. Tentatively, she moved her hips.

"Ah, God, Lilias." His lips claimed her in a drugging, demanding kiss that left her shattered. She opened her lips in a moan of primitive need, and his tongue slid between them, urging her to touch and taste him. His hand cupped her breast, squeezed lightly, and then his thumb brushed her nipple.

She cried out, a soft, needy sound. He did it again. Her hips moved in answer to the question his hands asked. "I never knew," she gasped.

His voice drifted to her out of the darkness, taut as his body while his head lowered slowly to the breast he fondled with such shattering skill. "Good."

His mouth closed over her.

She arched and cried out again, with that strange, muffled, animal sound from deep in her throat.

"You like that, do you?" He suckled, stroking the other breast, while she panted and hitched her hips beneath him. She hung on a wire of sensation, in thrall to his touch, his words, the brush of his lips.

As his hand delved farther down her side, he gave her other breast equal attention. Gently, he parted her legs. She jerked to attention, afraid and wanting at the same time. With each new touch, he invaded her body and her soul.

He touched her lightly, finding the moisture she couldn't control, and gave a searching stroke of his finger across a nubbin that made her twitch and ache beneath his questing hand.

"Aubrey, I . . . ahh. . . ." Dear heavens, it was more than she could take. Her hips hitched at the delicious torment. Something built inside, getting bigger and bigger, until she thought she would burst apart. His fingers paused, leaving her hanging, empty. And then, one finger, slick now, slowly entered her.

She was shocked, startled by the invasion. At the same time, her body clenched around him and she heard herself make a sound that beseeched. She felt the curve of his smile against the valley between her breasts.

"Do you want me, Lilias?"

He stroked again, a deep, lascivious claiming that satisfied and aroused her to fever pitch at the same time. He kept it up until she rose against his hand, while involuntary sounds wrenched from her.

"Tell me," he said, and removed his hand from her.

"Don't stop!"

"I won't. It's too late for that." He moved up and over her, his strong thigh parting her, the large, hard, mysterious part of him at the apex of her thighs, its head right against her opening. "You're so tight."

She stilled, felt the first, stinging stretch, felt him move cautiously, inch by inch. Felt him freeze, heard his muttered oath in the darkness, startled, joyous.

"My God."

It hurt. She whimpered. It hurt more as he nudged up right against the barrier Betty Mathers had described.

With a deep breath, he gathered himself, muscles bunching beneath her hands on his arms, his strong legs taut. He thrust through. She cried out in shock and pain. He lay still, breathing hard, his face against her neck.

Then he murmured, kissing her neck, her lips, her face. "Sweet Lilias, I'm sorry," she heard clearly. And again, "My own, my sweet wife."

It was so very . . . dear of him, so unexpected after all the heat and the passion.

Soothed by his voice and his kisses, her muscles relaxed and she lay beneath him with the slow realization that the pain was going away. She moved, experimenting, and with a hot, smooth glide, he filled her again in response.

"Yes," she whispered, as the pain was drowned in delicious ache and growing urgency. She lifted her hips to bring him closer. He groaned. His body answered hers in another stroking movement, but the muscles in his arms trembled, as though controlling his movements took great effort.

"Stay with me," he whispered, and rose above her, a swift, masculine shadow hovering, and spread his hand on her belly and downward, touching her again with that light, teasing brush of his thumb. Her breath caught in a sob as she arched to him, impelled forward by desire spreading in lightning bursts of sensation through her body.

It was too much, too frightening, the way she shuddered and ached and gasped, slung straining through space like a shooting star. Her arms wrapped about his broad shoulders as far as they could reach.

His arms slid beneath her, lifting her hips higher, closer with each stroke, until he was up against the mouth of her womb. He covered her everywhere, and she loved the pressure, the weight of his claiming. Her body yielded, each tissue throbbing with the glorious, surging rhythm of his invasion, and then all sensation froze on a shock of pleasure so fierce it sent her arching again in a burst of volcanic upheaval, ecstatic and wild.

She heard his muffled cry, felt the tremor in his thighs and within her as he drove into her one last time. While she clung to him, gasping and shattered like a shipwreck victim, the waves took her and took her and took her beyond herself into a place where the two of them made only one being, triumphant and complete.

Chapter Twenty

They lay like that for a long time until their racing heartbeats and ragged breathing calmed. Aubrey slowly came to the realization that he had done and said things that should have frightened Lilias enough to prefer a barefoot stroll through hot coals to taking her place in his bed. And now he was crushing the life out of her.

With a reluctant sigh, he rolled to his side, pulling her with him. Even though he knew he ought to be on his knees apologizing, he hung on to her, selfish and needy.

"Damnation," he caught himself muttering. Oh, better and better—his first gentle word to his wife after the most complete sexual experience of his life. He pulled her closer.

"Ow," she said into his shoulder.

He let go, and amazingly, she didn't leap out of bed. She just ducked her head beneath his arm and snuggled close, rubbing her nose with her forefinger.

"Did I hurt you?" he asked through clenched teeth.

"Not really. I just have a fear of bashing my nose. It's my only real beauty, you know."

"Your only . . ." He chuckled, drew her close, careful of the aforementioned nose. "My darling, if you only knew." He stroked her shoulder. Her skin was still warm and damp from their exertions. She smelled of him. His heart did a little half-thump of triumph. "I am sorry. I should not be surprised that there would be an original solution when the mystery pertained to you. But did I? Hurt you?"

She turned her head into the curve of his shoulder, seeming shy suddenly, after what they'd shared. "A little bit," came out muffled. "But it was, oh, it was . . ."

There was a pause as she lay in his arms. She stroked his chest, her fingers running lightly over the damp hair that curled there. With a secret thrill, he reveled in the sweetness and wondered if she even realized she was touching him so affectionately.

"Is it always like that?" she asked him finally.

"No." From the heady encounters of his earlier years to the perfumed boudoirs of Europe and Asia, it had never been like that.

"I didn't think so. Betty Mathers described the act, and she said it was important to a man to engage in it. But she never said that a woman might find it so powerful."

"Is that why you went to see her?"

Lilias shook her head and the long locks swayed in a silken wash over his arm. She sighed. "Pamela is increasing. She's afraid. I went to discover what I could. I told you, the medical books here glossed over the necessary information. It's a crime, you know. Doctors in this country should be more caring about mothers-to-be. Physicians should write texts designed for women to let them know what to expect, and when to be concerned."

"I've married a reformer, have I?" He rubbed his chin against her hair, breathed in the fresh scent of it.

"Knowledge is power, my lord."

"Aubrey."

"My lord?"

"Call me by my given name, Lilias. You've already done so once."

She gave a stifled laugh and felt for his hand, lacing her fingers through his. "Knowledge is power, Aubrey," she said in a musing voice. "And I think it gives one power over another to know, really know, that person without revealing oneself. You demanded honesty of me tonight. May I ask it of you, too?"

He froze, his hand suddenly stiff in hers. He had thought to marry a woman who would never interfere with his thoughts. And instead, due to his wasted anger and stupid mistakes, he found himself wed to a woman who sent him to heaven and hell on a regular basis.

For what little time they had before the maelstrom, let her be happy and at peace.

"What would you like to know?" He had become practiced in the art of dissembling in India. He could lie as well as the best of them.

She slipped away from him and sat up against the pillows. With care, he raised the quilt around her.

The first question, when it came in a faltering low voice, hit him right between the eyes. "Were you terribly in love with your first wife?"

Oh, God. Woman-like, she had gone to the heart of the matter, and most probably, the one thing important in all the mess ahead of them. He went into the answer he'd thought out on the voyage home—the one he hoped would bring him the sympathy of his eventual judges.

"The marriage was arranged, of course, by our parents. Susannah was quite beautiful, the English ideal, really. She had great charm. All society adored her. I thought I was very lucky."

He waited in the little pause, beginning to understand how

Lilias worked, and hating himself for this.

"It was a horrible accident. I was devastated, of course." This much, in spite of Susannah's constant vitriol, was true.

"You must miss her very much," came the small voice beside him. Her hand slipped into his again. "It must have been terrible for you." She lay silent for a moment. Lying close beside her, staring at the ceiling and praying that this conversation was over, he could feel her determined intake of breath.

"I shall try to be a good wife. I can be very helpful, you know."

"Oh, Lilias." Dear God, no more questions tonight!

He pulled her into his arms, the small body pliant and warm against him. Holding her face with both hands on her cheeks, his fingers thrust through the rich tresses he could only feel in the darkness, he kissed her fiercely, deeply, deliberately obliterating thought in the white heat of passion that sprang up between them.

"How much did I hurt you?" he demanded roughly, his lips feathering kisses along her cheeks, her brows, her lips.

"Not much. Hardly at all. Don't stop."

And he didn't, until she cried out again in the height of her release. Afterwards, she slept, warm and sated, in his arms, and his hands stroked her with an unconscious possessiveness. He stared straight ahead in the darkness, his mind busy on moves and counter-moves in some vast, implacable chess game, where in the end there was either all or nothing.

While Lilias lay beside him, trusting as a lamb. He stroked her hair, realizing with a pang that the stakes had risen. For the first time as he contemplated the future, Aubrey was afraid.

Chapter Twenty-One

When Lilias awoke the next morning, she lay alone in the lord's bed. She smiled and pulled his pillow close. It still held the indentation where his head had rested in the night. She buried her nose in it and breathed deeply. His scent was there—the strange mixture of medicinal balm and exotic spices from the ointment covering his cheek, the scent of woodland and fresh soap and a musky, male essence that was Aubrey.

The sun poured into the window, halfway up to its zenith. She had slept unusually late. At that realization, she buried her face in the pillow again. Heat rose to her cheeks. By now, the entire household would know where she had slept, and why.

For the first time, she realized that she was not just a guest in this house, but the mistress and a titled lady. The staff would scrutinize all her actions. No doubt, they had already discussed this last. Her stomach fluttered with a twinge of miserable unease.

How had she thought to step into this role of nobleman's lady, without beauty, without training, without background? After his magnificent lovemaking, she had been hopeful last

230

night. Before she'd opened her mouth and asked Aubrey that stupid question, that is. What had possessed her to think she could even try to take the place of a beloved, beautiful, charming wife?

"Knowledge is power." As she whispered the old mantra to herself, curiosity rose like the serpent in the garden. There were so many secrets in this castle—new, burly footmen who did not know the first thing about serving properly, men dressed in business suits coming and going at odd hours, and questions Aubrey refused to answer. If she could understand more about Susannah, perhaps she could learn through example, if not well, then at least adequately.

Jane arrived with clothing and a message from Aubrey. He would be ensconced in the study all morning.

After she had dressed and hastily breakfasted in the empty dining room, she returned to the earl's bedchamber and called for Mrs. Nettles to meet her next door, in the countess's suite of rooms. Excitement and anxiety filled her as she entered them.

Mrs. Nettles arrived a moment later. Her face was wreathed in a broad smile. "Good morning, my lady." Thank heavens she didn't ask Lilias how she'd slept.

As Mrs. Nettles led the way, Lilias walked through the rooms that were to be hers. The bedchamber held a four-poster bed with an airy, white-lace canopy. The inlaid vanity boasted silver-backed brushes and a gleaming mirror framed in silver. The room also held a cheval mirror, a comfortable petit-point library chair, and bookcases rising to the ceiling on both sides of a marble fireplace.

"The countess was that fond of books," Mrs. Nettles said.

"Lady Susannah liked books?" Lilias asked with a sinking heart, looking at the leather covers, some in French, some in Italian and Latin. It just got worse and worse. Aubrey's first wife was beautiful, charming, and a scholar.

Mrs. Nettles's mouth pursed. "Oh, no. Not her. I mean my mistress, Lady Christina, his lordship's mama. We've left them here for you. Being a teacher and all, we thought you might like to look through them. And if you'll come through here, you'll see the sitting room."

As a merchant's daughter, Lilias recognized the magnificent treasures that filled the chamber. A small Dutch painting of a young woman standing in pure light and looking straight at her with candid eyes was the work of a master. The arched ceiling's painted frescoes had a sophistication to match the work in the Royal Academy. The yellow satin wall coverings were of the finest French fabric.

"Lady Christina used to sit here writing her letters or visiting with her friends," Mrs. Nettles said. "You've met some of them already at the wedding."

Lilias had a vague recollection of several older ladies scrutinizing her, and now she knew why. They wished to know whether she'd measure up to Lady Christina's expectations. And, of course, Lady Christina had chosen Susannah for her son. Lilias wished she could control the anxiety that churned through her at that thought.

The housekeeper's face broke into a beaming smile. "As you can see, my lady, the rooms are all ready for you. With all the preparations for the wedding and, well, we expected that . . ." She broke off quickly, and Lilias felt her cheeks grow hotter.

"Other than moving my clothing and books, there is nothing to be done in these rooms?"

"That's it, my lady. There's a bit of your clothing in the wardrobe already. Lord Breme sent for the boxes from London and Jane put them there. You'll wish to look at them, no doubt."

Boxes? He'd bought more for her than the wedding gown? "I shall. These are beautiful rooms. I am very glad that the move can be made so easily."

Running her fingers idly along the top of a parquetry desk, she swallowed the lump of anxiety. "I suppose the late Lady Breme loved these rooms." She was pleased her voice showed only mild curiosity.

"Lord Breme's first wife?" Mrs. Nettles's lips curled. "She never slept in these rooms. Thought them too sweet for her taste. She had the rooms in the west wing. They're grander than these."

Mrs. Nettles shot her a look of uncertainty. "I've the keys, of course. Would you care to see them? I hadn't thought, but if they are more to your liking . . ."

Her mouth went dry at the thought of entering the beloved Susannah's chambers, but she had a terrible need to know just who Lady Drelincorte was. If her rooms held even a hint of the woman some said Lord Breme loved to distraction and others said he killed, she wished to see them. "Nothing could be more to my liking than this," she said. "Still, I should like it very much if you could show me her chambers."

"That would be fine, my lady." Mrs. Nettles's smile held a hint of relief.

They walked into the west wing together, Mrs. Nettles pulling her keys from her belt and chattering in a soothing manner that did not quite reduce the pull of nerves Lilias felt.

"The third Earl of Breme built this wing. He was an ally of Henry VII. Fought with him at Bosworth. See the dark wood-work and tall, mullioned windows? It all cost a pretty penny in those days. Oh, here we are, my lady."

Lilias nodded, half listening. After Mrs. Nettles fitted the key into the lock and swung the door open, Lilias forced her-self forward into the suite of rooms. She smelled a heavy, seductive blend of musk and spices. Mrs. Nettles crossed to the large bay windows and drew open the dark-green velvet curtains. Slowly, like a stage set in the first moment of a play, the room began to glow and come alive.

She had never in her life seen a chamber like this. The bedposts, covered in gold leaf, rose to a canopy made of green velvet interspersed with cloth of gold. The furniture was in the latest style—heavy, intricate, and crowded everywhere into the room. One couldn't walk without fear of bumping into something precious—an ormolu clock, a Chinese vase that looked to be Ming Dynasty, a dozen crystal perfume bottles set in finely-wrought filigreed silver.

On the far wall, clear in the light streaming from the windows, hung a portrait of Susannah. Lilias walked with care toward it and stared up at the likeness of her predecessor. Of course, she thought, in despair. Tall, blond, and mesmerizing, Susannah surveyed the room and this new interloper with an angelic smile. Lilias had thought her sister beautiful, but beside this wonder of womanhood, even Pamela paled.

Mrs. Nettles made a sound that closely resembled a *hmmpf*. Lilias glanced at her and was surprised to see her lips curved downward in a slight frown. "If I may be so bold to ask, what do you think of her, my lady?"

Lilias examined the portrait for another minute. Cherubs smiled up at Lady Susannah from the clouds at her feet, and light shone down upon her in a stream as it would on a saint. There was something slightly blasphemous about this portrait, just as there was something uncomfortably imperial about these chambers. The chamber weighed her down, as though it were judging her and finding her wanting.

In the waiting silence, enveloped by the heavy, Oriental scent of the room, oppressed by the blinding glitter of gold and the fussy furniture, she lost all sense of tact, and simply blurted, "I think the artist must have loved her to the point of obsession."

Mrs. Nettles gave a sharp nod. "Aye, you have a good understanding of these things, my lady."

Lilias only understood one thing at this point. Compared to Susannah Drelincorte, she was small and dark and common. "I've seen all I wish for today, Mrs. Nettles," she said, and navigated the tricky shoals of Victorian tables, tassels, and knickknacks as quickly as she could until she stood outside the room and took her first full, clean breath of air.

She would never question Aubrey about Susannah again. Why make him more aware than he already was of the humiliating comparison between them?

Mrs. Nettles followed her out. She closed the door and locked it. Lilias was startled to hear the housekeeper's voice cutting through her thoughts. "The one who painted that portrait was Mr. Rupert Hindley, Lord Breme's cousin, and a great admirer of the former Lady Breme."

A month later, Aubrey stared out the window of his study, contemplating the bleak landscape—the brown stubble of scythed lawn on this mid-March afternoon. "How is it possible?" he asked Ram.

"I'm sorry, my friend. There was a ship, one of those new steamers captained by a Scotsman, a pirate named Abernathy. It met Hindley in Suez. A skipper from America spotted the vessel and learned through the usual tavern grapevine that Hindley had booked a berth upon the ship. Those steamships are fast, Aubrey."

Aubrey's fist clenched. "There is a lesson for those of us who wish to play with fate. When did he reach Naples?"

"By our accounts, a short time ago," Ram said in a somber

voice. "He will no doubt arrive in England in another two weeks."

"Well then, we shall deal with this as we planned, only earlier."

"Yes, my lord." Will Lessing spoke up from the other side of the room. "I'll set things in motion."

Jeffries knocked on the study door. "Sir Samuel has arrived, my lord."

"Show him in."

For all that they called him the Fox, the canniest barrister in England who strode into the study looked a good deal more like a bulldog. Sir Samuel Paxton Green's stature was undersized and his rotund belly was the probable result of thousands of celebratory dinners in the course of his illustrious career. His steps were short and quick, his light hazel eyes sharp as he looked from Aubrey to Ram, whom he studied with a speculative gaze.

Then he turned to Aubrey. "Well, what have you remembered?"

Aubrey shook his head in frustration. "Almost nothing. Just snatches that don't mean enough. I try, but it won't come clear."

Sir Samuel frowned. "Try harder. Write down every snatch that comes to you. I don't care whether you killed her or not, Breme. I only care that you remember what happened and why. Blasted difficult to build a case without facts of any kind." Sir Samuel began to pace, belly leading the way, hands clasped behind his back.

"If you caught them together, if there was a fight with Hindley, if the gun went off, no man would convict you. So remember. That's the ticket."

"And in the meantime?" Aubrey asked him.

Sir Samuel raised his hand and counted off on his fingers.

"Go to London. Go to dinners, balls, your club."

Purposefully, Aubrey unclenched his fist. "That last is impossible. I've been asked to step down until this is over."

Sir Samuel's head whipped up. "Our lad's been busy, has he? Counter-moves, that's what you do. Give a dinner—your friends from Oxford and their friends. Peers, that's what we need."

Aubrey gritted his teeth. He'd been gone from home for a while. Would his old friends even accept an invitation to dine with him? "I despise toadies and I hate the idea of turning into one."

Sir Samuel looked him up and down coolly. "Hurts your pride, does it? Listen to me, my lord. Hindley wants you dead. If you wish to stop him, you are going to have to put up with a bit of toadying. These men will either see you as a jealous, murderous lunatic, or they will find you a good fellow with an excellent wine cellar. Given that we still have no concrete defense, I suggest you be a very good fellow for the next while."

Sir Samuel didn't stay long. Before he jumped into his coach and left Breme for Bath, in which Hindley was rumored to have amassed a great many debts, he looked up at Aubrey, his lower lip sticking out in a pugnacious manner.

"Get on with it, my lord. If you wish to enjoy that new bride of yours for a long time to come, be in London a week hence, and begin the campaign with the lords for the most important vote of your life. And Breme," he added after seating himself in the coach and leaning his head out the window, "do your damnedest to remember. Time's running out."

As the carriage drove out of the circle drive, Aubrey shut his eyes and rubbed his forehead with thumb and forefinger. Why in hell couldn't he remember? The harder he tried, the more elusive that night became.

He shook his head, rubbing his hand against the back of his neck.

Striding back inside, he entered the great hall, a room he'd always loved for its graceful, soaring arches, its tapestries, its minstrel's gallery with the intricately carved screen. This castle had stood for centuries, a haven. Breme was no longer a sanctuary, but a castle under siege. If he couldn't pull this off, Hindley would destroy it and everyone he loved.

The piece was a sonata by Beethoven. Despite the stifling heat of the evening and the dusty lawn outside the bungalow, he felt as though he were in cool, green England whenever he played it. The notes danced up and down the scale, rippling like the Cotswolds' racing streams.

Soon the monsoon rains would come, and the Indian earth would drink deep after the long drought. Soon his job would be over here. He could go home—could go through the humiliation of a divorce and bury himself at Breme as long as he wished.

"Aubrey! Open the door!" Susannah's voice, sharp, querulous, impatient.

He sighed and put down the violin. Why didn't she just leave him alone? Or better, just leave him?

He unlatched the door and it swung open on Susannah's gleaming hair, her flounced white gown, her beautiful, petulant face.

"It's a wonder you even heard me," she said as she wandered about the room, her long fingers aimlessly tapping against the music stand, the pianoforte's mahogany top, a little ivory statue on the desk. He watched, muscles tensing to swerve should she fling the statue at his head or catch it before it broke against a wall. He'd made the mistake of

telling Susannah that he was rather fond of it.

"How you can lose yourself in this nonsense—your music, your precious work with the government—good God, Aubrey. It's not as though the natives are civilized."

"And how would you know that?" he shot back. "Do you ever take the time or trouble to learn about this country?"

"Time and trouble! If you didn't ignore me constantly, perhaps I should be happier here." Her full lips pouted in what he'd thought a pretty moue, before he realized it, like all of her, was practiced and false. "If only you'd soften toward me, Aubrey. If only you'd pay attention to me."

"You have others to do that for you." His voice came out as cold as a Russian winter—as bleak as his heart.

"Come walk with me, Aubrey. Just this once, let us try."

He was empty. Drained after a year of tantrums, tears, and the knowledge that Hindley had arrived in Rajasthan two months ago. "There's nothing left to try for, Susannah. You know that as well as I do."

"Oh, there is, there is. Just let me tell you, and then you'll see."

He turned away from her and headed toward the door. She ran after him, already in tears, and for once, he heard desperation in her voice.

"You'd be happier if I died! You'd be free of me at last."

Freedom. He found himself hopelessly longing for it. He stopped, his hand on the latch, appalled.

"Come with me," she said, "just to prove you don't really feel that way."

He nodded, and turned to load his pistols.

"Aubrey." Another voice, musical, soft. A hand on his shoulder, small and strong. A reassuring caress.

Aubrey woke from the dream shaking and pulled Lilias into his arms. The nightmare was the first he'd had since his wedding. So lost had he been in Lilias each night.

"Bad dream?" she asked him.

He nodded and held on tight. Had he done it? Had he wanted so badly to be free he'd resorted to murder?

Lilias's hand stroked his cheek, then his chest right above his heart. Her touch quieted the self-loathing and kindled a spark of desire. He tipped up her chin and lowered his face, his kiss hungry and a little desperate. He would fan the spark into a flame that would light the darkness and keep the dreams at bay.

The next afternoon Aubrey raised his head and rubbed the back of his neck as he sat at his desk, having puzzled out the latest scheme to hide some of his fortune for Lilias should the worst come to pass.

He was frustrated by his own cowardice—his inability to decipher his dreams and to face what had happened on the night of Susannah's death. So he double-checked his figures to make sure he'd squirreled away enough currency in separate accounts to take care of his staff and tenants when—if he should be defeated.

He rose from the desk and walked to the window.

"Where is my lady?" he asked Jeffries, hovering discretely near.

"She's in the walled gardens, my lord."

"The gardens." The bare scrub of the lawn was all he could see from the high, mullioned windows in the hall. March did not seem the best month for strolling in the gardens. He started for the door and swung through it into the corridor. "Whatever for?"

"I'm not certain, my lord. But the sun's mild today and

the walls keep the wind out. She did take a cloak," Jeffries called after him as he strode down the corridor and grabbed a greatcoat from a footman.

Outside Breme Castle, Aubrey crossed the lawn, took the bridge at the head of the lake, and turned left on the brick path. Ahead, the brick walls rose ten feet high on both sides. There were kitchen gardens, and espaliered gardens of apple and pear trees, and rose gardens. Within the shelter of the walls, the wind became only a whisper, and the sun warmed his bare head.

"Lilias," he called as he walked, unable to keep the eagerness from his voice.

"In here." Her voice wafted high over the old red brick of the garden to his right.

The door opened with a rusty creak. His gaze lit upon his wife, cloak thrown off in the warmth of the sun, eyes shut, whirling about like a Turkish dervish. The skirts of her soft apricot wool gown flew out, revealing lacy crinolines and half-boots.

Lilias stopped abruptly. She wove a little as she took the first steps toward the door, a frown of concentration creasing her forehead.

Aubrey tried hard to suppress the twitch that begged to curve his lip into a grin. "My dear, if this is some scientific experiment, I can safely report that yes, spinning in circles with eyes shut causes dizziness."

"Shh." Cloak forgotten, she walked out of the garden, muttering to herself. Aubrey thought he heard "Left, then straight for eight doors."

He snatched up the neglected cloak and followed.

"One, two, three, four, five." Her five giant steps led her to the head of the smaller formal rose garden, laid out in a geometric pattern of crushed rock paths lined with statues. A fountain, silent now in the uncertain March weather, stood in the middle.

"Past Athena and to the right." Lilias made her way steadily forward on the central path, then veered off onto an angled walk. "Straight on to the maze," she muttered. They arrived at the maze. At its heart, Aubrey knew, was a large, complex folly of graceful ruins.

He glanced around. No one else disturbed the silence. They had the place to themselves. His breath came a little faster as he glanced sidelong at Lilias. She stood pondering the maze with narrowed eyes.

"You've been honing your sense of direction in your spare time, haven't you?"

She nodded. "Believe me, it was a victory to get from the walled gardens to here."

"Shall we?" he asked, indicating the entry to the maze.

"I don't know the puzzle yet."

He laughed outright at that. "I've known it forever."

He took her hand and began to tow her in. Her hand was warm and trusting in his. A picture flashed into his mind. Lilias, naked on the grass, protected by the maze's tall hedge from wind and prying eyes, her arms held out to him. Would her skin be golden in the clear light of day? He saw himself kneeling over her, watching her face for the exquisite ebb and flow of emotion, of passion.

At her wistful voice, he looked up.

"I got tired of ending up on the third instead of the second floor and in the east wing rather than the west wing," she said. "I know the castle fairly well now, I hope. Occasionally, it does seem to surprise me."

It was a hard thing to want his wife as badly as he did, to wish to see all of her, and to content himself only with touch and taste and the sound of her soft cries in the darkness.

In the light, she always looked straight at him. She allowed him to touch her hand, her shoulder in passing. When they walked together, when they dined and spoke and argued about books and politics, she never thought twice about how he looked, he knew that. But to take her, naked, exposed, for her to remember what she'd let him do to her for the past month—and oh, the things she'd let him do!

The hedge closed in around them, leading them deeper toward what Aubrey both feared and desired above all things. He found his hands were trembling.

The height of the hedges, that he had thought a welcoming shelter, covered them in shadows, blotting out light and warmth. Lilias shivered beside him.

He shook his head slightly like a dreamer awakening. What the hell was he doing here? He'd a firm and fast rule—only the nights were for Lilias. Here he was seeking her out by day.

Weakening. Would he turn coward, wanting a lifetime with her? Run from England with Lilias? Leave everything to Hindley and hide from the law on some provincial estate in Tuscany or America?

"I have something to ask you." She gave him a tentative smile. "We've been invited to hunt with the Malmsey, and to stay for a long weekend at Crestview Manor, John and Pamela's home. Here."

She fished into the pocket of her gown and showed him an invitation of ivory vellum. Attached was a letter from John Trevell, who with warm enthusiasm offered them the use of his house and stables for however long they wished to stay.

"I had wished to remain here, Lilias," he said, staring blindly at the invitation in her hand. Time to force himself to remember. Time to lose himself in his wife's arms.

She bit her lip and looked down at the ground they covered back across the wide expanse of lawn. "Normally, I wouldn't ask it. But the hunt season ends in two weeks and Squire Trevell is most comfortable upon a horse." She took a deep breath and glanced up at him. "I should like it very much if Squire Trevell and you could come to know each other in a situation where he feels comfortable. It will make him, and therefore Pamela, who looks to him as the last word on character, see you as you are and not as they might fear. Besides," she continued quickly, "I worry about Pamela and the baby. It would be so good to see her."

He thought of the next week, and London, and the calculating and condemning eyes upon him. "I'm sorry, my dear. I don't think it will be possible."

She bit her lip and nodded. "Very well," she said. No rancor, no tears. Just acceptance.

Which compelled him to hold out his hand. "Let me see the invitation."

She placed the heavy vellum missive into his hand. Her eyes held that clarity that always caught him by surprise.

"Greenleigh's hounds to hunt, as well," he murmured, staring at the invitation. Reggie Downs, Viscount Greenleigh, home early from France and Italy. He and Ram had counted up the lords and hadn't expected Reggie to return in time for the trial.

The Greenleigh hunt boasted another viscount, a couple of earls, and the Duke of Wharburton. Foxhunters invariably had a soft spot in their hearts for a good horseman, and Aubrey had ridden to hounds from the age of six.

He stifled the pang that hit him—that he could only give his wife what she wished when it benefited him. But he wasn't betraying her. He was making her happy. In a short time, she might well need her sister's comfort.

"I think it's an excellent idea," he told her. "Perhaps you'll write Trevell and make the arrangements."

"Oh, yes. Right away."

He caught his breath at the smile she gave him. Joy shone from her face. As though he had just given her the world. He turned his face away because it hurt too much to look.

He left her at the stairway up to the terrace and strode around the side of the castle, entering through a door that would take him straight to his study. A stray thought shocked him as he proceeded down the winding corridor, a musing as to when she would begin to change and become a bit manipulative. Nonsense. She might never change. She'd surprised him every time, he reminded himself.

Every time so far, a cynical voice whispered.

History has taught you it is only reasonable to beware, it argued. *When she changes, you'll not be caught unawares again.*

At eleven o'clock in the night, Richard Landham stepped into the darkened front room of the Green Lion at Blanfield, one town over from Tilden.

"Evenin', sir," a balding, portly man wearing a clean apron said, carrying a candle from what seemed to be a common room beyond.

"I'm to meet a man here at exactly this hour," Landham said, as the pendulum clock on the wall began to chime.

"Yes, he's expectin' you. Come you up the stairway then, sir," said the landlord, holding the candle high to light their way.

The stairs creaked a bit, but the inn was a tidy one, with decent ale and a good shepherd's pie on a cold day, Landham knew from experience. Even though the letter he'd received had been mysterious and the hour late, the promise of good money and Landham's familiarity with the neighborhood made him easy enough to ride over and hear what the mysterious correspondent had to say.

The landlord stopped on the landing and pushed at the first door to the left. It opened on a room dimly lit with a few candles. The man sitting in the chair at the table rose, motioning to a chair across from him. "That will be all," he told the landlord, who bowed and departed, closing the door behind him.

"Mr. Landham, I presume?" the man said as Landham took his seat.

"Aye. And you, sir?"

"Think of me as your unknown benefactor," the man said with a smile as he poured a glass of wine for him and pushed it over. He was of medium build, well dressed, with even features, but Landham couldn't see him as clearly as he would have liked in the dim room.

"You have considered my proposition?"

"Don't know exactly what yer proposing, do I?" Landham said, sitting back in the chair. "I'm here because yer letter mentioned that I might have good reason to take a bit of revenge on a certain lady and her husband."

"Indeed. The way I have heard it, that lady has injured you a great deal." The voice was pleasant, sympathetic.

Landham thought of the mocking jests from men who just a few months ago hung on his every word, of the mamas who now kept their daughters from him. "She's ruined my life in Tilden, and I've got no other," he said.

"Her husband has done me harm, as well. I thought perhaps we could form a partnership of sorts. With the money I'll be able to give you in a few months, you can go anywhere you wish and start again."

Something vaguely unsettling emanated from the man sitting opposite. But Landham didn't care. He tossed back the wine. "Tell me more," he said grimly.

So the fellow told him what he wanted from him. In the end, despite the cold chill that ran down his back, Landham agreed readily enough. He deserved the coin, and the revenge.

After closing the last trunk in preparation for today's journey to Crestview Manor, Lilias strolled downstairs toward the library, thinking to find a book to while away the time until Aubrey could join her. She shook her head, thinking of her husband's strange moods, and how they continued to confuse her. He could be impatient, or abstracted by gloom. And then he could change, lightning swift, a man of action and gay wit. And in the night, how deeply and thoroughly he could seduce her into behavior that shocked and titillated her in retrospect.

On her way to the library, she passed the ballroom, still rather heated as she remembered. Whoops of laughter from that large room broke into her thoughts and she paused by the ballroom door to listen.

"Brilliant botch of it, old fellow," someone said in a clipped, cultured accent. Ram's voice, Lilias thought in surprise. Again, his soft, native lilt was gone.

"Nonsense," Aubrey called out. "I said two of them in a row, and by God, that was two."

"Even with that sprawling dismount?"

"That was more your fault than mine! What say you, Jackson?"

"Aye, my lord. I'm with you."

"That's because he pays you, Jackson," the third man said.

"Not for this, he doesn't. He needs a stronger partner on the trapeze."

"The man must weigh fourteen stone! Only an ox could hold him properly."

"I say, Jackson, if we had one who could fling me a little farther, I bet I could make it three."

Whatever they were doing, they were enjoying it. Lilias rapped on the door.

"My lord?" she called, holding in a laugh. "What's going on in there?"

She opened the door slowly, took in Aubrey sprawled on his back on some kind of mat, and Jackson struggling up onto his elbows behind him. Sitting high in the air above her, on a strange swing with a very narrow seat, Ram was hastily wrapping his turban round his head, his dark eyes gleaming with laughter.

"We're playing circus. Jackson's teaching me a few tricks," Aubrey said, rising to take her hand and pull her to him. "And Ram's complaining, as usual."

"And you?"

"I?" He grinned, brushing back a lock of brilliant gold from his forehead, and bent, kissing her hand. "At this moment, my lady, I am the mountebank at your service."

Chapter Twenty-Two

Aubrey strode briskly toward the stables at Squire Trevell's Crestview Manor. The daylight was fast going into dusk, and he was eager to choose which one of the two horses John Trevell offered him for tomorrow's hunt. Tonight Pamela and John planned a dinner party in his and Lilias's honor for the local gentry.

Idly, he wondered if John would be late meeting him at the stables. He'd gone to the apothecary in Tilden for a tonic the doctor prescribed for Pamela. Fiercely protective of his wife, John wouldn't trust anyone else with the job.

Aubrey hurried along the path to the stable, passing through a small copse of trees before arriving in the stableyard, empty now as the grooms dressed in their livery. He understood John's concern.

Pamela had lost weight since the wedding. Her face was pale and drawn, and she seemed to drift about the large manor house like a wraith. Since they'd arrived, Lilias had barely left her side, agreeing only to whip in tomorrow at the hunt because a few of the hunt servants had come down with sore throats and fever.

A shadow rose in the darkening yard. A large, heavy-set

man stepped forward, and as he approached, Aubrey caught the feral grin on a face that some might call handsome. *A handsome devil,* he thought, and then the fellow spoke.

"Lord Breme?"

"What do you want, Landham?"

"I've a proposition for ye, my lord," the man said. "And ye'd do well to listen."

Pamela clutched the cloak tighter around her as she made her way through the little copse near the stables. She'd wanted to get out of the house for just a bit—at night, she lay awake, anxious and despairing about the baby. If she just got a little exercise, perhaps she'd be able to sleep. At the sound of male voices, she stopped, slipping behind the trunk of a tree at the shadowy edge of the copse. It was dark, and she was alone. Better to hide until she was sure who stood in the clearing beside the stable.

"It's about yer wife's sister." Landham's voice—on this land!

"What about her?" Lord Breme. Good God, were they in collusion?

"I had her, ye know. A month before she married the squire. Had her in one of his upstairs bedchambers. Oh, she was a sweet one. Eager as they come."

Pamela gagged, muffling the sound with her hand.

"She married him right quick after. Made herself part of the gentry. Wouldn't want it to get about, would ye? You being related and all."

"I'm sure you have a price in mind for your silence."

"Yer quick to catch on. I was thinking of relocating, almost immediate, like. Settling somewhere north. Far north. Maybe even go as far as America. I figure the costs to set me up—new home, a few servants and all, would take ten thousand pounds. A lot fer me, of course. But fer you, it's a pid-dling sum."

Pamela stared into the stableyard, horrified. Breme strolled over to the stable entry as though he hadn't a worry in the world. "Why would I put out that kind of money?" he asked in bored drawl.

Landham cleared his throat, an uneasy sound in the still twilight. "Are ye mad, man? To save her reputation."

Pamela watched, sick with shame, as Breme shrugged. "I wouldn't pay you two pence."

Dear God. Ten thousand pounds! She knew that Breme could have come up with the money, but John never could, unless he sold the land. She thought of him losing his new farmlands, and perhaps the house. How could she tell him about this? How could she have put him in such a position? It was all her fault, from the beginning. With a silent cry of an-guish, she slipped away through the woods and ran toward the house. She had thought herself safe. But now she was doomed. The baby, John, her hopes for the future—all gone, forever.

How cold, how uncaring Breme was. How cruel that this man of all men should know her shameful secret. She had to find a way to wrest Lilias from his clutches.

Landham looked driven, as though demons were after him. Aubrey leaned up against the wall of the stable and folded his arms across his chest, a mocking smile on his face while he seethed inside. Play the part, he reminded himself. If Landham thought for one minute he was anything but the heartless beast rumor branded him, he'd find a way to hurt Lilias and her sister.

"I wouldn't pay two pence to a blackmailer," he said softly. "However, I expect that you'll keep your mouth shut."

He pushed away from the wall. "If you ever breathe a word of what you have just told me about Mrs. Trevell, I shall call you out. You know my reputation?"

Landham nodded uncertainly.

"Lord Beast?" Aubrey continued. "The Demon Earl? The man who killed his own wife? I may die soon, you know. At the end of a rope. Compared to that, what better demise than to die while killing you in a duel?"

He rubbed his chin, smiling coldly as he pretended to consider the situation with a sangfroid he'd learned working with Ram. God help him, if he didn't convince this bastard to keep quiet, he'd have to fight him in a duel. Which would be one more black deed for the ton to grind in its rumor mills. "And you know, Landham, I might very well cheat. What's ten paces to a man like me? I'd just as soon turn on you at eight, or one, for that matter. Perhaps I'll bribe your second to mess with the powder in your pistol. Why not?

"The thing is," he said, stepping forward as Landham took a couple steps back, "I can make sure you won't live. Is that what you want?"

At the sound of boots on the path to the stable, Aubrey's head snapped up. "Breme, are you there?" John Trevell's voice rang out in the gloom.

Aubrey's smile was more a baring of teeth as he jerked his head in the direction of John's voice. "Shall we discuss this with the squire?"

"Ye've made yer own grave, Breme," Landham said in a voice that shook with something like desperation. "I have my scruples and my second thoughts. Knowin' I might have to pay, I gave ye a chance and ye threw it in my face. On yer own head be it." He slipped through the foliage at the edge of the woods and disappeared into the night.

Aubrey saw the glow of a lantern through the trees, and

then John walked out into the stableyard.

"Hullo. Wish you'd waited for me, Breme. Too dark to see your hand in front of your face. Have you had a chance to look at the mounts?"

Aubrey shook his head. "I was interrupted by Richard Landham. He had a rather troubling proposition."

John's face above the lantern grimaced in distaste. "It was a black day for us when we learned how close Lilias came to marrying the brute. What was the proposition?" John asked in a suspiciously casual tone.

"Blackmail," Aubrey said quietly, and the lantern jerked in John's hand. He wondered how much John Trevell knew of his wife's past before their marriage. Perhaps some, but he couldn't be certain. "He fancied he had some hold or other over Pamela, but he spoke in generalities."

"I see," Trevell said.

"I couldn't do it, John. To pay a man like that—it only encourages another attempt for money, and another, until you're trapped forever." Quietly, without giving the details of Landham's conversation, Aubrey repeated some of what he'd said, and why.

"It was the best I could do, with what time and knowledge I had. I hope it was good enough."

"If not, I shall see to him," John said grimly. "Don't mention it to Pamela, would you? She's very fragile right now. I wouldn't want to worry her."

Aubrey thought of Pamela's pale face, her nervous exhaustion, and nodded. It didn't seem that her mistrust of him mattered so much anymore. "Of course," he murmured. "Show me your stock, would you John? And then perhaps we'll return to the ladies."

The next morning dawned bright and clear at Squire

Trevell's new acreage. The ground was soft from the light rain that had fallen the night before. Aubrey, mounted upon a blooded bay, looked sideways at his wife, who sat Starfire on a sidesaddle with her usual ease and grace. Her blue velvet habit with black trim hugged her curves in a way that made him wish to haul her back to his chamber and take it off her.

For two nights they had made love in stealthy silence. Suppressing his desire to drown all conscious thought in her body, he was gentle with her, imprisoning her cries of ecstasy with his kisses as Pamela Trevell, one bedchamber away, no doubt sent frowns of disapproval toward him.

Last night Pamela's dislike had sunk to something entirely different. She was too polite to make it clear to the rest of her guests, but Aubrey had the feeling she loathed him. He had made a misstep somewhere along the way, and Pamela had passed judgment, perhaps for all time.

"I hope you enjoy this morning, my lord." Lilias gave him a look of concern and he realized he must have been frowning.

He gave her what he hoped was a reassuring smile. Just two more days and they'd be home again, alone for a few days before London. How odd to realize that home meant one bed, thick walls, and a whole night to share.

"I used to like this a lot," he said. "Remind me to tell you of the pack we kept at Breme."

Hounds barked and milled, sniffing at the new arrivals from the neighboring Greenleigh Hunt.

"Breme! Hallo, Breme!" Aubrey glanced over toward the hounds to see Reggie Downs, Viscount Greenleigh, waving to him enthusiastically from atop a small bay. Aubrey relaxed, glad to see he'd arrived. At Eton, Reggie had been a rather dim fellow with a pleasant word for everybody.

Reggie pushed his horse forward. "I say, Breme, what a

ripping day, eh? What luck to find you here. Haven't seen you for years, since you went off to India. All hush-hush, I heard. Great things done, they say. And this is your lady?"

"Good to see you, Greenleigh." Aubrey touched Lilias's elbow. He realized with a grin that he could do this, any time he wished—just touch her to get her attention in front of everyone. It baffled him, how much he liked it.

He made the introductions and watched her incline her head with a gracious smile. The little black net veil drifting from her beaver hat gave her an air of mystery and allure that Reggie responded to with the same fascination he'd seen on the other men gathered around her.

"Heard you agreed to whip in today, Lady Breme. Ripping of you to keep 'em in line. My hounds are young, some of 'em, and my huntsman down with the ague. If we can keep them together, we'll see some fine work. They're brave and fit, every one of 'em."

Someone waved to Reggie and motioned him over. "I'll see you at tea then, after. Aubrey, my lady." He smiled and tipped his hat, trotting away from them.

Aubrey smiled after him, thinking that conversation with good-natured Reggie and his friends at the elaborate tea would be enjoyable, even though his life might depend on it. Ah, English politics, served up with Devon cream and early hothouse strawberries, he mused. Sometimes interaction with British aristocracy could be intricate as that of Renaissance Italy.

Harnesses jingled as the horses snorted in the cool March air, eager to be off across the hilly stubble of the countryside.

The squire motioned Lilias over. He said something and she laughed, a carefree, happy sound that made Aubrey smile.

"Young Breme!" An elderly man across the way called out

to him, and Aubrey nudged his horse toward him, searching for his name. The fellow sat his horse with that old-school, straight backed perfection, much like Lord Brisbey, a friend of his father from the old days at Breme.

He grinned at the recollection. Good God, it was the Earl of Brisbey, replete with those fluffy side-whiskers that appeared to be the rage in England now. Aubrey greeted Brisbey and passed a few pleasant moments with the old fellow, cementing his reputation and watching Lilias, content within the moment.

To his left, Ned Bonney, the squire's tall, thin huntsman, gave orders to the whips gathered round him in their hunting pinks.

"Watch 'em near the edges of the property, Sam," he told a young man with a shock of red hair. "Our own hounds know their manners. But Viscount Greenleigh's pack is young. Who knows but they'll riot and chase after nothing for the fun of it. If so, do your best to turn 'em back to the rest of the pack. I don't want 'em going over that defile."

The squire nudged his horse over toward Aubrey just as Brisbey moved on to greet another group of hunters. "I'd rather Viscount Greenleigh hadn't brought his along, particularly since his huntsman can't lend a hand, but a joint meet's a joint meet," he told Aubrey. "My huntsman's the only one who really knows this property. I just purchased it some weeks ago, and have had no time to look it over.

"Still, we ought to have good sport today," he added, looking at the sky. "Cool enough, wet enough." Trevell gave a brusque nod to the huntsman, who raised the horn to his lips. As the mellow notes floated on the air, the hounds came to him, ears pricked in eagerness.

A moment later, Lilias joined Aubrey again. "We'll ride out together," she said.

As they trotted out toward the first wide field, Ned Bonney cast the hounds.

They fanned out, tails raised in a feathering motion, noses to the ground. It seemed only seconds later that the high, eager yelp of the lead hound shot out in the clear air. With a shock of recognition, Aubrey felt the familiar chill rise in the nape of his neck, the age-old rush of excitement. Lilias cast him a wide grin over her shoulder and took the first fence in front of him, galloping lightly over the field toward a rise. Beside her, sticking like a burr, was Reggie Downs, Viscount Greenleigh. If and when Reggie's hounds broke off from the pack, they'd be in position to follow them.

Aubrey passed Reggie, whose horse seemed to be suddenly flagging, and caught up with Lilias at the next fence. They took it in tandem, as neatly as a well-practiced duet. The pace was relentless. The fox, a gray, doubled and ran circles, leaving enough scent that hounds and horses madly followed.

Once, as Aubrey turned his head to find the rest of the field, he saw they had dropped back. Patting the neck of his mount, he felt the strong muscles beneath his hand expand and contract in a steady galloping rhythm. The horse had plenty left in him.

He hadn't remembered this part of life, Aubrey realized. How good it felt—the rush of cold air, the speed of a fine horse across the hills and valleys, the thrill of movement and color and sound. The huntsman's horn sounded again, this time sharply.

Lilias motioned to him. Above the wind, she cried, "Go with John. Stay right in his pocket."

Slightly ahead on a rise, John Trevell checked his mount and stood in his stirrups. Lilias urged Starfire on to the left and broke away, in perfect rhythm with her horse's swift canter. Aubrey let her go, and caught up with John.

Some distance ahead, the hounds had separated into two packs. One streamed off toward the left, the other circled to the right. John's huntsman lit out after the pack that went right.

Viscount Greenleigh, winded, his light complexion red with effort, was watching Lilias cross after his hounds. "Sorry, Trevell," he said with what breath he had left. "Must be two foxes out there."

"We've only viewed the gray," Trevell said with a frown.

"My hounds never riot," Viscount Greenleigh stubbornly insisted.

"Young Sam's gone to bring 'em back. And Lady Breme's coming on right behind him. A better whip you'll never find."

"You mean Sam?" Aubrey said as they cantered forward.

Trevell shook his head. "Lilias," he said. "She's got the best seat in the county and the best nose for where the fox will show himself."

As John turned his horse to follow his hounds, Aubrey followed, watching Lilias race over the stubble of last year's corn. She rode hell-for-leather, right behind young Sam, whose hunt cap had come off in the chase. His red hair blew loose in the wind.

Aubrey's gaze caught the small plume of smoke in the woods to the left. Sam's horse went down in a thrashing stumble. The boy landed spread-eagled on his back. Lilias shouted something back at him and he raised his head, nodding. She turned the horse and it broke back into a gallop, eating the distance between her and the Greenleigh hounds.

And Aubrey remembered the huntsman's voice, as he gave his orders to young Sam. "I don't want 'em going over that defile." His blood, so warm and carefree a moment before, froze and then ran cold in his veins. Sam had known the territory, but something that looked suspiciously like a gunshot had just felled his horse. That left only Lilias, who did not know it, to ride hard in his place. A precipice lay ahead, so overgrown with brush that an unwarned rider headed for it wouldn't see it.

He spurred his horse and charged down the hill to the left. "Lilias!" he shouted against the wind and the pounding of his heart. Unheeding, she galloped on.

Oh, God, oh, God. His breath sobbed in his throat as he rode, cursing, praying that his mount kept strength and wind. Lilias skirted a newly-ploughed field. Aubrey cut across and slowly—too slowly—began to close the gap.

The hounds, baying wildly, poured ahead. Lilias jumped a fence and galloped round the rise to spare Starfire the added effort. The horse was already stretched to the limit. Pushing his own mount with spur and crop, Aubrey took the hill to shorten the distance. From its height, he looked ahead and tasted the bile of horror.

For beyond the hedge jump, he saw what Lilias could not. Nothing but air. The deep defile the huntsman had spoken of lay immediately after the jump. If she took that jump, she would plunge down, down, into a ravine of rock.

To her death.

He galloped down the hill, shouting, mad to catch up. There wasn't time. The wind blew against him. His voice would never reach her.

Lilias raced after the screaming hounds, her whip cracking in the air above them. Maddened by a scent too strong to resist, they ran on, baying high and wild. The hedge was just ahead.

As he spurred his horse madly, the hounds disappeared through the hedge. Four lengths behind, now. He'd not reach her before she jumped off the end of the world.

Chapter Twenty-Three

No, no. Aubrey's stomach clenched.

Starfire gathered his powerful haunches to spring over.

"Lilias!" Aubrey shouted one last time for all he was worth. And the wind died. His voice carried across the field.

She hesitated.

Starfire caught her uncertainty, paused in mid-jump, twisted, and rolled to the side of the jump, throwing her from the saddle like a rag doll. She lay deathly still on the brown grass.

The bay slid to a stop by the jump and Aubrey leaped off, running, his breath sobbing in his throat.

Don't die, don't die, don't die.

He knelt beside her, hands trembling, fingers fighting with her stock, scrabbling for the pulse at her throat. And found one, strong and steady, beneath his questing fingers.

"Oh, dear love," he whispered, touching her brow, her cheeks, gently feeling each limb, looking for blood, for crushed or broken bone, finding nothing. His breath came choked. He realized he was holding in a sob of relief, and heard a whisper.

She raised a shaky finger to her nose. "Is it broken?"

He started to laugh, weakly, wildly, as he examined the One Beauty. "No, dear heart. If it were, it would be lopsided and you'd be bleeding like a stuck pig."

She smiled, eyes still shut. "Good." A moment later, she made another slight movement.

"Lie still," he said, still frightened. "Lilias, tell me what hurts."

She made a little moue. "Everything. Thank goodness the ground is soft." A heartbeat later, she narrowed her eyes. "Why in thunder did you stop me?"

"Give me a moment." *To breathe again.* "There's a cliff right beyond the drop jump." He could hear the tremor in his voice.

"The hounds, Aubrey! They went over," she said in a voice filled with sorrow.

"I'll see to them later," he murmured, stroking her cheek with trembling fingers. "All that matters now is you. Can you move your legs? Oh, that's good, darling. Now your arms. Yes. All right. Rest, now. Here, you're probably cold." As he placed his jacket over her, he heard hoofbeats behind him, and then John Trevell's voice right over his shoulder.

"Dear God, Lilias! How can I help, Breme?"

Aubrey gazed down into the dark, trusting eyes of his wife, his heart hitching in his chest, a painful sting at the back of his eyes. "Lend me your horse. I'll take her up in a few minutes. See if you can find the doctor while I take her back to the manor."

He stroked her cheek and murmured reassurance, barely hearing the low voices behind him. Someone brought the horse up.

"Can you put your arms around me, Lily?"

She nodded. "Of course. I just got the wind knocked out of me, that's all."

She lifted her arms and circled his neck while he bent to

her. "I'm going to lift you, now. If anything hurts more, scream immediately."

She smiled. "Right in your ear," she whispered.

He picked her up and she clung, light and willing. When he had lifted her to sit sideways on the squire's horse, he mounted behind and drew her against him, circling her waist to keep her there. She rested her head on his chest and put her arms around his waist. Her rakish little bowler had come off. Her hair fell down in the tumble and lay in a curtain of silk over his arm.

If he'd thought of Ned Bonney's warning a moment later, if he hadn't heard it at all—he could go mad thinking how close a thing this had been.

She fell off to sleep halfway back to the manor, scaring him with visions of concussion and worse. When they arrived, members of the field stood in the circled drive, talking quietly among themselves. It seemed the word had traveled on the wind. Pamela stood at the open door, her face drawn and white.

Ned Bonney took Lilias from him until he dismounted. Aubrey, bereft until he reached for her again, carried her into the house, following Pamela up the wide, winding stairs to their bedroom. Carefully, he put her down and brushed his hand along her cheek.

She opened her eyes and smiled at him. "You saved me, Aubrey."

He found himself trembling.

Dr. Thomas, who lived close-by, arrived shortly. Although fussy and overly obsequious, the man seemed to know his job.

"She'll have some nasty bruises to show tomorrow," he told Aubrey. "But there seem to be no broken bones. The best thing for her is quiet."

Aubrey lifted his head. There had been time for relief on the way home. Now, a churning anger goaded him. "I must speak to John," he told Pamela. "You'll watch her for me?"

Pamela nodded and took his place beside the bed. He heard her murmur something and Lilias answer in a soft voice as he made his way down the stairs. John Trevell was in the front sitting room, speaking to the huntsman in a low voice. His expression was serious as he turned to Aubrey.

"How is she?"

"The doctor says she'll be fine. John," he told the older man. "I need a horse."

The squire nodded. "I'll go with you. Aubrey," he said in a grim voice, "Ned's horse was shot."

Aubrey nodded. "I thought as much."

The huntsman accompanied them. When they returned to the field in which the line had split, Aubrey led the men left and retraced the line the runaway hounds had taken all the way to the hedge. Beyond and below it, they heard high, weak whimpers of pain in the defile below.

With axes, they pruned the hedge until there was a hole in it large enough for a man to go through. Aubrey tied a sturdy rope to a strong tree trunk near the precipice and lowered himself over the edge of the cliff. The earth on the side of the cliff was full of rock and clay made slick from last night's rain.

He landed amidst the dead and the suffering—all that young life setting off so bravely this morning, their white and tan coats glossy, their cries eager and strong.

Aubrey had seen death in many guises over the last few years, from sickness and snakebite to sudden death while on campaign with Ram. The worst—Susannah's eyes and the blood trickling from the bullet wound in her chest.

This slaughter sickened him to the point of near-retching.

With his pistols, he dispatched the hounds as quickly as he could.

An object fluttered nearby on a thorn branch. Picking up the ragged piece of material, he stuffed it into his pocket. It reeked of fox scent. Undoubtedly, it was a scrap of a long bag a man could drag along the ground from horseback, laying a line of scent strong enough to lure the Greenleigh hounds to hell.

Deep in thought, Aubrey made the jarring climb back to the top. John Trevell lay at the edge of the cliff waiting for him. His strong arm reached down for Aubrey, and he pulled him the last bit of the way up and onto solid ground.

Aubrey pulled the small patch of cloth from his pocket and handed it to John, who sniffed it.

"By God!" the squire shouted, his face red with fury.

The huntsman examined it and uttered a sharp, succinct oath. "Not a riot, then, but a drag, was it? When I get my hands on the bastard who did this . . ."

Someone had known that John Trevell would hunt this fixture on this day. Someone had known that Lilias would whip for him—had whipped for him in the past. And someone had known that John would ask Lilias to bring in any hounds that seemed to riot. But why was Lilias meant to go off that cliff?

Oh, God. He knew of only one person in Tilden who would hate them that much.

Chapter Twenty-Four

Aubrey walked slowly back along the line of the drag, his eyes trained on the brown stubble. John and the huntsman followed. Aubrey had a good idea of the man responsible for this outrage. But the planning was intricate, the execution, perfect or nearly so. Landham had not seemed that subtle.

There was something shining a little, brown like rust: one small drop to his left, another to his right, then again, about three or four feet from that. He bent, dipped his finger in it, looked at it against his skin, sniffed it.

If the day had been warmer and dryer, it wouldn't have still been slightly liquid. He wouldn't have been able to catch the scent, slightly metallic, slightly salty. He rubbed the dark red liquid on the white cuff of his shirt and looked at it. God, he'd seen enough of the stuff to last him a lifetime.

"Breme?" John asked, looking at his cuff.

"Blood," Aubrey told him, and kept walking. It was there again, four feet ahead, and then another four—large drops, parallel to each other, at about the distance of a horse's galloping stride over open country.

Taking great care with the powder and balls of lead, Aubrey reloaded his pistols and checked the knife at his belt.

"What man in this county hones his spurs to a point?" he asked John and the huntsman.

The two men looked at each other and frowned in unison. "Richard Landham," they both said at once.

The three men said nothing after that, but took to horse and cantered toward Tilden. Aubrey barely noticed the light rain falling as they rode. God, how he wanted the satisfaction of making Landham talk. He'd better turn that duty over to John.

They arrived at Landham's house in a raw, chill wind. Aubrey stared grimly at the sturdy half-timbered manor where Landham had planned to imprison Lilias as his bride. The house was eerily silent as they slid from their saddles and tethered the horses. The front door was open halfway.

"This is very strange," John Trevell said.

Aubrey was already at the door, pistol in hand. He swung it open the rest of the way and walked silently into the house. The only sound he heard was the ticking of the hall clock. His gaze swept the empty room to his left, a parlor with a sofa and two wing back chairs. To his right, the dining room, its Chippendale table and chairs a tribute to the farmer's wealth. That room was empty as well. Trevell and the huntsman followed quietly.

Stepping through the narrow hall, Aubrey slipped the latch and peered through the door into the kitchen, then swung the door open and strode to the table. Slumped over on it, the back of his head shattered by the ball of a pistol fired at close range, lay a huge, bluff man. Aubrey called out to John. He came at a run.

"Good God," John said. "That's Landham, all right. Or what's left of him."

Aubrey uttered a curse that even Trevell, open-minded as he was, no doubt took exception to. As he'd suspected,

Landham had not planned this day's work. Who killed him? Had there been a fight over his botched job?

"We have to tell the constable," John said.

"I must get to Lilias." Aubrey thought he'd go mad with the dread rising in him. Would Lilias be snatched from him, even as she lay helpless in her sister's bedchamber?

The pace back to Crestview Manor was as killing as the one they'd just run. Neither John Trevell nor the huntsman seemed upset with his silence.

At the manor drive, Trevell took the reins from him and said in a quiet voice, "Go up to your wife, Breme. Satisfy yourself that she is well. We'll discuss the rest later."

Aubrey nodded abruptly and took the stairs two at a time. Outside their room, he ran a hand through his soaked hair and glanced down at his filthy boots and his rain- and mud-splattered hunt clothes. Gently, he pushed the door open and walked in. With a quiet click, he shut it behind him, and leaned against it, just looking at her.

She was safe. Thank God, she was safe. She lay upon the pillows with eyes shut, the dark, silky fringe of her lashes against her cheeks. One arm lay upon the counterpane, the frilled lace of her gown halfway up to her elbow. As she stirred, her hand turned, palm up, and on the delicate skin of her arm above her elbow, a huge, dark bruise rapidly blossomed.

He stared at it, and then at Lilias, as all the cells inside his body vibrated in the aftermath of a shock something akin to an earthquake. He closed his eyes, as though blotting out the sight of his wife would negate what he had just realized. It did no good.

There was a chair somewhere behind him. He found it and sat heavily, looking at nothing, his hands limp on his knees. He had broken the cardinal rule in this match of wits he played for his life and his heritage.

He had fallen in love with his wife.

From the bed, he heard the first rustle of silk and linen sheets. She woke slowly, with a little moan, then a flutter of those delicate, blue-veined lids. When she saw him, her face lit up and a slow smile curved her soft lips. His heart gave a lurch.

"All's well?" she asked him.

"For now."

The smile faded and she looked at him carefully. "What is it? What's wrong?"

He came forward slowly and then knelt beside the bed. With a finger, he touched a springy lock of her hair that fell down over her shoulder.

God, it was over. For her own protection, for whatever chance they had, he had to tell her everything.

"We must talk. Tonight," he said, a promise to her and himself. "Now, I just want to look at you and hold you." He pressed kisses on her cheeks, the edge of her mouth, and when she sighed, he kissed the closed lids of her eyes and brushed his lips against the sweet, silky fall of her hair.

It was broad daylight. She could see him, and the dark scar that marked him for what he might be. He wouldn't press his luck, but this—the kisses, the stroke of his hands—she seemed to welcome.

For her part, Lilias felt she could breathe again. Her body opened beneath the sweetness of Aubrey's lips on hers and the claiming of his hands.

She had been afraid when he had gone. Because Pamela had clucked, muttering when she thought Lilias asleep, "Churlish, unfeeling man." Lilias could hear the scorn in Pamela's voice. "To rush out immediately after such an accident! His place is beside her now!"

And Lilias had turned her face to the wall, had held tight to the vision of Aubrey when she awoke on the ground to find him there, bending over her. Hadn't she seen terror, longing, and pain in his gaze before relief replaced them?

He had said things, hadn't he? Or had she dreamed the words that fell so sweetly from him in those first foggy moments of consciousness? Did it matter? He was here now, and she needed . . . she needed . . .

"Aubrey?"

"I'm here."

"I want you," she said, burning with embarrassment. "And what we do. At night. Please." She reached for the stock tie, pulling it and opening the first buttons at the neck of his shirt. He knelt beneath the workings of her hands, so still she thought he did not even breathe. She pressed her lips against the hollow of his throat, where his heart beat steady and strong. His scent was there, mixed with sweat and grit from whatever exertion he had been through as she lay in this bed, intensely grateful to be alive and missing him. "I want you to love me."

"Lilias." His hand swept from the long fall of her hair and hovered over the temptation of the buttons down her lawn gown. "You fell. For a moment, I thought . . . I can't be gentle."

"Good. I was scared, too, and I can't be gentle, either," she said in a voice soft with understanding. Beneath his shirt, her hands stroked the warm chest and tight belly. She heard his sharp intake of breath with delight. Still, by the tautness of his muscles, she could tell he fought the need they both felt.

"Aubrey, I'm fine. The soft ground cushioned my fall. If my arm hadn't landed on a rock, I'd barely be bruised."

He gently pulled up the sleeve of her gown, stared at her arm, and sucked in a harsh breath. She knew it was bruised badly from mid-forearm to the shoulder.

"Oh, sweetheart," he said, "you are very sore. I shouldn't."

She wouldn't have any of that, not when she needed this— this communion—so badly. Her fingers rose to his lips, cutting off his protests. Then she pulled his head down to hers. He kissed her, his lips soft on her mouth. The kiss deepened, became need and a heated, urgent call, soul to soul. *Yes, this way. Yes, touch me.* With passion, she could reach him clearly, and he would answer her honestly.

As he had said, it was a beginning.

"We shouldn't do this." Aubrey tried one last time, a man who'd already gone under twice, drowning in desire. But his words came out like the weak protest they were, while his blood raced hot and heavy in a terrible urgency. His heart pumped like thunder beneath her fingers.

She was his. *They were alive,* his heart beat in a strong, insistent rhythm. He pulled the gown from her, careful in spite of the need driving him. He had never seen her before in the daylight. He'd never realized how long and shapely her legs were, or how her waist tapered and her hips flared. He'd known the softness of her skin, but not that she was luminescent in the light.

His gaze held on her breasts. He made a sound, part laugh, part sigh. Her nipples, puckered from his lightest caress, were an apricot-tinged pink.

He cupped them in his hands, rubbed his cheek against them, watched when she rose to arch into his hands, the supple taper of her waist, the slim softness of her belly and the dark private curls, all only known in dim candlelight, until now.

He couldn't speak.

In the silence between them, her hands were busy with the

buttons on his riding breeches. He heard one of them rend, and then the shirt was off over his head, thrown to some corner in the room. Both of them breathed like runners at the end of the race.

"Come to me," she said, her arms open to take him, her slim legs restless on the sheets.

He didn't know how his boots and stockings and breeches came off or where they landed. He couldn't seem to stop looking at her, her face flushed, her dark eyes, her gaze stroking his body, her eyes hiding mysteries in their depths, her smile the most tempting since Eve.

In broad daylight, seeing him as he was, she still sighed and moaned as he cupped her. And deep inside, along with the delight, came niggling greed.

Yes, she looked at him and she still wanted him. But it wasn't enough.

He prayed silently that there would be a time when he could court her with the words of his heart. But until he played the game through and won, this was far, far more than he had ever hoped.

He slipped into the tight sheathe of her body. She wrapped her strong, beautiful legs around his hips, and he sank more deeply into her. He groaned once, and then, in a flare of pure lust, lost all control.

She gave beneath him, soft, pliant, the one woman in the world made for him. As passion swept him into the vortex, he heard her cries. He felt the quickening inside her, gripping him, tugging him forward into the torrent of his own release. He surged one last time, deep, part of her—heard his breath rasp rough and hard, and from his throat a muffled, ecstatic groan smothered against her neck.

He lay above her, spent, at peace, felt the heat and slick dampness of their bodies, still joined so intimately.

Like the crack of a pistol, the latch lifted, and the door burst open. Aubrey's arms tightened and cradled Lilias to him as he flung up his head toward danger, a snarl of warning grating past his throat.

At the same time, a woman said, "Lily, I heard you cry out. Shall I get the doctor?"

Pamela stood at the open door, her eyes wide, her hand raised, trembling, to her mouth. Her gaze scuttled from the ruined bed to the room strewn with discarded clothing. Aubrey knew what she'd seen—the little sister she'd raised and worried over, hurt, almost killed, in an accident just that day. To Pamela, Lilias no doubt looked like a helpless, wounded bird—bruised, stripped naked, and forced in bestial lust beneath her bare-arsed, scarred animal of a husband.

"Get away from my sister!" Pamela's voice rose in a breathy scream.

Aubrey shut his eyes against the look of revulsion and hatred on Pamela Trevell's face. "Get out!" he shouted.

"Pamela, come." John's voice this time, soothing and quiet. The door shut with a jarring bang.

Aubrey rolled over and drew his hand over his eyes.

"What was that?" Lilias whispered.

"That," he said, "was my good impression waving goodbye."

Chapter Twenty-Five

Aubrey slowly lifted himself away from Lilias. He rose and found his shirt. As he hitched it over his head, she heard him muttering to himself. It sounded suspiciously like curses.

The shirt fell about his body, cutting off her admirable view of his buttocks. He turned and glanced at her, a frown with something of abashed guilt to it, then came back to the bed and hovered, his fingers brushing her cheek with the utmost gentleness. "Do you feel well enough to travel?"

She wanted to tell him that if she could make love with the enthusiasm she had just displayed, she could most certainly travel. Any other day, she would have told him. But the set of his mouth, the glitter of rather frightening determination in his eyes, stopped the words before they could be spoken. She merely nodded, staring up at him in dismay at the change that had come over him since Pamela had burst in on them.

Pulling on his breeches, he grabbed the rest of his clothing and headed for the door and paused. He looked at her one last time, a fierce, possessive look, but one in which there was something bleak and lonely, as though he were somehow bidding her good-bye.

All the gentleness was gone from his face. Indeed, with his

height, his long legs, and broad shoulders, with his blaze of golden hair and his grim expression, he looked like a Viking warrior on the eve of battle.

A chill ran down her spine. "I'll call for Jane to pack," she said to him.

He nodded, a sharp movement of the head, and turned to go.

As Lilias dressed, she heard the murmur of John's voice from the upstairs study, and Aubrey's in response.

Jane curtsied and called a footman, who picked up her trunk and left the room. Jane followed quickly, giving the man orders as to where to put it. A low knock sounded at the door. Lilias paused in buttoning her glove and answered it. Pamela slipped into the room and Lilias blushed, remembering what her sister had seen the last time she'd entered the bedchamber.

She felt more awkward with her own sister than she had the night of the disastrous house party.

Then Pamela made it worse. "Lily," she said in a low voice. "I wish you to stay here, before it's too late. Do you understand?"

"But . . ." Lilias got no further. Aubrey, with that uncanny ability to hear even the softest sound, opened the door and, brushing by Pamela, crossed the room to stand behind Lilias. In a gesture so obvious, almost crude in polite company, he stroked the back of her neck and gently clasped her shoulders. She stood there, the stiff and uncertain spoils in a battle joined by the two people who could break her heart.

"She's not staying," he said in a cold voice, and led her downstairs.

He opened the coach door himself, helping her in with all courtesy.

They rode for a long while in silence, Aubrey grim, Lilias

afraid of what had changed him. The coach gave a hard jolt over a rut, and then turned right through the gates and down the long drive toward Breme Castle. Lilias tried to suppress the whimper of pain as her arm and shoulder connected with the seat.

"Damnation," Aubrey muttered, reaching to steady her. Then, slowly disengaging his hands from her waist, he said in a softer voice, "We're almost home."

She nodded, miserable and uncertain. How could the connection she felt between them dissolve into thin air as soon as he rose from their bed?

Sometimes at Breme he had been kind and funny, teasing her, touching her lightly in passing, making her wish for the night. But for the last hours of hard travel, he did not touch her, except to aid her as he would any other injured person. He simply sat with his hands very still in his lap, his mind troubled and busy, she supposed, from the look of intensity on his face.

The coach halted and swayed on its springs. Aubrey stepped down and called two footmen over. They, not he, helped her from the carriage and walked beside her up the broad stone stairway and through the tall, oak double doors.

She heard his quiet voice giving orders to Jeffries.

Almost as soon as she entered, housemaids scurried about on the inlaid tile floor, the ties of their caps and their apron strings flying. Two footmen came down the wide carved stairs bearing a trunk, and Aubrey's valet hurried after with a portmanteau. Aubrey spoke to them, indicating the area beside the front doors where he wanted his baggage stacked.

She hurried to his side. "What is happening?" she demanded.

He gave her a grave look, and suddenly she was afraid.

"I will tell you very soon," he said.

Again, without touching her, he opened a closed door to the right. She walked into a small sitting room and heard the door shut behind her, muting the sounds of midnight activity in the hall.

"You're weary. Please, go upstairs." Aubrey's quiet voice broke the silence between them. "First, I must speak to Ram Dass."

She trembled with weariness. Her arm was sore and bruised. But she lifted her chin and glared at him, as the anger snapped through her. "I'll wait here for you. And when you return, you'll tell me what in Hades is going on."

Aubrey shut the door behind him and crossed the hall in an agony of self-reproach. He could have kept Lilias safe here at Breme. But he had taken her into danger, exposed her to death, because of his own selfish plans to impress his peers. Never again would he use her. She was staying safe, no matter what she thought she wanted.

He opened the door to the study and found Ram pacing. Quickly, he told him what had happened. "The plan was too intricate for Landham to have designed," Aubrey concluded as Ram poured them both more brandy and handed a glass to him.

"And as you said, Landham spoke of plans to leave Tilden suddenly."

"I wonder," Aubrey said quietly, "what he was afraid of."

"My thought exactly."

"I believe someone hired Landham to plant that drag." Aubrey began to pace before the fire. "Someone who knew enough about me to realize that I'd whipped in for my father in the old days at Breme. John could have turned to me just as easily as he turned to Lilias. He could have picked me to bring back those hounds."

Ram nodded thoughtfully. "You or Lilias."

"Yes," Aubrey said. "If he couldn't kill me, Lilias's death would be just as devastating a blow."

And not necessarily because the bastard understood her real value to her husband, Aubrey thought, as his blood went cold.

They'd had more than a month together. She had not yet had her monthly flow. Someone would have counted the days of their marriage and realized what even now she might nurture within the protection of her body.

His child, the heir to Breme.

Hindley was back.

To Lilias, it seemed as if she'd paced for an eternity before Aubrey slipped through the doorway and entered the little sitting room. His face was pale but composed. Lilias stared up at him, her eyes narrowed, wondering how much of whatever was going on he'd share with her.

"Why is this house thrown into what looks like preparations for a retreat before a vast army?"

Aubrey's mouth quirked. "Not flight. I am running toward the enemy." He frowned at her. "Lilias, sit down before I pick you up bodily and put you into a seat."

She almost challenged him, just to have his hands on her again. Without his touch, she was bereft. But hearing his somber tone, she sat.

"I am going to London," he said.

"You? Not we?" She stared at him, and then her hands. Impatiently, she pushed aside the hurt and lifted her gaze to study him. "Why?"

His face was perfectly kind, she saw. He looked at her with the concern a man would show a ward, or a dependent of some other sort—a very young sister, maybe, or an old and respected servant. She had begun to hope for more.

"It's too dangerous to take you with me."

"Why?" She knew she sounded like a child, repetitively demanding to know.

"Someone tried to kill you today. I think I know who's responsible. I'll not have you hurt again on my account."

"It was an accident," she said. "And anybody could have been whipping in that spot."

He shook his head. "No. Ned's horse was shot. Somebody planted a drag to lure the hounds to the defile. To lure you there."

Her stomach heaved. "Why?" The blasted word was the best she could do.

He poured a dark, amber liquid into two glasses and brought one to her. "Drink it."

The first sip sent fire into her belly, and then warmth settled there. She took another sip, slid shakily into a chair, and stared up at him.

Aubrey grabbed the other glass of brandy and tossed it back. Crossing to the window, he looked out at the torchlit courtyard. "In a short time, a man will accuse me of murder. He was in India when I was there. He spent a good deal of time with Susannah. They were very close. Childhood friends, really."

His melodic voice had gone flat and toneless, automatically recounting the story of a stranger. It might have been the flicker of the lamplight that made her think she saw a very slight tremble across his shoulders.

"This man says I killed her. I saw her myself, lying in the jungle behind our bungalow with a bullet in her chest. I was shot that night, too, the night when the leopard found me. Ram Dass and the servants came for me in time. The story this man will tell is that I shot my wife in a fit of jealous rage and then turned the second gun on myself."

Aubrey turned and looked at her. His blue eyes were the color of midnight, deep and dark and empty. "He will tell this story on the witness stand, when I am put on trial for murder."

"No!" She rose and went to him in a rush. He backed away from her, his palms out. The silent gesture held her in place, transfixed by the look of suffering on his face.

"Lilias, the only reason I'm not in the gaol now is that I'm a peer of the realm, judged only by the lords. So while I'm free, he'll counter any moves I can make to regain my reputation. He has planted the filthy rumors through the ton already, but now he'll add embellishments to convince my judges that I'm steeped in degeneracy and one step from the madhouse. If I am to have a chance at acquittal, I must go to London immediately to offset these rumors."

Fear scuttled through her brain like mice across a pantry floor. "We could leave England—go to America, or to India, Italy, France," she said, pacing the floor. "We could make our way together. We could start again—I don't mind hard work."

Aubrey shook his head and smiled. "We'd have to live off your fortune."

She frowned at him. "This is no time to jest, Aubrey."

"I'm not joking. I settled a rather huge sum of money on you after you left Breme. Breme. . . ."

His mouth set in a line of determination. "You have to understand, Lilias. When I returned to England, I thought of Breme as a refuge, a place to hide. Then, when this assault began in earnest, I realized how fragile it was and how I would give my life to protect it." He gave her a long, straight look. "I can't leave. I can only stand and fight."

Her heart swelled at the sight of him, upright, stern, honorable.

"Who is this man?" she demanded.

Aubrey shut his eyes and rubbed his brow. "His name is Rupert Hindley. He is my cousin, and should I die, the next earl of Breme."

She nodded. "Of course. I understand. It's all a villainous plan to kill you, Aubrey. I knew it couldn't be anything else."

His face drained of color. The scars slashed, deep and black, across his cheek.

"It's not that simple, Lilias," he said in an expressionless voice. "There's a good chance that he's right."

Chapter Twenty-Six

"No." Lilias felt the first small shudder wrack her. But the shaking seemed to come from far away, as though this horror belonged to someone else. She looked toward the door. She was filled with an abrupt desire to move somewhere, anywhere, to escape. Instinctively, she turned to Aubrey. He would explain. He would make it all right.

The expression on his face was one of devastation. She stepped forward, intent upon going to him, to give him her warmth and her comfort.

But his taut stance was like an invisible shield about him, pushing her and her comfort away. She saw the subtle shimmer of his shoulders and feared he might crack in two if she came closer.

"I don't believe it," she said.

"I'm capable of anything, Lilias. If I hadn't found Landham already dead, I would have killed him, myself. And there's more." He turned away from her, placed his forearm against the wall, and leaned his head on it in a weary gesture of defeat.

"I can't remember what happened that night in the jungle, you see," he said in a voice soft with confusion. "No matter how hard I try, I can't remember."

She breathed a shaky sigh of relief. "It's all right," she said, the words tripping over themselves in her eagerness. "Things like that happen. Dr. Thomas told me about a case of memory loss from a blow on the head."

He swung round and pinned her with a flaring gaze. "Nothing hit me but a bullet, and that struck my chest. Don't you see? That time is a blank because I don't want to remember it. And what else would I hide from but my own criminal lunacy? I must have done it, Lilias. Hindley says he has proof. The ball that killed her came from my gun. And my dreams . . . I see her there, feel the gun in my hand, watch as her expression turns to horror. She has died before me nightly for months."

Lilias felt her heart stop for a beat and the blood seemed to pause in her veins. Could it be possible?

"But you loved her," she said.

His beautiful eyes were dead and empty in his pale face. "No. I hated her."

She recoiled, feeling the words like a slap on the face. "I need to think," she said. The vise around her heart tightened. If he were a murderer, how could she live with him? How could she still feel so much for him—pity and a desperate desire to ignore the damning words and beg him to take her to his bed and let her make it go away?

"We need to find proof, one way or another," she said in a voice that sounded preternaturally calm.

His mouth twisted. "*We* don't need to do anything. *You* are staying at Breme. I can keep you safe here, guarded by good men I trust. I must go to London, to face whatever Hindley sends my way. When it is over, if I'm still alive, we'll think what we're to do."

Oh, God. Was he talking about a separation?

A knock sounded at the door. Aubrey's hand went to the latch.

Lilias ran to him and clutched his outstretched arm. She didn't want to be alone to think about this, to imagine terrible things. "Everybody will want to see the woman you married. If I don't go, they'll think you . . . that I . . ."

Aubrey cringed, then quickly masked the naked flash of misery on his face. "They'll think you begin to fear me? If you were there, wearing the look you have on you now, they would know it."

"No. No. I just . . . you've dropped this on me suddenly. My mind is whirling. I told you. I have to think this out. Give me a little time."

He shook his head. "There's no more time." Gently, he took her hand and lifted it from his arm. He opened the door.

Ram stood there. "The coach is ready," he said.

"No, Aubrey," Lilias told him again.

He turned toward her, his gaze narrow and piercing. "You will stay here, do you understand?" he said with soft vehemence. "By God, you will not die!"

He strode out into the night. Lilias ran to a window overlooking the courtyard and saw only the swirl of his cape as he flung himself into the coach.

"Don't go," she whispered, staring after it as it vanished into the night.

The next morning, Lilias rose rather stiffly from a lonely bed. She had tossed and turned, waking often to tread the same path again and again.

Was it possible that Aubrey had killed his wife? And why? Hindley had said he'd been mad with jealousy. Why? What had Susannah Drelincorte done to arouse his jealousy?

She was beautiful, Aubrey had said. Although he hated

her. Lilias rose and dressed without calling Jane. She wanted no one to know where she was going, or why she felt she had to. Half an hour later, fighting the dread, she walked to the west wing of the castle to confront a ghost.

As soon as she opened the door to Susannah's chambers, the cloying scent of musk and expensive perfume pervaded the atmosphere. With haste, Lilias drew back the heavy velvet curtains. A shaft of sunlight illuminated the grand portrait of Susannah over the mantle.

Lilias gazed up at the magnificent blond. "Were you kind to him in the beginning?" she asked Susannah. "Did you care for him? Why did Aubrey hate you, Susannah? And why did Hindley worship you? The story still exists somewhere, doesn't it, Susannah? I intend to find it."

The sunlight dimmed. In a strange trick of light, Susannah's smile changed, became mocking, cruel. *"What can you do?"* it seemed to say. *"Poor little weak, plain creature. Give up. You can't win."*

Claustrophobia clenched at her belly, almost sending her to her knees. An evil essence seemed to mock her from the portrait—Susannah's spirit, sensing triumph.

Dizziness and nausea overcame her. It was just a nervous reaction—there was no malevolence in this room. She steered wildly for the door.

Tripping twice against the legs of impeding furniture, she ran into the corridor and slammed the door behind her.

I'd better sit down before I faint, she thought. Bracing her back against the wall, she slid down to the floor and slumped sideways. Laying her head on the floor, she gave in to the darkness.

"My lady, are you all right?" One of the newly-arrived, burly footmen knelt at her side and raised her upright.

"I may be plain," she said, blinking up as he stared down at her with confusion, "but I'm not weak." Fierce anger surged through her, and with it, common sense returned. She needed food. She needed time to think.

She took a deep breath and looked about her. "I feel much better," she told him, and began to rise.

"Wait, my lady," the footman said in concern, and stooped to aid her.

She hung on his arm, walking carefully, gaining strength with every step, while her mind began to work again.

Aubrey had thought she'd lied to him on their wedding night. He thought she might be carrying another man's child and planning to foist it off on him. Yet he couldn't hurt her. He listened to her. For heaven's sake, she'd been so sure he was sane and rational that she'd upbraided him. Under the worst of circumstances, he did not conduct himself as a man capable of murder in a jealous rage.

She thought back to his inexplicable behavior. The coldness, the irritation, the weariness, the sweet lovemaking until they fell, exhausted, into deep slumber. All of a sudden, the contradictions formed a visible pattern.

Aubrey wasn't mad. He was haunted. And hunted.

Oh, she realized he didn't want her help. His wary pride wrapped him as impenetrably as steel armor. It was almost impossible to think she'd ever get past it.

Something new and strong began to grow inside her. Susannah was wicked. Aubrey was innocent. It was her responsibility, her privilege as his wife, to aid him.

The footman helped Lilias down to the kitchen. Half of the servants sat about the heavy oak table, presumably gossiping about the last night's events. An instant hush fell when she entered the room. Then they rose as one and managed a hasty bow.

"Don't let me disturb you," she said with an airy wave of her hand. She took her place at the head of the table in Jeffries's usual seat. Mrs. Nettles brought her a cup of tea and a scone.

"I know you are all concerned about his lordship and probably wondering what you can do to help him . . ." She paused, letting the thought that they might be able to help sink in. "Perhaps there is someone who knew a good deal about Lady Susannah," she added helpfully. "Perhaps that person might know of somebody besides Lord Breme who might wish to kill her."

The footmen and the maids exchanged glances. One of them nudged Jane.

"She brought her own lady's maid," Jane said. "None of us liked her. Emma Pearson is her name. When the first Lady Breme died, she gave notice and sailed home from India. Said she'd come into some money and could quit service. I think she's in London."

"Oh, that's very good, Jane," Lilias said in an approving voice.

"She had us send her some of her winter things when she returned to England. I've got her direction somewhere," Mrs. Nettles said. "She wrote me that she got a pretty little sum. Got it regularly, she said."

"I should like that address," Lilias told Mrs. Nettles.

"I'll just go check my records. It'll take a bit of time, but I never throw anything away." Mrs. Nettles bustled off to her office, taking her tea with her.

Lilias returned to her room, deep in thought. The first business was to get to London. She needed to find proof of Aubrey's innocence, and Hindley was the key. But Roberts and the other new "servants" would no doubt refuse any request she made for the carriage.

Thus, at dusk, dressed in Jane's old cloak, she slipped out a side door with a small portmanteau and Emma Pearson's direction in her reticule. She saddled Starfire and arrived shortly thereafter at the gypsy camp.

"Lily," Val said, looking up from the campfire in surprise as she rode in. "How's life as a countess?"

"Complicated," she said with a grimace. Then she gave him her best smile. "I really, *really* need your help, Val."

He gave her a suspicious look. "What could you be needing that his lordship won't give you?"

He listened as she revealed her plans, his dark brows turning down in a deep frown.

"Not on your life, Lily. If he said stay put, that's what he meant. I'll not take you to London in the middle of the night with no guards to protect you and no permission from your husband."

"Oh, yes, you will." Gran Megan's voice came from the door of her wagon. "Go hitch the horse to your caravan, Val. She's takin' this journey, if I have to drive the wagon myself."

When Gran Megan spoke, her son listened, Lilias thought with a smile, as they pulled out of the gypsy camp in Val's caravan. But he didn't like it, that was certain.

"Don't you expect gratitude from his lordship for your tricks, Lily," he growled. "If you were my woman, I'd beat you."

"Nonsense!" She burst into a laugh at that thought.

"Well, I'd tie you to the wagon, at least."

"But then I couldn't cook your dinner," she said with mock innocence.

Val shook his head. "It's a wonder nobody's done away with you yet."

"Somebody tried," Lilias said with a shudder. "But

Aubrey saved me. He always saves me. Now I'm going to save him."

Val gave her a long look. "Lily, you scare a man half to death."

She thought of Rupert Hindley and pressed her lips together in determination. "I certainly hope so."

Aubrey shoved open the door to his chamber at Drelincorte House with a weary thrust of his elbow. His hands were full. The left held a half-empty brandy decanter and his glass, the right, a candlestick. Setting both with careful precision on the dresser, he shrugged out of his formal jacket and dropped it on a chair, then poured himself another glass. One more of these and he'd be drunk enough to sleep.

He didn't want to think about today, with its bloody frustration upon frustration. He had failed to remember anything Sir Samuel Paxton Green could use in his defense. The soiree at his godmother's townhouse had been miserable. Even old acquaintances had been cool. Their mistrust hurt and demoralized him more than he cared to contemplate. He began to wonder why he'd even bothered to come.

London was a dirty, foul place of coal dust, misery, and decadence of every kind. He missed Breme, with its clean, clear air.

He missed Lilias.

If she were here . . . He rubbed his face and sighed. If she were here, it would be worse. Somewhere on the ride to London, he realized that the only way to keep her safe from Hindley was to keep away from her bed. His widow would pose no threat to Hindley as long as she wasn't carrying his heir.

"What have I done?" he whispered. "If only . . ." If only he hadn't pushed Lilias to attend his blasted country weekend, if only he hadn't taken her to Crestview Manor, if only he hadn't grabbed at the chance to marry her, she'd be safe from all this.

The world shifted out of control. Sick with fear, he realized that she might have conceived already. From some hellish nether region, a secret, drunken hope surged. Maybe she'd already miscarried from the fall.

Then a picture rose in his mind. Lilias, alone, in pain, frightened, maybe worse—maybe her life was in danger, and he wasn't there! God!

No, he thought, scrubbing at his hair. They would have sent for him if she were ill.

He heard a sound—a groan of self-loathing coming from his own throat. Love and terror reduced him to a sotted, terrified beast.

Oh, Lilias, he thought. *Who will protect you if I die?*

The longing mixed with the fear, twisting him into knots. He wanted that sublime combination of soul's joy and completion in her arms. He tipped back his head and downed the drink. In the darkened room, he shut his eyes, breathing deeply. God, he was so gone with wanting, he imagined he smelled her scent in the air.

Dizziness hit him—too much brandy way too fast. He opened his eyes and the room swam into focus. At a soft sound of movement from the direction of the big four-poster bed, he tensed. Surreptitiously, his hand reached into his pocket for the pistol he now carried everywhere. Hindley, he thought, or more likely a surrogate.

"Hullo, Aubrey. I've been waiting forever." Lilias rose from the bed and walked toward him, a nymph in frothy, sea-green silk, all smooth skin and soft warmth as she drew closer to the light of the taper.

Carefully, he put the pistol down on the desk. Every beat of his heart said *mine*.

"Can't be you," he said, holding fast against the urgency racing through his blood as he crossed his arms and scowled at her for all he was worth. "You're a lu . . . illusion. I'm sotted," he explained to the vision of Lilias. Smiling, he swayed gently on his feet. "Nice dream. Stay around." The glass slipped from his hands. He squinted at it as it fell to the floor, the dark liquid puddling on the Turkish carpet. When he lifted his head, the simulacrum of Lilias had moved closer. His unruly gaze traveled over her like a starving man at a feast.

"I slipped the guards," she said. "Gran Megan's son brought me. You ought to travel in a gypsy caravan sometime. It's amazing how quickly one can get from Breme to London. Really far faster than the Posting Coach."

She came closer, lifting her slender arms, her fingers brushing his neck as she reached for his tie. He swallowed and licked his lips. The cravat slipped from his neck and slid to the floor.

"Can't do it." He shook his head staring at her. "No use, Lilias. You're not real." He waved his hand in the air, a grand gesture of negation. "If you were, my girl . . ." He lost the train of thought, then found it again. "Send you home at first light."

She frowned, intent on the buttons of his waistcoat. "But it's not light yet, is it? So I have time to tell you why you won't send me back." She bit her lip and ventured a glance at him. "You will listen, won't you?"

God, he must be very drunk. He felt every touch as the hallucination worked his buttons free and swept open his shirt, the palms flat on the tight muscles over his ribs. He could barely breathe from anticipation.

"I'll . . . try," he said, looking down past her bent head to the shadowed cleavage revealed by her gown. He shook with the need to grab her and follow her down into the heat swirling inside and all around him.

"All right, then." Her hands rose to his shoulders. His waistcoat and shirt slid to the floor. "First of all," she said in a thoughtful voice, "you didn't do it, Aubrey. I've thought about it very carefully, and you simply don't have the heart of a killer.

"You married me because you couldn't bear the thought of my ruin," she continued. "When you suspected me of lying to you about Landham, you could have beaten me or sent me out naked into the cold. Under English law, you have the right, you know. But you chose to believe I was 'an innocent, seduced and abandoned.' "

Oh, how this beautiful phantom's words could soothe his heart. "Jus' what I wanted you to say," he murmured, swaying on his feet. "Din't know I was a forchanut drunk."

With an amused sideways glance and a little shove, she pushed him into the chair and knelt before him on the carpet, her negligee frothing about her. One polished half-boot came off, then the other. His stockings followed.

"I've decided that you're the type who would rather believe there was something wrong with you than condemn someone else. You really do need me here, Aubrey," she said in a matter-of-fact voice as her hand rested on his thigh.

His muscles tightened as white heat shot through him.

"You're my 'lucination," he said through his clenched jaw, shaking his head.

She ignored him, running her fingers up his calves. He gasped, his legs tensing and stretching. If she'd just touch him a little higher . . . ah, God, that would be heaven.

"First," she continued, "there's society. I may not be quite the right sort, but it will look better if your wife attends these events with you. I wonder how many odd looks you got to-night without me on your arm, without me simpering up at you as though you were the sun and the moon."

He gave a breathless laugh. "You, simper?" he managed. "What a sat-ir-i-cal . . ." he blew out his lips, "performance."

"Don't be so sure," she whispered, laying her head on his thigh. "I could do a good imitation of a besotted wife, if you'd only give me the chance."

His breath caught in desire and hope. His hand hovered, yearning, above the gleaming flow of her hair, then drew back slowly. He waggled a finger at her. "Nursed me. Worried 'bout me. Just pity."

She shook her head against his thigh, and he groaned.

"And then, of course, there's the most important reason for me to stay." She nodded solemnly and looked up at him. "I believe you need an heir, and soon. It's so Hindley won't win, no matter what happens, isn't it?"

"No. Heir." The word was a strangled gasp.

The dream ignored his protest. "Well, how's that to happen if I'm at Breme and you're here?"

In a swish of silk, she rose and stood before him, all his dreams come to this drunken vision of heaven.

"You see," she said, "I really must stay."

He surged out of his chair, past caring what the hell they were talking about. Grabbing her hand, he pulled her the short distance to the bed and followed her down. He sank into her softness and her scent, the warm welcome of her arms, the dark heat that swirled around him. One more time . . .

"Can't stop," he said, kissing her everywhere. "Doesn't matter. My sweet 'lucination."

He's quite sotted, Lilias thought half in horrified amuse-ment. The sharp-sweet taste of brandy swirled with his tongue as he took her mouth in a deep penetration. But what did it matter? He was over her, his heat surrounding her, claiming her, filling her. His hands tugged at the gown, ripped it as he swept it off her shoulders and bared her breasts.

She laughed, breathless as his wild passion caught her in its fiery heat. He knelt above her, a smiling, tipsy Dionysus, his hands sliding down her side, pulling the gown from her hips to her feet in one jerk.

"My Lily. My 'lucination. Do what I want."

"Yes," she said. "Whatever you want."

"Up," he told her, dropping to her side in a quick flop. The mattress sagged beneath his weight. "Up above me," he ordered, grinning.

She knelt where he arranged her, knees inside his thighs.

"I lie here. You. Have your way. With me."

She looked down at his body, the muscled, rippling abdomen, the broad shoulders, the long, strong legs. She smiled as the sense of power rolled through her. Her turn to drive him wild—how delicious.

"Excellent plan." She stroked down his chest to his belly, one long, lascivious glide of fingers and palm. He sucked in his breath with a hiss. He'd been hard against her before, but the surge that lifted his trousers now caught her attentive admiration. She watched his face as her fingers slipped the buttons of his fly free one at a time. What a delightful look of torment. What marvelous sounds came from him—whispers and groans and incoherent pleas. She freed him from his trousers and touched him, wrapping her hand around him.

"Yes. Yesss."

He rose off the bed. Imagine that. As she licked her lips and stared at the long, hard, essence of his sex, her womb clenched in wanton response.

Then she lowered her head and touched him with her tongue.

"God, yes!" He panted, beautifully undone, straining beneath her. "Please, Lily." His face darkened, his nostrils flared, his eyes glazed with passion. "Your mouth."

She took him, nibbling gently, sucking, experimenting. The power rose in her, spilling out through her limbs. She could bring him to this extremity of lust, she thought triumphantly. She could arouse this desire in him. She aroused herself by doing it. She lifted her head. He moaned in disappointment. She rose on her knees and straddled his thighs, taking him in her hand.

He moaned again, this time looking hopeful. "Please, please, Lily. Inside you."

She placed him where he wanted to be, and began to move above him. His gaze swept up her body as it rose. "Don't leave," he begged. "Don't ever leave me."

She shook her head, smiling, and came down on him again, adding a little swirl of her hips that made him cry out. He clasped her hips, pulling down hard. She arched her back, brushed her hands up her ribs, lifting her breasts for him, preening like a wanton courtesan. He rose up, taking her nipple in his mouth, suckling hard. Her arms twined around his neck, and just like that, she lost herself, opening to him, gasping and mewling as his cries mixed with hers and the mattress sank as they rolled. He was over her again, pounding into her as she broke apart, and he came with a cry of completion, with his seed bursting high inside her as she shuddered and clenched him again, and again, and again.

Hours later, the gray light of dawn woke Lilias. She lay softly nestled in Aubrey's arms, one leg over his, her head on his shoulder. She raised her head and looked down at him. The view filled her with a heart-deep satisfaction. He was tousled from their lovemaking. His lips were relaxed in sleep, curved slightly in a smile. She had no doubt she'd put that smile on his face. Oh, he made her want to sing, to dance around the room.

She rose from the bed and donned his shirt. Then she slipped away through the door to the adjoining bedroom and found her dressing gown where she'd hung it the night before. She was too excited to sleep. She wanted tea and breakfast. She'd make notes on what she wanted to write to the maid who had Lady Susannah's letters. Then she'd go downstairs and wait for Aubrey to awaken.

How much of last night would he remember? Would he smile his bold pirate smile or flush? She couldn't wait to see.

Aubrey woke with a pounding headache, a mouth filled with cotton, and the relaxed ache in his muscles that he usually associated with magnificent sex. With a start, he reviewed his conduct last night. No, he hadn't gone to some stable of high flyers after the soiree. He'd come straight home and gotten soused in his own library. Fragments of a dream came back to him, full of lust and moonlight and a woman—*his* woman—above him, her arms raised, her breasts full and rose-tipped, her sinuous movements pulling him toward ecstasy.

Rising to ring the bell for his valet, he squinted and groaned as the light from the slightly-open maroon velvet curtains hit his eyes. Rubbing his face, he caught a familiar light, feminine scent on his hands, and frowned.

He looked back at the ravaged bed and grabbed the pillow beside his. He rubbed his face in it. Her scent was all over it.

"Hell."

"My lord?" His valet stood by the open door, hesitant.

As more of the dream came back to him, he groaned and

shut his eyes. "When did Lady Breme arrive?"

"L-Late last night, my lord." The valet stuttered.

"In what conveyance?" he asked gritting his teeth as those damning words, *gypsy caravan,* popped into his brain.

"A g-gypsy brought her, my lord. It was very dark. I'm sure nobody saw the . . . the vehicle." Try as he might, the valet couldn't keep a look of pinch-nosed disapproval from his face.

"And she is now . . . ?" Aubrey prompted impatiently.

"Waiting for you in the breakfast room, my lord."

He dressed in record time, barking at the valet because he didn't have Lilias to bark at. When he thought of her traveling in the middle of the night without guards! Of her arrival—stepping out into the street in front of anyone who might be watching the house—his blood ran cold. Little idiot with no thought to her safety!

When he entered the breakfast room, she looked up from the newspaper and gave him a brilliant smile. "Hullo, Aubrey. I assume you'd like coffee. A great deal of it."

He scowled, taking the cup she proffered. "Don't get too comfortable. I'm sending you back immediately."

She narrowed her eyes. "We settled it last night. Don't you remember?"

He remembered, all right. Exactly where her mouth had been, exactly how it felt. To his horror, he found that his face was on fire, while hers was firmly set in a look of determination.

"I can't keep you here." He took a section of the paper and snapped it open, hiding his face behind it.

"Whyever not?"

He grimaced at the wobble in her voice and peeked over the top of his paper to catch a glimpse of her face. She watched him carefully, just the tiniest hint of vulnerability in her eyes. He couldn't stand it. If she stayed, how long before he took her to his bed and endangered her again? Or was it already too late?

He folded the paper. "We won't need anything more, Frederick," he told the footman, who bowed and left the room, closing the door to give them privacy.

"Have you had your menses?" he asked abruptly, angry that he had to ask it, angry that, if the answer was yes, cold fear would swamp him again, and if she told him no, he'd have to send her back.

Lilias stared at the sweet man she'd made passionate love to just hours before and thought she was looking at an angry, cold stranger. "My menses?" They were back to the crude interrogation of the first days in their marriage. Had nothing changed for him in the last month? She looked down at her plate. "I don't know." Her voice faltered.

"Lilias. This is hardly something you wouldn't know. Either you're breeding," he said, and Lilias noted that he at least winced at the word, "or you're not."

She supposed the correct answer was "more or less," as her monthly had begun and then stopped. But she was not about to discuss such a personal function with this scowling brute. She shrugged.

"We'll have to assume you're not." He glared at her. "And last night you seduced me?"

She nodded, giving him a long, measuring look. *Seduced.* The word called up images of every Biblical villainess—Eve tempting Adam, Delilah shearing Samson.

"Hell." He got up from his seat and began to pace.

Refusing to give him the advantage of height, she rose as well. "You didn't mind much at the time," she said, crossing her arms over her chest. "In fact, you gave instructions!"

"I was sotted," he said.

Her mouth dropped open in shock. "Lord, Aubrey. You're whining as though you were some deflowered maiden."

At a discreet knock at the door, they both turned away from each other and stared in the other direction.

Frederick entered. He carried a silver tray stacked with wafers. "Sorry to disturb you, my lord, but the post arrived." He put the tray on the table and slipped out the door.

Aubrey strode to the table and sifted through the letters. He looked up at her in surprise and passed her one. She turned the heavy vellum over. The wax on the note bore the seal of the Duke of Ayres. She opened it and slid out an invitation from her Aunt Edith to be her guest of honor at her musicale for ladies being held the next day.

By the by, Aunt Edith wrote, *when you need to travel, our carriage is entirely at your disposal.*

"May I?" Aubrey's voice, his hand out commandingly. She passed the note back to him and bit her lip.

He cleared his throat. "Damnation. I'm surprised it's not in the dailies." He began to pace the room, tapping the letter against one hand. Finally, he turned to her, the frown still fixed on his face. "You can't leave. It's too dangerous."

He resumed pacing, first to the window, then to the door, then back again. "The gossip must be all over Mayfair by now. We'll have to do the best we can with what we've got. You won't ever leave this house without protection. Do you understand me, Lilias?"

She glowered at him. "I'm not an idiot."

"After your escapade last night, I'm tempted to contradict you," he snapped. "And you must accept the fact that I have more important matters at hand than paying attention to you."

She hid the stab of hurt and raised her chin. "I'll go with

somebody very strong. Perhaps one of the new footmen."

He raised his brows in surprise. "What do you know about the footmen?"

She rolled her eyes. Of all the arrogance! She was suddenly not only a seductress, but stupid. "Oh, for heaven's sake. They're sham, of course. Their livery is too tight across the shoulders and in the arms. They've broken two vases and five plates. They serve from the right and remove the dishes from the left. You would have given them notice long ago, if they didn't have another function."

He gave her a reluctant nod. Then, looking through the letters, he divided them into two piles.

Correction, she thought. She was a stupid seductress, not even worth his full attention.

"They're from Bow Street," he said, opening a letter and perusing it. "All right. You'll stay. As soon as your maid arrives, I'll tell her where to put you."

"Put me?" Her body drew itself together, tautened to take the blow. "I thought I would stay . . ." *in your bed* ". . . in the chamber next to yours."

He cleared his throat, his gaze fixed on the letter. "It will be better for both of us, if you're somewhere else."

Her lips wobbled. "Why?"

"It just will be." He looked up at her and his brows drew together. "Lilias, I must work."

"Yes. Well . . ." As stiffly as a mechanical toy, she turned and walked to the door. She couldn't quite take it all in—his complete transformation. After a month of the greatest happiness she'd ever known, he'd decided she was an unwelcome problem that needed sorting out in some far-away space, while he dealt with more pressing matters.

He gave her a strained smile. "You'll need new gowns. Go to the modiste this morning and order some. I'll tell two of the guards to accompany you."

"Yes, Aubrey," she said, turning away from him to hide the tears that threatened to spill over and down her cheeks. She walked out and closed the door behind her with a bang. What possessed men to think a new gown made up for a broken heart?

Chapter Twenty-Seven

Aubrey leaned his head against the door through which Lilias disappeared, fighting the desire to call her back and apologize. He hated how he'd deliberately hurt her in order to keep her safe. He wanted to take it all back and say other things, true things—like how much she meant to him, how her lovemaking had taken him to unimaginable heights, how much he needed her beside him. But then she would have thrown her arms around him and he would have kissed her and one thing would have led to another, perhaps even in the middle of the dining room.

All he had to do was remember the sight of her so still and pale on the ground at the edge of the precipice to realize that he had to protect her future. She was young, still full of foolish faith in him. His peers would feel differently, and she would be alone soon, and dreadfully vulnerable.

A little hurt now would protect her life. As long as they stayed away from each other as much as possible, he could control his lust and think at the same time.

At a knock on his door, Aubrey jerked back, rubbing his temples and swearing off hard liquor for the rest of his life. The door swung open on the butler and Sir Samuel Paxton

Green, who blew into the room like a small tornado. His bulldog expression was much in evidence as he growled his impatience.

"Hop to it, man. We have less than two weeks before we go to trial." Sir Samuel broke into his customary pace with the short, trotting stride of a hyperactive terrier, his cigar clamped firmly between his teeth.

He ruffled his hands through the fringe of wildly-grizzled gray hair that circled his otherwise bare scalp and shot Aubrey a sharp look. "And for the last time, sir, I ask you. Are you holding back any pertinent information?"

"I wish I were. It would be easier than the constant wondering."

"I take it you have tried to remember, and still are unable to do so."

Aubrey shook his head, trying to think of a way to describe the attempts and the frustration. "The details are just . . . gone."

Sir Samuel looked grave. "I cannot unearth anything legally damaging concerning Mr. Hindley, my lord. I can blast his character to smithereens in trial, yes. The man has gaming debts that will ruin him, unless he inherits Breme. But in the august House of Lords, that information alone will do us little good, unless your peers take a liking to you."

Aubrey nodded. After coming to London, he'd lost faith in his ability to win people over. He had begun to count his odd interests as flaws in other men's eyes—music, literature, friendship with men of other races, a sense of community with his servants. Every part of him that was most real seemed to damn him more.

"We must continue to look," Aubrey said.

"I suggest you and your lady draw as much favorable attention among your peers as possible."

Aubrey glanced at the salver on his desk. It overflowed with invitations to balls and routes. Everyone suddenly wished to view the mad earl and his new wife. He could envision the speculation. Was she an innocent victim or a grasping climber?

He covered his guilt with a shrug and a wry smile. After this morning's gossip about Lilias's unconventional arrival, he had to take her into the lion's den with him. "What else do we live for, but to provide grist for society's gossip mills?"

Later, when he heard the carriage wheels signaling Lilias's return from the mantuamaker, he met his wife in the hall. "We shall go to the opera tomorrow night. I'll be here at nine to escort you."

"Fine," she said in a hollow, empty voice.

Aubrey's idea of "somewhere else" turned out to be a chamber far down the hall from the master suite. Lilias paced as Jane, newly arrived from Breme, clucked and hung her gowns in the wardrobe.

"My, this one will need pressing, my lady, if you want it for tomorrow night." Jane sighed and smiled, as though everything were fine between her master and mistress. "The opera, just imagine!"

Nothing was fine—not the chamber she'd sleep in, and certainly not the look on her husband's face, as though he wished he were anywhere but near her. She'd put it about that Aubrey, busy with his preparations for the trial, needed quiet. It was the best she could do to keep the gossip down.

Why should she care, after he'd made it clear that the very sight of her made him flee the room? Her body wanted to shake with rage and hurt, and she controlled it, clamped down on all the emotions swirling around inside, pushing to get out. There was no moor here to ride until she was calm again. There was only the aristocracy, watching for any slip in her behavior, and the knowledge that she would have to face them almost immediately.

"His lordship was surprised to see us so soon," Jane said. "But I packed as quick as I could. And we traded horses at every posting inn."

Lilias was glad to have Jane beside her again, a cheerful, friendly face in this cold city of strangers. "Who's 'we'?" she asked.

"Oh, Roberts and that new fella, the one even brawnier . . . Jackson. We all came down from Breme last night, after I let them know you were gone to London," Jane said, as she began to brush the tangles out of Lilias's hair.

Lilias sat quietly, thinking hard beneath the gentle *shussh* of the brush. By all that was holy, she'd sworn she'd save this ungrateful clod, and she would. After that—well, after that, she'd go back to the country, where she belonged. She'd get a little cottage and raise herbs and nurse people who knew how to be grateful, and if he never came round again, she'd do just fine.

Aubrey awoke that night, gasping and covered in sweat. The last remnants of the dream seared his brain like the flames of hell.

Susannah, laughing in glee, challenging him in the midst of dark jungle. His hand raised the pistol— disgust, horror, rage, danger, fear. His hand squeezed the trigger. The gun bucked. Susannah stared at her chest in shock. A blossom of blood flowered there, poured from the wound. She looked at him, her eyes blank, and slumped slowly to the ground.

He covered his eyes. "My God, what have I done?" he whispered.

Lilias didn't see Aubrey until breakfast the next morning. He put down the paper and rose to help her into her seat. He looked much as he had when she'd first met him—a perfect, remote gentleman in somber dress. She'd had to stop thinking there was more between them than this polite dance between strangers. Every precise, measured move was another blow. She felt as though her heart was a bruised thing, each beat sore against her ribs.

It didn't matter, she scolded herself. She had a task to fulfill, she thought, as she poured tea for herself. One priority at a time. The important thing was to keep her husband alive. For that, he needed to remember what had happened, or she needed to find evidence to exonerate him. Afterward, she would think what to do.

"I must attend the musicale today," she said in a voice that was reassuringly brisk. "There's no other way to put an end to the gossip."

He frowned. "It's for ladies only. I can't accompany you."

Roberts, one of the new footmen, bent to serve from a tray of coffee and scones. The coffee sloshed from the silver pot.

Lilias whisked the scones off the tray in time to save them from a dunking and passed them to Aubrey. "Roberts could take your place. He's obviously got the qualifications."

Aubrey nodded. "Take Jackson, too." The other footman in the dining room, the tall, burly fellow Aubrey had played circus with, bowed slightly and grinned. "Jackson used to work with a circus. He can tell you all sorts of stories about circus life. I should like it if you could find some things to laugh about while you are here." His tone was tentative, but warmer than it had been.

She hated herself for the way her spirit lit at those few words. She was wasting her time, hanging on his every infinitesimal change of mood.

Lilias arrived early at Ayres House in a glossy, black closed carriage painted with the Breme coat of arms. Roberts and Jackson accompanied her inside, wearing jackets in the Breme green and gold livery that almost fit their huge frames. Their coat pockets bulged with things that Lilias preferred not to think about.

Lady Edith must have been watching for her, for she opened the door herself before Roberts had even plied the knocker. Her sweet, heart-shaped face was tremulous with emotion as she pulled Lilias into the large, ornate hall and rose up on her toes to kiss her cheek.

"I have hoped for this for many, many years," she said, blotting her tears with a lace-edged handkerchief. "Your grandfather has allowed me to write dear Pamela, as well. I think he has begun to realize that he has another chance with the two of you."

"Aunt Edith," Lilias said stiffly, "Pamela and I have no need of the duke's charity."

"It wouldn't be charity. I have something to show you, my dear." Lady Edith took her hand and led her into the formal sitting room, where the servants bustled about, setting up chairs and stands for the musicians. In the place of honor above the marble fireplace hung a large portrait.

"Oh, Mama," Lilias said softly. Her mother held her violin in one hand and her bow in the other. She looked so young, so happy, in the informal, lifelike painting. The duke stood beside her, a flute in his hand. In this portrait, he was a man in his prime, smiling and proud. He didn't look a thing like the stiff autocrat she had met at her wedding.

"He loved her dearly," Lady Edith said. "We all did. She was an extraordinary woman, strong and beautiful, with a talent that brought tears of joy to the eyes of everyone who heard her play. He used to listen to her every night, and the duets they played were so lovely. I think it was all that made him happy after my mother died. He wanted only the best for Gwennie. You can't imagine what it did to him—the estrangement. He was so determined that she should choose what he saw as her right and her duty. When she chose your father, your grandfather was devastated. He reacted too quickly and she took him at his word. She never spoke to him nor wrote to him again."

Lilias bit her lip. She thought of the nights when she stayed awake nursing Tilden's sick to put food on the table. She thought of the flight from Richard Landham, when she didn't know how or where she would find refuge.

"He's across the hall, in his study," Lady Edith said.

Lilias peered across the hall. The study door was open. Inside, she could see her grandfather, his tall, upright frame stiff with some sort of tension as he read, with seeming absorption, a book. She could just glimpse the title of the book, but she couldn't read it. It was upside-down.

She should ignore him. She should just get through this afternoon.

"Oh, thunder and blast," she whispered to herself.

The orchestra had arrived, and a few of the players set up their instruments beside the harpsichord—a base, a viola, a cello. She whispered a few words to them. With a shrug, one of the musicians reached into an open case and handed her a violin. The instruments took no time at all to tune.

None of them needed the sheet music. Bach's *Air on a G String* was a part of most musicians' repertoire. She shut her eyes, letting the music fill her until she was the music. Then she began, draining every drop from the melody as the counterpoint gave the beat. The acoustics in the room did not equal Breme, but the music flowed across the hall and through an open door, filling a study where one man sat alone, pretending to read. She opened her heart to the stately theme, sending it out to anyone who might be listening in spite of himself.

For that brief moment, the house sang.

The last notes soared and fell into silence. She opened her eyes. Her grandfather stood at the door, his lined face alight, tears streaming from his eyes.

The rest of the afternoon flew by. His Grace, Alfred, Duke of Ayres, remained to greet the guests and introduce his granddaughter to the ladies of British society.

Once, she heard his voice from across the room. "She's got her mother's talent," he said to some of the dowagers Aunt Edith had introduced earlier. "Of course, Breme is a virtuoso."

One of the ladies cooed something to him. "My conclusion exactly," he replied in a voice loud enough to carry. "It is not surprising they wished to marry so quickly, what with finding in each other the same gift of music they couldn't have found elsewhere."

What a tale! Lilias thought in amusement and some admiration. He was quick, her grandfather.

"I was just telling my sister how delightful it is to find a love match in polite society today," said the matron.

Included in the party were the Ladies Berring. After the Mozart, Lady Caroline came up to her, beaming. Her blue afternoon gown fell in graceful simplicity and her light brown hair was brushed upward into an attractive cluster of curls. In the month that followed that dinner party at Breme, she seemed to have gained a bit of polish.

"I was so happy to hear that you were in town for the Season. I've never forgotten what you said to that obnoxious Margaret Hall."

"She deserved it. What a harridan! I hope never to see her again."

"Unfortunately, you will. She's wed to old Lord Lazenby."

Lilias gave Caroline a rueful smile. "I'm afraid I don't know him."

"He's a viscount, aged about one hundred, with a penchant for gambling. Miss Hall, now Lady Lazenby, is thrilled with his title. She looks forward to a life in society, and Lazenby looks forward to a full purse."

Lilias burst into laughter. "You seemed so sweet. I never thought I'd hear you say a word against anyone. And now I find beneath that innocent façade lies a rather sharp mind."

Lady Caroline shrugged. "I spend a lot of time in the shadows watching others take the stage. I might as well get some amusement out of it."

Lilias's hand came out of its own accord and took Caroline's hand. "I'm going to need a wise friend with a gift for observation. Would you mind terribly if I ask you to fill the position?"

Her smile grew wider, revealing a charming pair of dimples that transformed her into a mischievous elf. "Call me Caroline. As do all my close friends, of which I now have one."

All in all, Lilias thought as she took leave of her aunt and grandfather, the afternoon had been successful. She hoped that she had left an impression of a happy wife with a small percentage of England's aristocratic matrons. She had found a friend with whom she could navigate the tricky shoals of the Season.

And best of all, she had managed to evade Jackson's and Roberts's watchful eyes long enough to give the butler a letter to post. The note, addressed to Emma Pearson, requested a meeting in which to discuss certain questions regarding her late mistress, Susannah Drelincorte, Countess Breme.

After writing to a number of his bankers, Aubrey turned to Ram, who'd been staring out the window at the carriage stopped before the townhouse on Berkley Square.

Ram frowned. "Lilias is home from the musicale."

Aubrey joined him by the window. A man in the Duke of Ayres's livery stood before the carriage in conversation with Lilias. He handed her something. She took it and spent a moment more with the man, apparently thanking him.

"How long has the footman been skulking outside the house?" Aubrey asked. "Why didn't he come in and leave the note for Lilias?"

"I don't know," Ram replied. "It looks as though he's coming in with her now, probably to wait for a reply. Are you going to ask her about this?"

Aubrey thought of the look in her eyes when he'd denied her the room beside his—the room that was hers by right. He shook his head. Why hurt her further with his mistrust? Better to keep it in, with all the other inchoate feelings rioting in his gut.

"I assume Ayres and his daughter incorrectly fear I'll keep their messages from her," he said. "I'll reassure them when all this is over."

If I'm still around to do so.

When he entered the upstairs study, he found Lilias at the desk, sealing a note. She gave it and another on her slant-top desk to the waiting maid, who curtsied to him and slipped out the door, presumably to deliver them to Ayres's man.

"Aubrey," she said rising. The soft rose silk of her gown whispered on the Turkish carpet. Her cheeks were bright with color, no doubt from her ride home from the musicale.

He fought the urge to touch her cheek, to feel its soft warmth.

Less than two weeks left.

"How was your morning?" he asked the floor.

"Fine," she answered without inflection.

"That's good. I'll . . . ah, I'll just . . ." He turned to the door to escape. He fumbled with the latch and finally had it open. He was out in the hall before he found he could breathe again. There were so many things he wanted to say. *I love you. You're not safe with me. I think I carry evil inside me. I'm sorry. I took what I wanted, and now you'll hate me for the rest of your life.*

Damn his brain, bottling everything up inside. Damn the dream. Was he a cold-blooded killer? Why couldn't he remember?

Almost running down the corridor, he flung the door open to Ram's office. Ram had taken the small room over when they'd arrived. The place was already filled with neatly-labeled test tubes and files of experiments. Myriad scents filled the air—rosemary, lavender, tansy, mixed with sharp, exotic eastern herbs. Ram looked up from the unguent he mixed in surprise.

"I had another dream," Aubrey said abruptly. "I'll go under."

"Tell me about it," Ram said.

So he did.

"Dreams can be tricky," Ram said. "They reveal reality, and hopes, and fears. You didn't necessarily do it, Aubrey."

Aubrey laughed, but it came out sounding more like a groan.

"All right," Ram said firmly, taking his arm. Somehow, the fact that Ram was still willing to touch him was infinitely reassuring. "When do you want to do it?"

"Now." Tremors wracked his body, and his teeth chattered as badly as they had at the height of the malaria attack.

"It'll just be me," Ram said gently. He closed the door.

Aubrey's legs were so rigid that they almost refused to bend, but he managed to sit on the couch Ram indicated.

"Don't be afraid," Ram said in that same gentle voice, sitting opposite and bringing out his pocket watch. "You know my professor worked with Mesmer in Switzerland. I've done this many times. The worst that can happen is that you won't remember."

"Just do it," Aubrey said between clenched teeth.

He lay back and concentrated on the golden glow of the watch. His eyelids grew heavy. Without his volition, they closed.

The next thing he heard was the staccato snap of fingers. He opened his eyes, feeling better. Hope surged through him, bringing him to his feet.

Ram shook his head. "I couldn't get through."

The buoyant expectation sank like a little skiff in an ocean storm. "Nothing?"

"Nothing. I'm sorry, Aubrey."

"Not your fault," Aubrey said, walking toward the door like an automaton. "It must be very bad if I could go under and not face it."

Ram gave him a long look. "Yes. Very bad. But not necessarily your doing."

Aubrey slowly turned his face away. "I wish I could believe that," he said.

As an antidote to the poison of his fears, Aubrey sent for the Drelincorte rubies. He couldn't sleep with his wife, he couldn't give her a child, his name couldn't bring her the re-spect her station should have guaranteed her. But these . . . He stared down into his gift of perfectly-cut gems strung glit-tering on gold between diamonds of equal brilliance. He bit his lip. It was something, anyway.

Aubrey arrived at Lilias's door as she was putting the last touches on her coiffure. He held out a silver box wrapped with a dark crimson ribbon.

She took it and opened it, staring down at its contents. She had never seen anything as magnificent as these jewels. Her skin went hot and cold with shame at her duplicity con-cerning Emma Pearson. She didn't deserve such generosity.

"I'll only speak to you. Bring no one else," Miss Pearson had written in reply to her letter. Lilias couldn't tell Aubrey. He would insist on accompanying her, or sending a squadron of detectives. And Emma Pearson would refuse to give Lilias the evidence that would exonerate Aubrey.

He stood very still, looking down at her bent head.

"They're beautiful," she whispered.

"It's a tradition. All the Drelincorte brides have worn them."

All the Drelincorte brides . . .

Susannah, too, she thought, and her heart gave another lurch. The beautiful, false Susannah, whom men adored, had worn these. And Lilias, keeping her secrets from Aubrey, would wear them next.

"The setting's old-fashioned, I know. If you want to change it . . ." His voice was hesitant, almost apologetic.

She shook her head without looking at him. "No. I meant it. They're beautiful."

Her body felt the change in him without her looking up—a stiffness emanating from every part of him. It was an elemental sense she'd developed, like a cat's whiskers in the dark. She wished she could lose it.

"You don't have to wear them tonight," Aubrey said. "But tomorrow night it would be helpful if you did."

She took a deep breath. "Tomorrow," she said. "At my first ball."

He gave a quick nod. "Yes. Several people will recognize the rubies and remember the tradition."

Of course, she thought. The necklace and earrings were a card of some value in this dangerous game they played with Hindley.

There was no real sentiment involved in this gift from Aubrey. The Drelincorte rubies merely gave her a certain legitimacy as a countess in the long line of Drelincorte countesses.

She didn't know whether she was hurt that she'd misconstrued the gift to mean more to Aubrey than it did, or relieved. She unclasped her mother's pearls and lifted the ruby necklace from its silken bed.

"Would you?" she asked him. She was doing the right thing. It wasn't deception, when she was now and always his ally. Was it? "The more often I wear them, the better."

She waited like that for what seemed an eternity, keeping her gaze on the hem of her dress. Finally, Aubrey took the necklace from her and clasped it at the back of her neck. His fingers never touched her skin.

Their carriage advanced in the slow crush of the Haymarket toward the entrance of the King's Theater. They were almost late for the first act of *The Magic Flute*, but from their box, Lilias searched the tiers of red and gold boxes that rose five stories high in a semicircle. She searched for faces from Aunt Edith's musicale. She smiled and inclined her head to several of the women just as the lights dimmed and the music began to swell. And then, sitting beside Aubrey, she tried to lose herself in the childlike, comical magic of the tale and the music.

It didn't work. She slid glances at her husband, sitting tall and still, like an effigy carved in stone. The heavy sense of loss weighed on her. She tried to remember why she'd come to London, and to comfort herself that, somehow, she might be helping him a little.

Intermission brought a noisy bustle to the floor below and several guests to their box, Caroline Berring included. Lilias tried hard to remember all the titles of the men who bowed over her hand, and succeeded only because she had done her homework in *Burke's Peerage* the night before.

Aubrey and one of the other men, a friend from Oxford, Lilias gathered, seated Caroline and her mother beside Lilias. "I received your note," Caroline whispered. "I'll meet you in Hyde Park at nine o'clock."

"You understand we'll have to slip the grooms," Lilias warned. "I don't want you falling and hurting yourself."

Caroline patted her hand. "Don't worry. I'm an excellent rider."

Lilias felt a pang of guilt. She had only told Caroline that she must meet a lady in the park, that it was important, and that she must tell no one. Without asking any questions, Caroline offered her the help of a true friend. Lilias only hoped she wasn't leading Caroline into danger.

Lilias surreptitiously poked Caroline. "Someone is staring at us from across the way. See? Second box from center." How odd. She couldn't see the man's expression, but there was something about him she didn't like.

Caroline glanced through her opera glasses and shook her head. "They're dimming the lights. All I can see is a head of brown hair and a pair of rather nice shoulders. He's not ter-

315

ribly tall, although he looks neatly built. He's probably looking for a mistress," she murmured with a shrug, but her voice held a hint of bitterness. "I'm not quite proper wife material."

"Don't," Lilias said, feeling hot with anger and protectiveness. She squeezed Caroline's hand. "You're pretty and bright and funny. And, to be quite practical, you have a fortune for a dowry. Don't let them forget any of it, and they'll all be lining up for your hand."

Even the magic of the opera dimmed. Lilias thought it odd that she and Aubrey must work so hard for the approval of a society that branded a wounded man a beast, his wife a harlot and a fortune hunter, a brilliant Indian doctor a barbarian, and an intelligent, kind young woman a bastard.

Tomorrow, because of this society's prejudices, she would lie to her husband in order to meet Emma Pearson. All she could do was pray that the maid's information would acquit her husband and not condemn him to death.

Chapter Twenty-Eight

The next morning, Lilias dismounted in an isolated area of Hyde Park, far from the well-traveled bridle trails.

"Are you sure you can hold both the horses?" she whispered to Caroline as they stood together, peering through the thicket. They had out-ridden their grooms and the ubiquitous Roberts, whose city-bred past did not include extensive riding lessons.

"I may be clumsy in society, but I'm fine with horses," Caroline whispered back. She pointed toward a fluted gazebo of worn, gray wood beneath the deep shade of several oaks. "You'd better go on. I think I see her."

As Lilias approached the gazebo, she saw a shadow move in the dim light. Her heart beat in her throat and her hands were clammy with anxiety.

"Miss Pearson?" she called softly as she climbed the stairs.

The gaunt figure rose in the shadows. "I am. You've come alone?" A woman dressed in black stepped forward from the gloom. Emma Pearson had a thin, hard face. Her black hair was streaked with gray and pulled back tightly beneath an unbecoming bonnet. Her eyes, with their dark, slashing brows, had a look of cunning in them that Lilias had never seen, even among the disreputable merchants she'd sometimes passed on the docks near her father's warehouses. And they were tinged with something else, a fanatical gleam that made Lilias shiver.

She took a deep breath and forced her hands to lie still at her side. "I left my friend at the far end of the copse."

"Let us discuss our business, then."

"You have information concerning the marriage between Lord Breme and his first wife. Letters, you said. I should like to see them."

"Oh, I've got them. The question is, how badly do you want them? It'll cost you a pretty sum."

"I am prepared to pay."

"You won't like what you read, you know." Her voice changed, grew dreamy. "My sweet lady was a goddess, she was. She was too good for him. She had the face of an angel and the charm to go with it. He was nothing beside her. Mr. Hindley was the only man good enough for her. It was tragedy that she should die and not that Lord Breme."

She gave Lilias a sly smile. "You'll have to read all that, you know. You'll have to see how low he was, how she despised him."

Lilias tried to keep her voice from shaking. "Nevertheless, I'll buy them from you."

"You'll wish you'd never cast your lot with him." Emma Pearson's eyes glittered with a mad light, and the smile grew wider with satisfaction. "You'll see why they're going to hang him."

Lilias felt cold as death. "How much?"

"Four hundred pounds," Emma Pearson said. "I'd take much more, but the satisfaction of causing his second wife to hate him as much as his first is almost compensation enough."

"How will I get it to you?" God, she needed to get out of this place. Now.

"Carry the money with you for the next few days. I'll contact you and let you know where to meet me. And be there. If you're not, I have other interested buyers."

Lilias walked back to the end of the copse on trembling legs.

Caroline took one look at her face and pulled her toward a fallen log, making her sit. "Put your head between your legs and breathe," she said. "My God, you're dead white."

Lilias raised her hand to her forehead. Drops of sweat came off on her fingers. She was still shaking. "What a horrible woman. You can't imagine." Caroline's hand appeared in front of her wavering vision. A linen handkerchief was hanging from it.

She took the handkerchief, wiped her face, and waited for the ground to quit rocking. When she could stand up again, she helped Caroline mount, and with the aid of the log, mounted Starfire.

Four hundred pounds, she thought. *Four hundred.* Where would she get a sum like that?

That afternoon, Lilias asked Roberts to accompany her to Herbert Adams and Son, one of the finer jewelers in London, with a shop in Ludgate Hill. It was a tidy-looking shop, with old, finely-polished brass fittings to the door, and a lovely bowed window in the front, its panes sparkling as much as the jewels displayed in their cases.

After holding open the shop door for her, Roberts stood guard outside. A chubby man in spectacles, dressed formally in a black frock coat with a high collar, bustled forward from the back of the shop. Taking in her fine, light woolen cloak and the fashionable blue silk bonnet, he gave her a broad smile.

"How can I be of service?" he asked in a quiet tone of dignity.

"Mr. Adams, I presume?" When the man nodded, Lilias reverently drew her mother's pearls from her reticule.

In the years after her mother's death, whenever she felt that there was nowhere on earth she fit, she'd open the box and look at them. Somehow, the pearls seemed a connection. As she softly touched them, she would almost feel her mother's sweet acceptance.

She bit her lip and held them out to the jeweler. "I should like to sell these," she said.

"I see." Adams's manner took on a subtle change from respectably unctuous to ever-so-slightly patronizing. He pulled a jeweler's glass from his vest pocket and polished it carefully with a handkerchief.

"Ah yes," he said with superior regret, putting the glass to his eye and examining the pearls carefully. "We must at times face these little trials."

Lilias stood in silence, waiting for his verdict, while Adams made all sorts of disappointed sounds.

"Well," he said, finally taking the glass down and shaking his head, "I wish I could give you more for them, but if you look here, and here, you'll see the imperfections. They're only worth two hundred pounds."

The merchant's daughter held out her hand for the pearls. "I know exactly what these are, Mr. Adams. They are South Sea, very rare because of their size and the perfection of each pearl. The luster is of the highest and they are beautifully matched. They're worth approximately five hundred pounds. I'm sure I could get that much by simply walking across the street to your competitor's shop."

Adams's lips thinned into a line. "Three hundred fifty," he said.

"I can't take less than four hundred fifty," she replied.

"Four hundred."

"Done," Lilias said. She hid her shaky sense of relief behind a cool inclination of her head. Papa would have been proud of her and furious with her for selling them, she thought ruefully. No matter. A few moments later, she walked out of the shop with one problem solved. But the more important one remained.

If the letters condemned Aubrey as a murderer, what would she do?

The ballroom of Lady Amelia's imposing townhouse was bright, with hundreds of candles in glittering chandeliers. The air was pleasantly warm and scented with exotic perfumes. Aubrey stood beside Lilias, accepting both the stares and the congratulations of people he'd known for many years.

He had to put behind him the niggling hurt at Lilias's reaction to his gift of the rubies. But he kept remembering her expression when he presented the rubies to her. She'd looked guilty and sad.

So it was easier to close off, to concentrate on the trial. He scanned the room for the men who would judge him.

Some of them he rather liked. Tomlinson was a friend from Oxford, with his head of prematurely white hair and his penchant for pretty tavern girls. Viscount Atherton, whose spur-of-the-moment challenges resulted in exhilarating cross-country chases or a fencing match at odd hours in someone's empty ballroom, shook his hand with enthusiasm. There were friends from school days and old friends of his parents, and they demanded introductions to his bride in tones of sincerity.

No one had given him the cut direct. The verdict must not be in yet. But he saw monocles raised appraisingly as Lilias stood beside him, beautiful and serene in an ivory brocade gown with full sleeves edged in lace, gathered at the elbow. The Drelincorte rubies sparkled from her ears and circled the creamy softness of her neck. She held herself proudly, her hand resting lightly on his arm.

After his rejection, she still stood close, but not clinging. She was remote, though, more like a comrade on the battle-field watching for the enemy than a wife in love with her hus-band.

Her discreet loyalty shamed him. Ideally, tonight should be magical for her. He had heard often enough from his mother how it was every young girl's dream to waltz in a ball-room. His reputation should protect her, not put her in danger from the rapier-sharp tongues of those judging them tonight.

Somewhere in the crush, there was a stir, and then the crowd around them parted. Margaret Hall, whom he had wooed and jilted, strode toward them, tugging an old man along beside her. Her chest dripped with diamonds and her peacock blue gown, no doubt from Worth, was trimmed about the neckline with the same. Perhaps his settlement had paid for it.

She stopped before them, eyes gleaming. Aubrey would take odds that she was up to no good. He bowed, only the slightest tip of the head, a condescension that she deserved in advance, he figured.

"Lord Breme," she said with a smile like a barracuda's. "And Lady Breme, I see. You of course know my husband, my lord Breme. I'm sure, however, that Miss . . . that Lady Breme does not. Fitzherbert, dear, allow me."

Old Fitz Carlton, Lord Atway, Aubrey realized. Old enough to be her grandfather, and a gamester at that. Well, Margaret should be pleased. She'd gotten her title, after all.

"My lord," Lilias said in her soft contralto, and Aubrey felt the tension in his neck ease at the sound. As Lord Carlton bent to kiss Lilias's hand, she executed the perfect curtsey. But Carlton was a creaky old thing who could only bend so far. Lilias's arm rose in his grasp. The lace on her sleeve fell back on the brocade.

A shriek erupted from Margaret's mouth. "Lady Breme, what is that horrible bruise on her your arm? Heavens, I am so sorry, my dear girl. How painful that looks!"

Aubrey's gaze flew to Lilias's arm. The bruise from the fall had blossomed into a riot of color, from purple to yellow, and all the shades in between. The skin looked tender and raw, as though someone had taken a stick to her there.

Margaret's hand snaked out. She tugged the sleeve farther up Lilias's arm in a blatant pretense of concern. Lilias winced at her touch.

"But I must not ask how you came by it," Margaret said, with a slow look at Aubrey. "It might make matters worse for you."

The hubbub in the room had ceased at her first strident scream. Monocles were clamped to the eye of every man in the room.

With her fan, Lilias slapped Margaret's hand away, and then pulled the sleeve down into place. "You encroach, Lady Carlton," she said with scorn. "I took a bad fall from my horse." Color stained her cheeks a bright red, and her eyes snapped. "It was an accident."

"Of course, my dear," Margaret said with a false show of sympathy and a voice that carried across the ballroom. "It's always an accident."

Aubrey heard a great intake of breath in the hushed room, as though the crowd had reacted as one. And then suddenly, a quiet voice in the back of the crowd said,

"Susannah's death was ruled an accident, too."

Aubrey caught a movement there. A man appeared, of medium height, with an athletic, trim body. He was impeccably dressed in black evening clothes. His brown hair was brushed to perfection. His face glowed with health and good humor. But in his eyes, malice and triumph gleamed.

And from his place behind the shocked and disapproving faces of the hushed group, Rupert Hindley raised his glass in salute and smiled, as though all his fortune had just been made.

Someone pushed his way through the group slowly backing off from Aubrey and Lilias. "What happened to my granddaughter?" Aubrey turned to see the Duke of Ayres frowning protectively at Lilias's right hand.

"It was an accident," Lilias said, and Aubrey could hear the anger in her voice as she pulled closer to him and deliberately placed her hand on his arm. "I was whipping-in, and almost went over a cliff." She looked at Lord Alfred with a plea in her eyes. "Aubrey saved my life, Grandfather. He really did."

Duke Alfred's deep frown smoothed over. "Breme," he nodded, and shook Aubrey's hand. The crowd around them murmured. In a low voice meant only for Aubrey's ears, he added, "My granddaughter's defense of you compels me to treat you like a man, not a beast. But if I ever see another bruise on her, I won't believe it to be an accident and I shall take measures to bring you down. Do we understand each other?"

"Perfectly," Aubrey said in a clipped voice. "I would do the same for any woman, and more for a child of my blood." He kept his face expressionless. In a frisson of fear, he wondered how, if Hindley chose to circulate another rumor, Duke Alfred would attempt to wrest Lilias from him. But for now, the duke stood at Aubrey's side, a man whose presence gave credence to Lilias's defense.

Aubrey glanced at Lilias, standing beside him, every stiff line of her body showing her distress. The crowd of people who had been backing away from him crept forward again with tentative steps. They would acknowledge him, but barely. He gripped the glass of champagne he held and raised it to his lips. Over the rim of his glass, he looked across the ballroom for Hindley, but he was gone. And so was Margaret Hall Carlton.

For her part, Lilias slowly lost the feeling that the earth was about to open and swallow her whole. She accepted the lukewarm compliments and answered polite questions by rote, for inside she was shaking.

If pride went before a fall, she'd blithely set herself up for a major tumble. Against his wishes, she had forced herself upon Aubrey, insisting that she could help. Then, like an idiot, she'd worn a gown that gave Margaret Carlton the chance to brand him a wife beater in front of the men who would judge him.

Hysteria threatened in the aftermath of the exchange. She needed a moment alone to deal with this before she began to laugh out loud, and then perhaps to cry. After another difficult half-hour mouthing pleasantries, she whispered a word to Aubrey and slipped away through the crowd to the ladies' retiring room.

Once inside the washroom, she stood alone by a large window overlooking the garden and stared into the night, letting the noise and the tension drain from her.

Ragged clouds scudded across the moon, and through their thin veil, the stars blinked at her. The heavens seemed remote and uncaring.

She reminded herself of Emma Pearson's letters. She had

to hold on to the hope of obtaining them. Leaving the room, she made her way through the crowded ballroom to find Aubrey. As she stood beside a pillar and searched for him, a small piece of paper was thrust into her hand. She turned to look, but the bearer of the note had disappeared.

Lilias felt her heart beat wildly, and she backed into an alcove behind a pillar to read the note.

"In the garden by the reflecting pool" was all it said, signed with the initials, E.P.

A sudden breeze drifted across Lilias's back. She stiffened and closed the note in her fist.

"Lady Breme?" Before she had a chance to take the first step away from the alcove, a man's hand cupped her shoulder, and she had not needed the voice to know that this was not Aubrey's hand. She wheeled at the stranger's familiarity, and found herself looking up into a handsome face, full of sympathetic charm. The man was of medium height. His body was well proportioned. His light brown hair had a slight curl and was trimmed perfectly. He looked absolutely angelic and kind. But his eyes, a hawk-like amber-yellow, added a jarring note of rapacity to the perfect picture he presented.

He executed a perfect bow. "I didn't mean to startle you, my lady. But I feared there was no other way to introduce myself. My name is Hindley. Rupert Hindley. I'm sure Lord Breme has told you of me, but you must not believe what he says."

She backed away, thinking wildly that Lucifer, too, had a pleasing shape.

He held out a hand, his deep brown eyes conveying a tragic concern. "Hear me out, my lady, I beg you, for your own safety. If your husband's venom affected only me, I wouldn't ask it. But I must warn you of the danger you are in, before it's too late."

"What danger?" Lilias forced her hands to lie still against her side. The muscles of her legs tensed for flight, but she had to stay and listen. If, even from this man, she could get a clear picture of Susannah's death, then maybe she could bring the truth to light.

"Breme's probably told you terrible things about his first wife. Lies, all lies. Susannah was wonderful. She was so sweet and clever and beautiful. Everybody loved her, and I most of all."

Hindley brushed his hand over his eyes and sighed. "We grew up together, had you known that? We were very close all our lives, soulmates really. Our love for each other was pure, a thing of the spirit. He hated her for it, and me too. He was mad with jealousy, you see."

Hindley leaned toward her, his voice low and throbbing with emotion. "You are an innocent, Lady Breme. You don't realize how that man can destroy everything you hold dear in life and cleverly get away with it. That is why I had to warn you. Don't trust him like Susannah did. Don't try to protect him. It will kill you." He looked past her, toward the ballroom, and raised his finger to his lips. "Shh. Someone's coming."

With a melting look, he squeezed her right shoulder, the one she'd fallen on. She bit her lip in pain. "If the time comes when you need a friend, send for me." Quickly, he passed her his card. Lilias glanced at the direction written on it and then watched him walk down the hall, head high and shoulders squared, looking for all the world a perfect, honorable gentleman.

Halfway across the ballroom, Lilias could see Aubrey lift his head, searching, probably for her.

She glanced back down at the note, her heart thudding. *Go to Aubrey,* she thought. *Tell him everything.*

But what if Emma Pearson left before she could get to the garden? Or if Aubrey would insist on coming with her? Emma Pearson would run off and sell the letters to somebody else. Hindley, maybe.

Clutching her reticule, Lilias felt the reassuring crinkle of bank notes. She peeked down the hallway to make certain Rupert Hindley was gone, then slipped out through the French doors into the darkness.

The wind whipped her skirts as she ran down the steps to the path leading out into the garden. The garden was silent, deserted, cold. The sniggling wind clutched at her hair, the bare twigs of the overhanging trees snapped and creaked. She hurried past them toward the reflecting pool. An unreasoning dread seized her.

The moon slipped behind a cloud, plunging the garden into darkness. The cold seeped into her bones. She stopped, her heart pounding against her throat, and hugged herself in an ineffectual protection against the wind.

Slowly, her eyes grew accustomed to the darkness. She began to move. The lapping of water told her she'd come close to the reflecting pool. A glimmer of light shone through the ragged edge of the cloud, dimly revealing the pool, the high evergreen hedge around it, and an upright figure sitting on one end of the high-backed, gothic bench beside the pool.

"Miss Pearson?" she called low.

The figure did not turn. Lilias crept closer. It was definitely a tall woman sitting on that bench, leaning a bit against the armrest.

"Miss Emma Pearson?" Lilias called again, walking forward until she stood in front of the bench. The woman did not stir. Lilias bent over her, worried now.

"Miss Pearson, are you ill?" She gently shook her

shoulder. The moon came out from the clouds in full force, flooding the garden with light.

Emma Pearson's mouth gaped in silent agony, as though she was straining for breath. Her sightless eyes, frozen in the moment of death, stared up at Lilias.

Chapter Twenty-Nine

Lilias screamed. A strong hand clamped over her mouth, cutting off the sound. She struggled, clawing and biting, mad with terror, but it was no use.

"Shh . . . it's me."

Aubrey's voice. She sank back against him, almost gagging with relief. His hand slipped from her mouth to her shoulders. She wheeled and flung herself into his arms. If she could have crawled into his body, she would have done so.

Glancing at the path behind him, he pulled her into the shrubbery surrounding the pool. She began to shake in belated reaction.

"My God, you've got goose bumps all over you. Here, I brought your cloak." He pulled away long enough to wrap it round her shoulders.

She tightened it around her, grateful for its warmth. He tugged her close, and rubbed his hands up and down her arms.

"Somebody killed her, Aubrey."

He kissed the top of her head. "I know. Can you stay here alone? I want to find out what happened, if I can. I'll be gone just for a minute."

"No, I'm going over there with you." She gulped and looked up at him. "She was waiting for me, Aubrey. She has some letters. They're important."

He narrowed his eyes. "What kind of letters?"

"They're Susannah's. From Hindley, I'd guess. They might be evidence for the trial."

His face went absolutely still. But the moonlight revealed his eyes. They burned down at her.

"Stay where you are. Do you understand?"

She nodded slowly, her gaze locked with his. Aubrey moved out into the dappled light, his movements lithe and absolutely soundless. Another figure appeared at his side, dressed in dark clothing, with a dark turban round his head. Ram and Aubrey spoke in low tones as Aubrey knelt by the body and swiftly examined it, checking the pockets of Emma Pearson's gown and her reticule.

"Get the coach," Lilias heard him tell Ram.

"And if there's trouble?" Ram asked him.

"You'll have to keep an ear out for it. If it's bad, try the Delhi Diversion. Somehow, we'll get to you at Pall Mall."

"All right. I'll use Boodles. They're always game for mischief."

As Lilias tried in vain to decipher this murky code, Ram disappeared into the shadows. Aubrey continued his search of the body for what seemed an eternity.

Then his head lifted. All his muscles seemed to vibrate with an alert attention, as though he were a wild animal scenting the breeze for enemies. It seemed but an instant before he was at her side again, grabbing her hand and pulling her farther along the path, toward the lawn behind the garden.

"Did you find anything?" Lilias braved his anger because she had to know.

"No."

She looked back over her shoulder. "Maybe she has them in her corset. I could go back and look."

"No." He tugged harder.

She picked up the pace, tripping a little as she tried to keep up. Then she heard what Aubrey must have heard before. Voices, coming from the house. Men's voices called back and forth, and someone's forceful tones rang out louder than the rest, issuing orders.

Aubrey grabbed her hand tighter. "Pick up your skirts and run like hell."

She sped beside him, breathless, confused. She heard a rip as the hem of her petticoat caught on the branch of a thorn bush. She tugged it free. In the darkness, something loomed in front of them, a thick stone wall at least eight feet from the ground.

"You don't mind heights, do you?" Aubrey said. In the moonlight, his eyes glinted dark and reckless.

She shook her head.

"Grab hold when you reach the top. Ready?" His strong hands clamped her waist and thrust. She hit the top of the wall, sprawled on her belly, scrabbled for a handhold to keep from pitching over, and felt him pull himself up beside her.

She glanced over her shoulder and saw men racing into the garden. Some had already reached Emma Pearson's body and knelt beside it. Others began to fan out, their lanterns held high.

An instant later, Aubrey jumped down the other side of the wall and held up his arms. "Jump," he said softly.

She took a deep breath and jumped. Aubrey caught her, fell back, and rolled to protect her. Behind her in the garden, one man called out close to the wall—"there's something here, a piece of white cloth, it looks, lacy—stuck on a branch."

The outcry grew louder as the men ran closer.

"He's got some of my petticoat," she whispered in fear as Aubrey grabbed her hand and pulled her along at a run.

"No matter. Much better than your gown," he said, as they raced down Grosvenor Place.

A whistle sounded from the top of the wall, and a man shouted, "There they are!"

Her heart leaped in her chest. Aubrey pulled her into a small side street, and kept running.

"Out there! They've turned down the street!"

Others must have joined the search, others fresh for a run. Lilias gasped in fear. The stitch in her side hurt with each painful breath.

"Come on," Aubrey said in a low command.

She clutched his hand tighter and they raced through Mayfair like foxes from hounds. With a burst of effort, they flew across New Bond Street and onto Piccadilly. As they zig-zagged onto St James, the men's voices behind them gained in volume. Lilias clutched her side and forced her feet to run. Her lungs strained for each breath.

Careening left onto Pall Mall, she noticed a wagon standing sideways, blocking the street. Behind it, a crowd of young men dressed in evening clothing sang and shouted together. They sounded drunk.

Aubrey shot her look and gave a breathless laugh. "Don't worry about them," he said, and kept running.

She didn't need to be told.

"Stop there!"

"Up ahead. Stop where you are!"

The men behind them shouted with voices hoarse from chasing them. She glanced back once and dread took her hard. Those men were gaining fast.

Aubrey clutched Lilias's hand harder. They sped past the drunks and the wagon, which at close range smelled rank.

Ahead of them, Ram Dass sat at the top of the carriage beside the coachman.

"Hie up, old chaps," one of the drunks said. "Put your backs into it."

"For Boodles and England!" The men cheered and heaved. The wagon overturned, spilling its contents into the street. The crowd of drunkards cheered and ran off.

Aubrey shoved Lilias into the coach and followed her, flinging the door closed as it took off down the street. As the coach wheeled around the corner toward home, Lilias stuck her head out the window.

In the dim lamplight, she saw the men who had been following them slip and fall into the contents of the wagon.

Aubrey collapsed in laughter beside her.

"What was that awful smell?" she said, feeling a grin spread across her own lips. He looked so young, so happy. It hit her that this is what he had probably been like before that terrible night in India. What he should be now.

Her heart wrenched with a deep, painful twist. In the clear perception of that instant, she nearly gasped out loud. Dear God, she loved this man. To the depths of her soul, she loved this man.

"The night soil wagon," Aubrey said, wheezing with laughter. "Oh, God, what a stench! Those uniforms will never get clean."

"Aubrey . . ." She turned in the coach and stared at him. "Were those men following us the constabulary?"

"Remind me to make a large donation within the week," Aubrey said with a grin.

"But how . . . and when . . . ?"

He shrugged. "As to how, it was the best Ram and I could come up with on the spot. As to when . . ." His face took on an ominous frown. "I saw you standing in that alcove talking to

Hindley. I saw you walking out into the garden and I followed."

In the dim light from a street lamp, Lilias watched Aubrey with a sort of awful fascination. The muscle in his jaw twitched in the most amazing fashion.

"Aubrey . . ."

He turned to her, fast as lightning, fixing her with a glare that ought to have burnt her to a crisp.

"What the hell were you doing out there alone?" The soft intensity of his words was worse than the loudest shout.

She pursed her lips and glared back. "Counter-intelligence."

He whipped toward her in one of those moves she could never anticipate. He grabbed her shoulders and shook her twice, none too gently. "What were you thinking, Lilias?"

"I'm doing my best to help," she said, and bit her lip to keep it from trembling.

"To help," Aubrey repeated. Everything he'd held inside him jumbled, hot, and about to boil over. "I can't deal with this," he said roughly. Worry and anger and lust rose in one molten force, thrusting for release.

"Foolish, brave, loyal wife," he said. He yanked her to him and kissed her, a deep, hard demand of lips and tongue. He kissed her face, her lips, the curve of her neck, drawing in the sweet taste of her skin, wanting her with an urgency that knew no bounds. His hands and his mouth roamed over her body, exploring every inch of her softness.

"Do you see?" he asked her. "Do you understand now?"

His hands feverishly tugged at the sleeves of her gown, bringing them down far enough to bare her breasts. He bent his head to it, licking, suckling without thought as he pulled up the skirts, the starched crinolines, found the tie to her drawers, and slid them off.

When he touched her, she cried out, that longing keen of desire he found the sweetest music in the world. "Do you know how much I want you? Put your hand on me." He was straining and aching for her. She touched him and he groaned, mad to get closer.

Her legs opened to him, cradling him, rising against him as he covered her, working the buttons of his trousers open. He pushed himself against her, wanting in, forgetting caution and duty in the need that clawed at him for culmination. His hands worked to help her, fumbling at the buttons. He sprang free, and rose above her, straining for some semblance of control, finding none. He stared at her face, her body there in the light of a passing lamp, then gone into shadow, illuminated, then dark like the deepest mystery. She was magnificent in her passion.

"Inside you, Lilias," he said, raising his head to look at her. In the dim light of the street lamps, her eyes looked back at him from a pale face. "I have to be inside."

"Yes," she said, solemn, deep eyes acknowledging.

The carriage swayed to a stop. The streetlight beside it shone down on them. Dazzled in the sudden light, he looked outside, then down at Lilias and his own body, frozen in shock at the near wreckage. Reality crashed down on him like a boulder.

"My God, what have I done?" he said, separating from her, rising on his knees and fumbling with his fly buttons. She lay beneath him, her dress a crumbled wreck, her breasts and her long legs exposed to the lamplight. She looked dazed, helpless to help herself. He pulled her to a sitting position and put her bodice to rights. Hastily, he straightened her skirt.

"We're at Drelincorte House," he told her, and smoothed back her hair. There was no time to fix it. He looked at the creases in his trousers, felt his tie askew. He wagered they looked drunk, untidy, debauched. With the ache in his groin, he thought it a rather tawdry joke.

"We're a mess," he said. *In more ways than one,* he thought.

The coach door opened. As more light flowed in from the lamps, Lilias glanced at Aubrey and winced. He'd gone back to looking grim.

Everything came back to her—misery at the ball, then terror, then the release in the carriage. Aubrey over her, kissing, touching, the madness, the glory of it. She couldn't keep up with all the changes, and now they were back to the beginning of the evening, only worse.

Aubrey led her into the library and closed the door with more force than necessary. In silence, he studied her face, tipping her chin this way and that, looking at the scratches on her cheek from the vines she'd run up against, and the scrape on her arm over the bruise. He swallowed convulsively, shaking his head.

His voice came out strangled. "You'd better begin at the beginning. And *don't* leave out any of the good parts."

A maid slipped in with a warm basin of water, soap, and a towel. At Aubrey's soft command, she returned with ointment for the scratches. After he dismissed her, he washed and doctored Lilias's face and her arm while she told him about Emma Pearson and the letters.

"I only wish we could have gone back and checked again," she said glumly.

"And gotten caught searching the body? She didn't have the letters anymore. Damn it, Lilias, don't you realize that's why she was killed? Whoever killed her knew she was to meet you. He left her there for you, or both of us, to find. I'll wager the constable, informed by an anonymous tip, showed up in that garden a few minutes later. I'd lay good odds he was to find us with her and come to his own conclusions. Counter-intelligence," he scoffed. "Counter-productive is what it was. Why the hell didn't you tell me about it?"

"She said to tell no one. And I thought . . ."

"Go on," he said.

"She hated you, Aubrey, and I think she was mad. I was afraid she'd destroy the letters if she thought I'd use them to clear your name."

Halfway through her recitation, Ram came in and quietly shut the door. Lilias told him and Aubrey about the meeting that took place in Hyde Park.

"You took Lady Caroline with you?" Ram's face was suffused with a ruddy color and his eyes were furious. His voice was as clipped and authoritative as any English aristocrat's voice.

It came to Lilias that there was something rather strange about how Ram Dass changed from Indian servant to English gentleman in the blink of an eye. How had he been admitted into Boodles, one of the most exclusive men's clubs? And how had he convinced those drunken boys to play that trick on the constabulary? But with her weariness and all the other frightening events of the night, this was just one more confusing puzzle. She blinked and tried to concentrate on Ram's question.

"Caroline came to hold my horse. Emma Pearson was adamant that I bring nobody to the actual meeting."

"Lady Caroline is a sweet, vulnerable young girl," Ram Dass said.

"Lady Caroline's as old as I am, and she's not nearly so vulnerable as you think," Lilias replied.

"Ram is very protective of Lady Caroline," Aubrey said.

"I am not," Ram Dass said through clenched teeth. "It's just that she's had a difficult life. And even though you weren't killed outright, if anyone had seen the two of you, and then seen you with a dead woman, Lady Caroline's already questionable reputation would have been in shreds. It was folly to involve her in your schemes."

"So the two of you out-raced your grooms and the detective I'd assigned to protect you." Aubrey threw those words into the mix, the muscle in his jaw still twitching. "You rode into a secluded area of Hyde Park, where anything could have happened to you. God, Lilias. I should just lock you in your room and be done with it. Or send you home to Breme."

"You can't send me home, Aubrey. You need me here to help you."

"As you did tonight?"

Lilias stared from one grim face to the other. Her heart sank. "I'm sorry," she whispered. "I wanted to help, and instead I've made of muck of it."

Aubrey poured three tumblers of brandy and handed them round. "That you did," he said, tossing the brandy down. "But Hindley is a clever enemy."

"Hindley killed her." Lilias swallowed in misery, letting the warm, sharp liquid burn its way down her throat and into her stomach.

Aubrey nodded. "Of course, there's the alternative."

She looked up sharply. "The alternative being?"

"That I killed her and took the letters, of course."

"Don't say that," she said low. "Not even in jest."

Aubrey shrugged. "With all the skulking about you've been doing, I'm surprised you haven't come to that conclusion yourself. Now," he said, cutting off her protest, "tell me again about your conversation with Hindley. Try to remember every word he said."

She did her best. They reconstructed the events of the evening until the clock struck the hour before dawn. Aubrey looked up, his eyes shadowed, the new morning's bristle on his chin gleaming gold in the lamplight.

"It's late. We've done what we can for the night."

"Aubrey, I think Emma Pearson's letters would have exonerated you. Otherwise, why would Hindley kill her? He wanted to stop you from getting them. We have to go to Hindley's house and find them. Here." She reached into her reticule and gave him the calling card. "I've his direction. He's near Mayfair, on the outskirts, in a townhouse."

Aubrey stared at her, his hands on his hips. "I am apprised of his direction," he said, refusing the paper. "And what is this *we*? *You* are going nowhere but to bed."

"But Aubrey—"

"Enough!" His shout stopped Lilias in mid-sentence. He rang the bell. "Because you kept vital information from me, we've already had one near-disaster. I'll not listen to another ridiculous scheme."

A footman knocked and entered.

"Have Lady Breme's maid attend her," Aubrey said, and turned his back to her.

Without a word, Lilias walked out of the library.

Jane was waiting for her in her chamber. She clucked over Lilias's cuts and her torn petticoat while Lilias's mind whirled.

Her scheme had gone wrong, but Aubrey should still listen to her. Hindley was obsessed with Susannah. And a man obsessed might well keep letters from the woman he loved, even if they exonerated his enemy. He'd simply keep them where he thought they'd never be found.

Jane helped her into her nightgown and gave her a drink of warm milk. "His lordship asked me to bring it to you. Anything else, my lady?"

Lilias drank the milk. It was soothing, with a slightly medicinal taste. Maybe Ram put something in it.

She was beginning to realize how intricate a mind Aubrey had. Tonight, he saw her in conversation with his enemy, saw her leave for the garden, and in the minute before he came after her, he planned a counter-strategy with Ram, just in case it was needed.

Perhaps he was right. She'd been nothing but trouble for him from the beginning. She wondered if he'd ever be able to look at her again the way he had before she'd disobeyed him and arrived on his doorstep in a gypsy caravan.

Chapter Thirty

Jane left. Lilias stared at the canopy above her bed. The . . . incident . . . in the carriage was an aberration. Nothing had changed between them. She tossed, hurting and restless, in a bed too large and cold.

Fury did not make Aubrey deny what he seemed to need so desperately. He was more than furious tonight in the carriage, and it didn't stop him. If they hadn't arrived home, he no doubt would have given them both some relief from the loneliness and the need.

Her head ached with unsettled questions and her eyes ached with unshed tears. But a great weariness settled over her. *Ram doctored the milk,* she thought and closed her eyes. At the edge of consciousness, the answer hovered, but she gave in to the medicine and let sleep take her.

The next morning she awoke heavy-lidded and still cold. Dully, she dressed and called for tea. But the very thought of swallowing anything sent her racing for the chamber pot. She felt somewhat better afterward.

Jane came in with the tea service, her face serious, as though she were entering a sickroom. "I'll just put it here, my lady," she said, and poured tea into the fine porcelain cup.

"Jane, where is his lordship?"

Jane finished pouring. "He left early this morning, my lady."

"Was there a message for me?"

Jane shook her head, her eyes on the tray. "No, my lady."

She slipped from the room quietly.

Aubrey was gone. And he'd left no message.

Lilias took up the teacup in a jerky movement.

"My lady?" Roberts entered the dining room and came toward her, holding a silver salver with a letter on it.

She thanked him and opened the letter. It was from Squire Trevell: *We have lost the child. Pamela begs you to come at once.*

Aubrey returned to Drelincorte House that afternoon, drained by another tension-filled meeting with a worried-looking Sir Samuel. He waited impatiently as Ram rapped on the front knocker. The butler seemed to take forever to open the door.

He wanted to see his wife. Once again, he'd been a beast. She was scarce more than a girl, and she'd braved the barracudas of the ton and the horror of coming upon a corpse in the darkness. She had trusted him enough to follow him in a terrifying chase through the London streets as they tried to escape from men who could have killed them or caught them at any moment. And what had he done to reward her courage and loyalty? Almost ravished her in a carriage and yelled at her afterwards.

When he wasn't crazed with fear or lust or self-disgust, he was a rational man. He needed to explain to her, but he didn't know where to start. He didn't even understand himself, anymore.

The butler opened the door hastily upon a scene of chaos resembling his flight to London from Breme not so long ago.

Carrying a small trunk, a footman ran down the stairs. Jane followed him, rapping out instructions and folding a warm woolen shawl.

"What is this, Hibson?" Aubrey demanded of the butler.

"I can explain." Lilias ran down the stairway. "Come into the library."

He followed her inside and shut the door on all the noise and confusion outside in the hall.

Lilias's face was pale and drawn. She had deep circles beneath her eyes. With a pang of guilt, he saw how much thinner she looked.

She handed him a letter. "I must go to her immediately," she said.

He read the letter carefully, and looked up, confused. "But Trevell says in time she'll recover. There's no doubt of that. Surely, you can wait until the trial is over."

She shook her head. "She's suffered terribly throughout this pregnancy, and not just in her body." Lilias's lips trembled as she took his hand. "Her mind is not steady, Aubrey. I'm the only one she can turn to. And more importantly, I made a promise to her. I can't break it, or she'll have no one she can trust. I have to go."

He shook his head slowly. "John says she will recover. You can be with her in three weeks, Lilias. I want you here until then."

She stared at her hands. "I can go to Tilden and be back in four days, five at most. No thanks to me, it went better than it might have last night. Your old friends are still gathered around you. You don't need me, Aubrey. But Pamela does."

"Don't need you?" *I need you just to breathe.* He clasped her arms, saw her flinch, and realized he'd just squeezed the bruise. He dropped his hands and stood like a stunned bull, with nothing and nobody to fight. The days were ticking down. His life was trickling away to nothing, and she said her sister needed her more.

He drew himself up. "Where does your allegiance lie?" He couldn't beg. He wouldn't.

She gestured toward him, a supplication that made him want to go to her and hold her and tell her it was all right. Desperate to push through to her, he tried again. "Pamela despises me. She'll do her best to turn you from me. All she needs is time and your sympathy."

Lilias shook her head and looked at him in anguish. "No one and nothing could turn me against you, Aubrey. You have to know that."

"I know nothing," he said, hot with misery and frustration. "As my wife, you owe your first loyalty to me."

She gazed at him for a long moment, her eyes large and tragic. "You have it. But I must go," she whispered.

He was losing her. He wanted to howl his fury, to smash something huge with his bare hands. His voice was a harsh, bestial cry. "It's either me or her, Lilias. Choose."

Tears welled in her eyes and ran down her pale cheeks like silent rain. "I can't."

The world turned cold and lifeless. He tried to shut himself off from it and all the hurt it contained. "Then you've made your choice," he said.

She started to speak, then shut her mouth with an audible click. Her brow wrinkled, as though she had just now begun to work a knotty problem. He could almost feel the wheels whirring in her brain. *She's going to change her mind,* he thought with a welling of relief. But when she looked at him again, her eyes narrowed.

"Why didn't you come to my bed, Aubrey?"

"What?" Where the hell had that come from?

"I'm trying to figure out why you sent me to sleep as far

away from you as possible, yet wanted me with rather amazing insistence on the seat of a carriage."

"I'm sorry for that," he broke in. "I should never have begun what would only endanger you."

She nodded slowly. "Yes. That's what I'm beginning to see. You won't make love to me because carrying your child makes me a target?"

"Yes," he said.

"Did you never think that I might see it differently? That no matter what happens, I would want your child to love? That I would want every chance I could get to sleep in your arms?"

He wanted to throw his arms around her, but half of him wanted to shake her, too. "That's not what we're talking about here," he reminded her. "We're talking about you leaving me today."

But her gaze held wisdom and understanding and a little bit of anger "No. It's exactly what we're talking about. You don't trust me, Aubrey. So you make all the decisions—to come to London without me, to send me down the hall with no more explanation than 'it's better this way.' That I must stay, because if I go, I have so little judgment that Pamela will convince me not to come back." She moved closer and raised her hand to his cheek, a soft benediction. Her eyes were sad. "Until you learn to trust me, Aubrey, we have nothing much to hold on to. And we must hold on very hard."

His heart twisted. She would leave him when he needed her most.

Trust.

"You'd better go," he said, staring at the floor. "Only, come back to me. Please."

She flung herself into his arms. "I love you," she whispered. "I shall always be with you."

Her fingers traveled over his cheeks, his brows, his lips. He looked up to find her eyes filled with tears. And love.

Blindly, he pulled her into his arms and lowered his head. Her lips parted in a sigh and he took the sweet balm of her spirit. Please, God, it would be enough to hold him until her return.

Late that night, Aubrey worked the pick delicately until the lock on the back door of Hindley's townhouse gave a click. He and Ram had watched Hindley's carriage pull away, then waited for half an hour until they heard no sounds at all from the house.

Lilias had been right about Hindley. When she returned, he'd have the letters and they would open them together.

Ram moved in the shadows behind him, ready to signal him at the first sign of Hindley's returning carriage. "Good luck," he said low.

Aubrey slipped through the door. The house was silent and dark, the servants all asleep. He slid noiselessly through the kitchen and the pantry, into the long, narrow hallway. It gave off onto several rooms, but he'd been in enough of these buildings to know approximately where to find the library, halfway down the hall.

He opened the door and slipped into the room. From the corner of his eye, he caught the movement of something behind him and swerved to his left. A hard and heavy club glanced off his head. As he fell to the floor, hands seized him. He fought, getting in a good clip to the stomach of one thug, kicking another's groin. There were too many of them, and they made him pay before they trussed his legs and arms tight, the rope stinging through his clothes.

"Go see if he's brought his men," a voice rapped.

Aubrey raised his head and gave a long, loud whistle

through bleeding lips. Outside the house, he heard running steps, and then Hindley's hired crew returning to the house.

Struggling, shaking his head in an unsuccessful effort to clear it, Aubrey squinted up into sudden light.

Rupert Hindley smiled down at him, his hazel raptor's eyes gleaming in satisfaction, a brace of candles in his hand. "My dear cousin, did you think I wouldn't expect you?"

Someone else in the carriage, then, Hindley's height, and dressed in his clothing.

"How courteous of you to take the bait," Hindley continued. "For what reason do you come, I wonder?" Hindley knelt, and fumbled in the pockets of Aubrey's jacket. "You wish to rob me of some letters, perhaps? Poor, helpless madman, with no memory of the murder he committed. What a shame you had to ruin the picture you and your wife presented last night. Ah, here we are."

Smiling, he lifted the pistol from Aubrey's right pocket. "No, I think the story's better if we say you came to kill me. With me gone, there would be no case against you, would there? But luckily, I was awake. A struggle ensued, and you know the rest."

Hindley aimed the gun at Aubrey's head.

Aubrey shut his eyes and waited, sick and numb. Lilias, he thought in despair. What will happen to her?

Nothing happened. He opened his eyes and tried his best to turn his aching head in Hindley's direction. He glared at him.

"Do it," Aubrey said. "Get it over with, you son of a bitch."

Hindley smiled. "Oh, no, old fellow. A quick demise would be too easy for you. You deserve to suffer the public shame and the private agony."

Removing his coat, Hindley hung it neatly from a wall

sconce. He aimed Aubrey's pistol, and shot through the edge of the coat's arm.

Then he put the coat on again and called the men who'd knocked Aubrey down and tied him up. "Get the constable," he told them. "This man shot me. You saw it and came to my aid."

"Yes, Mr. Hindley."

"Not for long, Smythe," Hindley said to the burly footman. "Soon, you'll address me as Lord Breme."

"Thank God you've come, Lilias," John Trevell said as they stood outside Pamela's door. "She grieves so hard, I'm afraid she will never recover. Please, help her."

Lilias nodded and entered the room quietly. Pamela lay silent in the bed, pale and exhausted, staring at the wall. Tears slid down her cheeks, unnoticed. Lilias felt the first stirring of fear as her mind raced through all the illnesses she'd nursed, and what possible symptoms the doctor might have missed. From what she'd read in the case history he had left for her, there were no physical problems.

"My dearest sister," she said, coming close. "Let me help you."

Pamela closed her eyes and took a deep breath. "There's nothing you can do, Lily. But I'm glad you're here, anyway."

"Pamela," Lilias said, "why won't you try? The doctor said that you'll have healthy babes someday. All you have to do is get well."

"I can't ever have a child," Pamela said in a choked whisper.

"Of course you can. Your body is perfectly capable of it."

Pamela shook her head. "God won't let me have another child. I don't deserve one."

As Lilias tried to understand, her stomach churned with anxiety. "Why not?"

Pamela turned her face to the wall.

Lilias took Pamela's limp hand and stroked it. While Lilias tried for calm, she felt the fear coil in her belly. Something far worse than a miscarriage was destroying her sister. "If you don't talk about this, you will never be free of it."

Pamela shut her eyes. "I cannot tell you."

"If you love John at all, think of how he feels, watching you like this, fearing you'll never get any better."

The struggle wracked Pamela's face. "He'll hate me when he knows."

"Then I won't tell him."

Lifting her gaze to Lilias, Pamela took a deep breath. "I'm a murderer. I killed my baby."

Lilias grabbed her hand. "No. John told me what happened. You were fine one minute, and the next, in pain. You miscarried. You didn't do anything to hurt your baby."

Pamela's eyes were wild with guilt. "I did," she insisted. "Half the time, I hated it. I never wanted it to be born." Her voice dropped to a whisper. "I hated it for what its father did to me."

"Good God," Lilias breathed. The world turned upside down on its axis. "John?" she asked. "Did John do anything to hurt you, Pamela?"

"Not John," Pamela said in a dead voice. "Richard Landham."

Chapter Thirty-One

Lilias choked down the bile that rose to her throat. "You have to tell me what happened."

"It won't do any good," Pamela said in a hopeless voice. "But you should know everything. You should know how wicked I am." She paused and plucked at the sheet with restless, thin fingers. "Do you remember the card party, when John kept me here for a week after and told everyone I was sick?"

Lilias nodded, not daring to breathe for fear Pamela would stop talking.

"I flirted a bit that night. With Richard Landham. I felt pretty and I'd had a glass of sherry before dinner. I knew Papa liked him. You had done everything for the family while I had just sat at home, sewing and helping with the cooking. I'd seen him looking at me before. I thought maybe he'd offer for me and Papa would have a bit of money from the marriage settlement and you might have a dowry. He seemed to like how I looked that night. He'd chosen me for his partner at whist. I left to use the ladies' retiring room upstairs. He was waiting when I came out. He . . . he kissed me."

Unaware of her movements, Pamela rubbed at her

mouth with the back of her hand.

"I allowed it because I thought he would ask me, after. But it scared me, the way he did it."

Lilias put a hand up to her mouth, remembering Landham's assault.

"I told him to stop," Pamela said. "He laughed and grabbed me. He pulled me into a bedchamber. It was dark." Her voice rose in a wild quaver. "I tried to fight him, but I couldn't. I couldn't stop him! He hurt me. Laughing all the time. He told me I wanted . . . that."

Pamela shuddered. "I felt as though he'd ripped me in half. There was blood after, all over me . . . on my gown, on the bed. What would people have thought if they'd seen me?"

Lilias couldn't stop a cry of pain and fury.

"He left me for John to find," Pamela said and covered her face. "I have never gotten over the shame of that. The best man I know found me lying there, knowing I'd done *that thing* with Landham. John was so good to me. He kept me with him until I could go home again. He told me he would marry me, in case there was a child. That he would love the child for its mother's sake, because he said . . ."

A sob escaped her lips. "He said he had always loved me. That he would always love me and protect me. And he has." She stared up at Lilias with a look of guilt and sorrow that wrenched Lilias's heart.

Pamela's voice throbbed with fierce emotion. "When I heard Landham was dead, I was glad. Glad, I tell you! He deserved it. But I was afraid the child would be like him. I knew I had to sleep, to eat, for the baby's sake. But I couldn't, worrying about it, not knowing whether it would be a demon child or it would be the sweetest babe in the world because John and I would love it."

In the long pause that followed, the only sound in the

room was the dripping of rain from the eaves. Lilias sat silent, afraid to speak, praying that Pamela would get it all out.

"But how could a child learn to be strong and good with a mother like me, Lily? I thought about it all the time. I should have fought harder, I should have screamed, I should have found something—a weapon—or used my nails. I was nothing—a helpless, useless creature. I failed my baby. I don't deserve to be a mother. I don't deserve to live. Never once," she whispered, "in all the time we've been wed. Never once has John come to my bed and demanded what was his by right. Because he can't bear to hurt me. Because he thinks that someday I'll be able to look upon the act with joy. Why would he be so good, when he should despise me for what I did to my baby?"

"You didn't kill your baby. Landham did, because of what he did to you." Lilias felt the rage rise in her, hot and eager. If Landham weren't dead already, she'd have taken a gun to his head. "Did you have a chance to scream?"

Pamela shook her head, her eyes wide. "He put his hand over my mouth. I could barely breathe."

"How big was Landham? How big are you?"

Pamela stared at her. "He *was* big, Lily, and so heavy. I struggled against him. I tried to kick him, but my skirts were in the way. I tried to get my hands free. He held them over my head and he covered my mouth with his own. My lip bled. My God, he hit me. I saw stars. I'd forgotten all that."

Lilias nodded grimly. "You could never have stopped him, Pamela. The only thing that would have stopped him was a bullet." Then she gave a start.

Pamela, victimized and ravaged, forgot the details. Pamela blamed herself.

Lilias had once read that victims often did that.

353

She'd been right all along. Aubrey was innocent.

By the next day, Pamela asked to see John. Lilias never heard what they said to one another in the quiet bedroom, but when she entered afterwards, Pamela smiled for the first time.

Dr. Thomas came and pronounced Pamela on the beginning of the road to recovery.

But as grateful as she was, Lilias had a difficult time pretending to be cheerful when she was so miserable inside.

Her parting from Aubrey tore at her heart.

"You've done me so much good," Pamela said. "If I could just have another day with you, Lily, it would mean so much to me."

"I have to leave."

"Can't you stay for just one more day?"

Lilias shook her head. "Aubrey needs me."

John Trevell stepped quietly into the room. Love softened his gaze when it met Pamela's. Then his look turned sober. He held out the paper from London. "Lilias, the newspaper just came by post. You need to read this before you go back."

She took the *Times* from him and scanned the headline. "Earl Imprisoned for Attempted Murder," it read. A drawing of Aubrey was placed right beneath the headline, his scars grossly exaggerated to make him look indeed a beast. She read on, her hands clenched on the paper in an effort to keep it from shaking. When she was through, she shut her eyes and brought her hands to her lips.

The story said he'd gone to Hindley's townhouse and tried to kill him.

No, no. She couldn't imagine Aubrey shooting anyone in cold blood. She reread the article to make sure.

There was no report of letters or their damning evidence.

If the constabulary had found them, they would have told the world.

She read the article a third time through. Hindley said there was a long, terrible struggle and the pistol went off in Aubrey's hand and the bullet went through Hindley's coat sleeve.

And then Hindley's servants came in and subdued Aubrey.

This story was making less and less sense. The servants should have heard the struggle before the gun went off. And Lilias would lay a hefty wager that if Hindley and Aubrey struggled at close range, Aubrey, taller, stronger, and faster than any man she'd ever known, would have been able to plant a facer that would have leveled Hindley. If he had wanted to kill the man, he surely would have shot something more substantial than a coat sleeve.

Her shoulders straightened and a strong, steady sense of determination filled her bones and her will with iron. She looked at John and Pamela, sitting side by side in the bed, holding hands and gazing at her with such concern.

"Please have the coach prepared, John. I must go home at once."

"Yes, of course." John sprang into action, ringing for a footman and issuing orders. "Her ladyship must stop at a posting inn and get some job horses. Have Cook pack a lunch— she'll not want to stop for more than a short respite while they put the fresh horses in the traces."

Later that day, the coach swayed as it rattled along the London road. The city lay just to the east of them, perhaps an hour away now.

They were holding Aubrey at Newgate, the paper said. Lilias shuddered, thinking what misery and filth must surround him in that squalid horror of a prison. She would take what money she could for bribes and pack anything for him from home that might make him comfortable.

She was so deep in her thoughts that the first shot from a pistol only half-pierced her consciousness. But when the second gun cracked sharply, she jumped and looked out the window. As the coach slowed to a halt, she saw a large group of men surrounding the vehicle. Black handkerchiefs masked their faces and their hats were pulled low over their heads.

"What the bloody hell's the meaning of this?" Tom Coachman roared.

"If ye don't shut yer trap and follow orders, we'll finish off the man we just shot and kill you, too." The thug brandished his weapon. "Ye come with us," he told Lilias.

As she watched, horror-stricken, Tom leaped from the coach box straight down on the highwayman. The force of his weight carried both bodies to the ground. Horses milled, kicking and prancing around the heaving duet, while Tom pummeled the man.

"My lady," Tom yelled at the top of his lungs. "Run!"

Lilias didn't waste any time. Sliding to the far side of the coach, she hit the ground at a crouch and took off for the trees to the left of the road. If she could only get to the woods where she could hide, Tom's sacrifice would not be in vain.

Her breath came sharp in her lungs. Her feet stumbled over briars and rocks, slowing her. Her hair had come down and flew wild behind her. Her eyes stung from the wind. She didn't dare look behind her, not on this uneven ground. Despite the pounding of her heart, she heard curses and the thud of shod hooves over the ground behind her.

She ran low and was almost to the woods when a hard arm caught her up, grabbing at her hair and her arm. She screamed in pain and rage, but the man hauled her up onto his horse. She fought, turning to claw his eyes. From somewhere, a cloak jammed down over her head, muffling her cries.

Someone roughly tied the cloak around her flailing arms, imprisoning her within its folds. She choked and struggled against arms that flung her face-down over the saddle. A moment later, someone dumped her onto the floor of the coach like a bundle of rags.

A moan from the other corner of the coach told her she was not alone. "Tom?" she whispered.

"Here . . . my . . . lady," he said in a halting voice. "Roberts is hurt bad . . . but I'll do."

"Get me free," she said.

Tom's fingers fumbled with the rope.

She heard the crack of a whip. The coach jerked forward, flinging her against the opposite seat.

Her head hit the wall. Stars bloomed beneath her shut lids. She struggled for consciousness. It seemed horribly important that she not fall into a faint. The nausea peaked and then receded, and she could think again. Tom shoved his way over to her, his fingers busy at the cords that held her prisoner.

All of her life, Lilias had found navigating her way about London or Paris a puzzle difficult to solve, even when she was on holiday with her father. She had passively accepted direction from others, rather than fight with maps and compasses.

But now, still blinded by the cloak, she paid attention with every sense she had left. The coach turned off the road and raced across an arched bridge, its wheels rumbling over cobblestones. It jolted and swung as it took a hard right turn. The force threw her against the wall, but she had been expecting it, nay, hoping for it, and took the hit with her shoulder. They were still heading east, toward London. She remembered the bridge from the night she'd come with the gypsies.

Tom wrestled clumsily with the cloak. "I'll be done in a minute. But you'll have to slide free of it yourself," he said.

Silently, she gave thanks to whatever angels were watching over her that she'd spent so much time trying to learn a bit of navigation at Breme.

They turned again, once to the left and once, after a journey of some three miles, to the right. They continued on for another half-hour, the cries of the eel men signaling a passage through Chelsea. Soon after, the coach halted.

Mayfair, she guessed, or very near to it. The ropes fell from about her. She slid free of the cloak. Two of her fingers bled from abrasions she'd suffered in the flight from her kidnappers. She took her hatpin from her bonnet, pulled a five-pound note from her reticule, and found what she needed to write.

She knew where she was. Quietly, quickly, she gave the note to Tom and told him what to do.

When the coach door opened, she was ready. With all her strength, she shoved and kicked, gouging an eye with an elbow, raking a face from cheek to jowl, using everything she had to give Tom time.

She felt a sharp crack, and then the world went black.

Chapter Thirty-Two

Two days after Lilias should have returned to London, Aubrey paced his cell in a welter of emotion like none he'd ever experienced before.

Four days, Aubrey. Trust me.

She must have read about him in the papers. With the shame of his arrest, of course, she wouldn't come back now. But he had expected a letter, at least. He felt like a beaten dog, wishing only to find a place to crawl into and die.

"I love you," she'd said. It was betrayal as false as his dreams of happiness had been.

"It's my fault," Ram said, leaning his back against the bars of Aubrey's cell. "If I hadn't pushed her on you, you wouldn't be in this situation." Ram sighed, then straightened his shoulders. "But it's too late for self-recrimination."

Aubrey raised a brow. "When have you ever indulged in that? No, this is my fault." He should never have trusted her words, the tears. It was not really so shocking, he realized. He'd simply dropped his guard and let her in.

Ram scowled and banged his fist against the stones of the cell. "You cannot give up. You cannot let Hindley win, just because Lilias ran away at the first sign of trouble."

Aubrey stopped pacing and stared at the mean little cell, the dripping, cold walls, the barred window. He straightened his shoulders and took a deep breath. Beast or not, he was still Breme.

"No," he said. "There's Breme to save, after all. Somehow, some way, I'll get out of this mess. And then I'm going to Tilden. I shall divorce Lilias, despite the public humiliation. She can remain with her sister all her life, if she wishes." He shrugged. "I'll go away and forget her, and then I'll make the best life I can for myself."

"Is that the best you can do to the woman who betrayed you?" Ram asked, watching him with what seemed great concentration.

He thought for a moment. No woman had ever made him feel like Lilias had. He had spent endless hours plotting and hoping to keep her safe. He had wanted a lifetime to shower her with everything good he could give her. Even now, the thought of living without her made his life empty of color, of harmony. The pain of her rejection was almost more than he could bear.

Aubrey shrugged, turning his face away so Ram couldn't see what must be plain upon it. "Divorce seems the worst a man can do to his wife."

"Oh," Ram said casually, looking down at his fingernails. "I can imagine better than that."

"What?" Aubrey narrowed his eyes.

"Think about it."

The water dripped down the dank stones, marking time as Aubrey thought about it. Slowly, realization struck and took his breath away. He shook his head to clear it. The fog of guilt he'd been living in suddenly lifted.

It would still be a long shot—no proof, only his word against Hindley's, and the break-in to his townhouse would prejudice the case—but now, by God, he could at least go down fighting.

A smile spread as relief and energy flooded his body.

"Ram, please fetch Sir Samuel," Aubrey said. "Tell him, I remember."

Lilias awoke to a blinding headache. Her throat felt like she had been swallowing pebbles, and every muscle in her body was crabbed with pain. She tried to move her arms, but they were tied with rope. When she moved her foot, the heavy links of chain pulled at her ankle.

She opened her eyes and caught the pin-prick brightness of a single candle at the far end of the room. A figure stirred in the chair at that end and rose, walking, in a nauseating wave of movement, toward her.

For some time, she'd been a prisoner in this room. A grimy serving woman had been the only person Lilias had seen. Suffering from the constant throbbing in her head and the nausea that accompanied it, she drifted in and out of a dark, dim sleep. Concussion, she noted dispassionately.

Now, looking at the figure walking toward her, she pulled control from deep inside and slowly sat up on the bed, the chain clinking from the leg iron.

"Who are you? Why do you hold me here?"

The man stopped just a few feet from her, his one hand held behind his back. He smiled in a pleasant way, as though this were a tea party. "You don't remember me, Lady Breme? How discourteous."

The face swam into focus. Her guess as she fled from the thugs had been right.

"Rupert Hindley. How long have I been your prisoner?"

"Three days. You've not been the most sociable of guests, but that has kept my men much happier."

"What have you done to my coachman and footman?"

"Oh, the one's a bit battered, but right enough, for the moment. But the coachman, stocky fellow—short?" His hand snaked from behind his back and a coat of green and gold livery, covered with blood, fell to her feet. "My men killed him three days ago, somewhere near Newgate." He wagged a finger at her. "You ordered him to escape, didn't you? Naughty girl."

Oh, God, what had she done? Tom couldn't be dead. He couldn't.

"They left him there after looking through his pockets. There wasn't anything of much value, except for this." Hindley's fingers opened and drifting toward her lap was a five-pound note, with words written on it in blood.

He shrugged. "The authorities will find him in a day or two. Or maybe what's left of him."

Oh, Tom. She struggled to keep the black, dull sickness out of her expression. She fought the nausea to think about where she was and what she could do to avenge one of the kindest men she knew.

She remembered, then, the foggy trip through the house, up two flights and to the left. She remembered passing a small room with a desk in it—one of those secretaries from the last century, covered in parquetry and odd patterns of veneer, a puzzle desk with a hidden drawer for valuables.

She had looked at it, half out of her mind with pain, and for some reason, ordered her sluggish brain to memorize where it was—three rooms down the hall from her.

She had to think. She had to plan. She had to get Hindley out of the room. His evil sapped her will.

"I wish to see my servant immediately."

Hindley gave her a look of deep amusement. "You were wasted on Drelincorte. As a tribute to your spine, I'll tell you what's going to happen to him and to you."

She swallowed, the movement almost causing her to gasp in pain. "When my husband learns of this, he will kill you."

"Your husband will do nothing, Lilias. I may call you Lilias, may I not? We're related, after all. Although he currently resides at Newgate, his next address will be the gibbet."

She shook her head slowly. "He'll find a way."

"In a few hours there will be nothing left of this house, my dear. There will be nothing left of you. The trial will take place. I shall, of course, be the Crown's star witness."

He smiled, his eyes dreamy with visions only he could see. "Aubrey will be found guilty. He cannot remember anything that might exonerate him, poor madman. Even his new wife is nowhere to be found. The lords who judge him will surmise that she's dead, another victim of the lunatic Lord Beast. But Aubrey will believe you fled him in fear and loathing. He will lose everything, just as I did that night in the jungle, and the last thought he shall have as they slip the rope round his neck will be of the woman he loves and how she betrayed him."

The horror grew, chilling her to the bone. "You're mad," she whispered.

"Just satisfied, finally, although not completely, my dear." Hindley bent toward her. With a smile, he brushed his hand over her throat. She turned her face away in disgust. "I had hoped to have a few days to enjoy you as your husband no doubt enjoyed Susannah. It seemed only fair. Breme took Susannah from my bed. Although you're not nearly in her league, there is something about you . . ."

Her throat clogged with bile. She struggled against the chains.

"You have no idea, do you, what he took from me? My love and my child. Yes, Susannah had just told me she'd conceived. What else could I do when I knew Aubrey would disgrace her with a divorce? When she deserved to be a countess and my unborn son a future earl."

He shook his head, his glittering eyes perused her from her chained ankle to the bruise that throbbed on her head. "I warned you, Lilias. I told you that night at Lady Amelia's ball that if you stayed with him, you'd be killed.

"You must understand," he continued, "I have nothing against you. But since you remained loyal, and since he's obviously mad—hah! Perfect description, eh? . . . about you, I have no choice. An eye for an eye, you see. His woman and his child for mine. But you've taken too long to awaken. I must conclude my business and be off. As pleasant as it has been to speak to someone who understands everything, time is of the essence."

His gaze raked over her. Then he looked around the room. "I resent it bitterly that I, too, will lose something precious to me. But sacrifices must be made. Don't struggle when the fire reaches you, my dear. Just give in to it, like all those Indian wives on their husbands' funeral pyres."

Tom shuddered and sputtered as a cold wash of water swept over his head.

"Get up, you lazy sod," a voice said.

He squinted up into the face of a man wearing a dark blue uniform.

"Come on, there. We can't allow drunks here."

"Where's here?" Tom said in a slur. God, he couldn't have gotten drunk, not when he had to get to his lordship. He shivered in the cold air and realized he lay there without a warm coat and his jacket of livery.

"Wait a minute there," the man said, holding a lantern close to his face. "Ye've been coshed on the head, haven't ye?"

Tom felt for the lump and winced.

"That's a beauty, that is."

"Somebody grabbed me from behind," Tom said as he started to remember. "What's the day?"

"The twentieth of March," the man said, helping him to his feet.

Tom looked around him wildly. Three days gone and his lordship not knowing. "I've got to get to Newgate with a message."

"We're close. I was just going in for work when I found you. What do you want there, anyhow?"

"I have to tell my master. He has to know."

"Ye need a hospital, man."

"No, I got to get to his lordship."

"Lord Breme yer master?"

"Aye," Tom said. The guard steadied him with a hand beneath his elbow, and they walked toward the prison.

"A couple of thieves got me on my way to him. One of 'em about my size. The other taller. They had a knife and a club. I couldn't do nothing. I was backed against the brick wall over there, the knife to my throat. The one my size fingered my coat. He said to take it off and my jacket too. He took 'em and put 'em on, and my jacket had the note in it from my mistress! I have to tell him."

The prison rose before him, stark and grim in the lamplight.

"I'll get you to him," the guard said. "Breme's a good 'un, polite and nice-like all the time. I almost believe he didn't do it."

"He didn't," Tom said with feeling.

Striding across the grim cell in Newgate, Ram grabbed Aubrey in an awkward embrace, patting his back soundly.

Then Ram cleared his throat.

"I knew you'd remember," he said.

Aubrey grinned in relief. His whole body felt strange, light, free. He wasn't insane. He wasn't a brutal beast. He was just a man. *He was good enough.*

For what? he asked himself. The answer came from the deepest recesses of his soul.

For Lilias.

A terrifying thought entered his mind—a thought he wouldn't have entertained just moments before.

Trust me. Nothing can turn me against you.

"Oh, God, Ram. What have I done?" He covered his face with his hands, gripped with terror and foreboding.

"What? What?" Ram was at his shoulder, shaking him.

Aubrey looked up, sick with certainty. "Lilias," he said in a voice he hadn't heard for months—the guttural cry of a beast. "She promised." *She never broke a promise.* "Hindley has her. He will kill her. And I can't get to her in time."

At a clatter of keys opening the barred door to the prison wing, Aubrey turned. The guard walked forward slowly, his arm supporting a short, stocky man who limped with every step, his head bent in exhaustion. Blood flowed from his head, down his shirt, and dripped to the floor.

As he unlocked Aubrey's cell, the guard said, "My lord, I brought this man in to ye. Says he's got to talk to ye. He's near faint from a cosh on the head. But he raised a fuss when I said I'd get him to hospital, so here he is."

The guard half carried Tom into the cell and lowered him to a chair. Tom slumped in the chair, bleary-eyed.

Aubrey froze. "What happened, man?"

"I'll leave him with you, my lord," the guard said, locking the cell door. "Jest call when you're done."

Dread had Aubrey by the throat. "Where is my wife?"

"Kidnapped. She told me to run. To you." Tom paused to draw breath, and every second that ticked away seared fear into Aubrey's brain. "I tried to get here. But I kept blacking out." Tom's breath came in slow wheezes.

"Oh, God, man. Where did they take her? And when?" Every muscle in Aubrey's body screamed to break loose and race toward her.

Tom opened his mouth. At that effort, he slumped forward again in the chair.

"Tom!" Aubrey shouted.

Tom stiffened and opened his eyes. "Near Mayfair. Three days ago. Note was in my pocket, but they stole it."

"Three days, you say?" Aubrey's hands shook. His legs didn't seem to want to hold him up. He sat slowly, like an old man.

"I looked at it, my lord. I'm sorry. I had it in my hand. Wanted to make sure what it said, in case the blood smeared."

"What blood?" Aubrey wanted to pull the iron bars of his cell apart with his own hands.

"Her ladyship didn't have anything else. She was bleedin' anyway. 'Hindley's townhouse,' she wrote. And . . ." Tom cleared his throat and stared at his feet. "I beg pardon, my lord. And she wrote, 'I love you.' I thought you should know that last bit, in the present circumstances and all."

"I love you," she'd written. In her own blood. Aubrey stared at Tom, sick with fear for Lilias and loathing himself for having doubted her.

"Drink this." Ram pulled his flask from his coat pocket and poured brandy into a glass.

Aubrey drank the brandy down in one gulp. "Three days," he said in a tight voice. She wasn't dead. He'd know it if she was dead. The world would have stopped. "I have to get out of here. Help me, Ram."

A few moments later, the guard heard that Indian fellow call him. As he walked forward, he noticed the candle at the end of the corridor had gone out.

"I'm leaving with the coachman," the Indian said in his soft sing-song English. The guard nodded and opened the cell door. "Sahib needs his sleep and this man needs a doctor."

The tall Indian walked out and as the guard locked the door behind him, the Indian lifted the wounded bloke and half-carried him, moving quickly ahead down the hall.

"Yeah. What with the trial tomorrow and all, his lordship needs his sleep," the guard said sympathetically.

The turban on the Indian's head glowed as the guard opened the door. The Indian was too intent on the wounded fellow to even thank him, but the guard didn't mind. His lordship paid him well enough for food and blankets. Besides, the little bloke was bleeding something awful. He needed help.

When the Indian and the little bloke were out on the dark street, the guard returned to his prison wing. He lit a candle and tiptoed down the hall to look in and see if his lordship wanted anything more. The cell was dark. His lordship lay beneath his blankets on his cot, his back to the guard. In the light of his candle, the guard could see the bright glitter of his lordship's hair.

Poor, miserable fellow. From what the guard had read, he didn't have a chance.

As his pounding shook the door of Drelincorte House, Aubrey heard running footsteps from inside. Hobson opened the door, blinked, and gasped.

"Lord Breme," he said, staring at Aubrey. No wonder Hobson looked upset.

Aubrey was dressed in Ram's turban and jodhpurs, and he carried the unconscious Tom into the house.

"Get a doctor," he told the footman, who gaped at him.

Three of the detectives appeared in the entry hall, the last of them tucking a pistol into his belt.

"Where to, my lord?" Jackson asked.

As he took the stairs two at a time, Aubrey barked orders. Racing into the study, he grabbed weapons. By the time he'd finished and run out the front door again, the horses stood in the street, saddled and waiting.

His heart pounded. Soon. He knew it. "Hurry up!" he shouted to Jackson. Grabbing the reins, Aubrey swung up into the saddle. He urged the black into a canter, down the streets toward Mayfair.

All the while his maddened heart drummed in his throat. The dark streets were deserted and the horses' hooves echoed eerily on the cobbles. His breath came in short rasps of fear and fury. His body contracted in fine tremors of emotion. "Faster!" he shouted, spurring his horse with hand and leg.

They raced into Mayfair and beyond, west toward the little street with wide lawns and small, decent houses. A glow appeared in the sky above the rooftops.

Not sunrise, Aubrey thought, staring at the reddish tint to the sky. This light, casting its color into the black, star-filled night, was not dawn.

Above the chimneys appeared the first frail flower of flame.

"It's Hindley's townhouse!" he shouted to the runners in recognition that cut like glass.

Not too late. Please, God, not too late.

He squeezed the horse into a mad gallop, down the street toward the flames.

Chapter Thirty-Three

The first tendrils of smoke crept beneath the door. Lilias felt her nostrils flare at the bitter smell and she doubled her efforts to free her hands. All the while, a ragged, muffled sobbing sounded in the room. Only vaguely did she realize it came from her own throat.

She hated her weakness, her inability to get free. She tugged at the leg-iron that rubbed her ankle raw, but there was no chance of slipping her foot through. Aubrey needed her! Why could she not get free?

The floorboards at her feet had taken on a frightening heat. It would not be long, then, until the house was an inferno. She tugged harder at the chain, frantic to free it from the ring bolted to the stone wall behind her.

Nothing.

Then in the distance below the room, a reverberation shook the timbers of the house. Had a wall crashed in? No. There were shouts, a pounding on the stairs so loud it sounded over the crackle of the flames.

"Lilias!"

A man's voice, a roar. A sob escaped her, of disbelief, and joy. She knew that voice. She'd heard it before, shouting in fear and love, over the noise of the hounds and the hoofbeats of her horse across a field, heading toward oblivion.

"Aubrey!" She screamed his name over the fire's thunder. She scrabbled off the bed and strained toward the door. On the other side, a crash sounded once, twice, and the blade of an axe splintered the heavy oak.

Aubrey stepped through the ruin of the door, a wet kerchief over his mouth, the axe in one hand and a coil of rope round his shoulder. His eyes shone with tears—from the fire, she supposed, or maybe from something else entirely. Then she was in his arms and sobbing even harder as he pressed kisses on her lips, her eyes, her tears coursing down her cheeks.

"I didn't leave you," she sobbed. "I was trying to get back."

"Shh. I love you, I love you." His hands were on the ropes binding her wrists. His knife flashed and they fell away.

He took the chain and spread it on the floor, then picked up the axe. "Look away," he said.

As soon as she turned her head, the blow fell. She felt the jar in the bones of her foot, and glanced down. Aubrey was already bending to pull free the severed link. Some of the chain still hung from her ankle, but she was free.

"I'm sorry, darling," he said as he ripped away part of the bed sheet, wet it in the pitcher beside the bed, and wrapped it between her ankle and the fetter. "It's the best I can do for now."

He handed her another piece of wet linen to wrap round her like a mask.

"You're always saving me," she said.

He grabbed her hand and pulled her toward the door. He reached for the axe as he pushed her into the hallway. She peered down the stairs. The front hall below them was a raging inferno.

"We'll try a window," Aubrey said through the smoke and flame, and he tugged her to the left.

"No, this way," Lilias said, taking the other direction.

His muffled voice, close to her ear, was calm, even amused. "Darling, we haven't time to get lost tonight."

"No. There's something I have to show you. Please, Aubrey, just this once. I know what I'm doing."

He turned right and ran beside her across the landing. One, two, three doors, she counted, and pushed the last open.

"In here," she said, and raced to the desk, with its intricate inlay and its secret compartment. "Hindley's mad. He was obsessed with Susannah." Her fingers touched all the knobs and buttons of the desk, opening drawers and small doors in an attempt to find the secret compartment. "He said he was losing something precious, but sacrifices had to be made. I think he saved all of Susannah's letters in this desk. His letters too, the ones he took from Emma Pearson. Don't you see? He'd never burn them unless they contained evidence of his guilt the night Susannah died. He must have been afraid you'd ask the court to search his house for them."

Desperately, she looked through the drawers. She found nothing but a list of Hindley's gaming vowels and unpaid bills. "Emma Pearson came into some money and no longer worked as a lady's maid. She must have been blackmailing him and he must have threatened her. So when I wrote her, she got one last chance to make some money and leave London."

"He might have hidden them all here, to read again," Lilias continued, "his and hers, as a sort of lover's conversation. But then he realized we knew." She coughed at the pall of smoke thickening the air. "He had to let them go, in case we sent somebody to find them here. I think he meant for them all to go up in flames with me. Oh, bloody blast!" she said impatiently. "If I could just open this, we'd have proof, don't you see?"

Aubrey looked over his shoulder. Fire danced along the stairway, licking the banister. With a huge roar and a crash, half of the balcony outside the room fell to the floor below in flames.

Lilias jumped at the sound and looked up from the desk in shock as the flames leaped higher, eating at the doorway. She felt Aubrey's hands drawing her aside.

He grinned down at her. "Beloved, at the moment the subtle approach will not do."

He pulled her to the window. "You first, understand?" he said, attaching the grappling hook on the end of the rope to the casement.

Lilias glanced over her shoulder, through the open doorway into the hall.

"I've found her," Aubrey shouted, leaning out the window. A detective appeared a moment later beneath them. At his side was Roberts, wounded and coughing, but alive.

Aubrey turned to Lilias. "I'm going to tie this end of the rope around you and lower you down. All right?"

She nodded and held her arms out from her side so he could secure the rope. "I still think those letters are in the desk, Aubrey," she said.

"Lilias, they're not worth dying over." His voice was strong and calm as he lifted her up and over the edge. "Now."

As he lowered her, Lilias kept her gaze on him all the while, loving his fierce smile, his midnight eyes shining with encouragement.

Jackson caught her and she looked up. The fire shrieked as it devoured the house. Aubrey was gone from the window. Where was he? She stared upward, willing him to come. She heard a crash as something smashed and she let out a cry. Had the floor of the room in which they'd just been standing broken free and dropped into the ravenous flames? Where was he? Where?

Vaguely, she heard people muttering in the street behind her. A bell clanged and men with axes and buckets ran toward the conflagration. The stench of fire rose in the air. Sparks glittered in the night sky like fireworks.

"Aubrey," she cried, choking with terror. She'd killed him, she thought, and agony clutched at her throat, stopping her breath as the smoke had not done.

The flames licked at the window where the rope lay. "Jackson!" Aubrey shouted from the window. Then Aubrey flung his body over the sill and hung for a moment; below, the red plumes reached for him. The rope smoked where it hung from the sill. Lithe as an acrobat, Aubrey slid down the rope, hand over hand, legs racing down the side of the burning house, the fire racing after him.

"Here, my lord!" Jackson ran toward him and stopped some feet out from the house. "Use yer legs, full swing out."

Aubrey was halfway down when the flames from the window licked at the rope. Hanging, he twisted his body until his back was to the house. Then he kicked off the wall, hard, and at the upswing of the rope, let go.

Lilias screamed and heard it echoed by the crowd below.

Aubrey flipped, somersaulting down through the air twice, thrice, hitting the ground in front of Jackson. The runner held fast to his wrists, falling and rolling with Aubrey's sudden weight, the last few feet away from the flaming coil of rope.

Lilias ran toward them, sobbing with relief. Jackson sat on his rump, shaking his head to clear it—and grinning.

In one movement, Aubrey rose and lifted her in his arms.

He was laughing. She smelled singed hair and sweat and Aubrey, praise God.

Jackson yelled as he pointed to the wall. The flames crackled and roared, devouring the house. Lilias and Aubrey raced away from the wall, Jackson beside them. She buried her head in Aubrey's shoulder, clinging, and heard the crash as the roof caved in and thundering flames shot up into the night.

Slowly, Aubrey lowered her to the ground. She shuddered, pressing against him as she stared at the conflagration. "I'm sorry," she said, and held Aubrey tight, afraid and chastened. "You almost died in that fire, and all because of a packet of letters. I was so stupid. I just couldn't let it go."

She held on tighter, then looked up at him, willing him to see her love, her gratitude. "Hindley told me you'd hate me, that you'd believe I betrayed you. I kept thinking he was right, but he wasn't! You had faith in me. Oh, Aubrey, you saved me when you should have thought the worst."

He brushed her hair back with a gentle caress of his fingers. "Sorry? Not nearly as much as I am."

Jackson tapped his shoulder. "My lord, I'm sorry to interrupt, but there's a newspaper man there, takin' notes. Somebody's going to tell him about this." He looked at the fire, and then the two of them. "I think it's in your best interest to talk to him first."

Aubrey nodded and kissed Lilias one last time. "Go with Jackson," he said.

Jackson led her away from the crowd. From the dark shelter of the trees at the back of the lawn, she watched Aubrey and the newsman speaking. Nodding eagerly, the newsman shook Aubrey's hand and walked away from the smoldering ruins of the house.

Aubrey turned and ran toward her. Within moments, he'd

lifted her onto the back of the black and mounted behind her. As he gathered the reins, she leaned against his warm, hard chest and shut her eyes. The cool night air soothed her throat. She was safe. She was free. And maybe, just maybe, she'd heard correctly over the roar of the fire, Aubrey loved her.

After they'd reached home, a blacksmith, hastily summoned, cut and filed off the leg iron. After Lilias had hastily bathed, she met Aubrey in the first-floor sitting room. He had bathed too, and changed into a long white outer jacket and long pantaloons, very much like those Ram Dass wore.

He took her in his arms, holding her close, her head against his chest. "I have a confession to make," he told her.

Dear God, had he remembered? Had he killed his wife? No. She wrapped her arms around the man who had saved her from death, who had managed to laugh when it was all over. She didn't believe him a killer.

"After we got out of Hindley's house, when you said I never doubted you, I thought—hell, like Shakespeare said, 'The better part of valor is discretion.' But I've let too many lies come between us." Her head rose a little with the deep breath he drew. "At first I was furious with you. I thought you were going to leave me. You may as well know the worst of it now."

"Oh," she said, holding on to him even tighter. "What a relief. I would have hated living with a saint."

"Lilias." He bent his head and, in gesture of grave formality, took her hand to his lips. "The prison is not a pretty place. But I need your help. I should be so very grateful . . . Would it be too much to ask that you come with me?"

"Wherever you go, I'll go with you," she said. She pulled his head down and kissed him in a moment of sweet communion. For the first time in seven days, she felt right.

The carriage was halfway to Newgate when, drugged with his kisses, she suddenly sat up in his arms, remembering.

"Aubrey, what did you say to that newspaperman to make him go away?"

Aubrey smiled at her. "I told him if he didn't print a word about our presence at the fire, I'd give him an exclusive interview immediately after the trial."

Dawn was breaking when they arrived at Newgate. Inside the carriage, Aubrey's face looked drawn and grim as he stared up at the prison. With easy haste, he tied a white length of material about his head and fastened it with a ruby pin.

"Ready?" he asked Lilias. She nodded and stepped down from the carriage, a handkerchief held to her nose. The guard who let them in gave Lilias a sleepy, curious look.

"Lady Breme to see my master," Aubrey said, pressing several coins into the man's hand.

The guard smiled at her and led them toward the cells. "You're back in London, are you, my lady?" he said. "Well, that's all right, then. He's a right easy one, Lord Breme. Never complains, pays well. I'll be sorry to see the last of him."

Aubrey's hand cupped her elbow in support. The dampness, the chill, and above all, the stench, was so strong it cut through her handkerchief and almost gagged her. She heard cries and moans from the cells to her right and left. She felt Aubrey's reassuring squeeze and pressed her lips shut.

"Yer lordship, her ladyship's here, and the wog," the guard called into the cell farthest down the grim corridor.

Lilias cringed at the ugly word, and wondered how many times men like Ram Dass had to hear it.

"Let them in," a clipped, aristocratic voice replied from within the cell.

The door creaked open. In the dim light a tall, well-built man stood in Aubrey's clothing, his back to her. His hair was blond.

"Well, if that's all then, I'll leave you to say yer good-byes," the guard told her, and then shut the door firmly behind him.

Lilias stared speechlessly at the man while the guard left the cell wing.

Then the tall blond man turned, and Lilias saw his face, golden and tanned. Eyes the color of rich coffee smiled at her from beneath dark, emphatic brows.

"Ram Dass?" she said.

"Darling," Aubrey said softly. "Allow me to introduce you to Ramsey Dassan Carmichael, Marquis of Headleymoor."

Ram frowned. "I hate that bloody title and you know it."

"Shall I try again?" Unwinding the turban, Aubrey grinned and handed the length of cloth to Ram. "May I present Prince Ramsey Dassan, grandson of His Majesty, King Dassan of Zaranbad."

Ram's frown had become a full-fledged scowl. "I don't like that one any better. I'll do this myself, Aubrey, if you'll permit?"

Lilias simply stood beside Aubrey and stared.

"My name is Ramsey Carmichael, Lady Breme. My business for the last three years has been to make peace between the world of my father and the world of my grandfather. Aubrey, as secret representative of Her Majesty's government, has helped me, in India and Zaranbad."

Aubrey cupped her cheek with one warm palm. "Let Ram take you home, now. Try to sleep. And Ram . . ."

His gaze fixed on Ram Dass—*Dassan*, Lilias corrected herself. Or perhaps just Carmichael.

In the process of adjusting the turban round his own head, Ram looked up.

"Ask Sir Samuel to come early today," Aubrey said. "We have much to discuss."

Chapter Thirty-Four

Lilias was too tense to rest. This morning, as with every other morning in the last two weeks, she awoke to run for the chamber pot and succumb to the nausea. Only this morning, on Ram's urging and his conclusions, she actually consulted a doctor. Which made her even more tense about the outcome of this trial.

With Jane's help, she dressed.

Jane looked up from her jewelry box. "Would you rather the pearls or the rubies, my lady?"

"The pearls?" Lilias said in surprise. "But they're gone, Jane."

Jane shook her head. "His lordship got it out of Roberts that you'd sold them. On the morning you left, he went to Adams, and bought them back."

He'd bought them back. For her. Lilias's eyes stung. She blinked quickly and straightened her back. No tears today. Only loyalty and pride in her husband and all that was Breme. The rubies were sumptuous and fit for balls. The pearls would be in better taste for the trial.

"I shall wear the rubies," she said, and lifted her chin as Jane clasped them about her neck.

She paced the house, in spite of Jane's clucks of disapproval, until it was time to leave the house. Dressed in proper English garb down to his dark green waistcoat and coat, Ram escorted her to the carriage. His brows were no longer as dark as they had always appeared. He must have dyed them, she realized, to play his role of Indian servant.

As the carriage stopped before the Gothic edifice of Parliament, Lilias noticed a small horde of men gathered on the curb of Whitehall Street.

She lifted her chin and descended from the coach. A murmur began among the men in the little crowd. "It's her," one said to the others. "I saw her at his side on the night of Lady Amelia's ball."

Ram grabbed her arm and propelled her forward. She hurried to keep up with him as the men raced after them, calling out, "Lady Breme, care to comment about this trial?"

"Where've you been, Lady Breme?"

"Did your husband do it?"

"Come to see him sentenced to hang?"

Ram thrust open the large doors and pushed her through. Silence descended, broken only by the quiet voices of the officials. Ram kept going, past the doorway to the House of Commons, and then across the hall to the Lords' chamber. Softly, he opened the door and slipped inside. She followed, joining him in a little alcove where she could hear everything, but all she could see was the majestic, empty throne at the end of the chamber and the angry faces of the lords sitting to one side.

The trial took on a nightmare atmosphere. "I call Rupert Hindley as witness," the prosecutor for the Crown said in stentorian tones.

She could not see Hindley, but she could hear him, and his voice dripped sincerity as he described the scene he had come upon that night in the jungle.

"Cousin Aubrey stood over his wife, a smoking gun in his hand. There was blood everywhere. I begged him to help me or to let me carry her to safety, where she could get help . . ." Hindley cleared his throat on a sob.

"Would you like a moment, sir?" the prosecutor said in a sympathetic voice.

"No." Hindley sounded determined, a man pulling himself together after an unspeakable crime, intent on getting through his testimony. "The truth is too important."

"Very well, sir. What did Lord Breme do when you asked him for help?" the prosecutor asked.

"He turned to me with eyes that absolutely glittered. He grinned, one of those horrible expressions one sees sometimes on lunatics. But his words were perfectly lucid. 'Never,' he said. He pulled out a pistol and aimed it at me. 'She'll die here and so will you, my only witness,' he said."

Hindley's voice shuddered at the last words. Lilias heard him draw a shaking breath. In the absolute silence of the chamber, the gasps of the lords were audible.

"I don't know how I did it," Hindley continued, "but somehow I had my pistol in my hand and I shot him. I admit it, I shot him, but only to wound. Then I ran as fast as I could to the bungalow, in order to alert the servants. I wanted to bring her back, you see. And Aubrey, too.

"Halfway there, I heard another shot in the forest. The servants passed me, running toward it. I knew they would find Susannah and Aubrey. And by now I was shaking so badly I went directly to the bungalow. I sat in the darkness, waiting, until they returned with the bodies."

His voice broke again. "Ram Dass, Aubrey's man, came to tell me that Aubrey would live, but Susannah was . . . was gone. It was then that I understood what Aubrey was about to get away with. I couldn't stand it. You have no idea how wonderful Lady Breme was. There was not a man or woman in the English community in Delhi or Rajasthan who didn't adore her. Someone had to stand up for Susannah and tell the truth. At the inquest I tried to do so, but the government of Rajasthan turned a deaf ear on my testimony. They wanted Aubrey's continued support in their negotiations with the crown. Some of them wanted his money."

Hindley's voice softened, and grew bitter. "I had nothing, you see, with which to bribe the native officials."

Lilias shut her eyes, but she couldn't shut out the offended muttering from the lords. A few hissed. If only she had been able to find the letters before the fire destroyed them. After Hindley's damning testimony, she might convince them that Aubrey had never hurt her, but she could never prove that he hadn't killed Susannah.

There was a long pause. "I fear," Hindley concluded, "Aubrey must have done the same thing to the new Lady Breme. She's gone and nobody knows where. We can only pray that, in avenging Susannah's death, you will also avenge hers."

Sir Samuel asked permission to call his first witness.

"If you must waste our time, do go ahead," the prosecutor said in a bored tone, only to be rebuked gently by the Lord Chancellor.

"I call Reginald Downs, Viscount Greenleigh," Sir Samuel said.

Lilias recognized Reggie Downs at once, from the hunt at Squire Trevell's. He stepped down from his seat among the lords, nodding and smiling at acquaintances, as if this wasn't a trial at all but a rather pleasant social event. At the witness box, he disappeared from her obstructed view, but she could still hear his tone of voice. Even giving his oath, he seemed to radiate good will rather than solemnity.

"Viscount Greenleigh, Mr. Hindley has given us a portrait of a man gone mad with jealousy and power, a man who would leave a woman to die in the middle of a jungle simply because he thought he could get away with it. Is this the man you have seen quite recently, in similar circumstances?"

"Breme?" Reggie laughed. "Ripping fellow. I'd say he was the exact opposite sort."

"Can you tell us how you came to that conclusion, my lord?"

"Certainly, Sir Samuel. Saw him just weeks ago, at Trevell's new fixture. Lost my best hounds on that hunt," he said glumly. "Almost lost Lady Breme, too. Terrible accident. Why, if it hadn't been for old Aubrey, things would have been quite different. Hounds rioted, dashed in full cry toward a cliff. Couldn't see the ravine. And Aubrey here, you ought to have seen him. Raced like a fiend to save his lady. Nick of time . . . her horse wheeled and stopped. Lady Breme had to step down, of course."

A murmur rose through the House. Most of the lords, hunters themselves, knew the genteel euphemism for what was, in reality, a fall that could have broken bones at best.

"Brave show she made of it, having her come-out so soon after. Best of all, the horse came through it all right. Not more than a little swelling on the near fore," Reggie finished triumphantly. "But Aubrey, he's just as he was in school, first to get there, saving everybody's hide. Dashed fine fellow, ain't he?"

"So Lord Greenleigh," Sir Samuel said, steering Reggie back to the subject at hand, "do you believe Lord Breme capable of wounding a woman and leaving her in the jungle to die alone?"

"Aubrey? Never! Why he's, you know, honor, duty, country. He's England, through and through."

"Thank you, my lord," Sir Samuel said. "You may step down."

The crown got nowhere with Reggie, whose bonhomie, while it proved nothing about the past, certainly painted a favorable portrait of Aubrey in the present.

John Trevell was the next witness Sir Samuel called. He asked John to recount the story of how he and Aubrey found the drag and then Richard Landham, shot dead in his kitchen.

"So you see," John concluded. "Someone wished to kill either Lord Breme or Lady Breme that day. Had it not been for Lord Breme's swift action, the fiend would have succeeded."

Again, all the crown could do was to point out that these facts were irrelevant to the murder committed in India a year past.

John stepped down, and Sir Samuel cleared his throat. The room stilled.

"I call Lilias Drelincorte, Lady Breme, to the box," Sir Samuel announced.

She heard a murmur of surprise flow along the benches like a wave sloughing into shore.

On wobbly legs, she entered the long chamber with its packed tiers of seats facing each other across the long aisle and its ceiling stretching toward heaven like some secular cathedral of justice. She kept her gaze firmly on Aubrey. Elegant in a black coat and dark gray breeches, he stood rail straight on a small, hastily-erected platform halfway down the aisle, a wooden rail surrounding it. Shackles bound his hands.

His face was composed and proud. He had left off the black ointment today. His scars, barely noticeable, crossed his cheek in thin, silver lines. Ram's impressive knowledge, gleaned from ancient Eastern texts written in Arabic and Sanskrit, had accomplished a miracle. She found herself transfixed by the beauty of her husband's face—and by the wrenching of her heart.

After incarceration in that hell hole, he'd ridden through the night, saved her from a raging fire, and raced back to gaol to meet his fate. And then, he had to stand, bound in chains like any common felon, subject to the stares and condemnation of the men who filled the benches.

Aubrey's gaze never left her. His lips curved in a private smile, giving her courage. She stopped before his platform. His hands rested on the balustrade. Despite the heavy chains, she raised them to her lips and kissed them both. He lowered his head, and the sun caught his hair, gilding it like precious ore. Some of longer strands, frizzled from the fire, gleamed like twisted wire from a jeweler's table. He gazed at her, midnight blue serenity and love together.

She gave him a tremulous smile and whispered, "I am carrying your child."

Joy flashed in his eyes, and determination. He cupped her cheek. The clerk cleared his throat and helped her to a long table in the aisleway, between the rows of seats that faced each other.

She stated her name for the record. Sir Samuel, belly holding his robes well out in front of his short, stocky frame, came forward. He adjusted his wig and bowed to her. It was coming now, she thought. They didn't have proof. The letters were gone. Her testimony was all they had.

"Lady Breme, you look somewhat weary." Sir Samuel's voice alerted her to the job ahead. "Will you tell this House what befell you four nights ago?"

A commotion to her left made her turn her head. Two constables held a struggling Hindley.

Sir Samuel and she had gone over her testimony this morning. Lilias stuck to the plan, determined to play the scene for all it was worth. She pointed dramatically in his direction. "Rupert Hindley and his ruffians kidnapped me," she said. "And then he tried to kill me."

The murmurs she had heard at her entrance rose to a babble of voices.

"Could you tell us, in great detail, what happened the night of April twenty-fifth?"

Lilias spent a great deal of time on the leg shackles and rope. Raising piteous eyes to the lords, she pulled up her cuffs to display the raw flesh of her wrists, where she had struggled to get free. In a broken voice, she described Hindley's glee at destroying Aubrey through her absence and her death.

She spoke of her terror as the flames rose and the joy she'd felt when she heard Aubrey shout her name. She spoke of his courage and his protectiveness.

Modestly, she lowered her eyes to her gloved hands. "Lord Breme is a man of great honor. He has saved me from death twice, as you now know. He has never evidenced anything but regard and affection for me."

She raised her eyes to the lords sitting before her, and looked at them for a long moment. "He is not the sort of man who could hurt anyone, especially a helpless woman."

A hush fell over the House. Then the prosecutor, resplendent in wig and scarlet, stood slowly.

"You speak of Lord Breme as though he were the perfect gentleman."

"I don't know how to answer that," Lilias said, biting her lip. "I have sworn to tell the truth, and so must tell you that, when ill, Lord Breme can be cross, even rude at times." She paused and glanced at the lords again. "But I have known many ladies who have confided that this is so with their husbands."

Feminine laughter erupted from the visitors' gallery above. The lords followed with their own rueful chuckles. Hope rose inside her. Oh, perhaps, just perhaps, she had succeeded in painting a realistic enough portrait of Aubrey to the lords. How could they not believe that Hindley was as false as Lucifer?

"Lady Breme, your testimony seems honest, even to me," the prosecutor said. "I am willing to believe that in your short marriage of only two months' duration . . ." his meaningful gaze swept the benches, "that Lord Breme has treated you gently. However," he continued in somber tones, "can you give us any proof that Lord Breme did not kill his wife, Susannah Drelincorte?"

Dread seeped through her.

"Shall I repeat the question?"

She shook her head. "I cannot produce proof. But I cannot believe—"

"That is all, Lady Breme. You are dismissed."

Aubrey returned her despairing look with a calm one of encouragement. She walked slowly out of the chamber, sick with apprehension.

Although Hindley would no doubt be accused of kidnapping and murder, Lilias had failed to clear Aubrey.

As she rushed up to the gallery, Aubrey was sworn and allowed to take his seat in the witness box. His gaze rose to the gallery and locked on hers, again with that reassuring serenity that made her bite her lip in order not to cry.

Sir Samuel stood before him, wig askew, looking like a pouter pigeon from the gallery above. "I wish you to clear up matters as quickly as possible, my lord. Will you tell this august body who shot your first wife, Susannah Drelincorte, on October the fifth, eighteen forty-two?"

The lords sat back in their seats, expecting, she knew, the negative reply.

Aubrey straightened his shoulders, composed as ever. "I shot her," he said.

Chapter Thirty-Five

Pandemonium burst forth from the gallery, from the benches.

Aubrey watched it, gauging his time as Sir Samuel sent him a nod. Well, he certainly had their attention now.

"Will you tell us, in your own words, what happened that night?"

Aubrey took a deep breath and stood very straight to control the shudder that threatened. Even now, when it meant his life, remembering was wrenching.

"Susannah came to me in the library. She asked me to walk with her on the grounds past the verandah. I said it was dangerous this time of night. Too many animals came out to hunt at dusk. Even the bats in that area could kill."

He barely noticed the hush that settled upon the chamber. He was reliving the night, and the terror. "She clung to my hand, insisting, half-hysterical. I had two pistols with me—I always carried them in India. I thought we'd be safe enough, so I followed her.

"The dusk came up quickly that night. Once we were halfway across the grounds, a mist circled our legs. She began to talk, to tell me things that I had mostly guessed before. But she told them in such a way, with a look of such contempt and triumph, that I found myself in the jungle before I knew it."

He paused, took a deep breath. "She said she was with child by Rupert Hindley, my cousin and heir and her lover from well before the first day of our marriage. She told me how she hated me, how she and Rupert wished me dead, and how they were going to make sure of it."

Humiliated, betrayed, and now the whole world knew it. He heard a soft cry from above and knew it was Lilias. He tried to swallow. Someone handed him a glass of water.

He could get through this. For her. For the child of their love.

"I heard a sound, a snap of twigs. Rupert Hindley appeared. I could make out his smile and the pistol he carried. I reached for mine, very slowly. 'Nobody will find you before the jackals get to you,' Hindley said. 'Nobody will ever know how you died.' "

Aubrey wanted to get through the rest quickly. "He raised his arm. I raised mine and shot. And at that instant, Susannah screamed and threw herself in front of Hindley. The ball hit her in the chest. I think she died instantly. Because of Susannah's lunge, Hindley's shot went wide and struck me in the shoulder. It was close enough to do damage, but not to kill me. I fell, and must have blacked out. When I came to, Hindley was gone. A leopard stood over Susannah's body."

He cleared his throat. "I startled it and it transferred its attention to me. I shot it before it could finish me off."

"Why did you not tell your story to the officials at the inquest, my lord?" Sir Samuel asked.

Aubrey stared at his hands. "I couldn't remember. Doctors tell me now that I probably could not face the fact that my cousin and my wife attempted to kill me for my fortune, my lands, and my title, and that they had planned it well before the marriage. I knew only two things when I awoke: that Susannah was dead, and that she had been unfaithful from the beginning."

He sighed, empty now. "I learned later, at the inquest, that Hindley was intent on revenge. I came home as quickly as I could, and tried to remember. But it wouldn't come, until finally, four nights ago, when my wife had not returned."

"How convenient," the prosecutor said, rising to object. "Are we to really swallow this Cheltenham tragedy on your word alone, Lord Breme?"

Sir Samuel's mouth spread in a grin that seemed to take up his entire countenance, jowls and all. "Oh, no. Certainly we must have proof."

Sir Samuel reached into his gown, fiddled about his jacket pocket, and pulled forth a packet of letters, wrapped in a slightly-singed blue ribbon.

"I present in evidence to the court the correspondence between Susannah Drelincorte and Rupert Hindley." With a flourish, Sir Samuel handed them to the Lord Chancellor, who adjusted his spectacles, opened the first, and perused it.

"The letters begin a year before the death of Susannah Drelincorte and end the week before her death," Sir Samuel said. "They are, for the most part, love letters. However, the last three reveal the lady's delicate condition and entail the plot to murder Lord Breme on the fifth of October, eighteen forty-two."

Sir Samuel smiled benignly at the prosecutor, whose mouth opened and shut in a fish-like motion. "I have witnesses who will testify that this is, indeed, the handwriting of both Lady Susannah and Rupert Hindley. I believe the Lord Chancellor may have a few words to say at this time."

The Lord Chancellor glanced up from the last letter, his mouth grim. He rose to his feet, a figure of pomp and dignity in his crimson robe and old-fashioned wig. "Aubrey Drelincorte, Lord Breme, it is the decision of this court that you are innocent of all charges brought against you. Release the prisoner."

A cheer rang through in the hall. Members of the lords swarmed from their benches, converging on the bailiff, who was attempting to unlock Aubrey's handcuffs. Reggie Downs plucked the keys from the man's hand and opened them. Some of the lords at the back of the crowd jumped over the platform in an effort to pat Aubrey on the back and to yell their congratulations over each other.

Aubrey stood in the midst of his peers and looked up into the gallery. Lilias had risen and taken the first steps toward the stairway to join him. She must have felt his gaze, for she turned as though he had called her name. Her smile lit her face with joyous incandescence. He could see the tracks of tears on her cheeks.

Damn, he thought. Why in thunder didn't men cry? His body felt like a dam holding back turbulent emotions that roiled and shook inside him. He supposed at times like this, his fellows would expect him to resort to drink, or a wild celebration at any one of his clubs.

Or, he thought, gazing at his wife while his mouth widened in a slow grin, he could take Lilias to bed and bury himself in her body until he'd purged the fear and the shaking.

He nodded, and she turned again toward the stairs. In a moment, he would be able to touch her, to speak to her.

He barely heard the Lord Chancellor's instructions to the guards to take Rupert Hindley to Newgate. It didn't matter anymore. It was finished.

The crowd around him parted, making a path from the dock to the space where Lilias stood waiting. He moved, slowly at first, still finding it difficult to realize that one night had changed everything, that he was free and he was innocent.

That was when she started to run and he opened his arms, and she flung herself into them. His arms locked about her.

"Still here," he said in a shaking voice. It was his affirmation, his triumphant cry to the Universe.

"Come with me, you two," Sir Samuel interrupted, scowling about at the milling crowd of reporters busily sketching the two of them locked in each other's arms. "Brilliant work, Breme, if I do say so myself. Excellent of you to have found the letters, what with the fire all around you." Sir Samuel patted him on the back as they walked, wig askew over his bald pate. "How you kept your head and solved the puzzle of the desk is quite beyond me."

Aubrey looked up from the illumination of Lilias's face and grinned. "I didn't solve it. I smashed the desk apart with an axe." He gave a deep sigh of pleasure, remembering the splintering of the wood and the packet of letters falling neatly to the floor. "Bloody satisfying sensation."

Sir Samuel left them in the privacy of a little chamber off the Lords', where Aubrey pulled Lilias into his arms again. He bent his head to the tender curve of her neck and breathed deep, taking in her scent as though it gave him life.

"All the days and all the nights of my life," he whispered against her.

"No," she said fiercely, and her arms tightened around him. "Longer. You're mine forever."

Epilogue

Every room of Breme Castle was decorated for Christmas, a few days away. The servants had done it all the week before, as Lilias had been rather busy at the time with the birth of Alexander David Arthur Drelicorte, Viscount Linton.

Ram had left today to spend Christmas with his father. He'd mumbled something about facing the onerous duties awaiting him, at which point Aubrey had laughed and said, "I assume you mean the Season. Planning a campaign, are you?"

"Perhaps," Ram had replied.

"There are compensations for being a titled English gentleman," Aubrey told him.

Ram had grinned, thinking of something or perhaps someone.

Lilias wondered if she should warn Caroline that the Season might hold some surprises.

"Which do you like the best, little one, the flutes or the strings?" she asked her son, who was nursing in sleepy contentment at her breast.

They lay in the large Tudor bed in the lord's bedchamber, surrounded by the scent of red beeswax candles and evergreen boughs. Breme was home as she'd never known one—a place where she found love and acceptance from its extraordinary inhabitants, and above all, from her husband.

The door opened quietly. As though her thoughts had summoned him, Aubrey slipped in. He stood still for a moment and just stared at Lilias and little Alex. He seemed mesmerized by the sight of her nursing their son. The sheen of the candles played on the gold of his hair and the soft gilt down on their baby's head. Alex burped and lay replete in her arms.

She gave Aubrey a worried look. "Have Papa and Grandfather come to blows yet?"

Aubrey grinned. "Your grandfather is rehearsing with the orchestra in the ballroom. But before that, your father and grandfather were together in the blue drawing room. Your father observed that the railways would make the carriage obsolete and discussed the comparative merits of each line. Duke Alfred was pleased to listen, as he wants to invest a goodly sum in the best of them."

Now, from the ballroom, Lilias could hear the servants rehearsing a piece Jeffries had written, a lyrical lullaby. She let out a breath of relief. She had been anxious about this visit for the last month of her pregnancy. But Aubrey had been adamant with both men. If they wanted to see Lilias, they must agree to put up with each other at the same time. He'd gambled on their affection for her—and won.

"Will miracles never cease?" she asked him, shaking her head in amazement.

"Not while you're here," Aubrey said with a smile. He bent, took Alex from her outstretched arms, and cradled the small, perfect body in his strong hands. He couldn't seem to stop looking at the baby. And when he wasn't looking at his son, he was looking at her with the same awe and wonder in his eyes.

"You're the miracle worker," she told him softly. He'd even won Pamela over, receiving a shy kiss on the cheek from her last night when she and John arrived, both of them heady with excitement because Pamela, glowing and healthy, expected her own babe in another five months.

At Lilias's praise, Aubrey gave her a skeptical smile and a quick shake of the head, but she knew better. Less than a year ago, she had expected a life of service—to her father, to the village of Tilden, to any nieces and nephews Pamela might give her. She had thought herself too abrupt, her hair too dark, her coloring too bright for the current ideal. She had thought no one could love her for herself.

Aubrey's attention swung back to his son, stirring in his arms. "All that potential in such a fragile package," he said. He shuddered to think of himself those months ago, plotting to wed and have an heir—an innocent pawn in a deadly game. No wonder he felt so protective, now that this miracle he held in his arms was here. Alexander was not just an heir but his beloved son.

The baby's tiny hand wrapped itself round Aubrey's finger and gripped. Aubrey's eyes widened in surprise. "Maybe not quite so fragile as I thought. Good. I want him strong—strong enough to survive in spite of anything. Strong enough to find what he wants."

"You'll give him what he needs to make it through, Aubrey."

In the midst of climbing into bed beside his wife, Aubrey shifted little Alex so the baby lay against his chest. He glanced up at Lilias, surprised, as he often was, at how well she understood him. The shameful trial and the nightmare that had gone before it faded a bit with each passing day, but there were times still when he recognized with a mental shudder how close a thing it had been. At those times, Lilias was there, opening her arms as though she knew he had to hold onto her in order to dispel the darkness.

His wife's lips curved. Her smile was almost a tangible thing, warming him and their son like the rays of the sun.

One arm cradling the sleeping baby, he curved the other around her and drew her close, where he could feel the softness and warmth of her body. She seemed to know just what he needed. He felt it often these days, the surge of communication without words. It had always been there, he realized, waiting to be tapped, first by longing, then by music, and then from a flood of words explaining everything, and words given back, understanding.

He was not alone. He was part of something larger. His greatest wish for his son was that he would find the same communion when his time came. Until then, he would cherish him and teach him, and give him the gifts he had been given: of music, of friendship, of enduring love.

"What do you think of him?" Lilias asked, the smile still lingering in her voice.

Aubrey glanced up at her. "He's beautiful."

The smile grew deeper. "Beautiful. Just like his father."

A Note on Malaria

Malaria is a pathogen that's common to the tropics. After being bitten by an infected mosquito, the patient's red blood cells become hosts for the Malaria organisms, called plasmodium. As part of their natural life cycle, the plasmodium develop inside the red blood cells until they reach maturity. At that time, they cause the red blood cells to break apart. This life cycle predictably repeats itself every forty-eight hours, usually at night, giving the patient the classic cyclic fevers and shaking chills of Malaria.

When the blood cells are destroyed, they release their contents into the bloodstream. Their hemoglobin is converted by the body into a substance called biliruben, which is yellow in color. As biliruben levels rise, the yellow color can be seen in the patient's skin, eyeballs, and especially under the tongue. This condition, associated with advanced disease, is called jaundice.

Aubrey was lucky to have Ram as his doctor in those early times, when treatment options were limited. Ram's long visits at his grandfather's palace in India exposed him to Eastern medical practices, and particularly to Quinghaosu, a drug derived from the sweet wormwood plant and used in China for more than two thousand years to treat fevers and the most deadly forms of falciparum Malaria.[1]

[1]Desowitz, Robert S. *The Malaria Capers* (*More Tales of Parasites and People, Research and Reality*), W. W. Norton & Company, New York, 1991.

About the Author

Mary Lennox is the author of historical romance and fantasy novels. A storyteller from the age of seven, she now lives with her husband and assorted animals on an idyllic horse farm in Ohio. She divides her time between the barn, the garden, and the siren call of her computer. Visit her at www.marylennox.com.